PRAISE FOR *LOVE'S ENDLESS FLAME*:

"BETTY BROOKS' SWEET, TOUCHING ROMANCE WILL WARM THE HEARTS OF READERS."
— Kathe Robin, *Romantic Times*

"FAST-PACED ADVENTURE ... INTRICATE PLOTS ... HATED TO SEE IT END."
— *Inside Romance*

"SENSUAL MAGIC ... PAGE TURNER ... SUPERB CHARACTERIZATION."
— Billie Green, author of *Once in a Blue Moon*

EVEN IN THE DARKEST CAVERNS ... LOVE LIGHTS THE WAY

"Is it over, Rogue? Are we outside now?" asked Miranda, running her tongue over dry lips.

"I'm afraid not, baby," he said roughly, leaning closer to her. "We're just in the light-cave that you told me about." He wrapped his arm around her and pulled her to a sitting position, holding her there by his strength. "It shouldn't be long before we're out of here though."

Rogue's palm cupped her chin and tipped her head toward him. "What have you done to me, Miranda Hartford?"

Instinctively, her arms circled his neck and she moved her head until her lips were positioned beneath his.

"You feel so good," he groaned. "It's been a long time since I held a woman in my arms. Too long."

BETTY BROOKS

Love's Endless Flame

ZEBRA BOOKS
KENSINGTON PUBLISHING CORP.

ZEBRA BOOKS

are published by

Kensington Publishing Corp.
475 Park Avenue South
New York, NY 10016

First printing: October, 1992

Printed in the United States of America

Dedicated to Sharon Greer—who took the time from her own busy schedule to accompany me through many of the caves described in this book. Thanks again, Sharon.

A special thank-you to my editor, Alice Alfonsi Kane, who allowed me to write something different.

Special acknowledgments go to—John Anderson—who generously shared his knowledge of caverns with me, and to Kelly Whitehead, tour guide for Sonora Cavern.

Also, a very special thank you to my physician, Dr. David Ramsey, for his help with the medical problems involved.

One

Texas Hill Country, 1897

The western sky blazed with color as Miranda lifted the hem of her riding skirt to the edge of her boots, stepped on the bottom rung of the corral fence, and hoisted herself onto the top rail. Then, clinging to the fence post, she perched delicately on the rail. Her gaze was captured by the bull in the pen, and she focused on the tips of the wicked horns that gleamed beneath the setting sun.

The bull looked mad enough to gore anything fool enough to get in his way, but thankfully his anger was directed elsewhere. As he stamped the parched earth in the middle of the corral, the animal glared at the two cowboys who warily circled around him, their lariats coiled and ready.

Miranda hugged the fence post tighter. Did they really think they could contain the beast with their flimsy ropes? The bull was massive, magnificent in its raw power, and frightening in its anger. Thank God, it was penned.

Almost as if it had read her thoughts, the bull whirled toward Miranda. His eyes narrowed to malevolent slits, he lowered his head and snorted.

Behind her, someone shouted. Miranda swung a glance over her shoulder to see a man running toward the corral. He waved, shouted again. What in heaven's name was wrong, she wondered.

Then the bull snorted again. If possible, he looked angrier than before as he pawed the ground in front of him, sending dust clouds aloft. But what had she to do with it? It was the men in the corral who had been annoying him, yet the bull was charging toward her.

She swayed on the fence rail, her eyes widening with horror as she clung desperately to the post. She had to get down, but her limbs were frozen, like icicles in the winter. Helplessly, as though she were caught in the midst of a never-ending nightmare, she watched the bull come closer.

Distantly she heard a voice behind her — the man she'd seen running? She couldn't seem to focus on his words, couldn't respond. Instead, her whole being, her entire world centered around two thousand pounds of hurtling bull. Again she swayed, this time out, into the corral.

Then strong arms circled her waist, jerking her from the fence. Her head slammed against a solid male chest.

Momentarily off balance, gasping for breath, she clung to the muscular frame holding her tight, as she tried to control the trembling of her body.

She could have been killed! — would have been if it had not been for the man whose arms still held her. She tilted her head and looked up, way up, into a face devoid of color beneath the sun-bronzed skin of a ruggedly handsome face. Startled, she looked into cold gray eyes filled with an anger almost equal to that she'd faced only moments before.

"What the hell are you doing here? Don't you know you could've been killed? Who are you anyway?" He rapped the words out with caustic censure.

Miranda felt the heat rising in her cheeks. She didn't like being chastised by anyone. She certainly had no intention of taking it from a stranger.

Instead of thanking him as she'd intended, she pushed away from his chest. "Would you please turn me loose?" she snapped.

He released her instantly. "I'm still waiting for an answer," he growled.

Refusing to allow herself to be intimidated, Miranda swallowed back her fear, lifted her chin a degree higher and shot him a look of immense dislike. She realized she'd been careless, but he had no need to be rude. "I must apologize for my curiosity," she said, her frosty voice fairly crackling with scorn. "The commotion in the corral was hard to ignore. I wondered what was causing it." When he remained silent, she drew herself up to her full height of five feet two and allowed her gaze to sweep over the length of him, taking in the dark, unruly hair showing beneath his water-stained Stetson, the worn clothing and dusty boots, before she met his glittering eyes again. "Please excuse me," she said haughtily. "I have business with Rogue McClaren."

"What kind of business?" he asked.

"That is none of your concern!" she snapped, turning on her heel and heading for the sprawling ranch house. Miranda could feel the cowboy's eyes on her as she walked away from him. The effrontery of the man! Who did he think he was anyway? Granted, she had been careless, but he needn't have been so hateful toward her. She had a good mind to report him to McClaren.

Climbing the stairs to the wide veranda, she tried to put the odious man from her mind, turning her thoughts instead to the reason she'd come to the McClaren ranch — her anxiety over her father.

Immediately, fear reared its ugly head again.

Something had gone wrong. Miranda knew it just as surely as she knew she was breathing. She shouldn't have waited so long to come . . . should have set out as soon as she realized her father had missed her graduation. Instead, she'd allowed herself to be sidetracked by others. If anything happened to him, she'd never forgive herself.

Stop that! she silently chastised herself. *He's all right. You know how forgetful he is.*

Making a fist, she rapped on the door.

Silence.

Again, she rapped, and a moment later she heard footsteps approaching. The door opened and a gray-haired woman stood facing her. "Yes?" the woman queried.

Miranda introduced herself, then added, "I've come to see Mr. McClaren."

The woman stepped aside and bade her enter. "You can set in the parlor while I get him," she said, pointing out the direction.

The room Miranda entered was a formal room; the windows, completely drapeless, had only shades. The walls were papered to about eighteen inches below the ceiling. The floor was covered with carpeting, and the mantel over the fireplace bore a formal arrangement with a bouquet in the center, flanked by two urns and two figurines; but there were no pictures on the walls.

Miranda smoothed away the wrinkles in her dark green riding skirt, tucked a stray copper-colored curl beneath her trim bonnet and seated herself on the gold satin settee. She was reflecting on the absence of pictures on the walls when the door opened to disclose the cowboy who had been so rude at the corral. Even before he spoke she had had a sneaking suspicion about who he was—perhaps because his bearing was so confident, his attitude bordering on arrogance. It was certainly not what she would have expected from a mere cowboy.

Removing his Stetson, he crossed the room and stopped in front of her. "Why're you here, Miss Hartford?"

Oh, sweet mother of God, she was right! Miranda felt a flush rising up her cheeks. This definitely wasn't her day. "Before we go into it, please let me apologize for mistaking you for one of your men," she said stiffly, rising to her feet.

"Don't bother." He tossed his hat toward a nearby chair where it landed, squarely in the seat, with a soft plop. "It was a natural enough mistake. How's your father?" Although his tone was abrupt, the rancher was obviously making an effort to be cordial.

"Then he has been here!" she heaved a sigh of relief. "Thank goodness. You don't know how worried I've been about him. Isn't that just like Poppa? He gets so engrossed in his work that he'd forget his head if it wasn't attached to his body. Where is he? Still out at the cave?"

Realizing she was babbling, Miranda settled herself down on the gold settee again and smiled across at him.

"I haven't seen him since Tuesday," he said shortly. "Didn't he go back to town?"

"No." A flicker of uneasiness edged her voice. "And I *was* surprised to find he'd left so near my graduation." Realizing he probably didn't have the vaguest idea what she was talking about, she went on. "You see, I've been studying at the women's university in Austin. My father may have mentioned it?" Her eyebrows lifted, making it a question rather than a statement.

He nodded abruptly. "Yeah! He did."

She smiled again, refusing to be intimidated by his manner. "I'm not surprised. He has a habit of telling anyone who'll listen to him. Anyway, that's why I was so worried about him. He traveled all the way from Maine, just to attend my graduation." Her green eyes clouded with worry. "And when he didn't show up . . . well, I went to his hotel—the Menger Hotel in Austin—and the clerk said my father left on Tuesday with the express purpose of seeking permission to explore a cavern on your property."

"So you think he's still there?"

"He must be. He didn't return to the hotel."

"I'll send one of my men to check on him," he said gruffly, rising to his feet and reaching for his hat. He was on the point of leaving when his housekeeper walked in carrying a silver tea service. Mc-Claren frowned at the laden tray, obviously wanting to escape, but seeming also to be conscious of his duties as host. Finally, with a sigh, he sat back down and tossed his hat on the floor beside him.

"Martha," he said gruffly, "Give Colby a yell. Miss Hartford can serve us."

With a curious glance at Miranda, the housekeeper left the room.

Realizing the rancher's words had been meant for her as well as the housekeeper, Miranda served the tea, then sipped the hot liquid, trying to calm her jangled nerves. She controlled the urge to fidget on the couch, knew it was because she felt uncomfortable sitting across from the rancher and she wondered at the reason.

As though sensing her unrest, the rancher engaged her in small talk. "You said you were goin' to the women's college? What are you studying?"

Miranda looked at him from beneath thick, coppery lashes. Although she felt he was only being polite by asking the question, she felt inclined to talk. "I'm majoring in geology."

"Geology? I wouldn't've thought a woman would be interested in rocks and such." His lips curled at the edges, and when he spoke again, his tone was slightly contemptuous. "You wouldn't be one of those suffragettes, would you, Miss Hartford?"

Miranda stiffened immediately, taking offense at his tone. "I'm afraid I fail to see the connection be-

13

tween geology and the women's movement," she said coolly. "My father is an archaeologist, Mr. Mc-Claren, as well as an experienced cave explorer. And, since I often accompany my father on his journeys, my interest is quite natural."

"You go in those caves with your father?"

His tone of voice implied he found something wrong with that. Was he one of those men who felt a woman should have no interests outside of home and family? She suspected he was, but before she could reply, a wiry, gray-haired man with a handlebar mustache of the same color stepped through the door.

McClaren put his cup down with a snap, picked up his Stetson and stood up, obviously feeling that his duties as host had been completed. "Colby," he growled, "this is Hartford's daughter."

Colby stopped beside her chair and held out his hand. Miranda's lips curled at the edges. The foreman had manners, even if his employer did not. She set her cup on a nearby table and allowed her hand to be shaken.

"Miranda Hartford," she murmured.

"Nice to meet you ma'am. Colby Turner's the name." He threw the rancher a reproving glance. "Rogue's manners ain't always what they should be. Which is partly my fault, I guess, since I had a hand in raisin' him. Martha said you was Professor Hartford's daughter. How's your pa doin'? Did him and that nephew of his'n find what they was lookin' for in that cave?"

"Apparently they're still there," Rogue McClaren said.

14

Colby narrowed his faded-blue eyes on Miranda's face. "I thought the professor said they was goin' to explore it last Tuesday."

Miranda nodded again. "They left town on Tuesday, so they must have. That's the reason I came here, Mister Turner. I was worried when they didn't return to the hotel."

"Well, ma'am," Colby said. "It's only a little bitty cave. I've been in it myself, and there ain't nothing in it to worry over. Your folks are prob'ly just takin' their time lookin' around out there."

"That's the way I figger it," Rogue McClaren said. "But send Rusty out to Squaw Mountain. Just to make sure nothin's gone wrong."

"I got Rusty busy already," Colby replied. "But I'll go myself. You gonna wait here, Miss?"

Miranda immediately rose to her feet. "I'd rather go along with you if you don't mind."

"Suit yourself," McClaren said, obviously already dismissing her and her problems from his mind. "Do you need a mount?"

The question served only to irritate her further, because it pretended concern where none existed. He had to know she'd come by horseback. How else could she have gotten there? Nevertheless, she managed to keep her voice neutral when she replied. "No, thank you. I have my own." With her gaze steady on his, she crossed the room and stopped in front of him. Grudgingly, she offered her hand to the rancher. "It was nice meeting you, Mr. Mc-Claren," she lied.

He nodded his head, his gray eyes glittering with amusement. "Same here." He turned back to the other man. "Colby, stop by Spring Creek on the way back. Tell Jack and Clem to beat the brush around Bear Mountain for strays." He gave every appearance of having already forgotten Miranda's presence as he jammed his Stetson on his head and stalked from the room.

"Rogue don't really mean to be rude," Colby apologized. "But it's calvin' time and he's got a lot on his mind."

"You have no need to apologize for him," Miranda said. "I'm sure he's a very busy man." But even though she said the words, pretending to understand, she didn't mean them. Any man with an ounce of sympathy would have shown a little concern in the face of her anxiety.

She tried to put the overbearing rancher from her mind as she followed the grizzled foreman to the corrals where her horse waited quietly.

As Miranda and the foreman rode away from the ranch, she felt a sense of relief that she'd soon see her father again. She'd been so worried about him, needlessly, perhaps, but she couldn't help the way she felt. Discounting Roger—for she'd never been able to get close to him—since her mother's death several years before, her father was all she had.

Shadows covered the land by the time Miranda and the foreman reached the cliffs where the cavern was located. Tension pulled her nerves taut, like cold wires touching her skin, as Miranda entered behind Colby. Immediately, her nostrils were assailed by the musty smell of freshly turned earth.

Moments later they found the rockslide.

Miranda's heart gave a crazy little jerk. Fear

washed over her as she stared at the rubble blocking their way.

It was obvious what had happened. Somehow, there had been a landslide. And, since there was no sign of her father or her cousin, they must be under, or on the other side of the pile of rocks!

Two

God! Please let him be on the other side!
"Poppa!" she called. "Poppa! Can you hear me?"

Cocking her head, she listened to the silence.

"Poppa's in there," she told Colby. "I know he is."
Miranda pointed at a large slab of rock — at least six
by four feet — on the cavern floor. Raw white marks
marred the sides, as though crowbars had gained
leverage there. "It looks as though that slab has
been moved."

"Yep. It sure does look thataway," Colby
growled. "If my memory don't fail me none, that
slab was standing upright the last time I was in here.
And they was a narrow split behind the slab. Appears to me they was tryin' to make the crack wider
and brought the whole roof down on 'em."

Although that was exactly what Miranda
thought, to hear the words spoken aloud caused her
face to become pale. "Oh, God!" she whispered.

Desperation sent Miranda scrambling up the
rockslide, trying to push the obstruction out of her

way. "Poppa's not dead," she said fiercely. "He can't be." She clutched at the rocks, caught one in her hand and flung it aside, heedless of her manicured nails, then grabbed another, only one thought driving her, she had to get to her father. She must find him!

"Don't, Miss," Colby said gruffly, his fingers wrapping around her right wrist and pulling gently at her. "We can't dig through all that by our lonesome. We're gonna need some more help."

Miranda looked at Colby through a water mist, turning her wrist this way and that as she tried to free it from his surprisingly strong grip. "You don't understand, Colby," she cried. "Poppa's all I have! I won't let him die! I have to get him out!"

"Ain't no need to take on so," he soothed. "We're gonna get him out. Don't you worry none about that. But we can't do it without some help. One of us has gotta go back to the ranch an' tell Rogue what happened out here."

She swallowed around the lump in her throat and with the back of her hand swiped at the tears coursing down her cheeks. "You're right, of course," she said, forcing herself to speak calmly. "I'm sorry I went to pieces. I don't usually do that." She gave a shuddering sigh. "You go back for help. I'll stay here and clean some of this rubble away."

"Uh huh," he grunted. "It'd be a whole lot better if you was to go. It's a cinch I can do a whole lot more here than you can."

Although Miranda didn't want to leave the site, she had sense enough to realize Colby was right. He would be able to accomplish much more than she could. "All right. I'll go. But—maybe if you call out to them every now and then, they might hear you. If—if Poppa's on the other side, it would make him feel better to know we've found him."

He nodded his grizzled head. "It prob'ly would at that," he said. "Now you quit worryin' about your pa, an' ride on back to the ranch. You can't never tell . . . by the time you get back here, your pa's likely to be standin' here beside me waitin' for you."

Praying to God that Colby was right, Miranda scrambled from the cavern. As she hurried to her mount, she tried to control her fear, but it continued to haunt her.

God! She couldn't lose her father! He was all she had! *Please let him be all right,* she silently prayed as she stopped beside the horse and caught up the reins. Putting her foot into the stirrup, she swung into the saddle. Fear for her father made her dig her heels into the animal's flanks, urging him toward the ranch.

She felt his muscles bunch as he gathered speed. His hooves pounded in time with her fear-ridden heart as she bent low over the stallion's neck to decrease wind resistance. Horse and rider seemed as one as they raced like the wind. Bent on reaching help as soon as possible, they went flying over scrub cedar that grew in their path.

When the ranch house came in sight, Miranda's gaze flew to the man who stood near the corral. She knew it was Rogue McClaren. Even from this distance, she recognized his large frame, and she knew in an instant that he saw her coming. There was disapproval in every line of his body as he turned to watch her approach. Her heart thumped loudly in her chest as she pulled up beside him.

With a whinny of protest, the stallion reared high, pawing at the air before him, forcing Miranda to dig her knees into her mount's sides in order to retain her seat. "We need some help!" she cried.

"What's wrong?" His voice was curt, hard.

"There was a landslide in the cave! We think Poppa and Roger are trapped on the other side." She wouldn't allow herself to consider any other possibility.

"Dammit! I should've known something like this would happen!" He barked orders at his men. Horses were brought forth, as well as picks and shovels. "Rusty, get some lanterns," McClaren growled. "It's gonna be dark before we can get out there!"

Miranda didn't wait for the others. Although her horse was tired, she reined the gelding around and headed back to the cavern. She was nearly there when McClaren caught up with her.

Colby had apparently heard them coming, because he was waiting for them outside the entrance. He pulled Rogue aside but even so, Miranda could hear them speak.

"Ain't heard nary a sound from in there," Colby said. "Might be the girl orghta be sent back to town."

Miranda had been on the point of entering the cavern. His words halted her in her tracks and she spun around to face the two men. "I won't be shut out of this," she said fiercely. "I intend to stay here until my father is found."

"We'll find him faster if you stay the hell out of the way!" McClaren snapped.

Instantly, anger surged forth. He had no need to tell her that. She had no intention of hampering the efforts to rescue her father. But there was no way she would leave.

Miranda stepped into the cavern and stared at the pile of rubble. Although there were signs of Colby's efforts to move the rocks, he'd barely dented the surface of the slide. She was unaware of the two men behind her until Colby spoke. "The men are here, ma'am. It'd be better if you was to wait outside."

Miranda knew better than to protest while McClaren was standing there. Anyway, it made sense. If she wasn't allowed to work, then she would only be taking up room. Nevertheless, she shot McClaren a heated glance of dislike on her way out.

Hours passed and, although the night was warm, Miranda felt chilled to the bone. She realized it was fear for her father that made her feel that way and she tried to take her mind off what was happening inside the cavern, but it was impossible. Dammit! Why had this happened?

Miranda looked up at the stars, twinkling brightly in the night sky overhead. They were the same stars that glittered over their home in Maine. If she'd gone to college there, they'd be home right now . . . her father safe within their parlor. Anguish twisted her heart. Why had she insisted on coming to Texas? Even as she asked herself the question, she knew the answer. She'd wanted to be on her own, wanted a chance to try her wings before becoming her father's assistant, a job designed to keep her constantly at his side. Had her fight for independence cost her father his life?

God! She hoped not.

She shouldn't have come to Texas. Shouldn't have been so stubborn. But he'd been so insistent about her choosing a university closer to home that she'd immediately rebelled.

Perhaps she wouldn't have been so obstinate if her future hadn't already been so cut and dried. But it was.

Miranda remembered the day Silas Hartford told her of his plans for her future. He had learned of a site in Egypt and was eager to excavate. But it could wait, he told her, until she had her degree. Then, with her knowledge of geology, of history recorded in rocks, added to his ability to study the past through relics left by ancient peoples, they would probe the mysteries of the past.

He hadn't taken into account that Miranda might have wanted more from life.

Was that so wrong?

Miranda's hands clenched into fists and her knuckles showed white, as her fingernails dug into her palms.

Perhaps it *was* wrong.

And perhaps she was being punished for being so selfish, so uncaring of her father's wishes. If she hadn't come to Texas her father wouldn't have known about the cave!

Hearing footsteps, Miranda turned around to see Colby approaching.

"Have you heard anything yet?" she asked hopefully.

"No," he said gruffly. "But that don't mean a thing. You just rest your mind easy about your pa. He's gonna be just fine." He picked up a canteen, lifted it to his mouth and took a long swallow. Then, with a sigh, he set it down again and went back in the cave.

An eternity seemed to pass while Miranda waited. Occasionally, one of the men would step outside to report on their progress and mutter reassurances to her and she felt grateful for those times.

Finally, Miranda heard a cry. "We're through!"

Dread mingled with relief as she hurried into the cavern. The lantern light flickered across the dirty faces of the men, but Miranda paid them little attention as she pushed her way across the cavern. At first she saw nothing but rock . . . then her gaze caught in the crevice, hardly more than a split in the rock, some eight feet high by a foot and a half wide — a narrow fissure which angled sharply down.

"Is — do you see anything?" Miranda asked timidly.

"No," McClaren replied. "Looks like they went down the passage. You wait outside while we check it out."

Miranda was tired of being told to wait outside. But she remained silent, standing aside to allow McClaren to enter the narrow tunnel.

"Professor Hartford!" His voice was taken up by others as several of the men followed him inside.

Miranda felt a cold chill creep over her when there was no answer. She started toward the passage, but a redheaded cowboy—she'd heard the others call him Rusty—stopped her.

"Better wait here," he said kindly. "If your pa is in there, then Rogue will find him."

Swallowing back the bile rising in her throat, Miranda stayed where she was, realizing the cowboy was worried about what condition her father would be in when he was found.

The voices continued to call out to her father, and they seemed to be getting more distant all the time. Miranda was almost overcome by anxiety as she waited. After what seemed like hours, she heard the men returning.

Her heart beat wildly beneath her ribs, like a frenzied bird trying to escape from the confines of a cage, as she peered through the opening, waiting for them to come into view. *Please, God!* she silently prayed. *Let Poppa be with them. He must be with them.*

But the moment Rogue came into view, the expression on his face told Miranda her prayers had been in vain. He shook his head. "I'm sorry," he said. "We didn't find him."

"Then why did you come back?" she asked. "He has to be in there and you must find him."

"The cave's bigger than we thought," he said. "That passage over there . . ." He jerked his thumb at the split in the rock, ". . . leads to a huge room, and there's a bunch of tunnels leading away from that." He sighed deeply and ran a hand through his dark, unruly hair. "Looks like we're goin' to need some more help. And the lanterns need to be refilled."

"There was no sign of Poppa or Roger?"

"No," he admitted. "But since they weren't under the slide, they have to be in there. They must've gone down one of the tunnels. But don't ask me why. It was a damn fool thing to do. Would've made more sense to wait close by."

She breathed a heavy sigh and nodded. "Poppa would have had a lantern so he could study the rock walls. If the lantern was still intact after the rockslide, Poppa's interest in his surroundings might have overcome his good sense. But I cannot understand why Roger didn't intervene and make him wait. Unless something happened . . . perhaps one of them was injured and they were looking for another way out." She bit her lip, feeling the need for urgent remedies. "Mister McClaren, we must find them . . . and quickly."

"Don't you think I know that?" he growled. "Dammit! As if I didn't already have enough to worry about!" He turned to face his men. "Looks like we're not done here yet. But I don't expect you boys to keep working without food in your bellies. Most of you haven't eaten since breakfast."

He turned back to study Miranda for a long moment and when he spoke again, his voice was almost gentle. "I know this is hard on you, but you'll feel better after you've had a hot meal." He patted her shoulder awkwardly. "Don't worry. We'll find him."

A lump filled her throat and to her consternation, tears filled her eyes. "I have to believe that," she said huskily. "I have to!"

"Take it for the gospel," he said, wrapping his fingers around her wrist to lead her out of the cavern. "Let's go."

"I'd like to stay here," she said, pulling her arm free. "Just in case my father comes back."

"No," Rogue said, his voice gentle but firm. "We'll need your help. The cave is big . . . there's no way of knowing how far those tunnels go, or what we'll find in them. I couldn't see any sign of bats in there. I think this is the first time the entrance has ever been uncovered." His voice became persuasive. "You said you'd been exploring caves with your father, so you'll know what we're gonna need in the way of supplies. You'll be more help to your father if you come with us."

Miranda could see the sense of his words. "There was no sign at all of bats?" When he shook his head, Miranda felt a surge of excitement. She knew from past experience that the absence of bats meant the cavern had never been opened before. God! *A cavern that is completely unexplored.* There was no way her father could have resisted the temptation of being the first to see — the first to learn — what this particular cave had to offer. "You're right," she said. "We are going to need supplies." She flicked a quick look at the rancher. "But . . . you'll leave someone here, Mr. McClaren? Just outside the entrance? My father might return, and if he needed help, then . . ."

"I'll stay," Rusty quickly volunteered. "Somebody can bring me some grub."

"Thank you," Miranda said. "You can't know how much I appreciate it." She began to make a mental list of the things they would need. "Mr. Mc-

27

Claren. Could you estimate how many tunnels branched off the big cavern?"

"I didn't stop to count," he said dryly. "But it won't be long before we find out."

No, it wouldn't be long. And she, for one, could hardly wait. Despite her worry over her father, the thrill of discovery surged forth. Only once before had she been in an unexplored cavern of any size. Now, when she least expected it, she was being given the opportunity to explore another one.

Suddenly, Miranda controlled an inward shudder.

She had barely survived the last one, but she refused to think about that now. The important thing was to get her father out . . . and alive.

God willing, it wasn't already too late.

Three

Although Miranda had thought she wasn't hungry, the first bite of the steak sandwich Rogue's housekeeper served in the parlor proved her wrong: she was utterly famished — unlike McClaren, who seemed too edgy to eat. Instead, he supplied her with pencil and paper, then began to pace the room.

With the aroma of freshly cooked meat teasing her nostrils, Miranda applied herself to eating. Between bites, she prepared a list of the supplies they would need.

First she listed lanterns. Then matches, followed by torches and candles. McClaren paused behind her chair and peered over her shoulder at the list.

"Are you sure we need all that?" he asked. "I would've thought lanterns would be enough. Why the torches and candles?"

She spared him a brief look, then reached for her sandwich again. "You said the cavern was extensive, riddled with tunnels. If we lose the lanterns, then any other equipment we take could be rendered useless in the dark." She met his eyes with a long, thoughtful look. "Do you know what it means to be in total darkness, Mr. McClaren?" Without giving him a chance to answer, she continued, "Well I do. It's a dark like no other . . . You can't even see your hand if you hold it in front of your eyes. We would be lost in there without some kind of light." She set her sandwich down on her plate, her appetite suddenly gone, taken away by a memory from the past. "I know what it means to be lost in a cavern . . . lost, with no light at all . . . with complete darkness all around you. It's a smothering, confining blackness that covers you like a heavy blanket that you can't throw off when it gets too warm, and all the while you're wondering if you'll ever see daylight again."

Even as Miranda spoke the words, she felt claustrophobia sweeping over her. Her stomach clenched with fear and she broke out in a cold sweat. The feeling was so strong that it threatened to overwhelm her.

Shut it down, Miranda, she silently urged herself. *Don't give in to it.*

"What's wrong?" McClaren's voice was harsh, questioning, and it brought her back to reality.

"Nothing," she muttered. "Nothing at all." She bent her head and concentrated on the task ahead of her. Drawing a deep breath to clear her head, she put pen to paper again and continued her list as though she'd never stopped writing.

Okay, she told herself. *We'll need matches and candles.*

Her glance flicked to the line above and she swallowed hard. She'd already listed the items once before. But, instead of erasing the extra listing, she left it to remind her. Then she wrote down twine, chalk, ropes and rope ladders. Compasses, boots for mountain climbing and pickaxes.

Pausing, she put the eraser end of the pencil in her mouth while she considered the chances of making alpenstocks. Then she added them to the list. When she had listed everything she could think of, Miranda handed the paper to McClaren.

He studied it silently for a moment, then looked up. "What in hell is a Ruhmkorff lamp? And where am I supposed to get rope ladders and equipment for mountain climbing?"

"We could get by with carbide lamps," she said.

"Carbide?" His voice was dry. "I don't have those either."

She heaved a resigned sigh. "The lanterns will have to do, but it's hard to pack enough fuel for them. We'll need plenty of candles. If that cave proves to be very deep, then every item on that list may be necessary to our survival."

"You might just as well cut out the 'our' stuff," he growled. "You're not going in the cave."

Anger surged through Miranda. Surely he was jesting. She had more at stake here than anyone else. And he wasn't about to leave her out of the search party. "I *am* going," she said, forcing her voice to stay calm. "You need me, McClaren. I'm the only one here that's experienced in cave exploration. You haven't the slightest idea what you'll encounter beneath the earth. There could be unexpected drops, or landslides. You have no idea what's down there!"

"And you do?"

"I didn't say that," she said sharply. "But I do know what can happen down there. As you apparently do not."

"Lady," he said grimly. "I don't have time for any of this. But I'll do what's necessary to get your father out so I can forget about the pair of you. In case you haven't noticed, we're busy this time of year and we—" He broke off as the sound of hoofbeats reached them. "What in hell is going on?" Two long strides carried him to the doorway, then he took off at a run.

Miranda's heart lurched. Hope mingled with fear as she hurried after him. Could her father have returned?

Rogue was halfway to the corral when Charlie hollered at him. "Better come quick, boss. Jack's all shot up. Looks like rustlers."

"Damn!" Rogue exclaimed, hurrying toward the small knot of men bent over the figure lying prone on the ground. Nearby stood a saddled horse with head drooping tiredly, his neck and withers white with foam.

Rogue knelt beside the fallen man, his gaze going to the bloodstained shirt. "What the hell happened, Jack?" His big hands were gentle as he pulled the shirt aside to check the extent of the man's injuries.

"Rustlers got Clem, boss. I . . . think he's dead. D-don't know how many cattle they got away with."

"How many rustlers?" Rogue asked.

"D-don't rightly know." Jack's breath whistled

through his throat, and his glazed eyes locked on Rogue's. "Am I gonna die, boss?"

"You're not gonna die," Rogue said, lifting his eyes to search the crowd, passing over Miranda's tense form to stop on his foreman. "Colby, send for Doc Stevens. Tell him to get out here on the double." When he returned his attention to the fallen man, he realized Jack was unconscious. "Let's get him inside," he said harshly. "Then get your rifles and some fresh horses out here."

Miranda Hartford stepped forward. "What are you going to do?" she asked quickly.

"What do you think?" His voice was harsh. "I'm going after the men who did this."

She clenched her elegant hands at her sides. He could read the tension in the way her stubborn chin rose half an inch, could even sympathize with the snap in her green eyes. But, dammit, what the hell could he do?

"What about my father?" she asked in measured tones.

He sighed and raked a hand through his dark hair. "Dammit, lady, can't you see I have enough to worry about already? You're gonna have to get someone else to help you. I have an emergency on my hands here."

"My father's situation isn't an emergency?" she asked, her eyes sparkling angrily.

"Maybe it is," Rogue said, "but somebody else will have to handle it." He realized he sounded harsh, but he had no time to think about her problems. The rustlers who'd shot Jack and Clem were probably the same ones who'd been stealing his stock for the past two months. He'd have to get on their trail right away, while whatever tracks they might've left were still fresh enough to follow. If he didn't stop the rustlers soon, he wouldn't have any stock left, and there was no way he could recover from such a loss. He would lose the ranch.

He took the reins from the man who brought him a fresh horse. "See that Miss Hartford reaches town safely," he said.

"No!" she snapped. She grabbed his arm, her nails digging through his shirt. "I'm not leaving this ranch until my father is found. And I can't do it alone. If you won't help me yourself, at least leave some of your men to help me search."

He pried her fingers loose. "I need my men," he said harshly. "All of them. Ask the town sheriff to help you."

"Dammit!" She seemed unaware of the startled looks the men sent her way. "There's no time. It's a six-hour ride back to Austin and another six back. That's twelve hours of riding time. By then my father could be dead."

He gritted his teeth and sucked in an impatient breath. "Lady, I'd like to help you, but you're askin' too much. If you want to wait until I catch the rustlers who shot my men and ran off my stock, then do it. But whatever you do, I'm going after the rustlers." He put his foot in the stirrup. "If I don't stop them, I stand to lose everything I own." He felt like a callous scoundrel when her eyes misted over, but he couldn't relent. There was too much at stake.

"Is that all you care about?" she cried. "Isn't there anything I can do to change your mind?"

"Afraid not," he said shortly. "You'll have to find somebody else to help you." He knew he sounded hard, but he couldn't help it. He had a duty not only to himself, but to his men.

Suddenly, a change came over her. She squared her shoulders and stared up at him with stormy eyes, her expression hard and unyielding. "I suggest you change your mind," she said in a voice as cold as a winter storm. "Otherwise you won't like what happens."

Rogue didn't cotton to the tone of her voice. "Spell it out, lady! What're you saying?"

"If you don't help me, McClaren . . . you're going to be sorry you put your stock before the welfare of my father. You're responsible for whatever happens on your land. If anything happens to my father, the rustlers won't have to ruin you. I'll do it myself. I'll file charges against you and see that you lose everything you own."

His breath hissed through his teeth. "Are you threatening me?" he asked softly.

"It's not a threat," she said, her voice wavering slightly. "It's more in the nature of a promise. Either help me find my father or I'll do whatever is necessary to ruin you. You can bet on it."

He studied her for a long moment. The woman had courage, but she was bluffing. He ought to leave . . . just ride off away from her, but he couldn't do it. Not with her looking like that, standing there with shoulders squared, her gaze stormy, trying her best to control her shaking voice long enough to intimidate him.

Dammit!

Why'd she have to come here anyway?

He looked at Zeke Raglan who stood nearby. "Get Colby out here!" he snapped. Then he turned to the Hartford woman. "You've made your position clear enough. Now wait for me at the house."

I'll do whatever is necessary to ruin you . . . ruin you . . . ruin you. Miranda's words echoed over and over in her mind as she walked stiffly away from him. But she wasn't the least bit sorry she'd made the threat. She'd do anything in her power to save her father's life. Even if it meant going into the cavern alone.

She gave a shudder of fear. Even the thought of such an event caused her to break out in a cold sweat. Her hands curled into fists and her fingernails dug into her flesh, but Miranda welcomed the pain it caused.

God! Please let McClaren help me, she silently prayed. *Don't make me have to go alone.*

Rogue explained to Colby what had happened.

"She threatened to ruin you?" Colby said, his eyes glinting with amusement. "Wisht I'da been here to see that." Suddenly, his expression became serious. "Why'd you wait until she did that afore you told her you was gonna send somebody to get her pa out?"

"Dammit, Colby!" Rogue exploded. "You know as well as I do the rustlers have to be stopped. And we have to act now while there's a trail to follow."

36

He raked a hand through his unruly dark hair and sighed. "Trouble is, we've got to do something about the professor too."

"How about we send one of the boys for the sheriff. He can see about gettin' her pa outta that cave."

"She's already pointed out the time involved!"

Colby gave him a long look. "Nothin' for it then." He spat a long stream of tobacco toward the ground. "Guess I'd better quit wastin' time and mosey along after them rustlers."

"You sayin' you'd rather go after the rustlers instead of lookin' for the professor?" Rogue asked.

Colby nodded his grizzled head. "I figger I'm too old to start learnin' about caves. If I gotta die, then I want it to be *on* the ground, not under it."

"Don't talk about dyin'," Rogue said brusquely. "You got a lotta years ahead of you, Colby."

"Maybe. And maybe not. But I ain't gonna go worryin' about it none. How many men you want left here?"

"I'll keep Rusty and Charlie."

Colby nodded. "Good enough," he said. "You take care of yourself in that cave, Rogue. An' don't worry about what's goin' on up here." He spun on his heels and yelled at one of the cowboys waiting with the horses. "Hey, Dan! Saddle up that big gray for me. We ain't got no time to lose."

A few minutes later Rogue watched the men ride out with Colby in the lead.

"Don't worry about 'em, boss," came a voice from behind him. "Colby's got a good head on his shoulders. He won't take no chances."

Rogue turned to face Charlie. He'd been so preoccupied that he hadn't heard him approach. "I know it. But I should've gone with 'em." He narrowed his eyes on the man who'd been more like a father to him than an employee. "I hate to ask you to go in the cave with me, Charlie. But I need somebody I can depend on."

"You don't have to ask, Rogue. Like always, I'll do whatever needs doin'. Do you think the professor is still alive?"

"He must be. If the slide had killed him, then we'd have found his body. Looks like he went explorin'."

"Damn fool thing to do," Charlie said. "How long do you think it'll take us to get him out?"

"Let's hope it won't take long." Rogue's lips thinned and he swore softly. "Dammit! why does everything always have to happen at once?"

"Ain't no sense in moanin' about it." Charlie's eyes narrowed on the paper still clutched in Rogue's right hand. "That the list Miss Hartford gave you?"

Rogue nodded and looked at it again. "See what you can do about roundin' up this stuff. Looks like we won't have much of it, but do the best you can."

Charlie took the list from Rogue and gave it his attention. "Seems to be wrote in a foreign language. An' what do we need with boots for mountain climbing? I thought we was headed down, not up." He heaved a long sigh. "Guess the little lady knows what she needs, though. Accordin' to the professor, she helped organize a club for folks like them. The ones who like crawlin' around under ground. He said they call themselves spelunkers."

Rogue's lips tightened. So the Hartford woman

liked organizing clubs, did she? "You know, I never could abide useless females," he growled.

Charlie studied Rogue from beneath beetled brows. "I know you like I know the back of my hand, Rogue. And I know what you're thinkin'. But the professor's daughter ain't nothin' like Dallas. You ain't got no good reason for thinkin' she is."

"I've got plenty of reason." Rogue heard the bitterness in his voice and it made him angry. He had tried hard to forget Dallas . . . to forget what she'd done to his brother. And Rogue had almost succeeded in forgetting. But the moment he'd laid eyes on the Hartford woman, the past had reared its ugly head.

"Women like the professor's daughter serve no purpose, Charlie." A muscle worked in his jaw. "Don't tell me you don't see the resemblance between them. Not only in looks either. They were both schooled like a man."

"You can't hold her education against her," Charlie said. "They's a lotta women gettin' schoolin' these days. The professor was proud as a peacock that his daughter was graduatin' from college."

"I'd bet my life she's a suffragette," Rogue said sourly. "Organizing clubs like she's got nothin' better to do! Dammit!" He spewed out the words. "Why'd this have to happen right now? I've got enough trouble already. I don't need another Dallas to make things worse."

"There you go again, mixin' her up with your brother's wife," Charlie growled. "You keep lettin' it eat away at you an' you ain't gonna have no chance to find a good woman for yourself. Dallas was a bad apple right enough. But she didn't come from the same basket as Miss Hartford. Now that's all I got to say about it, but you mark my words and you mark 'em good." He scowled at Rogue. "Best you forget about Dallas and concentrate on gettin' the professor outta that cave. Sooner we get that done, sooner we can help Colby catch them rustlers."

"You're right about that," Rogue said. "You help the Hartford woman with the supplies. I'm goin' back to the cave to see if the professor's turned up yet."

Four

"Hold on a minute!" Charlie called as Rogue turned to leave.

Rogue spun on his heels to face the other man again. "Yeah?" he inquired.

"You better take Rusty some chow, boss," Charlie reminded. "Martha put some steak sandwiches in a paper sack and she's got some coffee in a canteen for him."

"Coffee will be cold, time I get there," Rogue grunted. "But he might appreciate it anyway." He changed direction and strode toward the ranch house. He was halfway there when he heard Charlie shout. "Hey, Rogue! What's a Ruhmkorff coil?"

Rogue's lips twitched and he looked back toward the other man. "Ask the professor's daughter," he replied. "She's the one that wrote it down."

Although Rogue had hoped to avoid her,

Miranda Hartford met him in the doorway. "What are you going to do?" she asked.

Her face was pinched and drawn, her green eyes anxious, but the memory of her threat hardened his heart. "Seems like you left me no choice," he said acidly. "Either I help you or lose the ranch. That *was* what you said?"

His words were no more than uttered before an unseen veil shuttered her expression. "Yes," she said stiffly. "And I meant every word of it."

"I figured as much." He studied her with hooded eyes. He had no intention of telling her that the threat she'd made had had nothing to do with changing his mind. Let her think what she would. He didn't like women like her. He'd had occasion to meet her kind before—Dallas had brought enough of them to the house when she'd lived there—and he hated everything they stood for. Instead of doing what God had intended—making a home for their husbands and raising a family—they were intent on pursuing their own pleasures.

"Is that what changed your mind?" she asked.

"What else?" he growled. "I hope you're satisfied now! I've sent my men after the rustlers, and there's no tellin' what they'll find." His voice was coldly condemning. "Now if you'll step aside, I'll do whatever I can to get your father out of that cave . . . and you out of my life!"

"You'll need me," she reminded.

"Why?" He pinned her with his hard gaze. "Do you think you're the only one around here with enough brains to find a couple of old gents who had no more sense than to wander off and get themselves lost? If you're really so smart, then I'm surprised you needed anyone to help you. I'm surprised you didn't go after him alone." He vented his rage on her, not caring if the words hurt.

"The first rule in spelunking, Mister McClaren, is never do anything alone. You'll need me to help in the search. But not for the reasons you stated. You'll need me because, by your own account, the cavern is riddled with passages—any one of which my father could have taken. When he enters an unexplored cavern, he always uses a system—a method that never varies. And since Roger is down there with him, I'm the only person left up here who knows how he operates."

"And you don't intend to tell me?"

"There wouldn't be time enough to tell you what to do in every circumstance, even if I could think of every problem you might encounter." Her voice dripped acid when she added, "Which I can't."

"Rogue?" The voice turned their heads. It was Martha, the housekeeper, and she carried a small sack and a canteen. "I have Rusty's food ready as well as the foodstuffs that Miss Hartford ordered. Where do you want them?"

Miranda Hartford met his look. "The food for the search party," she explained. "Where are you putting the rest of the supplies?"

"You were damn sure I was going to help you, weren't you?" he asked.

"No," she denied. "Only sure that a search would be made. And it made no difference to the supplies, whether I went alone or had help. They were still required, whether or not you chose to help me."

Rogue turned back to his housekeeper. "Give me Rusty's supper and wait for Charlie to pick up the rest. I'm goin' out to the cavern now."

"I'll come with you," Miranda said quickly.

"No!" His voice was abrupt. "Stay here! Charlie may need some help."

Without waiting for an answer, he took the box from Martha and strode out of the house to the corrals. By the time he reached the caverns, his anger was not so overpowering. He could understand the woman's concern over her father, but hadn't she learned yet that honey caught more flies than vinegar?

He was still stewing over the woman's attitude when he reached the cavern where Rusty waited.

"I was beginning to think I'd been forgot," Rusty said. "Is that my grub?" He pointed at the box. "My belly's done gone wonderin' if my throat's been cut."

Rogue handed the box over to the red-haired man. "Martha said there's steak sandwiches in there. Should be hot coffee too. At least, it was hot when I left."

Rusty was already opening the box. As he pulled out a paper-wrapped sandwich, he looked up at Rogue again. "Where is ever'body?"

"We got some trouble, Rusty. There'll only be the two of us and Charlie."

Rusty paused in the act of unwrapping his sandwich. "What kind of trouble?"

"Rustlers hit our stock again. They shot up Jack. He thinks Clem is dead."

"Damn!" Rusty exclaimed. "What're we doin' here, boss? We gotta go after 'em."

Rogue sighed. "Colby took the rest of the boys and went over to the line shack to see if he could pick up their trail. The doc's been sent for so as to take care of Jack, and someone will pick up Clem." He looked toward the cavern. "We've got us a job here to see to."

"But what about the rustlers?" Rusty protested. "We gotta stop 'em or they'll wipe us out."

"We've got no choice in the matter," Rogue said abruptly. "The professor's got to be brought out of there. I take it there's been no sign of him?" This was said hopefully.

Rusty heaved a long sigh. "Nary a one. Nor nobody else, neither. Except for Chance."

"Chance Carter?" Chance worked on the Circle D, a ranch that bordered Rogue's. "He was here?"

"Yeah. He'd been to town. Made a detour across here. He's gone on to the Circle D. Said he'd be back to give us a hand."

"Good." Although Rogue and Chance had had their differences, he couldn't afford to refuse any help that was offered. "Finish your supper, Rusty," he said. "I'm goin' to check out the cave again."

"Sure thing," Rusty said, seating himself and reaching for the container of coffee.

Rogue picked up one of the lanterns and made his way to the cavern entrance. Then he set a match to the wick and stepped into the cave. He moved carefully over the rubble left from the slide, turning sideways at a narrow passage that was smoothly roofed by a perfectly flat layer of limestone.

Suddenly a feeling of claustrophobia struck Rogue. He stopped, forcing himself to take long, slow breaths, reminding himself that the walls widened again a short distance in front of him. The thought had a great deal to do with his quick recovery, and it steadied his nerves until he reached the wider passage.

It seemed an eternity before he reached the vast, crescent-shaped chamber. Rogue could only guess what lay beyond the chamber, because the search party had gone no farther.

Holding his lantern at eye level, Rogue studied each of the passages that extended from the inner cavern. Some of them were large enough to enter while standing upright, while others were only big enough to wriggle through.

He entered the nearest passage, one of the larger ones, and went a distance of fifty feet or so, then stopped. Cupping his mouth, he called, "Professor Hartford!"

Silence.

"Professor Hartford!" he called again.

When there was still no reply, he went another

fifty feet or so. "Professor Hartford!" he shouted.

No reply.

He peered into the darkness ahead, but it was so thick that it was virtually impenetrable. As far as he knew, the tunnel could go on and on in a never-ending path. Professor Hartford might have gone this way, but there was no way of knowing for certain.

He called again, listened to the silence, then retraced his steps and tried another passage. It too, seemed to have no end.

Frowning, he returned to the crescent-shaped chamber again and took still another passage. He found the tunnel so narrow it nearly took his skin off, but he knew he couldn't rule the passage out. It was entirely possible the professor would prefer the narrower passage. As far as Rogue knew, it might be easier to gather data from the narrow tunnel with rougher walls.

God! The professor's daughter was right. He would need her. The thought caused him a great degree of displeasure.

"Dammit!" he muttered. *Dammit, dammit, dammit,* the cavern echoed.

Sighing heavily, realizing the magnitude of what he was undertaking, Rogue returned to the entrance, where Rusty waited with Chance Carter.

Fast-moving clouds that spoke of a coming storm darkened the morning sky as Miranda and Charlie reached the entrance to the cave. She had expected to see Rogue and the redheaded cowboy they called Rusty. But she hadn't expected to see the blond man standing beside Rogue.

"Whoa!" Charlie called, pulling the carriage up beside McClaren. "Didn't mean to be so long, Rogue," Charlie said, hopping down from the buggy and turning to help Miranda down. "We had a time roundin' up all the supplies."

"You goin' to introduce me to the lady, Rogue?" the blond man beside the rancher asked. He had a round face, giving the impression of immaturity, but Miranda knew it must be false, because of the tiny lines around his eyes — the wrinkles suggested he was at least thirty years old.

"Chance Carter, Miranda Hartford," Rogue said grimly.

Chance stuck out his hand and gripped hers hard. "My nature's just like my name, ma'am," he said, his blue eyes twinkling down at her. "Always willin' to take a chance. Especially when there's a pretty lady involved."

"If you're here to help, Chance, then help Rusty unload the supplies," Rogue snapped.

"Let me help," Miranda said quickly.

"You stay out of the way," Rogue ordered.

Although Miranda took offense at his tone of voice, she stayed where she was until the wagon was unloaded. Rogue frowned down at the boxes. "Why did you use so many containers for this stuff?" he asked Charlie.

"I asked him to prepare the supplies in that manner," Miranda said quickly. "We brought along some canvas to waterproof them as well."

Rogue pinned her with his gaze. "I suppose you've got some reason for makin' them so small?"

"Certainly," she said. "We may be entering places where the larger boxes won't fit." Although she expected a caustic reply, he fell silent. "The supplies will have to be divided into five equal parts," she went on. "Each one of us will carry our share."

Leaving the others to deal with the supplies, Miranda approached the cavern. She felt the same sense of excitement that she always experienced on such an occasion, but underlying the excitement, there was the fear . . . fear of the unknown, fear for her father, and the fear that had been with her since the last time she'd entered an unexplored cavern. The fear that caused her to break out in a cold sweat.

Don't think about it, she told herself. *Put it out of your mind.* She knew she must forget about the past. She must think of nothing but her father. Of his need. She felt an overwhelming need to hurry . . . to find him before it was too late.

"You're not really going with us?" Chance Carter's voice spun her around. "I've been through a lotta caves in these parts, ma'am. And some of 'em are pretty hard to get through. I went in this one before you got here . . . far enough to know it ain't gonna be easy."

"Don't worry," she said with a smile. "I'm quite used to roughing it. I've been exploring caves since

I was a child. Besides, I have to go. No one else knows my father's habits, or the way he would re-act in a given situation."

"That's the only reason I'm letting you go with us!" growled a voice behind them.

Miranda didn't have to turn around to know who was behind her. She would have recognized Rogue McClaren's voice anywhere.

She took her time facing him, meeting his eyes with a cold stare. "*You* are letting me go?" she in-quired sweetly. "McClaren, you would play hell, stopping me!"

A slow smile spread across his face. "You'd bet-ter watch that temper, professor. It just might land you in trouble someday."

Miranda gritted her teeth, barely curbing the impulse to slap the smile off his face. "I don't have a temper," she snapped, feeling a flush stain her cheeks. "And for your information, I don't lay claim to being a professor. That's my father's title."

His eyebrows lifted and his eyes glinted with sardonic amusement. "And you're not tryin' to prove you're just as smart, with that fancy educa-tion of yours?"

Her lips tightened grimly. "I don't have to prove anything," she snapped. "The facts speak for themselves."

Miranda found herself hating the arrogant man who faced her. She knew he was angry because he'd been forced to search the cavern for her father. But she couldn't help it. She needed the odious man's help. Even so, she knew it wasn't going to be easy having him in the search party. At least they wouldn't be alone. Miranda would avoid him as much as possible, and when it wasn't possible, the others would be there to act as buffers.

"We're wasting time," she said. "It's already dawn and we should have been in the cavern long ago."

"Okay, boys," Rogue said, turning to the other two men who were approaching. "You heard the lady. It looks like she's in charge of this rescue operation." He grinned wickedly. "At least until I say otherwise."

There was a general move to pick up the supplies and Miranda bent to hoist hers on her back.

"I'll do that," Chance said, hurrying over to her.

Miranda opened her mouth to say she'd carry her own, but before she could get the first word out, Rogue was beside them. His dark eyes glittered down at her.

"If the lady goes, then she carries her own weight," Rogue growled.

"Now wait a minute, Rogue," Chance objected. "You don't really expect her to do that. Those supplies are too heavy for any woman to lug around."

"You heard what I said. If she goes, she'll be treated just like everybody else."

Miranda's lips tightened grimly. "That's exactly what I intended," she said in an icy voice. "Thank you very much for your offer, Chance, but Mr.

McClaren is right. Everyone must carry their own weight."

Stiffly, she finished gathering up her supplies and moved with the others toward the entrance to the cavern.

Five

The cool darkness of the cave surrounded her as Miranda held the lantern up and studied the walls of the crescent-shaped chamber they had entered. The dull gray rock of the passage behind her was replaced here by a golden brown color. Although there were a few formations in the chamber—stalactites of calcite, huddled like gnomes—she could see at a glance they were completely dormant, no longer forming or growing. Obviously air had entered the cavern in some manner and stopped the growth.

Miranda wished she had more time to spend in the chamber, but with her father's need uppermost in her mind, she hurried after the others.

Stopping beside Rusty at the far end of the chamber, she saw the tunnels, twisting and snaking away in three directions, each one filled with seemingly impenetrable darkness. Miranda felt McClaren's gaze on her as she studied each of them in turn.

Turning to face him, she asked, "Have you been in any of these passages?"

"Yes. Only a little ways, but far enough to know the tunnels don't end very quick. They just seem to go on forever."

"The right one as well?"

He nodded.

"Then that's the one we'll follow. My father always made it a practice to work from right to left, whatever the situation. That way he would always know what passage he'd already been through."

"That makes sense," McClaren said grudgingly. "I'll take the lead. Charlie, you bring up the rear. Everybody but Charlie put out your lanterns." Without waiting for a reply, he held his own lantern aloft and entered the passage on his right.

Although Miranda wasn't happy about putting out her lantern, she knew it made sense to conserve the fuel. However, before she killed the flame, she checked to make certain she still had her canvas-covered package of matches in the left pocket of her jacket.

The two lanterns proved more than enough to keep the darkness at bay in the narrow tunnel. They traveled through the passage for what seemed like hours, until finally they were brought up abruptly by a large boulder blocking the way.

"Looks like that's it," McClaren said. "If the

professor came this way, he must've turned back at this point."

"Wait a minute!" Miranda pushed around the others until she reached the blockage. "We have to be sure," she said, kneeling beside the boulder. "Lower your lantern, McClaren. We must be certain there's no opening."

The disk of light from the lantern lowered, swept to the right, then to the left. Miranda almost missed the darker spot near the bottom of the tunnel. "Wait!" she exclaimed. "Shine the light there!" She pointed toward the spot.

"What is it?" asked McClaren, holding the lantern closer to the floor.

"A hole." She felt exultant. "They could have gone through there . . . in fact, I'm almost certain they did."

"You're crazy!" he snapped. "Why would they do anything like that?"

"Because Poppa is an explorer. And, like so many other explorers, he's driven by insatiable curiosity." She shoved her head into the opening, hoping to see a light from some distant lantern. But there was nothing but darkness. She sat back on her heels and looked up at McClaren. "He came here to study the rock strata and he wouldn't have left until he'd done it."

"Looks like he'd've found enough rocks to study before he got this far."

"He wouldn't have been able to pass up a chance like this," she said with a sigh. "Do you see a cross anywhere?"

"No," he replied. "Nothing there."

"Then he went on."

"How can you be so sure?"

She sighed with exasperation. Was it going to be necessary to explain every little thing to the man? "Because my father would have left a cross if he had chosen to abandon this passage. He never relies on his memory . . . too many times the tunnels look the same. Also, the cross is a way of letting a search party — should one become necessary — know the direction he's taken."

Rogue knelt on the passage floor and peered at the velvety black opening . . . no more than two feet high, partially hidden by a protrusion in the boulder. "You really mean for us to go through that hole?"

"I *am* going through there, Mr. McClaren," she said grimly, flashing him a dark look. "But you have my permission to turn back if you're afraid of the dark." Brave words, but she didn't know what she'd do if he took her up on them.

A muscle twitched in his jaw and his eyes flared, but when he spoke, his voice was even. "I'm not afraid of the dark, Miss Hartford. But credit me with a little sense. It could be dangerous to crawl in there. You don't know for sure you'll be able to come back out."

Anxious fear swamped her, quenching her anger like a bucket of water poured on a flame.

God! She couldn't possibly go on alone. She needed this man's help.

Miranda tried to keep the fear from her voice, tried to present a calm front. "How can you know the passage is dangerous unless you try it?"

"Dammit, woman!" He spewed the words out. "I have eyes in my head."

"The only thing your eyes can possibly tell you is that you're faced with a narrow passage. I've been through many others very much like it. Sometimes they become completely blocked, other times they turn into larger passages. My father would have entered to see what lay beyond." She took a calming breath, then added, "As I'm going to do. But I shall need a lantern to light my way."

He made no effort to stop her from changing lanterns with him. Then he stood silently as she shoved the lighted lantern into the hole. Miranda's heart began a slow thudding beat as she crawled into the passage and pulled her supplies in behind her.

God, please let him follow, she silently prayed. Even though she'd been in like situations before, she was overwhelmed by the feeling of being sucked into the dark tunnel, completely alone. The darkness seemed to be closing around her, smothering her, like black velvet pressing against her face.

She swallowed back the fear that threatened to

overpower her as she squirmed forward on her stomach like a crawfish, wriggling her way through the dark crawl way until, finally, the ceiling lifted several inches, allowing her to advance on her knees.

"Come on," she called back over her shoulder. "The ceiling has already lifted, and there's plenty of room in here."

Miranda heard the muttered oath that came from Rogue McClaren, then the sound of him entering the crawl way behind her. She could easily identify the familiar thump, scrape, scrape, thump, scrape, scrape, that meant he was throwing his sack of supplies ahead of him then crawling after it.

The passage gradually widened and the ceiling continued to rise until finally it was high enough for her to stand upright. Wiping beads of sweat from her face, Miranda hoisted her pack on her back and continued onward. She had no idea how long they had traveled in the tunnel, for time ceased to have meaning. Quite suddenly, the passage opened into a large chamber.

Miranda raised her lantern above her head, her gaze moving around the cavern, fastening momentarily on a tendril of helictite growing from a wall, before moving on to touch on the next fantastic stone decoration, which resembled a butterfly in flight.

"My God!" whispered a voice at her elbow. "Wouldja look at that? The ceiling must be fifty feet high. And them white things growin' out of it . . . I never seen nothin' like it before."

"Those white things are called stalactites," Miranda said, dropping her pack to the floor and arching her tired back muscles. "Anybody object to taking a break?"

"Sounds like a mighty good idea to me," Chance said, tossing his pack to the ground and slumping down beside it. "Besides, I want to set here and admire them things . . . stalac—whatever you said." He stared in awe at the dazzling display of crystal-like stalactites and stalagmites, ranging in color from pure white through shades of beige, pale rose, bright orange and deep brown. "Damn me, if that's not one of the purtiest sights I've ever seen, I'll eat my hat."

"You might just as well eat it," remarked Charlie. " 'Cause you sure as hell ain't gonna need it down here." He cast a swift glance at Miranda. "Pardon my language ma'am."

"Please don't apologize, Charlie," she said, seating herself on the cavern floor. "We're obviously going to be in each other's company until my father is found, however long that takes. And if you're bent on apologizing every time you get excited, then you'll never get anything else said, because I can promise that you *will* be excited by the sights we encounter down here."

"I dunno, ma'am." He scratched his grizzled head. "Maybe excited ain't quite the word I'd use. Though I can see how a body who liked

59

something different would sure like this place. 'Cause it is that . . . different."

Miranda's laughter sounded through the darkness, and it seemed to startle the three men. "Perhaps you won't take to spelunking, Charlie."

"I ain't so sure I will, ma'am," he said. "I sure don't like being under the ground. But I am wonderin' about the peculiar-looking rocks that's ahanging from the ceiling. They look sorta like icicles. How do they stay up there?"

"Hey, Chance," Rusty called from the other side of the chamber. "Come take a look at this rock. Looks like an elephant."

Miranda smiled at the enthusiasm displayed by Rusty, then proceeded to answer Charlie's question. "The ceiling formations are stalactites. They're formed there by water. One drop at a time. The water works its way from the surface through cracks in the limestone." She pointed to the ground. "See the columns on the floor? Those are called stalagmites. They're formed the same way. The constantly dripping water deposits calcium carbonate on the live cave formations."

"A drop at a time?"

"That's right. One drop at a time."

"Musta taken a hell of a long time to build them things."

She laughed again. "Yes, Charlie. It did. Millions of years."

"Thank you for that piece of information,

professor." McClaren's voice was a harsh intrusion. "The rest of us were just dying to hear it."

Miranda stiffened. What was wrong with that hateful man? Was he just naturally that way, or did he object to intellectual women. His next words gave her the answer.

"Never could stand a woman that believed she was smarter than men."

She stifled an outraged gasp. The nerve of the man! She *was* smarter than the average man, but, contrary to his beliefs, she did not go around lording it over mortals with less knowledge than herself. She knew better than most that she was among the few women who had had the privilege of acquiring a good education.

She bit back a sharp retort, realizing that this was no time to fight a battle of words with the rancher, but such a time would surely come, because, although the trip was just beginning, she had taken about all she was going to take from the ignorant man.

When she spoke, her voice was even. "I don't just *believe* I'm smarter than most men, McClaren. Due to Poppa's efforts and a good education, I most certainly am. And I find that most men, like yourself, object to that fact." She pushed herself to her feet. "But, deny it as you will, it is a reality. In addition I have a well of strength to draw upon. That strength will carry me through most situations I will encounter." She swung her pack on her back. "Now, if you're quite sure you've had enough rest, then we'll continue on our way." That should fix him. No man would like being thought the cause of holding the rest of the party up because of his own weakness.

"I've been ready since we got here," he said grimly. "Since you seem to know everything, which way did your father go from here?"

Miranda hadn't realized that, as before, there were several passages branching out from the chamber. "The right one of course," she said grimly. "Poppa would have gone no other way."

"Douse your light, Charlie. We'll use just one from now on." Without another word, Rogue took the lead into the dark tunnel. His long strides carried him forward at a pace that was hard for her to maintain with her much shorter legs, but it was her own fault. She had succeeded in making him furious, and now he made no allowance for the fact that she was a woman.

That's only what you've been insisting on, an inner voice chided.

They were in a wide passage which sloped gently downwards for several yards, then turned abruptly to the left. She trudged silently forward, doing her best to keep up, but each time she realized she was blocking one of the men, she stood aside and waved him past her, until finally she was bringing up the rear. The others seemed not to notice that she was falling behind, that the light was fast fading around her, the lantern McClaren carried seemed to be only a pale yellow glow in the distance.

Miranda was tempted to light her lantern, but knew the fuel must be saved until it was really needed. She wondered momentarily why the other men were unable to sense her distress, then she knew immediately that they had taken her answers to Rogue to heart and most likely thought her mental strength was physical as well.

So much for her runaway tongue.

They kept up the pace Rogue set for hours and the distance they traveled must have been great, but still the tunnel went on. At some point in time, about the time Miranda thought her legs would give way beneath her, Rogue slowed his pace and allowed her to catch up with them.

When she came up beside him she realized the reason he had stopped. They had come into another chamber.

It was huge, even larger than the last one; a great natural cavern the size of a cathedral, with a high curved ceiling that vanished into darkness, and clefts and recesses that swallowed the feebly probing lantern light. Gnarled calcite columns formed enormous pillars that stretched up into the darkness above them.

"My God!" Rusty breathed. "Who'd've ever believed this place was down here? All the time

63

I was punchin' cattle on the range, all the time I was huntin' strays on Squaw Mountain, I had no idea they was anything like this waitin' just a few feet below me."

"It is impressive, isn't it?" Miranda asked softly.

"What'n hell stops the ceiling from collapsing?" Rusty asked.

"It's all rock," Miranda explained. "This cavern was formed by water, probably a river, forcing its way through underground."

"Musta been a hell of a river," Charlie said. "Never seen the like of it before." He wiped the back of his hand across his forehead and Miranda realized he was sweating in the cool air of the cavern. "Am I the only one that's getting hungry?" he asked. "Must be way past time to eat."

Rogue looked at his watch. "It's going on two," he said.

"In the afternoon?" Charlie's eyes widened. "Well, I'll be damned. Here we been traveling in these tunnels for nigh on to eight hours. Time don't seem to have much meaning down here, does it?"

Miranda grinned at Charlie. She was glad he was with them. "It's easy to lose track of time underground," she said. "Not only is there no sun to guide you, but there's nothing at all to indicate the passing of time—except for Mc-Claren's watch," she added dryly.

"And that's a fact," Charlie said. "An' I ain't so sure I like that. I 'spect after we get outta here, I ain't never gonna want to come into one of these things again."

"You may change your mind before we're through," Miranda said, her gaze roaming the cavern walls. Suddenly her heart gave a painful little jerk of excitement as her eyes became fixed on a black spot to the left of a strangely shaped pillar, barely visible in the dim circle of light. Was it an arrow? A sign from her father?

She turned to McClaren. "May I have the lantern for a moment?" she asked.

Silently, he handed it over.

Miranda was aware of Rogue McClaren's curious gaze as she hurried across the cavern, intent on inspecting the mark up close. She was certain it was a marker, left there by her father.

Miranda was totally unprepared when suddenly her foot struck something hard and she lost her balance, flailing out with her arms to regain her footing. Her fingers lost their grip on the lantern and she heard it clatter against the rock floor. Without a warning the light went out, leaving them in complete darkness.

"Botheration!" she muttered, taking a small measure of comfort from the sound of her own voice. She tried hard to forget about the darkness that seemed intent on smothering her, tried instead to concentrate on retrieving the light as quickly as possible.

She heard a scraping sound, then Rogue Mc-Claren's voice coming from somewhere behind her. "Everybody stay where you are until I get another lantern going."

But Miranda couldn't wait. Her mouth was dry, her fear almost debilitating. God! She must find the lantern, must have light to keep the blackness away.

She stepped forward, sweeping her right foot across the rock floor as she went, hoping to find the lantern. When she didn't connect with it, she went along quicker. She had to find the lantern, must find it before she gave in to her ever-growing fears.

Miranda leaned forward sweeping her hand in front of her. She was totally unprepared when the floor dropped from beneath her feet and she plummeted into a black abyss.

Six

"Aiiiieeeee!"

Even as Miranda fell, she heard the sound of her scream echoing through the cavern. Terror pierced through her, intensified by the blackness surrounding her as she continued to fall into the seemingly bottomless abyss, knowing with a certainty that when she reached the bottom there would be nothing left of her to worry about bringing up.

"Miranda!"

Rogue McClaren's voice seemed to be coming out of a clammy darkness . . . the wet, oozing, sucking darkness that clutched at her falling body.

And then she reached the bottom.

Kersplash!

Water closed over Miranda's head, and she gasped with shock, breathing the liquid into her lungs. It was cold, incredibly frigid, and it enveloped her, swallowed her, sucking her deeper

and deeper into its icy depths. She acknowledged the panic as she twisted about, arms and
feet working frantically, fighting to reach a surface that seemed so far away. The frigid water
pressed against her ears . . . God! how deep had
she gone?

She felt almost separated in mind from the
girl who fought so desperately . . . as if she
were only a casual observer, not really involved
with the girl who fought against the weight of
water-filled boots.

Her lungs were burning! Screaming out for
air! She'd never make it to the top before they
burst, not with her waterlogged boots weighing
her down.

Miranda knew, with a certainty, that she was
going to die . . . die . . . die . . .

Suddenly, when she was certain she couldn't
hold her breath any longer, she broke the surface. Gulping in huge breaths of the life-giving
oxygen, she felt herself sinking again and sucked
in a mouthful of water. Kicking madly with her
waterlogged boots, she reached the surface again
and coughed, spewing the water from her
mouth.

Desperately, Miranda flailed out with both
arms, splashing wildly, attempting to keep herself afloat while trying to expel the water from
her lungs.

When her hands struck something solid, she
scrabbled for purchase, but there was nothing

there to cling to and her fingers slid off the smooth surface.

God! If only it weren't so dark. If only it weren't . . . something struck her legs and she shrieked wildly.

"Miranda!" came a voice from somewhere above her . . . so far above . . .

Still gasping and sputtering, Miranda pumped her legs, treading water to keep afloat. She looked up—God, it was so far up—like looking through the wrong end of a telescope. There was only a faint light in the distance, and everywhere else there was darkness.

Fear surged through her, cold, debilitating fear, even worse than what she'd experienced in the French Alps. The fear was so overwhelming that it swamped every other thought in her mind. "Rogue!" she shrieked. "Help meeee!"

"Mira-a-anda!" Even from this distance she imagined she could hear the relief in his voice, but what did he have to be so relieved about? "Are you all right, Mira-a-anda?"

"No!" she shouted back, still splashing wildly in the pool. She would drown down here . . . alone in the darkness.

Miranda realized that the fear of such an end had been with her ever since she had been lost in the cavern in the Alps. She was certain that to die alone in the darkness would be the greatest agony of all.

"—you hu-u-urt?" His voice seemed dim, far

away, but then, it was. How far, she had no way of knowing.

"I . . ." She swallowed a mouthful of water and gave a choking cough. "I fell into a pool," she yelled. "I'm all right."

All right. She wasn't really all right. She wasn't injured. At least not physically. But she might well lose her sanity at any given moment.

"—again!" he called.

Was he asking her to repeat her answer? "I'm in a pool of water!" she called.

"Can you . . . afloat until we . . . rope to you?"

The water seemed to roil around her, and Miranda swallowed a mouthful, then choked and went under again. She struggled wildly toward the surface again, felt something solid strike the side of her head, then there was a burning sensation at her right temple.

Gasping with pain, she sucked in another mouthful of water, just before she plummeted downward again. She felt the rushing waters cooling the heat at her temple, knew that she must fight against the weight of her boots . . . but she was so tired . . . so tired . . . what was the use of struggling against her fate . . . she had only to let go and it would all be over.

Rogue lay flat at the edge of the abyss, looking downward, trying to penetrate the darkness

70

with his gaze. But it was an impossible task.

"How in hell are we gonna get her outta there?" Charlie asked, crouching down behind him, making sure to keep away from the edge.

Good question, but Rogue could find no answer for it. He only knew that somehow he must get her out. He turned to Charlie. "Bring me the rope."

"Ain't so sure there's enough of it to reach her, boss," Rusty said. "From the sound of her voice she's a far piece away."

Rogue already knew that, knew also that it had been awhile since they'd heard a sound from the well cavern. Was it because she'd already drowned?

Miranda's lungs burned as she fought her way to the surface again and coughed, trying to clear the water from her lungs. Then she sucked in huge gulps of air as she fought to tread water, to keep herself afloat in the darkness. She wasn't sure that she was bleeding until something warm began to trickle down her forehead and cheeks.

"Mira-a-anda!"

The voice, Rogue McClaren's voice, came from the cavern located high above her. Miranda tried to answer him, but to stay afloat took all the effort she could muster.

"Dammit!"

For some reason, the word came clearly, even from such a great distance, and Miranda could hear the fury in the voice. Was he angry because she'd fallen in the well-cavern? Well, she couldn't help it. *She couldn't!*

"Miranda!" Rogue's voice came again. "If you can hear me, hug the far wall!"

"Don't do it, Rogue!" shouted another voice from above. "It's too dangerous!"

Miranda lifted her head, trying again to penetrate the darkness above. For a moment there was a pinpoint of light in the distance, then it completely disappeared. The next moment there was a splash, then the water heaved around her as though a great weight had caused it to surge forth. Terror struck deep as Miranda fought to keep her head above the water, feeling positive she was no longer alone in the darkness.

A moment later something warm wrapped around her arm. Miranda struck out wildly, uttering a terrified screech. There was something in the pool with her!

Something alive!

"Stop it!" a harsh voice said. "It's just me! Rogue. I came to help you."

"Rogue?" she whispered, hardly daring to believe her senses. But it was true. She could feel his body against hers now, and nothing had ever felt so welcome to her before. "God! Is it really you?"

"Yes," he answered gruffly. "Are you all right?"

Miranda couldn't speak around the lump in her throat. She moved convulsively, her left arm circling his neck tightly while she patted his face with her right hand, feeling the need to reassure herself of his presence. Like a blind man, her palm read his features, from the frown that drew his brows together, to his firm, set mouth. She still found it hard to believe that he was with her.

But he was!

The realization loosed a flood of tears and she wrapped her other arm around his neck, pressed her body closer against him and began to sob hysterically.

"Take it easy," he said harshly. "No need to take on so. We'll get out of here! You're gonna be all right."

Miranda only clung tighter.

"Stop it!" he growled. "Get hold of yourself before you drown both of us."

His words snapped her out of her terror. She tried to relax her hold on him, but her body shook with tremors that she couldn't seem to control.

"Keep still," he said calmly. "I'm gonna tow you to safety."

Safety? In this hell-hole? Although Miranda doubted they'd ever reach safety, she forced her body to go still. A moment later he gave a lurch and stopped moving.

"It's okay now," he muttered. "I'm holding to the rocks."

She wiped the tears from her face with the back of her hand. "I-I'm s-sorry." She choked the words out. "I-I g-guess I p-panicked."

"That's okay," he said quietly. "You're holdin' up just fine."

"Do you really think we'll get out of here?"

"Of course. Charlie's already makin' plans to get us out."

Miranda realized he was trying to calm her fears. She found his very presence reassuring. "I'm sorry I was so foolish," she said. "I thought Poppa had left a sign for me, and I was in too big a hurry to examine it. I suppose it must have been bat guano."

"Wouldn't surprise me none," he agreed. "But we didn't see any sign of bats in here."

"Rogue!" came a shout from above. "Are y'all okay?"

"Yes!" Rogue yelled. "We're safe enough." Lowering his voice, he muttered. "I can't quite figure this place out. Charlie's voice sounded real clear, but we could hardly hear you."

"It's the acoustics," Miranda replied. "Something about the rock that is—" She broke off as they heard Charlie's voice again.

"We're sendin' a rope down," he shouted. "See if you can tie it aroun' Miranda so's we can pull 'er out!"

"Hurry it up!" Rogue shouted.

"Do you think they'll get us out?" Miranda asked.

"They'll get us out. Charlie won't stop tryin' until he does." He pulled her closer against him. "You're shiverin'."

"The water's cold."

"Yeah," he agreed. "But I 'spect part of your reaction is shock." His voice held a slight tinge of amusement when he continued. "Maybe that's why you were so glad to see me . . . or was that just my imagination workin' overtime?"

He knew damned well she'd been glad! Somehow, just his presence had served to calm her. The memory of her terror made her press her body closer against him. "How can you joke about this?"

"What else should I do, Miranda?" he asked gently. "The situation is bad, right enough, but cryin' about it's not gonna help the situation any."

"I-I'm not crying!" she whispered fiercely. "B-but I'll admit this constant d-dark is getting to me. I'd feel better if there was even a little l-light."

"That's somethin' I can fix." No sooner had the words left his mouth, then he pulled at her hands, still wrapped around his neck.

"What are you doing?" she quavered fearfully.

Suddenly, she felt the rock beneath her hand.

"Hold on to that," he commanded.

75

Her fingers tightened on the outcrop of rock and she waited, wondering what he intended. The silence lengthened between them and all the time she felt the movements that told her he was still beside her.

Suddenly she heard a scratching sound, then light flared, illuminating the darkness around them. "There," he said. "Is that better?"

She stared in amazement at the match in his hand, then her gaze lifted and met his eyes and she summoned up a smile. "I have some matches in my pocket, but I didn't even think about them." She drew in her breath with a shudder. "Thank you. Now I can last awhile longer."

"Look, Miranda," he said. "Look just above your hand."

Her gaze lifted and her eyes widened. There, only a few inches above her right hand, was a ledge. If they could climb up on it, they would at least be out of the cold water.

Suddenly the light sputtered, then went out, leaving them in total darkness again. But in that brief moment of light, Miranda regained her courage. With a lunge, she sought to find something higher on the wall to cling to. Her searching fingers found nothing but empty space and she sank down into the pool and the water closed in around her.

With a swift kick she surfaced again and scrabbled upward, her fingers caught . . . and wrapped around a solid object.

"Take it easy," came Rogue's voice from beside her. "You were doin' fine. Don't panic on me now."

"I've got it," she sputtered. "I'm holding to the rock, Rogue."

"Good girl! Now hang on tight and I'll try to boost you up there."

His hands slid downward, slipping between her thighs and she gave a shocked gasp and kicked at them.

"Sorry," he muttered. "Can't see a damn thing in this dark."

Miranda knew his actions hadn't been deliberate and silently berated herself for her reaction. A woman's body was the last thing he would have on his mind right now. He seemed to be steadying himself in some fashion against the rough rock because his hands wrapped around her hips and he pushed upward.

Keeping a tight grip with her left hand, Miranda flailed out with her right, found another protrusion and gripped tightly with numb fingers. Using her knees against the rough walls, she pulled herself upright until she was lying across the ledge, gasping for breath.

"Miranda," Rogue's quiet voice came from below and to her right. "Are you set snug up there?"

"Yes," she said, feeling along the ledge with her arms and legs. From the best she could determine, the narrow strip of rock seemed to be about twelve inches deep, but she had no way of knowing its length. "There's plenty of room for both of us up here. Do you think you can make it without a boost?"

His laugh was husky. "Do I have a choice? Here, take this." He handed her a small, water-proof, canvas-covered package. "That's the matches. Strike one of 'em on the box . . . an' be careful not to lose 'em."

She did as he asked, feeling her way through as she'd had cause to do many times in the past. A moment later, a light flared and she could see him just below her.

"Hold the match higher," he said. "Look that ledge over good while you can see it. You're gonna have to remember the way it looks."

Realizing he was right, Miranda lifted her head, allowing her gaze to sweep the area in front of her. Rock, nothing but grayish green rock, except . . . her gaze stopped on the dark depression, wondering if it was only a hollow place, or if . . .

Suddenly the light sputtered and went out.

Seven

Miranda narrowed her gaze, trying to penetrate the thick blackness. But it was useless . . . like trying to see through black velvet. Had her imagination been working overtime, or—her heart gave an erratic jerk of hope—could the depression have been a tunnel?

"Miranda," Rogue's voice came out of the darkness. "Scoot over. I don't want to knock you down when I climb up there."

"Just be careful," she muttered, pushing herself to her hands and knees and creeping cautiously along the rocky shelf. "There's not much room up here, and I don't want to wind up in that cold water again."

She heard a couple of grunts, then the sound of sloshing water, accompanied by slithery squishing. Then he was on the ledge beside her. He reached out and slid an arm around her shoulder, pulling her firmly against him. Miranda wondered at her calm acceptance of his embrace. Not only did she accept it, she welcomed it, and only a short time ago, she could hardly stand being in his company.

She told herself it was a natural reaction. After all, his body gave off heat, helping to ward off the chill caused by her sodden clothing. Miranda knew she must look a sight, with her riding habit clinging to her and her hair hanging in wet tangles.

Her lips turned up at the thought. Although Miranda had never been vain about her looks, here she was, in desperate circumstances, contemplating her appearance.

"This ledge oughta keep us halfway dry until Charlie can get us out of here." When she remained silent, he said, "Don't worry, Miranda. He *will* get us out."

"Of course he will," she said, not allowing herself to even contemplate otherwise. "They should have enough rope up there. Even if they have to tie some of them together. I have no doubt your men will rescue us."

"What's botherin' you then?"

"Bothering me?" She gave a husky laugh. "Well, being in this cavern is not —"

"No." His voice was firm. "There's somethin' else. You've gone quiet all of a sudden . . . Were you thinkin' of the professor . . . of what's happened to him?"

"Of course I'm concerned about him. That's the reason we're in this fix. But I do have sense enough to know we can't help him until we get out of here. No, I was thinking about something else . . . puzzling over it really." She probed the darkness with her gaze, wishing she could see him. "Just before the light went out, I saw something."

"Saw something? What kind of something?"

"It was a depression in the wall . . . more like a hole. And I've been wondering if it could be a tunnel."

He was silent for a moment, then, "Where was it?"

She tried to imagine the position in her mind. "I think maybe . . . it would be a little to your left," she said.

"Rogue!" The voice came from the cavern high above them. "We made . . . harness . . . -randa. We tied . . . ropes . . . when . . . harness . . . you, . . . -randa loop . . . around her . . ."

The words were broken up, as though the rock walls had absorbed most of them.

"What did he say?" Miranda asked anxiously.

"I think they have a harness ready for you." Raising his voice, he yelled, "Okay! Just hurry up! Miranda's got the shakes. I think she's getting tired of this place."

"Hold on . . . -randa!" Chance shouted. ". . . soon have . . . out."

"Chance!" Miranda shouted, cupping her mouth with her hands. "Would you lower a lantern down on that rope?"

"Good idea," said Rogue. "I should've thought of it myself. It'll make getting you in the harness easier."

Miranda hadn't thought of that. Her reason for

wanting the lantern was her interest in examining the well-cavern before they left it. She certainly had no intention of coming back in after she was safely out. She'd regained enough composure to be curious about her watery prison.

She kept her head thrown back, her eyes fixed on the pinpoint of light so far above them. How odd, she told herself. It hardly seems to be moving at all.

When Rogue shouted again, Miranda gave a jerk of surprise. "What's the matter up there? Hurry up with that lantern!"

"It's on its way!" The voice belonged to Charlie.

A shiver of fear went through Miranda. "I think we must be a long, long way from them." Her eyes never left the lantern that appeared to be barely moving.

"We are," he admitted. "I found that out in my dive. But seems like it's takin' a long time with that light." He fell silent for a long moment. "It's funny how the sound carries in here. Sometimes we're hearin' 'em real good, an' sometimes it's like their words are bein' gobbled up by the walls."

"I noticed that," she said. "The acoustics in here are peculiar. I've been in caves where sound travels easily over great distances—with those you get a reverberating effect, like an echo—and I've been in other caves where the sound is completely absorbed by the rock walls. There seems to be a little of both in here."

Miranda sensed that she'd lost Rogue's attention, knew she had when she heard his shout.

"Hey, Charlie! How much rope is tied to that lantern?"

"About fifty feet!" Charlie answered, his words loud and clear.

"May not be enough!" Rogue shouted back. "But go ahead and try."

The lantern seemed barely to move while they waited tensely. Finally, it stopped moving completely.

"What's goin' on up there?" Rogue yelled.

For a moment there was only silence from above. Then, "We ran outta rope!"

Miranda was trying to measure the distance with her eyes, as was Rogue, she realized, when he muttered, "Looks like the lantern's about halfway down. Must be close to a hundred feet from that cavern to the water level."

"Near that anyway," she agreed. "Do we just forget about the lantern?"

"No. We'll have 'em drop it down."

"The glass will explode on impact."

"More than likely. But I'd rather take the chance. It's not as risky as puttin' a harness around you in the dark."

His voice was slightly grim when he told the men to drop the lantern down to them. Miranda clenched her jaws while she watched the light, wobbling back and forth as though pulled with haste. Then suddenly, the light went out. A moment later it was back again, plunging closer, closer, until there was a loud splash, followed by the sound of breaking glass. In that same moment of time, Rogue released his hold on her and slipped into the water.

"Rogue!" she cried in panic.

"I'm here," came a voice from the darkness below her. "Just had to get the lantern."

"Did you find it?"

"Yeah. Got it right here."

"Be careful. You might cut yourself."

"Here. Take it until I get up there."

Miranda leaned toward his voice, feeling around the edge of the rocky shelf until her fingers brushed against metal. She wrapped her hand around the handle, gripping it tightly, waiting for him to rejoin her. When he was securely on the ledge, she felt him moving and wondered what he was doing. A moment later she had her answer.

"There," he said, satisfaction in his voice. A match flared, sending a meager light around them until he put it to the lantern wick.

She stared at the knife he was holding. "You trimmed the wick."

"Sure did," he grinned, holding the lantern up. "Behold your light, my lady."

Her laughter filled the cavern, echoing off the walls, again and again. The man was confusing. Ever since she'd met him, he had been rude and annoying. Now, when their situation was almost desperate, he was showing a sense of the ridiculous.

"Feel better?" he asked gently.

She nodded her head, unable to find a response.

"Good. Then we'll get on with the rescue." Looking up, he cupped his mouth and shouted, "Charlie! Can you see the light?"

"Yeah!" Charlie answered.

"How far would you guess it is?"

"Hard to tell, boss! Seems a mighty long ways."

Satisfied that Rogue would handle their end of the rescue, Miranda directed her attention to her surroundings. As she'd already suspected, the cavern was shaped like a well, perhaps thirty feet in circumference. She studied the rocky walls. They were smooth, slippery, with very few outcrops or depressions that could be used to help them climb out.

Something tugged at her memory and she searched for the hole she'd seen before, and as she'd suspected, found it a little beyond Rogue. Her gaze narrowed. It could be a passage, a way out of this place without help from those above.

"Rogue," she said. "Look around to your left. There's the hole I told you about. Does it go back into the rock wall?"

He frowned and turned, his gaze narrowing on the opening. "Well, I'll be damned," he said. "That's exactly what it does." He shoved the lantern into the hole and looked inside.

"What do you see?" she asked eagerly.

"Looks like it goes on a ways," he replied, pulling the lantern out again. Suddenly, his eyes became fixed. "What's this?" he muttered.

"What?" she asked sharply.

"It's a black smudge. Looks almost like somebody made it on purpose. Like they put an arrow here."

An arrow? "Let me see!" In her eagerness, her foot slid on the slippery ledge and only Rogue's swift reaction saved her from toppling off.

"Be careful!"

"Move over so I can see the arrow," she said.

"I know what you're thinkin'," he said gruffly. "But you're dead wrong. It's not an arrow. Just a dark smudge."

"No." She shook her head to emphasize her point. "It's an arrow. My father made it." She pointed at what she knew to be the upper end. "See. Those two lines are the prongs."

"They're just smudges," he said grimly.

"No!" she said sharply, trying to push past him. "You said yourself it looked like an arrow. That's my father's mark. I know it is. He always carries charcoal in his pocket. He's trying to tell me he went through there."

"You're not thinkin' straight," he said, placing a hand on her forearm. "Just listen to yourself. How could your father have got down here anyway?"

"He could've fallen in, the same way I did. Now move out of my way so I can look for him."

He gave a long-suffering sigh. "If you're bent on goin' in there, then at least wait 'til I tell Charlie what's goin' on."

Miranda could hardly contain her excitement while she waited for him to explain to the others. She was so certain she would find her father before too much longer.

"I still don't think this is a good idea," he grumbled, crawling into the tunnel.

"I know. You've already said so." Miranda was close on his heels.

"Stay out there!" he snapped, turning his head to pin her with a glare. "There's no sense in both of us comin' in here."

"I don't want to be left out there alone," she said, making her voice sound reasonable. "I won't get in the way." She wouldn't be sent back, couldn't be certain he'd follow the tunnel to its end without her.

They'd only gone a short distance when the ceiling lifted enough for them to stand upright. A little farther on, the path widened until it was easily traversed by both of them. Soon, the tunnel took an upward curve, but it was a gradual climb.

Rogue had finally stopped grumbling, having obviously decided they might've found an easier way out of the well-cavern. Finally, he stopped, drawing his watch out of his pocket and studying it. "I don't know how long we've been walkin', Miranda, but we'll have to go back. Charlie will be worryin' about us."

Although she knew he was right, she also knew she couldn't stop now. "Let's just go a little further," she pleaded. "Just a few more minutes."

"All right. But only five more minutes. Then we'll go back."

All too soon he stopped again. "Time's up. We're goin' back now."

She gave a heavy sigh. "It looks like we have a problem."

"What kind of problem?" he asked grimly.

"I can't go back," she said, putting all the determination she felt into her voice. "I won't leave until I've satisfied myself that my father didn't go this way."

"That is a problem," he agreed. "Because—" His fingers snared her wrist, digging into the tender flesh. "—because, you're not leaving my side, Miranda. Not until we're back with the others."

Although she chafed at his words, she also knew he was right. As she'd told him herself, the first rule in cave exploration was never to go off alone. But she couldn't leave this place without at least checking the passage out.

Not when there was every possibility that her father had been here.

No! She must make certain!

Eight

"I must go farther," she said, trying to maintain an even, conciliatory tone. "Surely you can see that. And if you insist on staying with me, then you'll have to come too."

His penetrating gaze bored into her as he eyed her grimly. Miranda shuffled uncomfortably, but held silent beneath his gaze. She refused to be intimidated. Not when her father's life was at stake. Her determination was like a rock inside her, and perhaps he read it in her face.

Whatever the reason, he gave a muttered exclamation, then growled. "All right. But we'll first have to let the others know what we're about."

He didn't release her hand as he strode back down the passage toward the well-cavern. When they reached the spot where the ceiling lowered drastically, he turned to her. "You can wait here for me. But I don't want you budging an inch." Hs voice became steely, commanding. "Do you hear me, Miranda? Don't you budge an inch."

"All right," she said submissively, her eyes fastened to his. "I'll wait here for you."

With an abrupt nod, he released her, then dropped to his hands and knees and, pushing the lantern before him, he crawled away from her toward the well-cavern.

As the distance between them increased, the circle of light the lantern had given off became smaller and smaller until it was only a dim memory.

Miranda shivered with cold, realizing as she did that she'd found a certain warmth in his presence. With even that removed, and darkness pushing at her from all sides, she felt chilled to the bone.

Gathering a handful of sodden skirt, she wrung as much water as she could from it, then turned her attention to her jacket. It too, was still dripping water. She shrugged it from her shoulders and squeezed it out, then, hearing Rogue's voice hailing Charlie, decided she had time to wring her shirt out as well. Although she fumbled with the buttons in the darkness, she was fastening the last one when she saw the circle of light that meant Rogue was returning.

Thankfully, she watched him draw nearer, saw beyond the lantern to the dark figure behind it. Like herself, he was dripping wet. With his shirt plastered against his upper torso, the thick muscles in his chest and arms were sharply defined. His breeches clung to his slim hips and powerful legs, leaving little to the imagination. Her gaze continued down, touched on his powerful legs and his bare feet. Obviously he'd removed his boots before his dive into the well-cavern. Although he'd been able to swim better without the weight of his boots, his feet were likely to suffer—while traversing the tunnel—for the lack of them.

"Well, what do you think?" His amused voice interrupted her thoughts, jerked her eyes upward. "Will I do?"

He was smiling broadly, and his grin brought a flush to her cheeks. To cover her confusion, she spoke quickly. "Did you get everything we need?"

His smile faded and he frowned, his dark brows pulling almost together as he looked down at the dripping package in his arms. "Who can say what we'll need. Charlie tossed one of the packs down. There should be food, water and lantern fuel in it. Let's hope we get done before the supplies are gone." He gave her an enigmatic look. "Are you ready to go?"

She nodded her head and followed closely behind him as he led the way back up the tunnel.

They'd only gone a short distance from their first stopping point when the tunnel opened into a large high-ceilinged room, perhaps thirty feet wide and thirty feet from floor to ceiling at its lowest point. This chamber, like the one above, was decorated with gypsum crystals, hanging from the ceiling and the walls. The shapes of the stone decorations were fantastic, never before seen by Miranda in any of the other caves she'd been in.

The bright yellow glow of the lantern lit up the white calcite, highlighting a gypsum beard growing out of a rock. Beside it grew a formation whose spikes resembled a bottle brush.

"It's so beautiful," she whispered.

"Yeah, I guess so." Rogue swept the lantern across the nearest wall, then strode across the chamber, taking the light with him. Miranda hurried to catch up, unwilling to be left in the dark.

"I don't see any exit," she said in a hushed voice. Neither did she see any sign of her father, but she refused to give voice to her disappointment, feeling—although she knew it was absurd—that to do so might put her father beyond all reach.

"We can't turn back yet!" As she spoke her voice wavered.

Thankfully, he agreed with her. "No. We won't go back. Not yet, anyway," Rogue said. "Not until we've checked this place over good."

He moved closer to the wall, lowering the lantern and examining the rock thoroughly. Becoming aware of a shifting beneath her feet, Miranda looked down, saw she was leaving footprints where she walked.

"Look, Rogue," she said. "The floor is covered with red sand."

"Well, I'll be damned." He knelt down and scooped up a handful of the sand. "Wonder how that got in here?"

"There was probably a river running through this cavern eons ago," she said, looking up at him. Her eyes began to glitter with excitement. "And, you know . . . if Poppa and Roger came through here, then they would've left footprints behind."

Rogue began a systematic search that proved fruitless. There were no footprints in the chamber besides their own. The red sand was so smooth that it looked as though nothing had touched its surface in the past thousand years.

When they had completed a tour of the cavern, Miranda's spirits had run a gamut of emotions, ranging from certainty that she would find something to lead her to her father, to a dark feeling of dread that she might never discover what had become of him.

As though sensing her feelings, Rogue placed a gentle hand on her arm. "Don't give up on him," he urged. "All this means is he didn't come this way."

Despite herself, her eyes filled with tears.

"Come on," he said gently, pulling her into his arms. "You're not really going to cry, are you? You'll spoil my image of you." He stroked her hair lightly and she found his touch soothing.

"What image is that?" she mumbled, forcing herself not to burrow deeper against his chest.

Instead of answering her question, he said, "We're not licked yet, professor. See that big rock over yonder?" She lifted her head, her gaze following the direction of his finger to the boulder. "Yes," she mumbled. "What about it?"

"There's a big hole over there. On the other

side. You was so busy lookin' for tracks that you musta missed seein' it."

She pushed away from him. "Maybe that's where Poppa went," she said eagerly, hurrying toward the boulder.

"Miranda." His voice came urgently behind her. "The professor couldn't have gone in there."

"How do you know?" She turned to glare up at him, anger rising to the fore. Why did he always have to be so pessimistic? Just when she'd found something to hold on to, he wanted to take it away from her.

"Think about it," he said gently. "He couldn't've gone in there without comin' here first. An' there's no footprints."

"Then why did you even mention it?" she snapped, tears coming to her eyes.

"Because I thought it might be a better way out of here . . . a way to get back to the cave where Charlie and the others are waitin'."

He wrapped an arm around her shoulders. "I didn't think how you'd take it or I'da kept my mouth shut," he said, smoothing her cheek with his callused palm. Then, lifting her chin, he made her look at him. "I know you're worried about him, Miranda. But we're doin' everything possible to find him."

"I know," she whispered, her lips trembling. "I know you are, and I appreciate everything you're doing, Rogue."

He cleared his throat and released her as though he felt a sudden awkwardness. "We'd best check out that hole," he muttered. "You keep close behind me."

He stooped to enter the dark tunnel with Miranda right behind him. They followed the passage, kept following it for what seemed like hours. Time passed—an eternity it seemed—but still the tunnel went on. Miranda's eagerness had completely drained away, along with most of her energy. It became harder and harder to put one foot in front of the other, but soon it wasn't necessary, because the ceiling of the tunnel dropped, became so low that it was necessary to get down on her knees and crawl.

At times the tunnel became so small that they could hardly maneuver themselves through. Miranda's spirits, having lowered with the ceiling, lifted slightly when the passage did. Soon, the passage angled to the left and Rogue disappeared around it. Miranda followed closely behind, unwilling to be left without a light.

She rounded the curve and bumped into Rogue, who'd stopped in front of a wall of sheer rock.

"Looks like that's it," he said gruffly. "We've come as far as we can, Miranda. We'll have to go back."

"Oh, God!" she cried, disappointment sweeping through her. She slumped down against the wall and wiped at the moisture that suddenly filled her eyes. "What are we going to do?"

"What we're *not* gonna do is give up!" he said shortly. "Now, stop feeling sorry for yourself and get up from there!"

His tone brought her abruptly to her feet. "Damn you! I'm not feeling sorry for myself! But I'm worried about my father. And I'm tired and hungry and cold and I—"

"I know," he interrupted. "So am I." He expelled a heavy sigh and raked a hand through his tousled hair. "Look, Miranda. Just because we're turnin' back, doesn't mean we're givin' up. But we need food and rest. You've been doin' a lot of stumblin' . . . can't hardly put one foot in front of the other."

"I know," she sighed. "I know you're right. We've got to have rest." She faced the rock wall and gave it a hard kick, expending a small portion of her frustration as well as making her toes sting through her boots. "Dammit! There has to be another way! There has to—" She broke off as her sweeping gaze caught on a bed-sized crack about two feet above Rogue's head. "Look!" she said. "There's an opening up there!"

He swore softly and handed her the lantern. "Hold that a minute," he said.

Suddenly, she became aware of a muted roar. Excitement coursed through her. "Listen," she said, tilting her head toward the sound. It was coming from the crack.

"What is it?" he frowned down at her.

"It could be an underground waterfall," she suggested.

Putting a hand in the crack, Rogue placed his bare foot on a rough protrusion in the wall and hoisted himself upwards. Only moments later, he was peering through the crack. "Hand me the lantern," he said, turning to face her. "I want a closer look."

She handed the lantern up, her eyes glued to the hole in the rock. Although from where she was standing, her vision was limited to the crack, the disk of light from the lantern disclosed rounded walls, similar to the well-cavern, sparsely coated with dark, velvety moss.

Rogue pushed the lantern through the crack, then followed it with his head and shoulders.

"What do you see?" she asked impatiently.

"Looks like a rock chimney," he replied. "And the roaring is louder in here. The air smells fresher too. And wet, kinda like fresh laundry just hung out to dry."

He pulled his head back out and handed her the lantern. "Aren't we going through?" she asked.

"No. I'm still tired and hungry." He gave her a long look. "That chimney goes straight up. It's not gonna be an easy thing, climbin' it. We're gonna need some rest before we try." He jumped down, then grunted, "Dammit!"

"What's wrong?"

"Stepped on a sharp rock. I think I cut my big toe."

"You need your boots," she said with a worried frown.

"Yeah. I shoulda had Charlie drop 'em down. Come on." He took her arm, turning her around. "Let's go back to that big room. The

97

one with all the red sand."

"What time is it?" she asked.

Releasing her, her took out his watch. "Six o'clock. No wonder we're so tired. We been goin' all day." He sighed heavily. "I'd give a lot for a beefsteak along about now."

"Me too," she agreed. "But we won't find one in the pack on your back."

"I reckon I'm hungry enough to settle for anything. Just so long's it don't bite back."

Finding herself in complete agreement, Miranda silently followed him down the passageway.

Nine

"I'm starved," Miranda said, seating herself on the red sand and pulling the bag of supplies toward her. "I hope there's some food in here."

"There will be," Rogue said. "Charlie would've made sure of it."

Miranda pulled out a tin of sardines and eyed them skeptically. The canned fish hadn't been on her list of foodstuffs. "This contains a lot of salt. We'd better make sure we have enough water."

"I don't think we need to worry about that."

"Why?"

"There's water aplenty back at the well cavern."

She gave an unladylike snort. "You're right about that! But I'm not so sure I want to drink it. Not after we were swimming in it."

Rogue uttered a short laugh. "You surprise me, professor. I wouldn't've thought you'd be so squeamish."

"I'm not saying I wouldn't drink it," Miranda said. "Just that I didn't want to." She laid aside the can of sardines and pulled out a tin of biscuits. Her fingers fumbled with the lid, but it seemed stuck tight.

"Let me," Rogue said, reaching for the biscuit container.

After handing it over, Miranda rummaged through the pack again. "There's several candles in here. Bless Charlie for thinking of them." She looked up at Rogue. "They'll come in handy if we run out of fuel."

"Let's hope it won't come to that," he said, prying at the biscuit tin. Finally, the lid snapped off and he extracted two biscuits. "Here." He popped one in his mouth as he handed her the other. "Not bad," he muttered. "A little soggy, but not bad. Did you find any meat in there?" He reached for the sack.

"Nothing but sardines," she said, watching him dig through it with the same eagerness that she'd felt only moments before.

"Sardines are fine with me," he said, pulling a tin from the pack. "It's not beefsteak, but beggars can't afford to be choosers. An' right now my stomach's beggin' for food."

"God, I'm tired," she said, reaching for another biscuit. "I don't think I've ever been so tired before."

"I don't wonder," he said gently. "Nobody can keep up forever at the pace we've been goin'.

I've gotta hand it to you, professor. You don't do much complainin'."

Coming from him, that was a compliment. "If I thought complaining would help the situation, then you'd hear plenty of it," Miranda said. "But I've caused you enough trouble already, McClaren." She studied him in the lantern light. His face looked hard, chiseled, his body muscled and strong, a fact that, somehow, made her feel safe. "I guess I haven't thanked you for coming with me." Although her voice was hesitant, she knew the words must be said. She owed it to him. "I don't know what I'd have done if you hadn't come, and I want you to know how grateful I am."

His gaze swung up, met hers for a long, heart-stopping moment. "What's this?" he asked softly.

"Confession time, I guess." She lowered her lashes, finding herself unable to meet his penetrating gaze. "I just . . . that is . . . I would have gone mad had I been here alone."

"You? I'd've thought you could handle anything this place had to throw at you."

"Anything, maybe, except being left alone in the dark." Her voice was ragged and she shuddered in memory.

Reaching out, he placed a gentle hand on her shoulder. "Tell me what you're feeling," he commanded. "Get it out of your system."

"Sometime, maybe I will," she replied. "But

not now." She took a deep, shuddering breath and turned her attention back to the sardines. "Have you got that open yet?"

He allowed the change of conversation, picking up a sardine and handing it to her on the end of his knife. "Not so finicky now?" he chided.

"No," she replied. "I'm too hungry."

And she was. Sardines had never tasted so good before. All too soon they were gone. Miranda had turned her attention to their surroundings again, admiring the almost translucent sprays of gypsum crystal, when Rogue dug a canteen of water from the bag of supplies and handed it to her.

Closing both hands around the water container, she drank thirstily, then he closed the pack of supplies again and tied it securely with the rope that had bound it.

Miranda's eyes fell on an unopened tin of sardines lying on the sand. Realizing he had already secured the pack of supplies, she reached for it, scooping it up and dropping it into the pocket of her jacket.

"We'll have to put out the lantern," Rogue said quietly. "Will you be okay?"

She nodded and her coppery hair swept across one cheek. "Yes. I'll be all right. Just so long as you don't go anywhere."

"You keep the lantern on your side," he said, setting it down at her elbow. Then, a quick poof of air later, the darkness closed around them.

Miranda heard a whisper of sound, then felt Rogue beside her. Taking comfort from his presence, she curled up on the sand and closed her eyes. She lay there, trying to relax her tense body, listening to the silence, unable to fall asleep.

Finally, she could stand it no longer. "Rogue?" she questioned softly. "Are you awake?"

"Yes." She heard him turn over to face her. "What's the matter? Can't you go to sleep?"

"I am finding it difficult. I keep thinking about my father, wondering where he is, wondering if I'll ever see him again."

"Of course you will," he growled. "He struck me as bein' mighty smart. He would know what he's up against in here. He'll prob'ly get out on his own."

"I hope and pray so." She lapsed into silence, trying to force her tired body to relax. But still she couldn't sleep. "Rogue?"

"Huh?"

"Are you still angry with me for making you come?"

For a long moment there was silence, and when his voice finally came, it held a harshness that had been absent since he'd joined her in the well-cavern. "I wish you hadn't brought that up."

"Then you are."

"Go to sleep."

Miranda swallowed around a lump in her throat. Why hadn't she let well enough alone? Why had she reminded him of her threat? He'd been so companionable until she'd spoken so carelessly. But couldn't he see that she could have acted no differently? Surely now, after all that had happened, he could see how desperate her father's situation was.

Maybe he thought his situation was every bit as desperate, a silent voice said.

She uttered a long sigh and turned over.

"Dammit, Miranda! Go to sleep!"

"I c-can't," she said, blinking against the moisture that suddenly filled her eyes. "I-I was th-thinking about what happened. About the rustlers. I know I did you an injustice, but the situation—"

"I don't want to discuss it!" he snapped. "What's done is done. Nothing can change it now." His tone of voice demanded complete obedience. "If you have to talk, then for God's sake, choose another subject!" Without waiting for an answer, he continued, "I'd heard there was some big caves in these parts, but I never thought there was one on the Lazy R. I guess there's no way to fill it up."

"Fill it up?" Miranda wiped at the moisture clinging to her eyelashes, feeling grateful for the covering darkness, chiding herself for being such a crybaby. "Why would you want to fill it up?"

"Don't want my stock falling down here."

It was such a ridiculous notion that she laughed. "That's not likely to happen," she said. "You obviously don't know much about caves."

When he spoke again she heard the smile in his voice. "Don't know and don't want to learn. Everbody's not bent on crawlin' around in the dirt under God's green earth, professor. An' even if I'd had a mind to do it, there's been no time. My ranch came to me through a distant cousin and it was plenty run-down. It's said my cousin lost his son. The boy just disappeared when he was thirteen. I'm wonderin' now if he found a way down here and couldn't get back out."

A shiver of fear swept over Miranda at his words. She had to remind herself that the boy had been a teenager, very untried in cave exploration, which was a dangerous pastime for anyone.

"After that, my cousin—Robert McClaren— got kinda funny in the head. Heard he talked to his son . . . like he was standin' right next to him. I guess he went crazy. That boy was all he had—his wife had died when the kid was born. Anyway, he let this place go to the dogs. Wasn't so much as a head of stock left by the time he died. It's took all my time just to get it goin' again."

"But you finally did it?"

"Yeah. An' now a bunch of rustlers are tryin' to put me outta business."

"I'm sorry," she said in a small voice.

"Forget it!" he said abruptly, turning away from her. "It's past time we were asleep!"

He'd dismissed her again, and although Miranda knew she should try to sleep, she was still too restless. Uttering a heavy sigh, she turned on her side and closed her eyes, trying to force her body to relax. She lay there for long moments, then turned on her back, sighing again.

"Can't sleep?" His voice came out of the darkness, startling her.

"No. I'm exhausted, but I just can't relax."

"Maybe you're tryin' too hard. Or maybe it's just too damn dark."

"I ought to be used to that," she said. "After all, I've been exploring caves with Poppa since I was eight years old."

"Musta been years and years ago," he teased.

"Eleven," she told him.

"So you're nineteen?" He was silent for a long moment, then his voice came again. "I imagine you learned a lot about caves in those years, but somehow, I don't think you had much time left for other things . . . things you shoulda been learnin'."

"Like what?"

"Just how to be a woman."

"You think I'm not womanly enough?" She felt curiously hurt.

"Now you're puttin' words in my mouth. I

just think you haven't been courted very much."

"You're right. There hasn't been much time for things of that nature. I studied hard the last few years to gain acceptance into college. That was a condition Poppa made before he would allow me to accompany him to Europe."

"And what'd you do in Europe?" he asked.

"We explored the caverns there. God, Rogue, you'd never believe them unless you saw them yourself. I shall never forget the ice caves in the Pyrenees. Nor the Grotto Casteret. It was such a splendid cave. I saw stalactites of purest ice and huge ice crystals that were at least a foot in diameter. I climbed frozen, underground waterfalls. Their beauty would be impossible to describe."

"Is that all you did in Europe?" She heard something in his voice that she couldn't identify. "Did you only explore ice caves, Miranda?"

"There were other caves as well."

"But you only explored caves."

She heard it again, definite this time; pity. He didn't have to pity her. She'd had a good life with her father, an exciting life. "We didn't just explore caves. We met other people. It was a very exciting time for me. When we were in France I helped organize a speleology club. It's the first one of its kind, but soon there will be many others all over the world." Realizing he had fallen silent, realizing as well that she was still being pitied, she said, "Obviously my life has been quite dull compared with yours. I know very little about life on a cattle ranch. Although I did have occasion to see some cattle being branded." She shuddered in memory. "That seems such a cruel practice. Why do you do it?"

"It's been the way of cattlemen for years. It's the best way for a rancher to mark his stock, and believe me, Miranda, the animals hardly feel a thing."

"How do you know that?" she asked. "Did you ever ask one of them?"

He uttered a husky laugh and Miranda found she liked the sound. She settled into a more comfortable position and said, "Tell me about life on your ranch."

He obliged her, telling her about growing up on the range, about spring roundup, branding cattle, riding, roping, and trail drives where he had spent weeks driving the cattle to market and had slept with the stars twinkling high overhead.

Miranda found the droning sound of his voice soothing and her tense body slowly relaxed, her eyes closed and she slept.

Miranda didn't know how long she'd been sleeping, only knew that some sound had awakened her. Was Rogue up already? But surely, if he were, then he would have lit the lantern.

The sound came again, a soft, whispery sound, accompanied by a slight shuffling, scraping noise.

The hair lifted along her arms. "Poppa?" she whispered. "Is that you, Poppa?"

Cocking her head, she listened to the silence. Then it came again, faint, perhaps even farther away, but definite. Her heart gave a lurch. God! It must be her father.

"Poppa?" she whispered softly. "Where are you Poppa?"

Although there was no answer, she was certain the sound had been real and not imagined. And there was no doubt in her mind that her father was somewhere nearby. She reached out and felt into the darkness where she'd left the lantern. Her fingers touched and gripped it. She didn't think she'd been asleep long and hated to wake Rogue, but there was someone moving somewhere nearby, and she was determined to find out who it was.

Putting her body between the lantern and Rogue, she struck a match and held it to the wick. Light flared instantly. Blocking as much of the light as possible with her body, she moved to the other side of the large boulder and entered the tunnel. She made her way down the passage for a short distance, then realized the sound was coming from a gap, narrow, perhaps sixteen inches wide—a gap that had escaped their notice the first time through.

Her heart skipped a beat. Could her father be there?

Squeezing through the crevice, she whispered, "Poppa! Are you there, Poppa?" The echoes of her voice sounded queer. "Why don't you answer me?"

A scurrying noise was followed by silence. She realized the noise could have been made by a cave salamander, but there was also the chance her father was somewhere in this passage, perhaps unable to answer her call.

Dammit! She needed to know. But should she return and wake Rogue from his sleep before venturing farther? No, she decided. Not until she was certain. She took a step forward, then stopped. Suppose he woke up while she was gone and became alarmed. She must go back and leave him the lantern. There were candles in the pack that she could take with her to check out the noise. She certainly would not go very far alone. She knew better than that.

Retracing her steps, she moved silently across the red sand, opened her pack and took out a candle. Across the cavern, in the dark recesses, Rogue slept on.

Miranda struck a match and lit the candle, then she put out the flame on the lantern. After replacing the lantern where Rogue could easily grasp it, Miranda left the cavern and entered the passage again.

Fully realizing the danger of going off on her

own, Miranda found a stone and scratched the shape of an arrow on the rock floor. She pointed the arrow toward the crevice. Then, feeling satisfied that she had taken every precaution, she stepped inside.

The rock scraped at her, caught at her clothes, then let her through. She had only gone a few feet when she heard the noise again, scrape, shuffle, scrape shuffle.

"Poppa?" she called.

Silence. Then the sound came again. Scrape, shuffle, scrape, shuffle. Miranda hurried forward, intent on finding the source of the noise. The passage was wider now, leading upwards in a gentle curve and the floor was smooth.

All too soon, the passage narrowed again, and Miranda knew she should go back. *After I see what's around the next bend,* she silently told herself, turning sideways to squeeze through the rock walls.

The flame on her candle flickered and she realized there was a draft coming from somewhere. Could this passage connect with the rock chimney they had found earlier? It was entirely possible. It could be a way out of the cavern. Perhaps this was the way her father had come.

But when the passage had bottlenecked until it was so tight that it was hard for her to force her body through, she realized her father could not have come this way. Like Rogue, he was a big man. Too big to make it through this narrow rock passage.

The candle flickered, the flame bowing sideways in all directions, and Miranda shifted her body, intent on shielding the flame from the sudden draft. Her elbow struck a rock, dislodging it and sending rock fragments scattering.

Something fell onto her head with a sharp little rap of pain. A pebble. It was followed by a shower of dust and small stones, dislodged from somewhere above her.

Miranda heard a low rumble that seemed to take place inside her head. It was a sound that struck fear in her heart, a sound that built in volume until it seemed to be an echo that came from far and near, until it overlapped itself. It was real, she knew. Real, not imagined, and the reality was more terrifying than death.

Run, run! her mind screamed.

But she couldn't move.

Shock held her motionless as the whole passage trembled, then collapsed around her.

Ten

A loud crash woke Rogue, jerking him upright, his eyes straining into the darkness. He might've thought he'd imagined the sound, had it not been for the low rumbling in the distance . . . a rumbling that even now was diminishing, until finally it was gone completely, leaving the silence absolute, broken only by the sound of his own breathing.

Something about that very fact caused him to feel a sense of unease. Rogue worried it around in his mind for a moment, until finally, quite suddenly, he knew exactly why he was feeling concerned.

There was only the sound of his *own* breath. Why couldn't he hear Miranda?

Reaching out, he encountered only emptiness. His heart gave a jerk, then began to beat in double time.

Calm down, he silently told himself. *Nothing's wrong. She's gotta be here. She wouldn't have left by herself.*

113

Even as he chided himself, he was groping through the darkness, sweeping his hand in a wide arc, reaching farther and farther into the dark emptiness, but he found nothing substantial.

His anxiety grew by leaps and bounds. "Miranda," he said sharply.

Silence.

"Miranda!" His voice was louder, harsh with apprehension.

Still silence.

His hands trembled as he groped in his pocket for the box of matches. His fingers closed over it, pulled it out. He fumbled with the lid, finally managed to open it and a moment later a match sputtered, then flared, and he found himself staring at the imprint Miranda's body had left in the red sand.

Fear surged through him, pure, terrifying fear as his gaze swept the darkened corners of the cavern. He knew it was empty, except for himself. "Dammit!" he swore. "Miranda, where the hell are you?"

Rogue felt the stinging pain of the flame burning his fingers just before the match burned down, leaving him in total darkness again. He groped for the lantern, felt his fingers brush against it, heard the soft thunk as it was knocked away into the sand.

Muttering curses beneath his breath, he struck another match, found the lantern and lit it.

Holding the lantern before him, he searched every inch of the cavern for the girl who had been with him when he had fallen asleep, but his search was in vain.

"Miranda!" he shouted. "Answer me, Miranda!" As he paused to listen, the silence seemed to mock him.

Suddenly he remembered the rock chimney. Had Miranda been so eager to find her father, that she'd tossed caution to the wind and gone there? Could she really have been so foolish? God! It would seem so, for there'd be no earthly reason to have gone back to the well-cavern.

Feeling the need for haste, Rogue crossed the carpet of red sand, entered the narrow tunnel and hurried down it, calling out Miranda's name over and over again. But he was doomed to disappointment, because there was no answer. Only that same terrible silence . . . the almost unbearable silence, as though he were the only occupant of this underground world.

Miranda moaned and pushed at the confining covers. Why were they so heavy, so restricting? And why did they poke her with sharp points? Covers shouldn't have sharp points. They should be soft, warm, comforting.

She stirred, becoming aware of the silence . . . opened her eyes . . . and blinked into the darkness. Her eyes were open, weren't they? She blinked again, just to make sure. Yes, they were open. But it was dark, so dark . . . and quiet, so soundless that she felt threatened by the absolute stillness around her, felt almost suffocated by it.

While her mind tried to deal with the absence of sound, her hands pushed at the sharpness covering her body.

Rocks! God! Was she lying beneath a pile of rocks? Her fingers tightened around one, felt the rough edges. It had to be rocks.

Lifting her hand, she tried to see her fingers, but it was impossible. Her eyes could not penetrate the blackness that surrounded her.

Fighting back the panic, Miranda told herself she must be sleeping. She brought her hand forward, touched her face, and knew she was awake. This was no dream.

She was awake and she was lying in a bed of rocks that were digging into the flesh of her arms and legs, her back and buttocks! In fact, she didn't think there was any part of her that didn't hurt.

Suddenly, as though a door had opened, she remembered what had happened. *God! Why had she been so foolish?*

Light! She needed light! Where was her candle?

She tried desperately to keep hold of her sanity as her hands groped through the darkness, searching for the candle she'd dropped.

God help her! She was doomed to die in here! Alone in the darkness, as she'd always known she would die—ever since that time in the French Alps when she had been lost in a cave, alone with no light.

"No!" she said aloud. "Don't think of it! And don't sit here feeling sorry for yourself. Do something!"

"What can I do?" she argued with herself. "I can't see anything. I'll never find my way back to Rogue!"

Suddenly, as though a light broke through the darkness, she remembered the matches in her pocket. She laughed aloud and the sound startled her. Granted, the sound was slightly hysterical, but it was laughter. "You ninny," she muttered. "You'll be all right if you keep your head."

She dug in her pocket and extracted the canvas-wrapped matches. The twine resisted her trembling fingers until finally she used her teeth to bite through the string. A few minutes later she struck a match on a stone. It flared brightly, then sputtered, fizzled, and completely went out.

"Damn!" she muttered, her heart pounding loudly in her ears. "The rock's too wet!"

Realizing she couldn't afford to waste her matches, she scraped the match against the box. Again, the match refused to light.

When she realized it was her trembling hands

that were defeating her purpose, Miranda took several deep, calming breaths.

Don't think about the cavern in the French Alps, she silently told herself. *Shove it away, push it out of your memory. Get control of yourself. Count to ten, the way Poppa showed you. And if that isn't enough, do it all again. One, two, three . . .*

Miranda could actually feel herself calming. Only moments later, light flared, and in that same moment of time, as though God had seen fit to answer her prayers, she saw the candle; it lay only a few feet away, resting in a heap of rubble.

Heaving a heartfelt sigh of relief, Miranda lit the candle, then held it aloft to inspect her surroundings.

She wasn't the least bit reassured by what she saw.

Miranda could see at a glance that she'd been lucky. She was in a pocket of hard limestone, surrounded by rocky shale. The hard rock had held when the shale had given way. Loose rock lay everywhere, completely blocking the passage before and behind her.

Her heart quaked crazily, and her neck muscles throbbed with tension. What had happened anyway? What had she done to cause such a disaster? Try as she would, she couldn't remember!

"Miranda!"

Miranda's heart gave a crazy lurch. It was Rogue! He was searching for her!

"Miranda?" His voice came again, incredibly distant . . . so far away.

"In here, Rogue!" she yelled, cupping her mouth with her hands. "I'm in here!"

" — randa-a-a!"

She turned her head, this way and that, trying to determine which way the voice was coming from. "I'm in the passage, Rogue!"

" — da! . . . you?"

God! Was he unable to hear her? How could that be possible? If she could hear him, then he should be able to hear her as well. Shouldn't he? Was she mistaken, or was his voice getting even more distant?

"Rogue!" she screamed, crawling closer to the blocked area behind her, pushing at the rocks that closely resembled sponges. "I'm in here, Rogue. There's a crev — "

She broke off as his cry came again. It was obvious he hadn't heard her, and with each passing moment his voice was becoming fainter. He was going farther away from her all the time.

"Rogue!" she screamed, desperation in her voice as, frantically, she picked up a rock and flung it aside. "Rogue! Help me!"

But there was no answer, only the sound of falling rocks. It was then that Miranda realized that calling out to him was useless — she was only making herself hoarse by her screams — and she slumped down against the fallen rocks and wept uncontrollably until there were no more tears left.

When her sobs finally ceased, she became aware that breathing had become difficult. Only then did the gravity of her situation really strike her. She had almost used up all the oxygen in the chamber. She'd die if she didn't get out soon!

Chiding herself for giving away to tears, Miranda used her sleeve to wipe away the last sign of her weakness. Although she knew her candle was using up precious oxygen, she also knew she needed light to dig her way through the rubble.

She grabbed a rock and was intent on throwing it aside when something about it caught her attention. Although she'd already noticed that it was the porous, spongy type of rock that she had encountered before in caverns, the fact hadn't really registered. Now that it did, she realized why Rogue had been unable to hear her. The rock was very much like the sponge it resembled. It absorbed sound. Her voice would never carry more than a few feet this side of the barrier.

Bracing herself against the rock wall, Miranda struggled upright on reluctant legs. Her feet felt numb and her knees wobbled, threatening to buckle beneath her weight. She took several deep breaths to shore up her courage, rubbed at her aching neck muscles, then turned her attention to her surroundings.

There was rock everywhere, piled higher than her head. Where had it all come from? A foolish thought, she knew. She was covered by rock, surrounded by it, had been since they'd entered the cave.

Her gaze touched on a boulder . . . no use trying in that direction. It wasn't the way anyway. Thank the Lord for small favors.

You could be dead, she silently reminded herself.

Realizing the truth in that, she decided she'd been granted a big favor after all. She studied the rockslide again. If she moved some of the rocks at the top of the pile, then she might be able to crawl over them.

Her gaze measured the width of the passage. Was it wider than before? The ceiling was most certainly higher, but that was understandable. After all, it had caved in. Still, the rocks were piled clear to the top.

She gave a heavy sigh and stepped cautiously on the pile, realizing the necessity of being extra cautious. Something she should have thought of before. If she had done so, then the slide might have been prevented.

She'd made a giant-sized mistake, she realized, and it was a mistake that could still prove fatal.

Acknowledging her error, she began to work

on moving the rocks. Even as she worked she could feel the blood running down her arms and legs from tiny cuts inflicted by the rockslide. Her knees became raw, as did her hands and elbows, but she closed her mind against the pain. She would have to deal with it soon enough.

Later—she didn't know how long, maybe minutes, perhaps even hours, for she had no way of counting time—she was able to squirm through the hole she'd made at the top of the rubble. She was almost through when she bumped her head, hard, against the ceiling.

With a grunt of pain, she hugged the pile of rubble, scraping her already raw elbows and knees.

Her heart lifted with gladness as she recognized the passage ahead, its walls smooth, its ceiling slightly rounded. Her pulse quickened, as did her step. Miranda knew all she had to do was hurry, and soon she'd be back with Rogue.

Scratched and dirty, bleeding from her many wounds, Miranda limped forward, turning sideways occasionally to slide her bruised body through when the tunnel became so narrow as to make traversing it actually painful, but all the time telling herself that soon she'd be back with the rancher.

It seemed an eternity later when she saw a soft glow of light beaming from somewhere in the distance. Breathing a sigh of relief, she sent a heartfelt thank-you winging toward the heavens. It was obvious that Rogue had found the narrow entrance to the passage.

"Rogue!" she cried, the relief she felt sounding in her voice. "Thank God you found me! I was so worried!" Ignoring the pain from her many wounds, she hurried forward, stumbling in her haste over an unseen rock that sent her sprawling on all fours.

"Ooommph!" The sound burst forth, followed by a cry of pain as her raw knees came in contact with the rocky floor of the tunnel. She felt the warm flow of fresh blood trickling down her legs, but paid it no mind, her only thought to see Rogue again.

Pushing herself to her feet again, she hurried on toward the light ahead until finally, she burst from the tunnel.

Then, sucking in a sharp breath, Miranda came to an abrupt halt.

Eleven

The moon, a silvery arc in the sky, shone down on the restless cattle. There was not even a whisper of a breeze, and the unprecedented heat was unrelenting. Even so, Colby felt there was something else causing the cattle to mill around.

He had positioned himself on a slight rise in the ground, hoping to spot any trouble before it happened. He ground his teeth in frustration. He hadn't been able to find the men who'd shot Jack and killed Clem, but he'd be damned if he'd allow any more cattle to be taken.

He puzzled over the disappearance of the rustlers. All the luck had been on their side. Colby had been unable to trail them in the dark, and by morning the clouds that had been threatening rain had finally released their moisture. The result had been high winds, torrential rain and thunder and lightning that seemed bent on splitting the heavens apart with their fury. What tracks the rustlers had left had been completely wiped out.

Remembering his inability to catch the rustlers,

Colby's weary shoulders drooped even more. Dammit! He was getting too old for such long hours in the saddle. In another year or two he'd be worse than useless. Rogue might just as well take him out and shoot him for all the good he could do.

Realizing he was about to wallow in self-pity, which wasn't his style at all, Colby lifted his sweat-stained Stetson from the back of his head and slapped it against his thigh in disgust. The resulting sound, the soft thud, caused his mount to sidestep restlessly.

"Easy now," Colby grunted, tightening his left hand around the reins.

When the horse quieted, the old man wiped the beads of moisture from his forehead. Still hatless, he probed the darkness for some sign of trouble. His gaze found the four mounted figures circling the herd, not nearly enough to stop the cattle should they decide to run, but enough to stop rustlers from stealing them.

At least he hoped so.

Miranda's spirits plummeted as she stared at the large chamber. How had she managed to come back to the chamber with red sand, when she hadn't yet traversed the tunnel leading to the chimney rock?

"Rogue?" Her voice was questioning.

There was no answer. "Rogue!" she called again, louder this time. "Are you in—" She broke off abruptly as her searching gaze told her what she'd already begun to suspect. She was only wasting her time by calling out. Rogue McClaren couldn't answer her, because he wasn't there. She had *not* entered the chamber carpeted with red sand. Instead, she'd entered another, much larger chamber, and the light—the soft glow—she'd seen hadn't come from Rogue's lantern as she'd thought. Instead, it originated in the chamber itself.

"Oh, God!" she whispered, slumping down against the rocky floor. "Phosphorus walls!" There could be no other answer. The walls were composed of phosphor. But why did they glitter? Phosphor gave off a light similar to that of a firefly.

With her trembling hand holding the candle aloft, Miranda looked this way and that, swiveling her head back and forth, her gaze sweeping over the glittering walls. Millions of tiny reflections were scattered like glass beads everywhere the small circle of light reached, while before her, perhaps twenty feet distant, gnarled calcite columns stretched more than fifty feet to the ceiling.

Once before, several years ago, Miranda had been in a cavern where several chambers had been lighted by phosphor walls. But, without artificial lights, it had been a shadowy world at best. Certainly nothing as wondrous as this . . . this glittering, sparkling world seemed to be made up of millions of tiny diamonds. Never in her life had she seen anything like it. And, although there was beauty in the chamber, breathtaking beauty, Miranda wasn't in any mood to appreciate it.

She felt only sinking despair.

She was alone. Totally, absolutely alone in her isolation.

Her gaze touched on the flickering candle in her hand. It seemed to have diminished in size while she stood there. She was wasting it needlessly. With a quick puff of air, she blew it out.

Immediately, the glittering world disappeared, replaced by a soft diffused glow.

Miranda swallowed convulsively. Even though she hadn't been able to appreciate the beauty of the chamber, at least she'd taken some comfort from the light. Now there was little comfort to be found, because she'd suddenly realized what had happened, and that comprehension had been accompanied by a chill. It was apparent now that she'd mistaken the direction. Instead of turning back, she'd traveled the wrong way. The path to the chamber with red sand was still blocked . . . and she and Rogue were going in opposite directions.

Tears came to her eyes and she blinked rapidly to dry them. "Don't go feeling sorry for yourself," she muttered. "You've been in worse situations before." *Like the time in the Alps when I—* "No!" She spewed the words out. "I won't think of that! I can't!"

Miranda realized she'd have to return to the blocked passage, realized as well that she needed time to compose herself, to prepare herself before she entered the confining tunnel again. God! She didn't want to go back in there! Not ever again!

If only this wasn't really happening. If only, instead, she was reliving the nightmare. Perhaps she was! Yes! She squeezed her eyes shut. *Yes, yes, yes!* her mind screamed. *You're in your bed . . . asleep, just waiting for someone to wake you. None of this was really happening. Soon, Greta will come. She'll set your morning tea on the bedside table. She'll go to the window and fling open the shutters, then turn around and tell you to hurry, because Poppa is becoming impatient. You'll smile, as you always do, and say Poppa is always impatient and—*

Miranda opened her eyes abruptly, stared around her shadowy world. She wasn't asleep. She was in a cavern, and she was lost . . . and, God! She was so alone!

Unable to still the trembling of her body, Miranda indulged herself in a good cry. When it was over she rose and took stock of her situation. There was light in the chamber and she felt a desire to linger there, at least until her nerves calmed, but she knew she dared not. Miranda had no idea what lay ahead of her, only knew the path she'd already traveled.

She'd have to go back . . . must go back, else she might forever be trapped here . . . alone.

Unable to bear the thought of such an event, she swallowed her fear and turned to face the tunnel again. The dark mouth seemed to be beckoning her . . . pulsating with life, watching her, waiting for a chance to smother her with its blackness. She told herself she was just being fanciful, but she could almost swear she could hear it breathing.

Stilling her own breath, Miranda listened to the sound, her body tensed, her senses alert for some unknown, nameless thing.

Suddenly she became aware of sound, then a soft, feathery touch against her face, almost like the air moving around her, and there was a freshness about it, above the moist yet musty smells of the cave. And, God! There *was* sound. Granted, it was only a soft sound . . . muted . . . almost like softly flowing water.

Suddenly, as though she'd been hit by a bolt of lightning, she was certain she'd identified the sound.

Somewhere, nearby, there was a subterranean river; a river that was even now flowing through the cavern.

Recognition brought strength to Miranda's legs and renewed her courage. She hurried forward, knowing the river could be her salvation. If water flowed into the cavern, then surely it must flow out again.

Circling around a gnarled column, Miranda stumbled over an unseen object on the rocky floor, flailed out her arms to regain her balance, then slowed her pace, her eyes probing the shadows ahead, mindful of what her haste had already brought her to.

When she circled around another column, she

knew she was getting closer, because the sound of flowing water was louder. But now it seemed to be coming from below her.

Sudden realization brought her to a halt, fearful of taking another step, afraid she would fall to her death, because she was certain now that she stood facing a chasm.

After lighting her candle, she peered down into an underground canyon which plunged perhaps twenty feet below. Her eyes traveled up and down the gorge, trying to measure its length. She guessed it was two hundred feet long and perhaps a hundred wide, and in the center of the canyon, barely seen in the shadowy depths, was the underground river.

Could she reach it? Her gaze narrowed on the chasm; it was too steep at this point, but perhaps there was another way down. She curbed the impulse to hunt for one. It could take hours, and she knew she must return to the rockslide.

Even now, Rogue might've found the tunnel. He could be there, digging away the rubble, trying to find her. She'd have to hurry, must help him, after all, she was the experienced caver.

Little good your experience did you, a silent voice chided. *You've broken almost every rule in the spelunker's handbook. Even the first one, learned at your father's knee as a child . . . the rule about exploring in pairs.*

Silently cursing herself for not using her brains, she limped back to the tunnel, took in a deep breath of courage and entered the passage.

* * *

"Miranda!" Rogue shouted, having little hope of an answer. He'd reached the chimney rock again, and finding no sign of her there, he squirmed his way through the bed-sized crack until he was standing on the floor of the chimney. He lifted the lantern above his head, studying the hole above him that seemed to go on forever, becoming smaller and smaller as it did. Realizing it was only an illusion, he looped the lantern handle over his wrist, then, after bracing his hands and feet against the sides of the chimney, he began to climb.

He'd only gone a short distance when he found a hole, perhaps three feet high and two feet wide, leading from the chimney. Sticking his head and shoulders into the hole, he called her name. "Miranda! Are you in there? Miranda?"

He listened for a moment to the silence, then retreated and started climbing again. Soon, the chimney began to close in around him and he realized it hadn't really been an illusion. The chimney squeezed inward about twenty feet above him, until there was only about ten inches left of the opening, too narrow for Miranda to have passed through.

He had to go back.

"God, Miranda," he muttered hoarsely. "Where the hell did you go?"

Swiftly, he began to descend the chimney again until he reached the passage leading off from it.

131

This time, instead of passing by, he shoved the lantern into the tunnel and crawled in behind it. She had to have come this way, and by God, he was going to find her!

Sweat poured down Miranda's face as she crawled through the hole she'd made earlier and climbed over the rubble. The air was hot and heavy, and she felt incredibly thirsty, her throat dry and dusty. God! She'd give anything for just one drop of water.

She could almost swear she heard the sound of the river again, flowing softly as it made its way across the canyon, but she knew that was impossible. It was only a memory, a residue, left in her mind.

Heaving a tired sigh, Miranda turned back to the job at hand—clearing away the rubble. After dripping some candle wax onto a protruding rock above her head, she stuck her candle in the hot wax, then, with great determination, set about clearing the rocks from the tunnel.

She climbed to the top of the rubble, grasped the nearest rock, then flung it aside. Then, another and another. She didn't know how long she worked, wouldn't allow herself to even contemplate the time, her only thought was to make a hole that she could crawl through.

It was hotter near the ceiling, and there was less oxygen, a fact that caused her distress. Her breathing was heavy, her scrapes and bruises painful, and she was so damned thirsty! How much longer could she go without water?

"Rogue," she muttered, stopping to wipe the sweat from her brow. "Where are you, Rogue? Don't leave me here alone!" Even as she uttered the words, Miranda felt in her heart of hearts that he wouldn't leave her. She'd only known the rancher a little while, but she instinctively knew that he wouldn't stop until he found her, whether alive . . . or dead.

Miranda took a small measure of comfort from that knowledge. If worse came to worse in here, then she could at least die knowing she wouldn't be left in the cavern. Somehow, he would find her, and when that happened, he was sure to see that she was laid to rest with those she'd loved in life.

Would he care that she was dead? Even as she asked herself the question she wondered why the answer to it was so important to her.

"I'm getting morbid," she muttered with an unsteady laugh.

She grasped another rock, about eighteen inches across, and tugged at it with both hands. It was heavy, refused to budge. Her feet slipped against the rubble and she heard a shower of pebbles and rocks give way beneath her. She dug her feet into the fallen rock and renewed her efforts to free the rock. It moved ever so slightly and, feeling encouraged, she pulled harder. It moved again as did several smaller stones around it. Releasing the bigger rock, she worked at removing those around until she could slide her fingers behind it.

A moment later it was free, sliding down the pile of rocks behind her. It struck the passage floor with a heavy thunk. Immediately there was a shower of rocks from the left wall of the passage.

Her heart jerked crazily as she peered into the hole. But it was too dark, she couldn't see. She reached for the candle, noticing for the first time how small it had become. It wouldn't last more than another hour and then she would be in total darkness.

The thought terrified her.

She had to break through the blockage, must become reunited with Rogue. Holding the candle aloft, she peered into the hole.

"Oh, God, no!" All her efforts had been wasted. She'd never break through this tunnel. Not with the slab of rock facing her.

Twelve

Dawn streaked the early morning sky with shades of pink and gold, but Colby, finishing his coffee on the porch of the ranch house, paid no attention.

His grip tightened on his coffee cup and he glared at its contents as though he suspected the coffee was poisoned.

But he was unaware of his gaze; it was focused inwardly, his mind elsewhere, still puzzling over the rustlers' trail. If he wasn't mistaken, they were headed for the lead mine, but, for the life of him, he could find no earthly reason for their actions. Surely they knew there'd be men at the mine who'd question the presence of Rogue's stock with strangers.

He sighed, tossed the dregs of the coffee onto the ground, laid his cup beside his chair and, telling his creaking joints to behave, rose to his feet. Immediately, pain flared through his left thigh—the leg he'd broken when the bay fell on him last year—and he grabbed the porch rail with one hand while he used the other to massage his stiff leg.

"Gettin' too damn old to be chasin' after rustlers," he mumbled beneath his breath.

Straightening up, he let his narrowed gaze sweep the northern pasture—hoping to see Rogue riding in with Rusty and Charlie—then he expelled a frustrated sigh.

Where in hell was Rogue, anyway?

The three men who waited in the chamber that contained the well-cavern were wondering the same thing. A small, one-burner kerosene stove had been set up and an empty pot—containing only dried coffee grounds now—rested on top of it. Rusty sat on the floor near the abyss and Chance leaned against a nearby wall, sliding his fingers back and forth across a harmonica.

Charlie paced restlessly through the chamber, trying to control the fear that grew with each passing moment.

"You're gonna wear a hole in the floor if you keep that up, Charlie," Chance said softly. "Why don't you set yourself down and rest awhile."

"How in hell am I supposed to relax when Rogue an' Miranda's disappeared!" Charlie snapped, turning to glare at Chance. "They shoulda been back by now. They shoulda at least let us know what's goin' on down there."

"Maybe they can't," Rusty said, leaning closer to the well-cavern.

"Dammit, boy!" Charlie snapped. "Get away from there!"

"I was just lookin' to see if I could see anything."

"You ain't gonna see nothin'," Charlie growled. "You ain't been able to see down there for the last day and a half. Why should it be any different now?"

"If he comes back, there'll be a light down there," Rusty argued. "We oughtta at least keep an eye out for a light . . . just in case we can't hear 'em call out!"

Chance unfolded his long legs and got to his feet. "No sense in gettin' all het up, Charlie. We're all worried about Rogue. But there ain't nothin' we can do until we hear from 'em."

Rogue had found a series of dry tunnels that twisted and wound until he would have become lost if he hadn't used the professor's method of marking a trail by scratching an arrow to indicate the way he traveled.

His body was bone-weary and his eyes stung, feeling as though they were filled with pebbles as big around as his fingertips. Although he realized he needed to rest, he couldn't allow himself to do so. One thought pressed him onward. He must find Miranda . . . must do it soon, before it was too late.

He stumbled on, holding the lantern as far away from himself as possible, realizing the fumes from it were partly responsible for the stinging in his eyes.

"Miranda," he shouted hoarsely. *Miranda! Miranda! Miranda!* the cavern picked up his voice and sent it back to him, over and over again, but there was no other sound, except that of his own labored breath.

Suddenly, he stumbled and fell to his knees and the lantern was ripped from his hand. The light went out and left him in complete darkness.

Despairingly, Miranda stumbled through the darkness, headed away, again, from the chamber carpeted with red sand. But what else could she do? The tunnel leading to it was well and truly blocked. There was no way on earth she could move the slab of rock blocking it. No way at all. Although the humidity in the tunnel was high, and sweat rolled down her face, her body felt chilled and numb . . . as did her mind.

Miranda could hardly bear leaving the passage, realizing that every step she took put her farther and farther away from Rogue, but she had no choice. She still had enough sense to know she was dehydrating. If she didn't find some water soon, she wouldn't have strength enough to do so.

And she knew there was water in the phosphor cavern. There had to be! Hadn't she heard it with her own ears, seen it with her own eyes? All she had to do was reach it. She hoped the task wouldn't prove impossible.

* * *

Losing the lantern hadn't been what turned Rogue back; he'd had no trouble finding it. No. What had turned him back was the path around the next bend. He hadn't realized what he was seeing at first, not until he'd already cut his bare foot. That stopped him cold and he took a closer look at the tunnel floor. He'd only seen rock like that once before, held in the palm of a seafaring man. Coral. Razor-sharp coral. There was no way he'd cross it, not without slicing his feet to shreds. It was then he knew he'd have to go back. And he'd been away for so long, perhaps Miranda had returned by herself.

He'd almost convinced himself he would find her waiting for him at the well-cavern but the hope was in vain. When he left the passageway, his lantern illuminated the deep glassy surface of the pool and there was no sign of Miranda.

Dammit all! Where could she be?

Swallowing back the fear threatening to choke him, Rogue tilted his head and stared up into the inky blackness above him. Were the others still there? he wondered.

Rogue set his lantern down on the narrow ledge, and cupped his mouth and shouted. "Charlie! Charlie, are you there?"

There was a long moment of silence before the answer came. "We're still here, Rogue."

"Have you heard anything from Miranda?"

Silence greeted his question, a silence that

139

stretched out, lengthening like a ripple in a pond. When the answer finally came, it was the one he was least prepared for.

"No!" Just the one word, but it said everything, hid a world of feelings.

Rogue's shoulders slumped as though they could no longer carry the heavy burden of Miranda's disappearance. For the first time in his life Rogue was afraid that whatever road he chose to walk would be the wrong one . . . and the cost would be Miranda's life.

God! Why had he allowed her to accompany them into the cavern? He should have known something like this would happen.

"Rogue!"

The voice barely penetrated his consciousness, so absorbed was he in his dark thoughts.

"Rogue!" The voice belonged to Rusty. "Do you want me to come down there?"

Rogue knew he needed help badly, knew as well that Rusty would be risking his life by joining him, but he did need help. Miranda needed help.

"It's no picnic down here, Rusty," he yelled. "We don't know what we'll run into."

Rusty remained silent, leaving Rogue wondering if he'd had second thoughts about joining him. He certainly wouldn't blame him if he decided against coming down. "Charlie," Rogue called.

"Yeah?"

"I need some stuff down here." He went on to list several things, fuel for the lantern being the first, his boots the second item on his list. "Bundle it all up in some canvas and toss it down to me."

"Chance is already puttin' it together, boss," Charlie shouted. "An' Rusty's gettin' into that harness rig. Said he's comin' down there."

Feeling a measure of relief that he'd soon have some help with his search for Miranda, Rogue squatted down on the ledge and leaned back against the cavern wall, intent on taking a breather while he waited.

It was funny how well he could hear the others at this moment. As Miranda had said, the acoustics in the well-cavern were odd, sometimes allowing them to hear, and at other times seeming to swallow the sound.

He knew the exact moment when they lowered Rusty into the well-cavern, but it wasn't because of the acoustics, it was the accompanying shower of pebbles that spattered the water only a few feet below him.

Long moments seemed to pass before he heard a sudden exclamation. "Charlie look! The rope's fraying. It's sawin' against the ledge!"

Panic surged through Rogue. "Pull him back up!" he yelled. "There's a ledge down here. If he falls, he might hit it!"

But his words came too late. Rogue knew it when there was no answer from above . . . when he saw Rusty penetrate the illuminated portion of the well-cavern, falling with his head down in a diving position. Rusty's momentum was carrying him too close . . . too close to the ledge where Rogue was standing.

God! Rogue's stomach lurched and nausea swept over him as he heard the crack of Rusty's body striking the ledge, just before he slid into the pool of water.

Although Rogue felt with a certainty that Rusty was dead, he slipped into the pool, plunging into the watery depths, his hands outstretched, searching, finally sweeping across sodden fabric. Then he gripped hard, pulling the young man upwards, pushing and tugging until he had him on the ledge.

"Rusty." Rogue's breathing was harsh, ragged, as he heaved himself on the ledge beside the limp body. "Are you all right, boy!" Although he asked the question, he expected no answer, feeling positive the boy would never speak again.

"Dammit, Rusty," he swore softly. "What in hell am I going to tell your folks?"

Silence filled the cavern, and during that silence, Rogue bowed his head and said a silent prayer for the dead man. Although Rusty was only nineteen, he'd been working at the ranch for the past three years, ever since Rogue had inherited it. He was too young to die, but there was little time to mourn his passing, because Miranda was still lost. If he didn't find her soon, she could meet the same fate as Rusty.

He smoothed the red hair away from Rusty's eyes, the way the young man had always been doing. "You never could tame your curls, could you boy?" He sighed deeply. "Guess you won't have to worry about it no more."

Suddenly, unbelievably, Rusty coughed and breathed in a huge gulp of air.

"Dammit, Rusty!" Rogue exclaimed happily. "You're alive!"

"Can't prove it by me," Rusty muttered, attempting to push himself upright, and almost losing his balance on the ledge in the attempt. "What happened, anyway?"

"You fell," Rogue said gruffly. "I thought you broke your neck. It sure sounded like it."

"I think my canteen hit the ledge."

Rogue eyed the canteen strapped around Rusty's waist, dented now, and he realized what must have happened. It had been the canteen he'd heard. Just a few more inches and Rusty's body would have taken the blow.

"Rogue!" Charlie's voice sounded in the distance. "Did Rusty make it?"

Rogue threw back his head and stared up at the pinpoint of light so far above him. "Yes!" he shouted, hearing the gladness in his voice. "Yes, dammit! Rusty made it just fine."

"I wouldn't go so far as to say that," Rusty grumbled. "That water's some hard. And I think I swallowed half of it."

"But you're alive, boy," Rogue told him. "An' you still got enough strength about you to bitch an' moan so I guess you're doin' okay. Now hush up while I see what's goin' on up there." Throwing back his head, he cupped his hands around his mouth and shouted, "Charlie! Are you still there?"

"I'm still here!"

"Where's those supplies?"

"They're on the way now."

"Good! You stay put up there in case I need you. But send Chance back to the ranch. Tell Colby we need some more help! You gotta find another way down here! This one's too dangerous. Me an' Rusty's goin' to leave to look for Miranda. If you don't hear from us in another eight hours, then tear this place apart until you find her."

"I gotcha!" Charlie yelled. "An' Chance is already on his way to the ranch. You make damn sure you watch what you're doin'. I got a feelin' things ain't too safe down there."

Rogue didn't just have a feeling about the danger involved; he knew it for a fact. The professor and his nephew had disappeared and now, so had Miranda.

With her disappearance uppermost in his mind, he entered the dark hole again, hoping against hope that when he returned to the cavern with red sand, Miranda would be there waiting for him.

Thirteen

Despair settled around Miranda and she wore it like a mantle as she made her way back up the tunnel toward the lighted chamber. God! What could she do? The passage was blocked, effectively cutting her off from Rogue and the others.

Miranda swallowed around the lump of fear that clogged her throat; it felt raw, embedded with grit and dirt from the debris blocking the tunnel. Her tongue felt thick, swollen . . . her thirst had become almost overpowering.

Feeling the need to save her candle — it was growing smaller all the time — she extinguished the flame and was instantly engulfed by darkness. Her eyes strained through the heavy blackness, found a pinpoint of light in the distance and remained there as she stumbled forward, hurrying toward the chamber with phosphor walls.

There was water in the river, and by God, she'd find a way to reach it! Miranda had no intention of letting the cave destroy her.

Bursting into the lighted chamber, driven by her thirst and her determination to live, she hurried toward the slope, circling the huge formations, her ears tuned to the sound of softly flowing water.

Her nostrils twitched and flared, assailed by the fresh scent of water and her thirst increased tenfold. When she reached the edge of the upper chamber, she searched for a way down to the river. To her left she found a slope. Although it was steep, Miranda felt she could manage to descend.

Her first step down the slope became a skidding slide on loose shale and rubble that carried her forward at a startling pace. She landed in a sprawling heap, her breath whooshing out of her body.

Pushing herself to her elbows, she found she was only halfway down the slope, perched on a wide ledge.

Fighting desperately to retain her courage, she examined the area below her. Another slope. It seemed stable enough, but then, so had the area above her.

Carefully, she lowered her legs over the ledge, put her feet firmly against the rocky slope and, cautiously, fearfully, she descended, realizing the danger she faced if she injured herself. Trapped as she was, there would be no help for her.

Finally, when Miranda's feet rested on the canyon floor, she expelled a heartfelt sigh of relief. Her steps quickened as she limped across the sand to the river's edge.

Although the water had a green tint to it, she realized it was only an illusion — cast by the phosphor walls of the cavern.

Dropping to her knees, Miranda scooped up a handful of water and carried it to her mouth. The water was cool, refreshing, soothing to her parched throat. After she'd quenched her thirst, she lifted her riding skirt and waded into the water to wash her many cuts and bruises. Although most of her wounds were minor, on the calf of her right leg there was a long cut that still seeped blood.

Miranda frowned down at it. It needed stitching, but perhaps she could stanch the flow of blood by binding it. Wading to the riverbank, she tore a strip of cloth from the bottom of her riding skirt and wrapped it tightly around the wound. Since there was nothing more she could do for it at present, she turned her attention to her shadowy surroundings.

The river stretched from one end of the canyon to another, obviously exiting somewhere downstream.

The thought brought her to her feet again and she limped across the sand, headed downstream, intent on finding the river's exit. She was almost to the end of the canyon when she saw it . . . yawning darkly against the wall ahead of her.

How long was the tunnel, she silently wondered. Could she escape from this darkness there? Her question was quickly answered when she waded into the water, felt the tug of the current against her calves. She couldn't use the tunnel to escape . . . dared not. If she found it impassable, the force of the water might prevent her return.

No. She couldn't escape that way, but perhaps the entrance tunnel would free her.

Spinning on her heels, she retraced her steps, following the river upstream. The river ended abruptly at a waterfall about ten feet high. Although exhaustion weighed heavy on her, Miranda climbed the boulders until she reached the top of the fall where the river entered the cavern.

Stopping abruptly, she stared in dismay. There couldn't be more than six or seven inches between the water and the ceiling. Did she dare enter the underground river . . . dare to follow the tunnel that was almost filled with water?

Although the thought was frightening, the alternative—to stay in the cave alone—was even more so. She had to attempt it, couldn't pass over any chance of getting out of here.

Miranda's legs trembled as she entered the cold water again, feeling it lap against her ankles, then against her calves and thighs as she headed for the dark entrance. As she had suspected, the water was swift and she had to fight against the current, but if she could find handholds in the watery tunnel, then perhaps she could manage to travel through it.

Miranda allowed her body to be submerged up to her shoulders, and she tilted her head back until only her face was above the water. Grasping the rocky walls, she began her watery journey.

Rogue stopped in the chamber with red sand long enough to don his boots, then he entered the passage leading to the rock chimney. He would have missed the crevice again had it not been for his companion.

When he passed the projection, it seemed only a shadow. He'd already taken several steps when he heard Rusty's startled exclamation. "Hey, boss! Wait a minute! There's somethin' here!"

Rogue spun on his heel and found Rusty staring into a crevice. *Dammit!* he silently cursed himself. How could he have missed it?

He eyed the narrow opening—a crevice so thin that it seemed unlikely Miranda would have gone inside. Holding the lantern at arm's length, Rogue thrust it into the crevice, allowing the circle of light to brighten the walls of the tunnel.

"I don't know, Rusty," he said. "It don't make no sense that she'd've gone in there."

"They ain't been no rhyme nor reason for anythin' that's been happenin' down here," Rusty muttered.

"You're right about that," Rogue remarked. "I still don't know why she left in the first place." He spun on his heels to leave and the toe of his boot struck something hard.

Crack!

The object was flung against the far wall. Rogue's searching gaze found the small rock . . . located at the edge of the mark that had obviously been scraped into the rocky floor.

An arrow!

Dammit! Miranda must've scratched the arrow into the rock. She *had* gone into the tunnel.

"Miranda!" he shouted, poking his head into the crevice. "Are you in there, Miranda?" There was no answer. Only silence filled the darkness ahead of him. Holding the lantern in front of him, he tried to squeeze his large frame into the narrow crevice, but try as he would, it was too small.

"Let me do it," Rusty said. "I'm not as big as you are."

Rogue stood aside and Rusty pushed his lanky frame into the narrow opening. He went down it several feet, then called out. "It gets wider around the corner. She coulda made it through here."

But why in hell would she have wanted to? Rogue wondered. "Miranda!" he called again. "Dammit, Miranda, answer me!"

For some reason, he felt his voice wasn't carrying forward as it should have done. Rogue realized it was the acoustics again, playing a trick on their voices, something that seemed to happen with regularity in this underground world.

God! How could anyone actually want to explore such a place? His lips tightened grimly. He would damned well find Miranda, and when he did, he would take her out of this nightmarish world.

Rusty slid out of the crevice to stand beside Rogue. "If we chop off some of the rock around the entrance you should be able to get through."

Realizing that the other man was right, Rogue used the hammer and chisel in his pack to chop away at the entrance until it was wide enough for his body, then he squeezed into the crevice. Holding his lantern before him, he allowed the beam of his light to show him the way. All too soon they were stumbling over fallen rock.

The smell of freshly fallen debris hung heavy in the air renewing his sense of urgency. Hurrying forward, he rounded a curve and saw the pile of rock that blocked the passage.

"Dammit," he swore softly.

"What is it?" Rusty asked from behind him.

"It's a fresh rockslide."

Feverishly, he began working to clear the rocks that were blocking the passage, all the time fearing that he would find Miranda's cold body lying beneath the stones.

Miranda groaned and, with a cold, trembling hand, she pushed her wet hair back from her face, tucking a strand behind her ear. Her attempt to travel the watery tunnel had failed — she'd finally run out of headroom — and now she lay on the sandy river bank, feeling incredibly exhausted . . . and hungry, she realized suddenly.

Forcing her eyes open, Miranda stared up into the phosphorus glow, feeling not the slightest admiration for the underground world. She was beyond that, would give everything she possessed to be back in her room in the dormitory.

Suddenly she began to shiver. Pushing herself to her knees, Miranda wrapped her arms around herself. It was so cold — so cold. If only she had a fire.

Even as the thought came, something tugged at her memory. Hadn't she passed some dried wood farther down the river?

Jerking to her feet, she limped down the riverbank, intent on finding enough wood for a fire. She patted her pocket where she'd left the matches, but it seemed unnaturally flat . . . as though it were empty. Oh, Lord, no! Surely she hadn't lost them. Her heart beat in double time as she fumbled in the pocket. When her fingers brushed the canvas packet, she breathed a sigh of relief. She was trembling so much that when she pulled them out, she dropped the matches. She bent to pick them up and her eyes fastened on the soggy packet beside the matches. Good Lord! It couldn't be! Even as her eyes denied its existence, she reached for the small bag of tea that she'd shoved in her pocket when she'd eaten at the hotel. Just the sight of it caused her mouth to water. If she only had something in which to boil water, she could make a cup of tea.

And if the river washed wood up on the bank, then perhaps it would give up other things as well. She began a systematic search of the area around the river and came up with several mussel shells, a good stash of dry wood, some dried Spanish moss and the bottom half of somebody's woolen underwear.

Hardly able to believe her luck, Miranda clutched her treasures against her chest, carrying them to higher ground and stacking them in separate piles. After laying a fire, she added some of the dried moss for tinder and struck a match to it.

While the flames ate away at the wood, Miranda examined the mussel shells. Could she use them to heat water? Stripping off her boots and socks, she waded into the cold water and washed the mussel shells, then filled two of them with water. She was on the point of turning back when she saw another shell—half buried in the sand. Unlike the ones she carried, the shell was closed.

Miranda was nearly ecstatic when she found that it contained a live mussel. Carrying her treasures to the fire, she laid them as close as she dared.

Although the water soon grew hot enough for brewing tea, the mussel shells were so small, she had only a taste. But, she relished the tea, just as she did the small piece of meat she dug from the mussel shell.

Finding that the meager meal had only made her hungrier, she went back to the river. Since there'd been mussels in it, then there might very well be fish. And if there were fish, and if she could catch some, then she just might be able to survive until a search party could reach her. She must hold on to that thought. She *would* be rescued — as she had been that time in the French Alps.

But even as she clung to the hope that a search party would come for her, she realized it was very unlikely. There was every possibility that, even though she wasn't yet ready to depart from this world, she would have little say in the matter.

The death she had always feared might soon become a reality.

Fourteen

Don't let her be dead! Rogue silently prayed as he dug furiously through the rubble, grasping fist-sized rocks and flinging them behind him, paying little heed to where they landed.

"Boss," Rusty said from behind him. "Let up, boss. You can't clear it thataway."

Rogue ignored the other man, his movements never ceasing as he continued to dig at the rubble, the fingers of both hands clenching, grasping, then flinging the rocks behind him. But it was agonizingly slow work, so suffocatingly slow.

"Stop it, boss!" Rusty commanded gruffly, tugging at the other man's shoulder. "Can't you see you ain't doin' any good? You're gonna wind up bringin' the whole ceiling down on us!"

"I have to get her out!" Rogue snarled, jerking away from the younger man. "And if you're so weak-kneed that you can't help, then get the hell out of the tunnel and stay out of my way!"

"I ain't goin' nowheres!" Rusty snapped. "Not until you start thinkin' straight."

Rogue had his fingers latched around a rock about eighteen inches in diameter, but Rusty's tone of voice was so unlike his usual behavior that it brought Rogue back to his senses. Wrenching the rock loose, he flung it aside amid a shower of rocks, then turned to look at the other man.

"Sorry," he apologized gruffly. "Guess I went a little haywire there for a minute. But you can see we got no time to lose. We have to get her outta there before she suffocates."

"Yeah," Rusty agreed. "But there's gotta be a better way to do it. This tunnel is too narrow for us to work side by side. Besides, look around you, boss. Damn near every rock you're movin' is causin' two more to fall from the ceilin'. We gotta find a way to shore the tunnel up before we go any further. We can't be no use to anybody if we're dead."

"You're right. We need some logs to shore up the tunnel, but that's not possible. There's no way we could get any down here. Not the way we come in here and it's the only way I know." Rogue swallowed around his fear and sent his searching gaze around the tunnel, looking for an answer. The ceiling did look unstable, except maybe there—on the left side of the tunnel. If that huge slab of rock extended all the way to the floor—it was impossible to know, with the pile of rocks around it—but if it did, the ceiling would hold there.

Rogue pointed to the slab. "Maybe that's where we should direct our attention," he told the other man. "If we clear the rubble away from that, maybe we could find a way around it without bringin' the ceiling down."

155

"It's the only way I can see," Rusty said, his gaze following Rogue's finger to the spot. "We're gonna have to carry the rock out of the tunnel though. We won't have no room to work if we leave it here."

Rogue stripped off his shirt and tossed it to the other man. "Try putting both our shirts together and loading the rocks on them," he said. "Should get along faster that way."

He didn't wait for a reply. Instead, he began digging through the rubble again, flinging the rocks toward the shirts in order to expedite matters. But it all seemed useless. Again, as before, every rock he moved brought two more rolling down to take its place.

Rogue dared not even speculate on what was happening beyond the barrier. He knew Miranda could be injured, helpless beneath the rubble and unable to call out. His efforts to free her might very well result in her death.

That thought stopped him cold. "Miranda!" he shouted. "Miranda! Answer me if you can."

Tilting his head, Rogue listened intently, but there was no answer to his call, only the sound of Rusty's boots as he dragged rock out of the tunnel and the occasional plop, plop, thunk, of more rocks falling from above.

God! he felt so helpless . . . so damned helpless.

"Don't worry, boss. We'll get her out." The voice, coming from only a few feet behind him, spun Rogue around. He'd been so bound up in his own wretchedness that he hadn't realized the other man had returned.

"We're not even sure she's in there," Rogue said harshly.

"There was the arrow —"

"Who's to say she didn't come in the tunnel, then go out again." Rogue wanted desperately to believe what he was saying, needed to feel she was safe, wherever she was. "Maybe we better go back to the main tunnel and search again. We might've missed a turn someplace. Wouldn't surprise me none. I didn't see this one, so I could've missed another one. Damn! This whole area is honeycombed with tunnels. It would take years to explore them all."

"I hope not," Rusty muttered. "Somethin' tells me if we don't find her soon it just might be too late."

Rogue's exact thoughts, and knowing that Rusty felt the same way didn't help matters at all. God, what must Miranda be feeling? Lost and alone, more than likely in the dark. Yes, he decided. Definitely in the dark, because she could only have taken a candle and it would have played out long ago. How long could she keep her sanity? he wondered. How long before she went stark, raving mad. He wouldn't allow himself to believe her dead, but he did realize that she might be better off dead than crazy.

He must find her . . . and quickly.

The half-caste leader of the rustlers topped the ridge and pulled back on the black stallion's reins. Spread out below him, glinting like a silver ribbon beneath the sun, was Turkey Creek.

Wrapping the leather reins around the saddle-horn, Geraldo Mendez lifted the sweat-stained felt hat from his head, then brushed the sleeve of his bright red shirt across his forehead to remove the beads of sweat.

Swiveling in the saddle, Geraldo looked back toward the cattle. His mustachio twitched as the corners of his mouth tilted higher, his lips forming a smile. It was a good-sized herd and would bring them plenty of cash. It had been a good plan. But then, he reminded himself, wasn't he a brilliant man?

Geraldo was a swarthy man, his body built like a barrel, a heritage of his *indio* blood; but a lot of Latin showed in his swashbuckler style, in his taste for bright serapes and garish clothes. He was a cocky man, most vain about his heavy mustachio, under which there was almost always a perpetual smile, a broad, gleaming, mocking malevolence that could freeze a man's bones.

He was proud of himself; proud of his reputation as a ruthless cutthroat and terror. He told himself that where he and his band of equally villainous rowdies rode, the peasants trembled.

In the past, so had the law. But in these times, near the turn of the century, where a man had only to pick up the instrument called the telephone to summon a hundred lawmen, Geraldo made a point of being careful, of striking fast, then leaving a trail of dust behind him.

But today he was in no hurry. Geraldo knew that the gringo, McClaren, had done as they'd wished; he'd gone into the cavern to hunt for the professor,

158

and even though McClaren had left his foreman—the one called Colby—behind to track down the rustlers, Geraldo still felt no sense of urgency.

After all, why should he? The good rain had come and covered their tracks and it was sure to have left the old man's joints aching. By the time the old one was able to follow, Geraldo would have the animals across Turkey Creek and long gone toward the border.

Yes, it had been a good plan.

His eyes slid back to the creek in the valley. Although it was wide, it was only two or three feet deep. There would be no trouble crossing it with the cattle. Maybe he would stop long enough to rest the horses.

The corners of his mouth lifted again and there was a glint in his black eyes. Maybe it was a good idea. Yes, he decided. He would rest the horses, and he would allow the men to rest, for there was time. His lips twitched again. And there was even time enough to enjoy a few pulls on the whiskey bottle in his saddlebag.

Geraldo knew he needn't hurry. Why should he? There was only the old one and a handful of men to chase after him, and they'd lost his trail long ago.

Scrape, thud, clunk. The sound of the rocks being lifted, then tossed behind him was mingled with Rogue's harsh breathing as he continued to dig away at the rubble that blocked the passage.

He had to get through to Miranda. He must find

her! The need — the urgency he felt — was almost overwhelming.

Suddenly, Rusty spoke from beside him. "My lantern's runnin' out of kerosene, boss. It ain't gonna last much longer."

Rogue swiveled slightly, meeting the other man's eyes. "We shoulda brought the supplies with us instead of leavin' 'em in that big cave with red sand." His eyes slid to his own lantern. The flame was flickering madly. "Mine's nearly empty too," he went on. "Go fill yours an' bring the supplies back here." He brushed with a sleeve at the sweat beading his forehead, then slumped wearily against the pile of rubble. "God, it's hot in here," he mumbled, swallowing thickly. His mouth and throat felt stuffed with cotton. "I could use some water."

"You could use some rest too," Rusty said with a grimace. "You ain't gonna help her none by killin' yourself." He heaved a weary sigh and studied the pile of rubble facing them. "I ain't so sure we're doin' any good here, boss. I don't know where all them rocks is comin' from, but we ain't made no kind of hole in it. We're gonna have to have some more help."

Rogue rubbed his reddened eyes. "I know it. I've known it all along." His shoulders slumped tiredly. "Fill the lanterns. Then go back to the well-cavern. Chance oughtta be back by now."

Miranda, unwilling to give up, entered the river tunnel again. There had to be a way to go through it. She tipped her head back. Although there was no

160

more than three inches of space between the ceiling and the water, she could draw air through her nose.

It gave her a scary, claustrophobic feeling, but, Lord help her, she didn't want to turn back. Although she had no way of knowing, there was a possibility she was very near the entrance of the river tunnel. And without going on, would never even know how close she was.

Suddenly, water swept into her nose, causing a burning sensation, and she took a backwards step, then another and another until she had enough room to cough and expel the water. She sucked greedily at the air, filling her lungs, breathing in and out, her breath rasping harshly in the river tunnel.

Miranda tried to steady her nerves, realizing at once what had happened. The few inches of breathing space had completely disappeared and the water filled the tunnel from floor to ceiling.

She knew she must turn back, knew, yet felt unwilling to do so. Perhaps if she took a deep breath, filled her lungs with air, then she could go on a little farther under the water.

Suiting thought to action, Miranda gulped in a huge breath and went under, swimming as fast as possible against the current. All too soon her lungs began to burn, literally crying out for air and she knew she no longer had a choice. She must turn back.

But she couldn't! God, not yet! The entrance had to be near . . . just a little bit farther ahead. Although her eyes stung, felt as though they were filled with pebbles, she kept them wide open. Soon she would see daylight, the blue sky overhead. Oh,

Lord, how she ached to see the blue sky again . . . just one more time before she drowned.

Although Miranda's lungs felt as though they were on fire, sheer determination carried her forward—determination to see, once again, the blue sky over her head.

With his fuel replenished, Rogue held the lantern aloft and studied the pile of rubble before him. He'd managed to dig a hole at the top, but it was only a few feet in depth. He had no idea how much rock blocked the passage. There might be fifty feet or there might not even be another side. The rest of the tunnel might be completely blocked.

He shuddered at the thought, unable to bear it, because if it were true, then Miranda was dead. But, dammit! She couldn't be!

She *had* to be on the other side of the rubble. He wouldn't allow himself to think otherwise. But how could he get her out?

"Miranda," he muttered, still studying the pile of rocks. "Where are you? What have you gone and got yourself into?" Thoughts of her filled his mind. The way she'd faced him down, forcing him to come with her. She was such a spunky little thing, brave and independent. But a mind could only stand so much, and she was alone in this dark that was so black, this dark that had not even one tiny star to light the way, and she could be in pain, perhaps terrified.

"If you had to leave, professor, why didn't you take the lantern?" Even as he asked the question, he knew the answer. It was obvious. She had left the lantern for him in case he woke while she was gone. That, in itself, indicated she hadn't meant to be gone very long, couldn't have meant to go very far.

Obviously the accident — the landslide — had prevented her return. The landslide could, even now, be covering her dead body.

Even as the thought shuddered over him, he dismissed it. Miranda Hartford wasn't dead. He felt certain of it. If she was, then he would most certainly know.

Miranda fought against the water that seemed intent on drowning her, but there was no escaping it. She had gone too far in the tunnel. There was not even one inch of space left where she could breathe the precious life-giving air her lungs were craving. Instead, the water flooded in her nose, her mouth, her eyes.

Mustering every last ounce of strength she possessed, she turned around and swam with the current, hoping the combined efforts of the current and her weak limbs would see her to the end of the water passage.

Colby leaned against the corral, his hands clenched on the top rail while Mike and Little Joe worked with the big gray stallion. Although the foreman's eyes were on the battle going on in the corral, his mind was turned inward, focused on Rogue. Where in hell could he be? He'd had enough time to find the professor. In fact, there'd been more than enough time, so why hadn't he returned?

"The boy's gone an' got hisself in trouble," he mumbled. "I feel it in my bones."

Suddenly, amid the ruckus in the corral, there was the sound of thundering hooves. Colby turned to see a horse and rider racing toward him.

Recognizing Rowdy Granger, one of the Lazy R riders, Colby stood straighter, his body tense, expectant. He didn't know the other two men had joined him until Mike spoke from a few feet away.

"Who is it?" Mike asked.

"Rowdy," Colby said gruffly, his gaze never wavering from the man who reined up beside him and slid from the saddle.

"What's up, Rowdy?" growled Colby.

"We saw 'em, Colby," Rowdy said, his breath coming quickly. "It was Zeke that saw 'em an' sent me for you."

"The rustlers?" Colby inquired.

"No. Not them. Not yet. Zeke just saw the herd. But the rustlers gotta be there too. Zeke just figgered he better not wait around an' look for 'em."

"Where did he see 'em?" Colby asked.

"He said they was on the rise above Turkey Creek. Looked like they was bein' driven, but he couldn't see no riders from where he was at. He come lookin' for me, then went back to watch."

Colby nodded his grizzled head. "He done right. You able to ride?"

"Damn right I am. I ain't about to be left behind."

It was the answer Colby had expected. All the

164

hands were loyal to Rogue and they didn't want him to go under. "Mount up," he snapped. "We're goin' after that herd." Maybe his luck had changed. Maybe he might have the herd back by the time Rogue returned.

If he returned at all.

Fifteen

Miranda felt cold . . . so cold. And, Lord, she felt sick, so incredibly nauseated. In that same instant of time when she felt the sickness, she also realized she couldn't control it. But, finding her body unwilling to obey her mind, she could only turn her head and empty the contents of her stomach beside her.

When she'd finished retching, had completely expelled the river water she'd swallowed, she lay shuddering on the sand, coughing weakly, as water continued to stream from her nose and mouth. Miranda knew she must get up, but realized that something was wrong with her arms. Calling upon every ounce of strength within herself, she forced them to move, willed them to support her weight.

Her elbows refused to comply. They felt as stiff as a board. "Move, dammit," she muttered hoarsely. Although her lungs still burned and her throat felt as though it had been stuffed full of nails, the sound of her own voice gave her added strength. Her right arm moved. Immediately, pain shot through her arm . . . hot, stabbing pain that started at her wrist and continued up past her elbow.

Clenching her teeth, she tried again; numbly, creakily, agonizingly slow, she moved.

You can do it! That's the way. Miranda could almost hear her father's voice uttering the words he'd often said before. *If the mind boggles at the whole, Miranda, then forget the whole. Take it one piece at a time.* If necessary, one inch at a time.

Finally, after what seemed an eternity, Miranda was sitting upright, taking stock of her situation.

Apparently—although she was wet and filthy, her body a mass of bruises from bashing against the rocks—her limbs had managed to remain intact.

Miranda looked around her twilight world, feeling the incredible weight of total aloneness.

Rogue! she cried silently. *God, Rogue! I need you.*

She wondered momentarily why she called for the rancher instead of for her father. The shout, when it came, seemed to be in answer to her silent prayer.

Miranda! Where are you!

"I'm here, Rogue," she muttered weakly, her searching gaze scouring the edge of the cliff, searching for some sign of the man who'd called out to her. Her gaze caught momentarily on a dark shadow, followed it upward, too far, she realized. It had to be one of the columns . . . not a man as she'd hoped.

Miranda! The shout came again, ringing through her head. *Answer me, Miranda!*

"Rogue! I'm down here!"

Down here, down here, down here . . . her voice echoed back to her. Something about it puzzled her and her mind worried over what she'd heard. Or, she suddenly realized, what she *hadn't* heard. Why hadn't she heard the echo of Rogue's voice?

She waited, listening, hoping to hear his voice again, but only the sound of water, flowing across limestone as it made its way downstream, broke the silence of the cavern. Had she really heard Rogue's voice? she wondered. Or had it only been her imagination?

Sudden tears filled her eyes, welling over and streaming down her face. Lord help her! How could she endure it all again? How could she endure the pain . . . the deprivation . . . the eternal suffering. Even the thought of such an event caused her stomach to coil in a tight knot. She'd survived the ordeal before . . . just barely. But, God! How could fate be so cruel as to make her go through it all again?

Miranda knew she couldn't go through it all again . . . knew as well that this time she'd lose her sanity before death came to claim her. Wouldn't it be better if she died right now? Wouldn't it be better if she took her own life?

Her searching gaze swept the sand around her, looking for something . . . anything, that would accomplish the task. She saw the discarded mussel shell and reached for it. The edge should be sharp enough to cut an artery in her wrist.

Her fingers wrapped around it and she gripped tightly, testing its strength. Yes! She brought it against her wrist, pressed hard, feeling the sharpness against her flesh. A quick slicing movement produced several bloody beads.

Harder! You'll have to press harder! an inner voice silently cried.

She was on the verge of doing so when she suddenly realized what she was doing and flung the shell away from her. *God! Had she already lost her senses?* Just the thought sent fear shivering through her.

With her eyes glued to the bloody beads on her wrist, Miranda lifted her head and sent a long, terrifying scream throughout the cavern.

A scream, long and agonized, caught Rogue unawares. His reaction was instantaneous. He jerked spasmodically, then froze, caught in the act of flinging another rock aside. Fear sent icy fingers crawling through his body, clawing at his stomach and twisting around his heart. His fingers tightened around the rock he was holding, his knuckles showing white. He knew with a certainty that he hadn't just imagined the sound. Although it had been thin, diluted, and very, very far away, he *had* heard the scream . . . the *terrified* scream of a woman, literally consumed by pain.

"Oh, my God!" His voice was a hoarse rasp. "She *is* there! Dammit! She *is* alive! I knew it! I knew it all the time!" His heart jerked crazily with alarm. "But what in hell is happening to her?" Scrambling atop the rubble, unmindful of the shower of rocks he dislodged, he searched for a crack . . . some small opening that would allow his voice to reach her. "Miranda!" he shouted. "I'm here, Miranda! I'm in the tunnel! Just hang on until I get there!"

The slope seemed incredibly steep as Miranda literally crawled up it. She closed her mind to the pain of her flesh, ignored the blood trickling down her legs. She concentrated instead on reaching the upper level of the cavern.

If the whole boggles the mind, then forget the whole. Concentrate instead on one tiny part. In this case, the tiny part consisted of gaining inch after inch of ground, to satisfy the almost overpowering compulsion to return to the rockslide.

Finally, after what seemed like hours, she lay sprawled on the ledge that, only a short time before, had seemed unreachable. After taking only a short moment to regain her breath, Miranda pushed herself to her feet and limped across the underground canyon toward the dark, yawning mouth of the tunnel.

The blackness . . . the same dark nothingness that had seemed so threatening before, seemed almost to welcome her. Unhesitatingly, she entered, feeling her way through the darkness, palms pressed firmly against the rock walls around her.

Although Miranda heard no sound other than her own footsteps and the thud, thud, thump, of her own heart, crazily beating beneath the confines of her ribcage, she felt certain Rogue was in the tunnel. But even so, she didn't call out, knew it would be useless to do so. He'd never be able to hear her. Not with the rockslide between them.

Miranda continued to hurry forward, unmindful of the darkness that enclosed her, knowing only that somewhere, on the other side of the slide, perhaps, was Rogue. And she must get there before he gave up and left.

Rogue worked feverishly to make a hole near the large slab of rock, taking heart when his efforts finally uncovered a hole. Although it was only a small crack, perhaps four inches wide, at least he was finally showing some progress. His movements rarely ceased; he only paused occasionally to call Miranda's name and listen for an answer. On one such time the sound he'd been waiting for finally came.

"I'm here, Rogue! I'm here!"

"Miranda!" His heart gave a crazy jerk, skip, jump. "God, Miranda! I thought you were dead! Are you all right?"

"Yes." Her wobbling voice sounded tearful. "I guess . . . I'm all right, but . . . but you don't know how *glad* I am you finally found me."

"Why the hell did you leave like that?" he asked, his relief suddenly turning to anger. God! The ache in his gut was almost more than he could bear. And he had this stubborn little chit to blame for it.

"Do-don't y-you y-yell at m-me," she stuttered, then, to his everlasting shame she began to cry. Harsh, rasping sobs came from her, seeming to be torn from her body, and he felt like a mean, heartless bully.

"Stop it, Miranda," he said, wishing he could pull

her into his arms and comfort her. "Don't cry like that. I didn't mean to yell at you. It's just that I thought you might be dead and I—oh, hell!" The words spewed forth, his voice ragged, harsh with remembered fear.

But she seemed not to notice. Instead, she continued to sob, frantically, desperately, with broken little cries that stabbed through him like a knife digging away at clay. "Stop it, Miranda!" he commanded gruffly. "I'm here now! There's nothin' to cry about."

He wondered if she even heard him. If she did, she paid not the slightest attention. Her wretched little cries continued, ripping away at his gut, wrapping around his heart and threatening to tear it out of his body, leaving him helpless and weak-kneed.

Swallowing around the lump in his throat, he spoke in a cold, steely voice. "I'd never have suspected you were such a crybaby, Miranda. I thought you had guts." He knew he was being cruel, but knew as well that if she didn't stop crying soon, he would be unable to withstand the pain her tears caused him.

"I-I'm n-not a crybaby," she said fiercely, between hiccups. "I-if y-you'd b-been through what I h-have, then m-maybe—"

"I know, I know," he soothed gently. "But it's over now, professor. I'm here, and I won't stop until I have you outta there."

"D-do . . . do you really think you can get me out?" she asked hopefully.

"I'll get you out!" He *had* to get her out, would be unable to rest until he'd done so.

When she spoke again, her voice was steadier. "I'm s-sorry for b-being so s-stupid. I never cry." When he didn't answer, she said, "What do you want me to do?"

He gave a long, shuddering sigh. "I don't know," he admitted. "Whatever it is, we'll have to take it slow. The roof of the tunnel is shaky." He didn't want to tell her just how unstable the roof really was, that it could easily collapse at any moment. He was afraid the news would bring on another flood of tears.

But he needn't have worried. Her voice, when it came, was calm and steady. "You can't dig through to me, Rogue. There's a boulder wedged between us that will be impossible to move."

"Do you have any idea how big it is?"

"No, but I'd guess there's five to ten feet between us."

"You sound closer than that."

"It's the acoustics on your side of the tunnel," she explained. "Our voices carry easily from here. But if I step back a couple of feet, then you won't be able to hear me. The rocks in here are like sponges. They absorb the sound of my voice." She paused for a long moment, and when she spoke again, her voice was edged with pain. "I don't think you'll be able to reach me. I'm afraid . . . afraid I'm stuck here. But, McClaren . . . please d-don't go away yet. Stay with me for awhile longer. It helps to know you're over there, just a few feet away from me. Maybe it will give me the courage to face whatever I must."

Her words stabbed through him. She was so

173

small, so fragile, and yet so brave. God! He had to get help for her. "Miranda," he said gently. "Don't talk like that. You'll soon be free. Just stay where you are. Stay right there, and I'll go back to the well-cavern and—"

"No," she cried. "Please, Rogue! Don't leave me alone yet." Her voice was husky with tears and there was no way he could make himself leave her.

"I won't go anywhere," he said softly. "Not until you're ready for me to leave."

She laughed shakily. "In that case, you'll never leave me."

Rogue felt a pain in his chest. Her words sounded strangely intimate, as though they'd been lovers. It was hard to believe they'd known each other such a short time. He leaned against the rockslide, wishing he could reach out and embrace her.

"Are you still there?" she asked. Something about her voice, perhaps it was the very calmness of it, told him she already knew he was.

"Yes. I'm still here." He searched for something else to say, something to take her mind off the circumstances. "Are you hungry?" Immediately, he cursed himself for being a fool. Of course she was hungry! She couldn't be otherwise.

"Not so much now," she replied.

Although he wasn't sure why she replied as she did, he didn't pursue that line. Better not to remind her of her hunger. "Your candle must be nearly gone."

"It burned out long ago," she replied.

His heart gave a crazy jerk, something it had been doing a lot lately. He should have expected

174

that, but he hadn't. "We'll soon have you out of there," he said, forcing a cheerful note into his voice.

She was silent for a long moment, then she spoke. "McClaren . . . don't blame yourself if you can't do it. I won't."

"Don't be stupid!" he said harshly. "We're gonna get you outta there! Rusty's gone back to the well-cavern to see about gettin' some more help to dig you out." Where the hell was Rusty anyway? It shouldn't have taken so long just to go to the well-cavern and back.

"Rusty came down to help you?"

"Yes. And so will the others."

"You can't dig through here," she said. "You'll only risk your life unnecessarily. There should be another way to get in here, with so many tunnels riddling this cave system. I thought I could get out through the river tunnel, but it didn't work out. I ran out of breathing room before I got to the end of it."

"What river tunnel?"

"The one that's in here. I didn't tell you, did I?" Her voice lifted with excitement. "Rogue. You should see this place. You'll never believe it. At the other end of this tunnel is a huge, glittering chamber. Like something out of a fairy tale. The cavern walls are made of phosphor and crystal. Combined, they create light in the chamber. It's an underground canyon really, with a river running through it."

She continued to babble about the river and the sand and the valley. Was she mad? No! He wouldn't accept that. But perhaps being alone for so long, in total darkness, had made her build a fantasy world.

"Miranda," he said gently. "This world of yours sounds fantastic, but are you sure . . ."

"I thought I was going to drown in the river," she babbled on. "I guess I almost did. I was so intent on not giving up, so sure that I would find a way out, but the roof was only inches above the water and the space kept getting smaller and smaller until finally I took a deep breath and started swimming. When my lungs filled with water . . ."

As she babbled on, Rogue began to realize that what she was describing sounded all too real. If she was building herself a fantasy world, then why would she include a near-drowning episode?

"Miranda," he said. "Listen to me."

"All right."

"You must not go into that river again. Do you hear me? If it's really there, the danger is real. You were obviously lucky this time. The next time might prove fatal."

"I know that," she said. "But can't I go into it to catch some fish?"

"There's fish in it?"

"Yes. I'm not sure how big they are. But I did see fish there. And mussels too." Her voice sounded grieved. "The mussel was only enough to make me hungrier, but it tasted good with the tea."

Now he knew it was her imagination. Tea and mussels? There was no way she'd had either one. It was only her mind trying to take the edge off her hunger.

Dammit! Where was Rusty?

"Miranda," he said hesitantly. "I should go and tell the others I've found you. Will you be all right until I get back?"

"I'll have to be, won't I?" Her voice was choked now. "But don't go yet, Rogue. Wait a little while longer. Talk to me. I like the sound of your voice."

"What do you want to talk about?" he asked.

"Nothing. Anything. Just talk. You could tell me more about sleeping out under the stars. That's something I've never done."

"Not even at the beginning of an expedition?" he asked. Although he felt the need to hurry, he also felt her need for companionship. Perhaps he could ease a small part of her pain by indulging in memories of the past for a short time.

"No. Poppa always started our cave explorations at dawn. We never set up camp outside." Her voice was suddenly wistful. "I think it would be nice to be able to open your eyes at midnight and see the stars overhead."

"Yes," he agreed. "It is. They look like millions of diamonds glittering on a bed of dark velvet. After we get out of here, then I'll show them to you one night."

"Would you really do that, Rogue?"

"Of course," he said gently. "You have my promise on it."

"Rogue. Is your mother alive?"

What a funny question. And yet she seemed very serious. "Yes, of course. Why do you ask?"

"I just wondered." She gave a husky laugh. "It's hard to think of you as someone's baby."

"Did you think I was born fully grown?"

She laughed again. "Where is your mother?"

"She lives with my father in Montana," he said, still wondering at her curiosity about his parents.

"Then both your parents are still living?"

"Yes."

"I've always wondered what it would be like to have a mother."

"Would you like to share mine?"

"Do you think she would let me?"

"Yes. I'm sure she would," he said. "Some day I'll take you to meet her."

Even as he said the words she wanted to hear, Miranda knew it would never happen. She would never go to Montana, never meet his mother, because she would never leave this cavern alive. She swallowed back her fear and spoke again. "What does she look like, Rogue? Describe her to me."

"She has . . ." His voice broke suddenly and he cleared his throat and began again. "Mother has curly brown hair and brown eyes," he said. "She's a little taller than you are and more rounded, of course."

" 'Mother' sounds like such a stiff, formal word, Rogue," she said, leaning her head against the side of the cavern. "Is your mother a formal person?" His use of the word "mother" had conjured up visions of a dark-haired woman with a cool expression, a woman who never allowed her children to dirty the house.

"Mother, formal?" Rogue gave a husky laugh. "She'd love that. No. Mother isn't formal. Mother

178

is . . . well, how can I describe her? Mother smells of vanilla and spice, of cookies and cakes left cooling on the kitchen table, of . . ."

"Stop, stop!" she cried, laughing until tears rolled down her face. "Rogue! How could you? I'm starving to death over here and you start talking about food."

"Oh, damn," he said forcefully. "I never even thought. But you did ask, and I have no other way of describing my mother."

"Don't worry," she said. "You were describing her just fine." She fell silent, knowing she must let him go. But it was hard. Oh, Lord! It was so hard.

Drawing a deep breath of courage, she pinned her gaze on the lantern light filtering through to her through the cracks. "Thank you for describing her to me, Rogue," she said softly. Rubbing her silent tears away, she added, "I know it's past time you went. And, don't worry about me. I'll be all right now."

He cleared his throat. "Are you sure?"

"Yes. Just talking to you for awhile has given me the courage to go on. You go on back and do what you have to . . . but, Rogue?" She could hear the tears in her voice.

"Yeah?"

"Would you come back later? Not right away, of course, it would be foolish, since there's no way through here. But if you can't find another way soon, then would you come back and talk to me again?"

"Yeah. I'll just do that." She heard him clear his

throat again and the light on the wall shifted. "Do you want me to leave the lantern?"

"No. Don't do that. You'll need it more than I will." Her fingers dug into her palms and she stifled the sobs that shook her slender frame. "You go on now, Rogue. I'm just going to stay here awhile." *And watch the light go away,* she silently added. And it did, growing dimmer and dimmer, until finally she was left completely in darkness . . . alone.

Sixteen

Geraldo lay amid a bed of wild flowers, his head propped against a log, to make it easier to swallow from the bottle he held. He contemplated the blue sky overhead while he silently congratulated himself on acquiring such a healthy-looking herd of cattle.

Turkey Creek was only a few feet away; he could hear the water as it flowed gently downstream and he had not a care in the world. Hadn't he outwitted the old one?

It was as the stupid gringos had said, when they'd come to him, hats in hand.

His lips pulled into a wide smile as he remembered the meeting with the gringos. They'd thought him stupid, saying their names were Smith and Jones, thinking to deceive him when Geraldo knew the names were not their true ones. But who cared what they were called. The only thing that mattered was the gold they'd offered.

Geraldo smiled again and took another pull at the whiskey bottle. Imagine . . . they were paying him for this raid that was pure pleasure anyway. He guessed their purpose was revenge against the rancher McClaren, a man they were too white-livered to go against themselves. But that was good. They'd wanted Geraldo, wanted him bad, and he knew it, so he'd set a high price in gold, but the stupid gringos had not even tried to bargain with him.

Geraldo shoved his hand into his pocket and brought out a handful of bright silver dollars and fixed on them with avid eyes. There were more of them in his saddlebags, plenty more. He rubbed them sensually between his palm and his blunt but supple fingers; with the other hand he poured whiskey into his throat.

This was indeed a good day. Not only gold, for which no lawman might foolishly come looking, but this dividend, the herd of cattle as fat as any he'd ever seen.

If there was any cloud on his enjoyment it was only that the raid had been too easy, with too little excitement to make his blood tingle, too little killing to add the spice that any good dish needs, like a steaming pot of beans with no fine hot chilies to satisfy the belly.

He turned his head toward the creek to see how his band was coming with the watering and found them moving the animals back, regrouping them as they finished drinking, getting ready for the crossing. Except that one man wasn't working. He was standing, looking startled, off up the slope that lifted gently from the stream. Geraldo turned his

182

head again, without haste. And he found five mounted men, sitting abreast, dark shadows against the blue cloudless sky.

Although every part of Rogue's mind and body screamed out against leaving Miranda alone, he realized, as she obviously had, that there was nothing else he could do.

He sighed heavily, raked a hand through his dark hair and tried to focus his thoughts on the job at hand . . . he must find a way to break through to Miranda. God only knew what she was having to endure, trapped alone there in the darkness. She'd tried so hard to be brave, to hide her fear from him, but he'd seen past her efforts, had heard the shaking in her voice when she'd teased about his mother. Poor brave, little thing.

Dammit! He should never have allowed her to accompany them on the search!

Even as the thought came, Rogue knew he could not have stopped her from accompanying them. Her fear for her father had been uppermost in her mind and it had overcome her good sense.

Professor Hartford.

What in tarnation had happened to the man anyway? Even as the question rose in Rogue's mind, he pushed it aside. Whatever the professor's fate, he would have to wait. Rogue intended to concentrate all his energy . . . all his efforts on rescuing Miranda before something worse happened to her.

He was halfway to the well-cavern when the light from another lantern told him someone was approaching. Only moments later he saw Rusty.

"Where in hell have you been?" he rasped harshly.

"You told me to go —"

"Never mind that!" Rogue snapped. "I found Miranda!"

"You found her! That's great!" Rusty looked past the rancher's shoulder as though expecting to see Miranda there. When he didn't, his gaze flicked back to the other man. "Where is she?"

"In the tunnel as we suspected. She's alive, and she said she's okay, but . . . I'm not so sure about that. She sounded all strung out."

"It's no wonder," Rusty said. "Not after all she's been through."

"We don't really know what she's been through," Rogue muttered. "We're not even sure how long she's been lost."

"More'n three days, boss. Charlie said you been down here for more'n three days now."

"Three days! God! No wonder I'm so damn tired! We gotta get her outta there, Rusty, an' we're gonna need some help doin' it."

Rusty sighed and raked his free hand through his copper curls. "That's sure gonna be a problem, boss. We ain't got no help."

"What do you mean?" Rogue snapped. "Charlie was supposed to send Chance to the ranch for more help."

"He did. But Chance ain't come back yet."

"He didn't come back? Why in hell not?" Without waiting for an answer, he went on. "Then Charlie's still up there alone."

184

"Yeah."

"Dammit!" Something must have gone wrong at the ranch. The thought was only a fleeting one, gone as quickly as it came, because Rogue's mind was already turned in another direction, trying to devise a plan to rescue Miranda. "There has to be another way in there," he muttered. "Miranda said there was a huge chamber back there, and an underground—"

"Back where?" Rusty interrupted.

"A little farther on in the tunnel. On her side."

"If she's up to explorin' boss, then it must mean she's okay."

"All it means is she don't have no broken bones," Rogue replied. "What's got me worried is her state of mind. She was talkin' kinda funny . . . babblin' on about a big room with glittering walls with an underground river with mussels and—" He broke off suddenly, hearing the words he was saying, realizing how crazy they sounded.

"Maybe she's right, boss. Maybe she did see a river. You gotta admit we seen sights down here that I ain't never even heard of before. Who's to say they ain't a river too?"

Rogue shrugged his shoulders. "If that chamber is as big as she says, then it's more'n likely there'll be tunnels runnin' out of it. And it's up to us to find those tunnels."

"You reckon she's gonna be okay until we find a way to get to her?"

"I don't know," Rogue said grimly. "I got a feelin' that she's afraid of the dark."

"That don't make no sense. Somebody that's

185

afraid of the dark sure wouldn't be hankerin' to mess around in caves."

"I don't know, Rusty, but I think she was more afraid for her father, than she was of the cave. You gotta admit she has spunk. She's already showed us that. Let's just hope she can hold onto it, 'cause it's gonna take plenty of it to see her through this."

Rogue sent a silent prayer winging toward the heavens. *Don't let her lose her senses, Lord, and please, please, keep her safe.* He didn't even stop to wonder why it mattered so much to him. But it did; it mattered desperately. Rogue knew she was already imagining things. Weren't the diamondlike walls—the ones that lighted the chamber she babbled about—weren't they proof enough that she was inventing stuff to help her keep her sanity? How long could her imaginary world sustain her? Would she—by the time he was able to reach her— be stark, raving mad? Just the thought of such an event was almost more than he could bear.

Miranda limped slowly through the tunnel, making her painful way back to the phosphor cavern. "Things could be worse," she said aloud. "He knows where I am now. He'll find a way to get me out of here." *Please, Lord! Just let him find me in time!*

A memory flashed into her mind; a memory of Ruben, of Professor Dometrius . . . and Jane. "Don't do that," she muttered, grinding her teeth together. "Don't think of them! You're going to get out of here! Rogue will get you out!"

But she found it wasn't so simple to dismiss them from her mind . . . especially Jane Alexander, and the way she'd looked the last time Miranda had seen her, so thin, so . . . broken, so . . . dead.

"Stop it!" she cried aloud, her voice filled with anguish. "It wasn't my fault!" *My fault, my fault, my fault,* echoed the cavern. Miranda sank to her knees, pressing the heels of her palms over her ears as hard as she could, trying to shut out the sound of the cavern accusing her.

She lay there for a time, long after the echo had died away, sobbing out her anguish. Finally, when there were no more tears left to cry, she gave a shuddering sigh and pushed herself to her feet again and continued through the tunnel, intent on reaching the underground river again. Miranda still retained enough sanity to realize that she had a better chance of survival at the river. There were mussels there, and although they made a meager mouthful, if she could find enough of them, she wouldn't starve to death. And if she could devise a way to trap a fish—

Just the thought of roasted fish lent strength to Miranda's legs. Moments later, she saw the soft, diffused light of the cavern ahead, and already, in the distance, she could hear the sound of falling water, could envision it as she'd last seen it, tumbling down a series of ledges that made up the underground waterfall.

Paying little attention to the columns and other formations, Miranda skirted around them and hurried toward the sound.

* * *

"What in hell is that?" Rusty asked, swinging his lantern out at arm's length to study the coral-studded cavern better.

"Some kind of cave coral," Rogue replied. "And it's sharp as hell."

"An' we're gonna cross it?" Rusty turned questioning eyes on the rancher.

"Yeah. It's goin' in the general direction of Miranda's cave. It just might lead us there." He eyed the younger man. "You don't have to go across, Rusty. You could go back to the well-cavern and wait for the others. Maybe that would be best anyway. Maybe—"

"I didn't say I wasn't gonna come," Rusty interrupted. "I just asked if we was gonna cross it." He raised a booted leg and studied the sole. "Just had these things resoled by that new bootmaker in Austin. I guess this is a way to find out if he's any good or not."

"I don't think you oughtta be holdin' the bootmaker to blame if they don't hold up," Rogue said abruptly. He studied the floor ahead of them, noticing how the light played across the sharp points of the coral. "Just be careful and don't slip," he muttered. "A fall could slice you to pieces."

"You ain't tellin' me somethin' I don't already know," Rusty muttered.

Rogue started across the coral, testing the floor as he went, praying that he wasn't wasting his time, that the tunnel would lead to Miranda's underground cavern. If the path he was taking proved to be the wrong one, he'd have to retrace his steps again. And God only knew how much longer

Miranda could keep her sanity, trapped alone in that damned cavern.

Colby's group looked down from the hilltop. The cattle were there, raggedly bunched, with saddled horses roaming among them that didn't belong to the Lazy R. As they watched, a dozen men in brightly colored shirts eased back into the herd or clustered between it. One man got up from where he had been lying against a log.

Rowdy mumbled, then said more distinctly, "I've seen him before, Colby. That's that bastard Geraldo. I wouldn't've thought he'd have the guts to come this far from the border."

Colby made a grunting sound. "He'll find out soon enough the Lazy R ain't such easy pickin's."

"How we gonna play it?" Colby asked.

Without looking away from Geraldo, yet taking in the whole picture below, Colby told him, "Guess I'll just mosey on down there. The rest of you cover me with your rifles."

He urged the big gelding on down the grade, slowly, but deliberately, his body adjusting to the gait as the animal's descending forefeet made one shoulder drop and then the other. Becoming aware that Rowdy was following him, Colby spoke without turning; "I said—"

"I heard what you said, Colby, but I reckon I ain't the rest of 'em."

Colby's lips twitched slightly and he let it go and continued on at his unhurried pace.

* * *

Rogue McClaren and Rusty had made it safely across the coral tunnel but now they were at a junction where several tunnels branched off from the one. Keeping in mind the professor's way of eliminating tunnels, Rogue chose the right one. The passage curved and wound, climbed, then dropped, but always leading in the general direction of Miranda's cavern. Rogue's steps quickened; now he was sure he was on the right track. He rounded a curve and was suddenly brought to an abrupt stop. His shoulders drooped tiredly as he stared in dismay at the rock wall facing him.

God! Had it all been in vain? He slumped against the limestone wall, then slid to the floor and placed his head on his bent knees. He was tired! So damned tired!

"Maybe it ain't so bad," Rusty muttered. "There's them other tunnels. One of them may lead to her. We could—"

"I'm beginnin' to think we'll never get through to her," Rogue said harshly. "I'm beginnin' to think we're just wasting our time."

"How long's it been since you ate, boss?" Rusty asked gruffly.

"I don't know," Rogue replied. "But I can't think about eating now." He looked up and glared at the younger man. "How could I when she's starvin' to death in there?"

"You ain't gonna help her by starvin' your own self," Rusty muttered. "All you're gonna do is make yourself so weak you won't be able to keep on lookin'!"

"Dammit, Rusty! Don't tell me—" Rogue broke off abruptly, suddenly realizing what he was doing. He was lashing out at the man who'd volunteered to help him . . . a man who, despite his youth, had been a friend. And what Rusty said made sense. If he didn't eat, if he didn't keep up his strength, then Miranda was already as good as dead. "Dig in that pack over there," he growled. "There's some sardines in there and—my God! Miranda has some sardines in her pocket! She's not totally without food." He curbed the urge to return to the blocked passage to remind her about the tin of sardines. Instead, he made himself wait. It was entirely possible she'd already found them. Anyway, another couple of hours wouldn't make that much difference to her, but it would allow him to search another one of the tunnels while he was here.

Moments later, Rogue decided sardines had never tasted so good before. He wasted little time in consuming them and as he ate, he examined the rocky wall ahead of him. Something about the rock was different. It was pitted, gouged out, until it looked very much like a sponge. Could it be the same type of rock that made up Miranda's tunnel? Digging into his pocket, he extracted his knife and dug the tip of his blade into the rock. It crumbled easily beneath the sharp blade.

"Look at the way it crumbles," he rasped hoarsely. "We just might be able to dig through this stuff."

With a muttered exclamation, Rusty dug out his knife, and, choosing a spot about two feet away from the rancher, he began digging into the porous rock. Their efforts were punctuated by harsh breathing, and soon beads of sweat dotted both men's brows, but they ignored it, their movements never ceasing, not even when the first trickle of water appeared.

"I think we're on the right track!" Rusty grunted. "Looks like there's water on the other side."

"It could be Miranda's underground river," Rogue replied, shoving his knife deeper into the porous material and yanking another chunk out, intent on widening the gap.

He was unprepared when suddenly, with a groaning sound, a crack appeared in the rock wall. It widened, then abruptly gave way and he was engulfed by a flood of water that struck him like a blow, sending him crashing against the far wall. Water flooded his mouth and nose, choking his breath off until he felt as though he was drowning in an ocean. He was vaguely aware of being tossed about, his body spun over and under, crashing against rocks, bouncing against one wall, then the other. A sudden sharp blow against his head sent his senses reeling, and although he fought to remain conscious — knew he must if he was to survive — he fought in vain. A red haze slowly formed before his eyes . . . his lungs felt as though they were on fire, then blackness overcame him.

Seventeen

Miranda stood helplessly on the riverbank, watching in horror as Rogue's limp body was dashed against the rocks over and over again. She knew he was drowning . . . knew if she didn't get to him, didn't pull him out of the water, he would die. But she couldn't help him, her legs were frozen to the spot; all she could do was utter a silent scream and watch him drown.

Miranda.

She tried to answer him, but her jaws seemed locked in place. The current brought him nearer to the bank where she stood watching. The flood was twirling him around and around, like driftwood caught in a raging torrent. His eyes . . . so dead, so lifeless, turned toward her. As she watched, his mouth opened and he uttered her name again.

Miranda.

She was so overwhelmed with the scene that her throat moved and she was finally able to force sound through it.

"Aaaa-iiii-eeee!"

The sound jerked her eyes open and she pushed herself to her elbows, her frantic gaze searching the shadowy world around her. Although the horror of the dream was still with her, she realized it had only been that . . . just a dream.

Miranda.

Her heart gave a crazy little jerk. *Rogue?* Realizing no sound had passed her locked throat, she swallowed hard and forced the word out. "Rogue? Where are you?"

Although she waited for him to call out to her again, there was no sound other than the muted roar of the river.

But she hadn't been mistaken, she was almost certain he'd called out to her. Or had it all been in her mind?

Suddenly, she had a terrible premonition that something was wrong . . . that something terrible had happened to him, that the nightmare hadn't been a dream, but a forewarning . . . a terrible prediction of what had already happened, or was certain to come.

Oh, God! She had to warn him that he was in terrible danger. But how could she?

The passage . . . must go to the blocked passage.

Miranda didn't know where the words came from, only knew that she had an overpowering compulsion to return to the tunnel. The urge was so strong, so compelling, that she struggled upright again, her every thought focused on finding the strength to climb the slope again.

Her legs were soft and rubbery, seeming to be almost boneless as she took a wobbling step forward. *Please, Lord,* she silently prayed. *Give me the strength to get there one more time.* She stumbled, tried to lift feet that were so heavy they felt as though they weighed a ton. As if that were not enough, her knees refused to lock in place.

Tears rolled down Miranda's cheeks as she realized hunger had finally taken its toll. She hadn't the strength to go one more step. But she had to! She must! One more step! Just one more!

Although her body moved forward, her legs seemed stuck in place. Losing her balance, she fell forward, giving a cry of pain as she struck the sand with a heavy thud that knocked the breath from her body and dissipated the strength she'd managed to retain from her limbs. Miranda realized she'd never be able to regain her feet, much less climb the slope. To continue to try was useless.

Rogue's spirit was as battered as his body as he stared down at Rusty's lifeless body. This time there was no mistake. The boy was dead, his body stiff and cold. Rogue didn't know if the cause of death was drowning, or if it had been the blow Rusty had obviously received on the back of his head. Lord knew it looked bad enough to cause his death, but it really didn't matter. Dead was dead.

Suddenly, the match Rogue was holding sputtered and went out, leaving him in total darkness again. His trembling fingers extracted another match from the waterproof container in his pocket and he struck it, hearing the fizzle just before a flame sparked and light flared again. He turned away from Rusty. He had no time to spare, would have to find his lantern as quickly as possible . . . before he wasted his matches looking for it.

Five matches later he found the lantern, resting beside a four-foot rock. A moment later he held the lighted lantern before him, taking the time to study his surroundings. The flood of water had washed him past the coral-covered chamber and he'd have to cross it again before he could enter another tunnel. Instead of turning that way, he went on down the tunnel toward the chimney rock. Rusty's death had increased his anxiety for Miranda. He felt a need to be with her again—or as close as he could get to her—to assure himself that she was all right before he continued his search for a way into her chamber.

"Be there, Miranda," he muttered hoarsely. "Be there waiting for me."

Miranda became aware of something sharp digging into her hipbone. Squeezing her eyes shut, she tried to stem the flow of weak tears, but they continued to creep down her cheeks.

Miranda allowed herself a moment of weakness—who would know anyway?—then she attempted to gather the shards of courage around her again. It would be easier, she told herself, if she didn't hurt so much . . . if she weren't so damned hungry . . . if something sharp, something hard hadn't been poking holes in her hipbone.

Curiosity rolled her over so she could sweep her

hand over the sand beneath her, but there was nothing there . . . nothing except sand, and that couldn't have been the culprit. Realizing the object was in her pocket, she dug her fingers in it and grasped a hard, metal object . . . and sucked in a sharp breath.

God! It was the sardines! She'd been slowly starving to death with a tin of sardines tucked away in her pocket.

Shoving her hand into the pocket of her riding skirt, she curled her fingers around the folding knife resting there, uttering a silent prayer that the blade wouldn't break.

Geraldo's black eyes were expectant, his smile unchanging as he watched the men come closer. He jingled the gold pieces in his pocket, enjoying the sound of them. Suddenly, a movement on the hill caught his attention. Four other riders had come up the far side and joined the two left there. But still that made only eight men. And he had twelve. Nice odds, he decided, his smile widening a trifle. The men on the hill pulled their rifles out of their boots, but that was all right too. At this distance, with the two men riding toward him—the ones on top couldn't be sure they would hit what they were aiming at. They wouldn't shoot. The knowledge sent Geraldo's tongue, red and stiff, sliding out of his mouth to caress his full, warm lips. His blood began to pound with life as his eyes went to the dark-haired youth that rode beside the old man. When the newcomers reined in some yards away Geraldo called a happy greeting to them.

"Good morn-ning," he said, speaking with an ex-aggerated accent.

The man who responded, the older one, was not so polite and his voice was flat, abrupt, without a trace of inflection.

"The name's Colby Turner. I'm foreman of the Lazy R an' those animals you're holdin' are carryin' our brand."

"No, *Señor.* There is a mistake here."

"You're the one that made it."

Geraldo's grin was only a little misshapen by his talking.

"No, *Señor* Colbeee, you make the mistake. You don't bring enough men." His smile disappeared, then just as suddenly came again. "But I tell you what, we have a long way to go and cattle are much trouble to drive . . ."

Geraldo's black eyes glittered, as they fell like a snake on the grizzled foreman. But he also saw the dark-haired youth step his horse in on Colby's left side and Geraldo did not miss the barely perceptible glance by which the older man acknowledged the new arrival while keeping his attention where it should be, on Geraldo himself.

". . . so if you want these cattle . . . I will sell them. Maybe you brought some gold with you?" Geraldo's left hand tossed a coin that winked in the sun and clinked back against its fellows as he caught it.

"No."

"Silver?" This was very good play.

"Just lead."

Geraldo put on a face of disappointment. "Oh-ho . . . Well, *Señor* Colbeee, we cannot make a bargain with lead. I have enough of that." He shut off his smile abruptly. "It looks like we will have to kill you and take the cattle too."

The whiskey bottle dropped from his open hand and his fingers closed on his gunstock, snapping it out of the holster. A shot exploded and all hell broke loose.

Miranda stumbled through the blackness, intent on reaching the rockslide as soon as possible, afraid that Rogue would decide she wasn't coming and that he would leave the passage again.

She was certain he'd come into the tunnel, had heard him calling her again before she'd finished the tin of sardines, but she'd forced herself to ignore the calls, because she knew she'd have to eat to regain her strength.

The passage seemed longer than usual, and with each bend she negotiated, she expected to catch a glimpse of the light from Rogue's lantern. She didn't know she'd reached the rockslide until she bumped into it.

Sudden fear streaked through her, washing over her in cold waves. *No, Lord, no! Don't let this be happening!* Rogue hadn't waited for her to come. He'd come to the tunnel and, not finding her there, had gone away again.

"Rogue!" she screamed, curling her hands into fists and beating against the rocks, unmindful of the pain she was inflicting on herself. "Come back,

Rogue! I'm here! Come back!" She could hear the hysteria in her voice, but could do nothing to curb it. "Dammit, McClaren! You come back here! Don't leave me alone like this!" Tears streamed down her face but she paid them no heed, her only thought was to make him hear her. He had to come back!

"Miranda!" The sharp voice, sounding almost angry, penetrated her hysteria.

He had come back! He'd heard her and returned to the tunnel. Miranda wiped the tears away and fixed her eyes on the small pinpoint of light streaming through the crack at the top of the tunnel.

"R-Rogue?" Her voice wobbled slightly, even as she kept her eyes fixed on the light.

"Yes, Miranda. It's me." He sounded strained, and weary, as though he'd been through a terrible ordeal and, she realized, he also sounded angry.

Was it because she hadn't been here when he came? She took issue with his reasoning. How was she supposed to know when he was coming? She didn't have a timepiece, no way of telling what time it was. Not even the sun or moon to help her. "You shouldn't have left."

"I had to, Miranda. You know that. I thought you understood."

"I-I—" sniff, sniff. "I'm t-trying—" sniff, sniff. She wiped at the tears still streaming down her face. "But—but you shouldn't g-go away so soon."

"I didn't want to," he said gruffly. "You know that. But it had to be done."

"No," she exclaimed. "Not before we had a chance to talk."

"We did talk," he chided. "Have you forgotten already? We talked about my mother."

"Th-that was last time," she said. "We didn't talk this time."

"You're not making sense." His voice was gruff, yet kind. "But we're not going to think about anything except the here and now. You're not alone anymore. I'm here with you. And I aim to stay here until you're ready for me to go."

"Then you may not leave at all." The thought struck her as funny and she added, "You may have to spend the rest of your life here in this tunnel." She realized as soon as she'd uttered the words that she shouldn't have said them. They brought the presence of death much too close.

"Guess what I've been doing?" she said.

"There's no tellin'. I've only known you a short time, professor, but I've already found out how unpredictable you are."

She was silent for a long moment. "I guess that's why we're in this mess."

"Don't blame yourself. It's already done, an' there's no way to change what's past. You were going to tell me what you've been up to."

She allowed the change of subject and when she spoke again, she tried to infuse a lighter tone in her voice. "It's nothing really," she admitted. "And yet, it's everything to me. I found a can of sardines in my pocket. That's why I didn't come when you first called out to me. I was busy devouring the whole can of sardines. God! They were so good!"

He was silent for a long moment.

"Rogue? Say something. You're still over there, aren't you?"

"I didn't call out to you, Miranda." His voice sounded strained.

"But you must have," she insisted. "I heard you. At first, I thought it was a dream. It was all mixed up with you drowning and all. But the urge to come here was overpowering. I knew you'd be waiting for me. I must have heard you call . . ." Her voice trailed away.

"It must've been a dream," he said. "You were just havin' a nightmare."

"You're here, aren't you?"

"Yes. I'm here. And I've already said I'll stay awhile. I'm so damn tired I don't think I could move anyway."

"So am I. I feel like I've been in here for years already. Talk to me, Rogue. Take my mind off this . . . this damnable darkness that's all around me. Tell me more about your family. Do you have brothers and sisters?"

"One brother and two sisters."

"Where do they live?"

"In Montana." The answer was abrupt, barely finished when he asked a question of his own. "You said you felt the urge to come here . . . just felt it."

"Yes. But I heard you calling me."

"I had been thinkin' about you real hard . . . kinda worryin' about how you were . . . makin' it. But you can't hear thoughts, Miranda."

Thoughts? He'd only been thinking about her, hadn't really called out to her? How could that possibly be?

202

She worried the matter over in her mind. Rogue said he hadn't called to her, and yet Miranda knew she'd heard him.

Since he had no reason to lie, then there could be only one answer. She must have heard his thoughts. Impossible! Thoughts can't be heard. Even as she denied that possibility, she remembered the Beauregard twins. Suzanne Beauregard had known the exact moment when her sister, Simona, had fallen from her mount and broken her leg.

"Rogue," she said hesitantly. "Have you ever heard about thought transference? About twins that knew when one or the other was in trouble?"

"No. And we're not twins, Miranda. I'm right proud of that too."

"Why? Would it be so horrible to be my brother?"

"Yes, it would. Because the thoughts I have of you aren't the least bit brotherly."

Miranda felt a flush darken her cheeks and chided herself for the reaction. He hadn't meant it like it sounded. He'd made it plain enough in the past that he didn't even like her. It was only their circumstances, their total isolation from others, coupled with the damnable, smothering blackness surrounding them, that made his words seem so intimate.

"Talk to me professor. Tell me about yourself."

"There's not much to tell," she said. "I'm just about as ordinary as you can get, and my life has been pretty dull."

"Ordinary and dull?" he questioned gruffly. "Is that the way you see yourself?"

"It's the way I am," she replied.

"Ordinary people don't spend their lives in caves," he replied.

"Most of the people we — Poppa and I — associate with do. Either caves or archaeological digs. Months . . . sometimes even years, are spent digging in the ground without anything to show for your efforts." Her voice became wistful. "Poppa wants me to be his assistant on his next dig."

"Is that what you want?"

"It's better than being a gofer," she said, then hastily explained. "A gofer is the one who fetches and carries for everyone else."

"And those are the only choices you have? Your father's assistant or a gofer?"

"They are the only ones Poppa would consider." She heaved a long sigh. "He's kept me with him since . . . since I left boarding school — except for college of course — and he expects things to continue as they always have."

"And you're willing to go along with him?"

"Poppa's all I have," she replied. "My mother died when I was a child." Her voice became wistful. "Sarah, our housekeeper, has never forgiven Poppa for being away when Mother died. She shouldn't blame him though. Poppa can't help the way he is. Exploring is in his blood. It's what makes life worth living for him."

She could hear the wistfulness in her voice and hated herself for it. She didn't want him to think she'd been deprived of love. She hadn't. Poppa did love her, he just didn't know how to express that love.

He'd never held her in his arms, never told her he loved her. Perhaps she had been deprived in that way. Maybe that was the reason she felt such a longing to be held in Rogue's arms, to feel the warmth of his body next to hers.

But that was impossible. McClaren would never want to hold her that way.

Why would she even consider such a notion?

Even as she asked herself the question, she knew why.

Impossible as it sounded, she cared about the rancher.

Cared too much.

But, then, it didn't really matter. Miranda realized she would probably die in here.

God, no! Don't let that happen! Not now! Not when I'm just beginning to know love.

Eighteen

Charlie's expression was grim as he paced the underground chamber. Back and forth he went, unable to stop—even though his arthritic hip was paining him something fierce—for any length of time. He had no idea how long he'd been pacing; it could have been hours, or it could have been days. He didn't know. He only knew that he was worried. Too worried to settle himself down.

He'd sent Chance for help hours ago; six hours, in fact, and still, he hadn't returned.

"Dammit!" He smacked his fist into his left palm. "Where in hell is he? And where is Rogue and them others? What's happenin' down there?"

His steps brought him up beside the well-cavern and he stopped, dropping to one knee beside the black, watery pit. Carefully, mindful not to lose his balance, he leaned over to peer intently into it.

But it was no use. Try as he would, he couldn't penetrate the absolute darkness inside its watery depths.

Cupping his mouth, he called out, "Rogue? Are you okay?" He listened for a moment to the silence, then tried again. "Rusty? Where are you, boy? Answer me!" Again, there was only silence. Not even the echo of his words; the watery pit seemed to have swallowed the sound of his voice.

With his shoulders slumping wearily, Charlie rose to his feet, his thoughts returning to the man he'd sent for help. Charlie's searching gaze probed the mouth of the tunnel that led to the exit. "Where in hell are you, Chance? What's takin' you so damn long?"

Unable to find an answer to his question, Charlie resumed his pacing, trying to work off his worry by exhausting himself in that manner.

Rogue found the sound of Miranda's voice as soothing as a gentle summer rain while she continued to speak of her childhood. As he listened, his muscles slowly unknotted and his fingers uncurled. He shifted his body slightly, leaning his head against the hard rock, picturing her in his mind's eye. He remembered the way she'd looked when he'd first seen her, with her face softly framed by loose tendrils of rich, auburn hair, turned a fiery copper by the setting sun.

His lips twitched slightly as he remembered her anger. Even in the grip of that very strong emotion, the corners of her mouth had turned upwards more than they turned down. His eyes had been drawn to them, to the fullness of her ruby lips, to the dainty straight nose that tilted slightly at the tip. He remembered how a flush had darkened her cheeks, like the flush of sunset against freshly fallen snow. But it had been her flashing green eyes—so much like those of his brother's wife—that had brought him to his senses. That same resemblance was the reason he'd lashed out at her, the reason he'd tried so hard to deny the feelings she'd aroused in him from the beginning. Even now, just remembering the way she'd felt as he held her fast in his arms, her taut, rounded breasts pressing so firmly against his chest, caused a reaction in his lower body. He'd been so aroused . . . so totally, so intimately, aware of the sweet womanly scent of her. But then, she'd allowed her temper free rein and they'd got off to a bad start.

He expelled a long sigh, wishing he could hold her again . . . wishing this damned mountain of rock wasn't between them. But there was no wishing it away, and at the moment there was nothing else he could do, so he settled into it, shifting his body around until he could relax and allow her soft voice to wash over him, cover him like a soft, velvety cloak. Then, with Miranda's features firmly embedded in his mind, he allowed his eyelids to droop . . . then to close. His pulse slowed to a steady beat and he was hovering on the edge of sleep when she stopped speaking.

The cessation of all sound jerked his eyes open and Rogue blinked at the circle of light dancing on the opposite wall. Something about it bothered him.

Shaking the cobwebs from his mind, Rogue studied the lantern. Was it his imagination, or was the light dimmer? He sat up straighter. Was he running out of fuel again?

Hooking his fingers in the handle, he shook the lantern. Instead of a heavy slosh, it made a soft, swishing sound and he realized it was almost empty.

"Dammit!" he muttered. He'd have to return to the well-cavern for more fuel since he'd lost his pack of supplies in the flood.

"Rogue?" Miranda's voice was questioning.

"Yeah?" he asked gruffly.

"What are you doing?"

He forced a husky laugh. "Nothing right now. But I was nearly asleep."

"You must be exhausted. Was I boring you?"

"I like hearin' you talk." He looked at the lantern again. How long did he have before it went out? He didn't want to leave her, but he'd have to. He tried to sound casual when he spoke again. "Looks like my lantern's just about outta fuel, professor. I'll have to go back an' get some more."

"Now?" Her voice was fragile and shaking, edged with fear. "You have to leave now?"

"Not just yet," he replied. "I reckon it won't hurt to stay awhile longer."

"Rogue?"

"Yeah?"

"You mentioned before that you'd sent Rusty for help."

"Yeah." He tried to keep all emotion from his voice.

"Where is he now?"

Rogue swallowed around the lump that suddenly formed in his throat. How could he answer her?

Should he lie? Should he say that Rusty was still checking out some of the other tunnels?

"Something's happened to him, hasn't it?" He heard the intensity in her voice and realized she'd already guessed at the truth.

"Why should you think that?" he asked, trying to stall . . . trying to think of the best way to reply.

"He's dead." This time her voice was flat, completely emotionless.

Since she'd already guessed Rusty's fate, it would be useless to lie. Anyway, he'd never been any good at telling tales. "Yeah, Miranda. He is. There was an accident a little while ago, an'—"

"Was it a quick death?" Her voice was hollow—it sounded to him as if it were an echo coming from a dark tomb.

"Miranda! Don't do this to yourself. I'm gonna get you outta there. Just—"

"I have to know," she said shrilly. "Just tell me! Was it quick? Did Rusty suffer before he died?"

"No," he replied gruffly. "He didn't suffer at all. He died real quick-like from a blow to the head." Rogue didn't mention the water; he felt it would be better in the circumstances if she didn't know the details, because her own experience—the near-drowning—was still too fresh in her mind.

"Thank God for that! At least he didn't have to suffer. Not like Jane and the others." Her voice was ragged with emotion. "Maybe it would be better if you forget about me, McClaren. I don't want to be the cause of any more deaths. There's already been too many on my conscience. Far too many."

"What are you talking about?" he demanded

harshly. "You're not to blame for Rusty's death. It was an accident. If anybody's to blame, then it's me."

"No. I was the careless one. If I hadn't been in such a hurry, I wouldn't have fallen into the well-cavern, an-and, th-then none of this would've happened." She began to sob quietly and the sound was like a stabbing pain in Rogue's heart.

"Stop that, Miranda," he snarled. "What's done is done! Cryin' about it won't help, an' Rusty would be the last one to blame either one of us." Realizing the truth of his words, Rogue felt as though a great weight had been lifted from his shoulders. Despite his youth, Rusty had had an enormous amount of courage and his death had been a freak accident, nothing more.

Miranda snuffled a few times, then seemed to get control of herself. "You—you d-didn't intend to tell me about him, did you? Why not?"

"Because I figgered it wouldn't do no good, an' I had an idea you'd blame yourself. Just like you did."

"I *am* to blame," she said fiercely. "No matter what you say, he wouldn't be dead if he hadn't come down here to help me."

"You're bein' plumb foolish, professor. Rusty died because his time was all used up."

"What does that mean?"

"A man's only got so much time to live. When that time's all gone—when he's used it all up—then he's gonna die. No matter where he is, or what he's doin', he's gonna die. Looks like Rusty was just meant to die young."

"That's nonsense!" she snapped. "You can't really believe such a thing?"

"Why not?" he asked, just barely managing to keep the satisfaction out of his voice. He had succeeded in taking her mind off Rusty's death.

"I credited you with more sense, McClaren. If our lives were already laid out before we were born, then there would be no purpose in life."

"How do you figger that?"

"Just think about it for a minute," she said urgently. "If everyone believed as you do—that fate had everything already planned out for us—the world would likely come to a standstill. Farmers wouldn't try to save their crops from the weather, believing they would either survive, or perish, as fate had ordained. Even cattlemen, like you, would have no reason to tend their stock, feeling they would either die . . . or survive as fate decreed. Hope is what makes the world go around, McClaren. Sometimes it's all that keeps us going. Lord knows, if I hadn't had hope to cling to during that time in the French Alps, then I'd have taken my own life before they found me." Her words sent a chill over him. "Hope," she said softly. "That's all I had. Just a little word, but without it, without hope, I'd have gone stark, raving mad."

"You're too strong for that," he said gruffly, hoping that he was right. What was she babbling on about anyway? What in hell had happened to her in the French Alps? Whatever it was, it was eating away at her, like a worm slowly chewing its way through a green apple. "What happened in the French Alps, Miranda?"

212

She drew a long, shuddering breath. "I don't want to talk about it," she said grimly. "Lord knows, I try hard enough to forget it ever happened. But that's impossible. No matter how hard I try to push it back down, it's always there, lurking just below the surface, like some monster in a nightmare, just waiting to catch you when you're most vulnerable, before it gobbles you up."

"Then don't try to keep it down," he said gruffly. "Tell me about it. Face up to your fears while you've got the strength to overcome them." Even as he said the words, he was wondering if he should be encouraging her to think about something she'd obviously tried hard to forget. He had no idea what could've happened to her, only knew that, whatever it was, it had left her with a deep and abiding fear. "Tell me about it, Miranda," he said again. "Tell me, and remember that—even though we can't touch each other—I'm just a few feet away from you."

She uttered a heavy sigh. "Only a few feet, and yet, so far away. But perhaps you're right. Maybe it is time I talked about what happened in that cave. Maybe it's even way past time."

Then she began her story.

Nineteen

Even now, after all these years, Miranda could still feel the intense excitement she'd experienced when they'd first entered the cavern. Professor Dometrius had led the way, followed by Miranda, then her best friend, Jane Alexander, with Ruben, the professor's young assistant, bringing up the rear. Miranda remembered Jane's reluctance — she'd only gone at Miranda's urging, and that was the reason Miranda suffered from such feelings of guilt.

The two girls were only thirteen. They attended the same private school in France, and from the beginning, had been drawn to each other. Perhaps because, like herself, Jane was motherless. It had seemed like a stroke of good fortune when Miranda heard about the professor's proposed exploration. Since he was a close friend of her father's, Miranda prevailed upon him to allow her to accompany him into the cave. Being cognizant of the fact that she'd often accompanied her father, the professor had agreed. The cavern was known to be small, not more than two hundred feet deep and the professor believed there would be no danger involved. But fate had taken a hand.

While crossing a narrow ledge, the rock had given way beneath them, sending them plunging into a deep chasm. None of them were lucky enough to escape injury. When Miranda regained her senses, she found herself in total darkness, with both her legs broken. At first they thought the professor's injuries were the most serious, because it was soon obvious that he'd broken his back. Miranda could still hear his moans as he lay dying, but above that, she remembered the sound of Jane's voice as she spewed forth words of bitter hatred, cursing Miranda over and over again for talking her into joining the expedition.

Although the professor's and Ruben's deaths had been slow and agonizing — Ruben had suffered internal injuries — their demise was still not as horrible to Miranda as Jane's. No. Janie's death was even worse, because she died by her own hand, using a jagged rock to cut her wrists, then continuing to spew out her hatred for her former friend until death finally claimed her.

One by one they'd passed from this life . . . first Jane, then Ruben, then the professor, until finally, Miranda was left alone in the darkness, hurting not only in body, but in mind as well. It was only as the professor's last breath left his body that Miranda found the courage to drag herself away from the others, to leave the place where death hovered around her.

Later . . . she didn't know how long it had been, she became aware of a dripping sound and realized that somewhere, not very far away, she'd find the water that she badly needed.

Gathering up the food that was left — and with nothing to guide her but the sound of dripping water — Miranda slid along the bottom of the chasm, painfully dragging her broken legs behind her until finally she found the source; water seeping through limestone, dripping one drop at a time, onto a stalagmite growing from the floor. Miranda stayed there, catching the water in her mouth time and time again, as it came, one drop at a time. Never enough to quench her thirst, but enough to keep her alive.

She'd lost all count of time — it could have been weeks, it could have been months — when she woke to the sound of voices in the distance. At first she thought she was hallucinating. When she realized the voices were real, she tried to call for help . . . and found she couldn't. Her throat was so dry, so parched, and she was so weak that she couldn't utter a sound. But Miranda refused to give up. She found a stone and managed to make enough noise to catch their attention. She was lucky, the others weren't.

She stopped talking, unable to go on.

"My God, Miranda," Rogue said. "It's a wonder you didn't go crazy. How long were you in there?"

"Just over six weeks. The food ran out — I was near starvation when they found me — but that was the least of my worries." She shuddered in memory. "I couldn't see when they brought me out, but the blindness was only temporary. I'd been in there so long that the bright sun burned my eyes. They said I was lucky to be alive." She didn't tell him about the months in the hospital. Her legs had to be broken all over again so they could be set straight. For a time she'd thought she would be lame. But her father had hired the best physicians Europe had to offer, and eventually her legs had healed.

"It's a wonder you still have the nerve to go in caves after an experience like that."

"At first, I didn't want to, but Poppa made me. He said I had to face up to my fears, that it was the only way I'd ever put it behind me. And I thought it had worked."

"Until this mess brought it all back."

"Yes." She uttered a long, shaky sigh. "God, Rogue! I wish you didn't have to leave."

"I wish I didn't either, baby," he said, his voice rasping hoarsely. "God, how I wish I didn't. But there's no other way. You know that, don't you?"

"Yes, I know." Had he really called her "baby"? "And I know I'm being foolish. Don't worry about me. I'll be all right. I know you'll get me out sooner or later." She forced a laugh, biting her bottom lip to stop its quivering. "I—I'm prepared to wait, Rogue. But please . . . don't make me wait too long."

"I wish to hell I was over there with you."

Her mouth twisted wryly. "You couldn't do much from here."

"I could hold you," he said, his voice soft as velvet. "You could put your head against my chest, professor. I think that'd be kinda nice. I'd like to have my arms around you right now."

His words sent a tingle through her body and she

217

felt heat rising in her cheeks. "Would you, Mc-Claren? Would you really like that?"

"Yeah," he admitted. "Much as it surprises me, I would like it. What man wouldn't feel proud with you in his arms?"

Her mouth lifted at the corners in the tiniest smile. "You didn't feel that way when we first met," she said. "In fact, you took an instant dislike to me. Was that yesterday? Or the day before? Just how long has it been since we met?"

"I don't know how long it's been," he replied. "Only that it's more'n three days. It's hard to keep up with time since we came down here. As far as dislikin' you, professor, well, that just ain't so. Not any more. Maybe once, that was the way of it, but not anymore."

"Why didn't you like me?"

"I guess it was like somebody once said. Something happened in the past that colored my way of thinkin'. I guess I *was* worried that you'd prove to be like *her.*" His voice changed, became hard. "Hell! You're nothin' like Dallas. I can see that now."

"Dallas!" Her heart gave a crazy jerk. Who was Dallas? Was it possible he had a wife? She hadn't seen any sign of another woman, except for the housekeeper, but that didn't mean there wasn't one. Miranda was afraid to ask, but wanted desperately to know. "Who is Dallas?"

"My brother's wife," he said gruffly. "And don't ask me about them. The past is better left alone."

Perhaps now, she allowed silently. *But one day, maybe, you'll be willing to talk about it.* "I'm glad you didn't really dislike me," she said aloud.

"Somehow, that makes me feel better."

"Then think about this too." His voice had a ragged edge. "Maybe I was worried about likin' you a little *too* much."

"What do you mean?"

"Think about it for awhile. You're smart enough to work it out on your own. When you come up with the answer, then hold onto it until I get over there to you. Maybe we can do something about it."

Although he spoke in riddles, she gave him the answer she sensed he needed. "All right. I'll think about it."

"Good," he said. "Now, I'd better leave. This damn light's about gone."

"Go ahead," she urged. "I'll be fine."

"I'll be back soon," he said gently.

Then the tiny pinpoint of light that was all she had of him began to wobble, and she could hear the sound of his footsteps moving away from her.

Suddenly, remembering she hadn't told him about the nightmare, she felt panic wash over her. "Rogue!"

His answer was instant. "What?"

"I forgot to tell you. I had a dream. Actually, it was more like a nightmare." Speaking about it brought the nightmare to the surface again, reminded her of how he'd looked, his eyes open . . . so dead, so empty. The memory was so fresh that she shuddered in remembered terror. She took long, deep breaths through her nose, releasing them through her mouth, as her hands clenched into tight fists against her breast. "You . . . you were d-drowning, Rogue," she finally managed. "You

219

. . . you were d-dead, floating face up in the river."

"Stop it!" he ordered gruffly. "Forget about it. It's not going to happen!"

"I—I know," she said, her voice barely above a whisper. "I know it was j-just a d-dream. But, Rogue. You will be careful? Won't you?"

"I'll be careful, Miranda. You can count on it."

She swallowed hard around the lump in her throat. She must keep the fear out of her voice. "I will. I'll count on it. You go on now. Do what you have to do. But . . . when you come back in the tunnel, call me. Then don't go away. Just wait until I get here."

"I will," he said. "Don't worry, Miranda. I'll wait. No matter how long it takes. I'll call, then wait for you to come."

"All right. Goodbye, Rogue."

Miranda was proud of the steady sound of her voice, even as she wondered how it could sound so with the tears streaming down her face. She stood where she was long after the sound of his footsteps had disappeared. Then, turning around to face away from Rogue, she limped through the tunnel, toward the cavern with phospor walls.

Dammit! Dammit, dammit! Rogue cursed inwardly as he made his way across the chamber with red sand. He had promised her he would get her out, but how in hell could he keep that promise?

With his heart pounding furiously in his chest, he entered the tunnel leading to the well-cavern and hurried forward. Soon, he was standing on the ledge, peering up into the darkness above.

"Charlie!" he yelled.

Instantly, he saw a lantern in the distance. It was followed by Charlie's angry voice. "Where in hell have you been? Don'tcha know I been wearin' this cavern out up here, pacin' back and forth worryin' over the lot of you?"

"Sorry about that," Rogue called. "I couldn't get back no sooner. How many men you got up there?"

"Nobody but me," Charlie called. "Chance didn't come back yet."

"Dammit!"

"You want me to go see what's holdin' him up?"

"No!" Rogue said sharply. "Stay there! If somethin' happens to you, we're stuck down here. Just stay where you are! Chance won't let us down. He'll be back. Just send me down some more supplies! I lost mine in a flood." He waited a short moment, then added, "We lost Rusty too."

"What? Say that again!"

"Rusty's dead!"

There was a long silence from above. Then Charlie spoke again. "That's a damn shame." Although the words seemed to make light of Rusty's death, Rogue knew the depth of Charlie's feeling for the younger man. The old man would grieve in his own way for Rusty, but while there was a job to be done, he would do it. "When Chance gets back with the others, I'll send word to his ma and pa," Charlie continued. "You mind your step down there, Rogue. You're all that little girl's got now. She's dependin' on you."

"I know," Rogue muttered.

Realizing there was no way Charlie could hear him, Rogue raised his voice. "Hurry up with those supplies, Charlie. Send down plenty of fuel."

A few minutes later he fished the new supplies out of the water and hefted the pack on his back. After calling a goodbye up to Charlie, Rogue set out toward the chimney rock. There were still several narrow crevices leading away from it and he would try every damned one of them until he found a way to reach Miranda. There was no way in hell he would leave her alone with the nightmarish memories of another time plaguing her. He only hoped he could reach her before she lost her mind.

The diffused light from the cavern with phosphor walls was a welcome sight for Miranda. Speaking of the past had brought everything back to her as though it had happened yesterday. Even now, she could hear Jane cursing her, spewing terrible words into the darkness. Miranda shuddered in remembrance.

Stop it, Miranda! she heard her father scolding. *You couldn't know what was going to happen. She might have lived if she'd had your courage. Her death was her own fault.*

Realizing it was useless to blame herself, she turned her thoughts to her injuries. The cut on her leg seemed more painful than usual, and somehow she'd started it bleeding again. She knew how easily a cut could become infected and she was hurrying across the cavern toward the river—intent on washing it—when a scurrying noise caught her attention. She stopped, narrowing her gaze on the shadowy darkness only a few feet away.

Was there something alive beneath the fallen rock? Curious, she moved closer and a white salamander darted out, shooting between her feet and scurrying as fast as it could toward the safety of a crack in the wall. Then, as though curious about her, the creature turned around and poked its head back out.

"I wasn't going to hurt you," she chided. "Don't you know that I'm glad to see something alive and breathing down here? I don't enjoy being alone. Even a salamander would be company for me."

Apparently the creature had no use for her company, because it pulled its head back into the crack; its tiny claws scraped against rock as it disappeared into the darkness.

Feeling slightly disappointed, Miranda circled a gnarled calcite column and limped toward the canyon. She could hear the river in the distance and took comfort from the sound. When she reached the river, she would gather wood for a fire then search for mussels in the shallows. Perhaps she would be lucky enough to find several. Five or six would be enough to fill her stomach, shrunken as it was.

Her nostrils dilated—she imagined she could almost smell the mussels, steaming in their heated shells.

Her eagerness quickened her steps as she limped toward the river canyon.

Cra-a-a-ck!

The lower half of her body came to an abrupt

halt as her right boot struck something hard while the upper half continued its forward movement.

Flailing out with both arms, Miranda tried to right herself, but her efforts were in vain.

"Oooofff," Miranda's breath whooshed out of her lungs when she struck the debris-strewn floor and skidded toward the edge of the canyon.

Scrabbling for purchase, she stopped a mere foot from the edge and lay there, nerves quivering, eyes filled with grit, pulling quick breaths into her lungs while her heart beat wildly in her chest, thudding like a herd of stampeding horses.

When Miranda was finally able to move, she pushed herself to all fours, gritting her teeth against the pain burning through the calf of her injured leg. Her gaze probed the shadows around the floor and pinpointed the rocks that were large enough to trip over, and had to be avoided. She was on the point of rising when the shadowy darkness near her right hand suddenly moved.

Had the salamander returned?

Curious, she lowered her hand until she felt the rocks beneath her fingers.

The shadows flickered again, then she felt something crawl onto her index finger.

A chill swept over her. Was it a spider? Although she felt the urge to shake the creature off, her curiosity overcame her fear. Miranda moved her hand closer to her face until she could see what she held.

A cricket! It was only a cricket. And a crippled one at that. Somehow it had lost one of its jumping hind legs.

"Oh, you poor little thing," she said, transferring

4 FREE BOOKS

TO GET YOUR 4 FREE BOOKS WORTH $18.00 — MAIL IN THE FREE BOOK CERTIFICATE T O D A Y

Fill in the Free Book Certificate below, and we'll send your FREE BOOKS to you as soon as we receive it.

If the certificate is missing below, write to: Zebra Home Subscription Service, Inc., P.O. Box 5214, 120 Brighton Road, Clifton, New Jersey 07015-5214.

FREE BOOK CERTIFICATE

4 FREE BOOKS

ZEBRA HOME SUBSCRIPTION SERVICE, INC.

YES! Please start my subscription to Zebra Historical Romances and send me my first 4 books absolutely FREE. I understand that each month I may preview four new Zebra Historical Romances free for 10 days. If I'm not satisfied with them, I may return the four books within 10 days and owe nothing. Otherwise, I will pay the low preferred subscriber's price of just $3.75 each; a total of $15.00, *a savings off the publisher's price of $3.00.* I may return any shipment and I may cancel this subscription at any time. There is no obligation to buy any ship-ment and there are no shipping, handling or other hidden charges. Regardless of what I decide, the four free books are mine to keep.

NAME

ADDRESS _____ APT

CITY _____ STATE _____ ZIP

( )
TELEPHONE

SIGNATURE _____ (if under 18, parent or guardian must sign)

Terms, offer and prices subject to change without notice. Subscription subject to acceptance by Zebra Books. Zebra Books reserves the right to reject any order or cancel any subscription.

the creature to her left palm. "You're hurt." She stroked it with her right index finger. "Was that nasty salamander chasing you? Don't worry," she murmured. "You're going to be all right now. I'll take good care of you." She closed her fingers around the insect, making a cage for it. "Do you like mussels? You can help me find some big, juicy ones and we'll have a feast."

Suddenly, to her great surprise, the cricket began to sing. It gave off a steady, almost musical chirruping, and Miranda found the sound pleasing to her ears. "I'm glad you can sing," she said, holding the cricket closer to her face while stroking its velvety coat of hairlike setae. "My, my. You are a big one, aren't you? Why, you must be at least three inches long. I suppose you'll make a pig of yourself over my mussels, but I won't mind. Not in the slightest."

Miranda kept up a running, one-sided conversation with the cricket as she limped back to the canyon, then made her way down to the river. The cricket's song had lifted her spirits, had lightened the atmosphere around her, had made it less fearful. Even though her only companion was a cricket, she was no longer alone.

Frustration filled Rogue as he came to the end of another passage. "Dammit! Not again!" he swore.

Knotting his hand into a fist, he struck the obstruction savagely, welcoming the pain he inflicted on himself. "Damn you!" he swore at the rock, hitting it over and over again. "Damn you! Damn you."

Suddenly, realizing that he was damaging his hand—a hand that he would need to free Miranda—he slumped against the rock wall and took several deep, calming breaths. There was nothing else he could do here. The passage had proved as disappointing as the others he'd already tried.

Expelling a heavy sigh, he rose to his feet. He would return to the blocked passage. Maybe there was something he'd missed before, maybe he hadn't checked it close enough.

Dammit! There must be a way through it. There must be a way to get past the slide without bringing the whole roof down on them.

Since he'd been through the passages so many times, the journey was made in record time.

"Miranda!" Rogue shouted as he neared the rockslide.

"I'm already here, Rogue," her calm voice came from beyond the barrier. "I've been waiting for you."

"You didn't go back to the river after I left?"

"Yes. I went," she replied. "I was searching for mussels when I felt the urge to come here. You're dreadfully tired aren't you?"

"Yeah. I'm beat." Setting his lantern down on the floor, he surveyed the pile of fallen rock, searching for something he might have missed. But, except for the small hole at the top, there was nothing.

The problem seemed insurmountable.

"What are you doing?" she asked.

"I'm trying to find something . . . anything, that I might have missed before. Some way to get

226

through this damn pile of rocks without bringing the ceiling down on us."

She was silent for a long moment, then suddenly, he heard a loud *Thunk, thunk, crack!*

"Miranda!" he said sharply. "What are you doing?"

"I'm moving rocks!" she snapped. "I don't care anymore. If the ceiling is going to collapse then it will, but I'm tired of doing nothing."

"Wait!" he commanded. "Stop that! Let's think about this for a minute."

"I told you I'm tired of waiting." Her voice was edged with hysteria.

"Calm down!" he growled. "I intend to dig through here, but I'd rather have you out of the way while I do it."

"I'm not afraid," she said, her voice calmer. "I'd rather take my chances here and now."

"Just hold on for a minute," he said, his gaze probing the pile of rocks, searching for the weakest places. "Miranda, there might be a chance. The boulder is on the right side of the chamber. There's a chance it might hold the ceiling up if we dig directly to the left of it."

"Do you really think so?"

"It's worth a try."

"I'll dig from this side," she said eagerly. "But first, let me take Peter back to the phosphor chamber. I don't want him hurt if there's another rockslide."

"Peter?"

"My cricket. I guess I didn't tell you about him. He was in the phosphor chamber. He has a broken hopper, but he has a beautiful voice."

A cricket? God! Her words tore the heart from him. "Go ahead," he said gruffly. "Put the cricket where it'll be safe. And maybe you better stay with him."

"No. I'm coming back to help."

"I'll work on these rocks while you're gone."

"Rogue? You will be careful? You're all I have left . . . my only hope of getting out of here."

"You don't have to worry, professor. I know what I'm doin'." He began to pull at the rocks again, weighing the position of each one before removing it and tossing it aside. His urgency drove at him. He wanted to get as many rocks as possible out of the way before she returned. That way, if the roof did collapse, she wouldn't be caught under the rubble.

His urgency made him less cautious than he should have been.

Rogue pulled out a stabilizing rock, only realizing his error when it was already too late . . . when he felt a shower of rocks, just before he heard a rumbling sound that became a thunder of falling rock.

Immediately he jumped backwards, and he felt a sharp blow to the head just before darkness closed in around him.

Twenty

Rogue kicked out at the debris covering his legs, relieved to find nothing solid had pinned them down. He coughed, spitting dust from his lungs, then wiped one hand across his eyes to clear them.

God! His head hurt something fierce.

"Rogue! What happened?" The sound was muffled, the words barely discernible, as though the distance between Miranda and himself had widened even more. "Rogue, are you there?"

Struggling to clear his head of the gray mist that blurred his mind, he hastened to reassure her. "Yeah," he muttered. "I'm okay."

"Rogue!" Miranda's voice rose, became high-pitched, bordering on hysteria. "Can you hear me?"

"Yeah, I hear you," he called, scrabbling in the darkness for the lantern. His fingers brushed against cold metal and, realizing it was the handle, he closed his hand around it. Moments later he held the lighted lantern aloft and took stock of the situation.

"Rogue!"

"Just a minute, Miranda," he called irritably, frowning at the fresh slide. It didn't really look too bad. Not much worse than it had before.

"Dammit, Rogue! Answer me! Please . . . answer me . . . please . . ." The last word was a wailing plea and her anguish penetrated his concentration.

"I'm here, Miranda," he called, even as he realized she couldn't hear him! The knowledge sent his narrowed gaze over the rubble, searching for the hole that had been there, but he searched in vain, the hole was gone, covered by the fresh slide.

"Rogue!" The anguish contained in the one word was like a steel rod in his chest that stabbed through flesh and muscle and worked its way slowly through his midsection. "Rogue!"

Clutching frantically at the rocks where he thought the hole had been, he flung them aside without a thought to where they landed, calling to her over and over again, trying to calm her hysteria. "Miranda! I'm okay, Miranda." Dammit! Why couldn't she hear him? It didn't make sense when he could hear her, hear the fear in her voice.

Sweat beaded his forehead as he worked to expose the small hole that had allowed them to communicate with each other . . . and all the time he could hear her screaming out her terror.

"I'm here, Miranda! I'm here!" He continued to call, hoping to send his voice beyond the barrier.

Suddenly, almost miraculously, he moved a rock

and uncovered the small, black hole and heard the sound of low sobbing. "Miranda! Are you all right?"

"Rogue? Is that you? Oh, God, thank you. He's alive. Rogue? Are you all right?"

"Yeah, I'm all right. How about you?"

"Yes. Now that I know you—you aren't—" She broke off, apparently unable to follow that line of thought. Heaving a sigh, she asked, "What happened, Rogue?"

"I don't know. I must've pulled a rock loose that was holdin' up the ceiling."

"But you're not hurt?"

"No, I'm not hurt. Miranda! Don't worry about me." He could hear the ragged edge to his voice. "I shouldn't've messed around with it. Dammit all!" He slammed his left fist into his right palm. "I knew the whole thing was unstable. I should've left it alone."

"Don't blame yourself." Her voice was forlorn. "We both knew the risks involved."

His eyes stung and the back of his throat burned. He swallowed thickly before he spoke again. "Miranda. I'm going back to the well-cavern. I need to talk to Charlie. You've been over there too long. There's gotta be somethin' we can do . . . somebody that knows somethin' about these damn caves, an' it's past time we sent for 'em." When she remained silent, he spoke again. "You know that, don't you?"

"Yes. I know. But I don't think there is anyone. Not around these parts." She gave a jerky laugh.

"Look at me. I thought I knew it all. Everything there was to know about caves, but here I am, trapped again." Her voice became bitter. "I was so smart . . . so certain I could handle anything that came along." Her voice became forlorn. "You were right about me, McClaren. I thought my education elevated me above others. I was so damn smart, and so self-satisfied . . . and now I'm sorry." The last words were said softly. "Please forgive me."

"There's nothing to forgive," he said roughly. "You made a mistake. That's all." He knew he had to leave, but God! He didn't want to leave her alone. It had been hard enough when he hadn't known what she'd been through in France. He gave a sigh. "Will you be okay until I get back?"

Her laugh was husky, almost jerky, certainly not a very happy sound, although he was almost certain she'd intended it to be encouraging. "Of course I'll be okay. I'll have to be, won't I?"

He didn't answer her. After all, what could he say? How much more could her mind take before it snapped? Had the mishap in the French Alps made her stronger, or had it only made her more susceptible to ghosts from the past? God! If only she wasn't alone! If only that damn cricket that she'd named Peter was a dog, or a cat, or something more substantial than an insect. Hell! he swore silently. While he was wishing, he might just as well wish that he, himself, was Peter!

A sudden thought struck him. "Miranda," he

said, his heart giving a crazy jerk. "Is Peter . . . is your cricket okay?"

"Yes." Her relief was evident. "I left him in the phosphor chamber. He didn't want to stay there . . . he hung onto my shirt pocket."

"Smart cricket," he said gruffly. "If I was in your pocket I'd prob'ly feel the same way."

She gave an unsteady laugh. "Do you know something, Rogue McClaren? You try to act tough . . . try to act mean and uncaring, but I'm beginning to see through you. Underneath that tough exterior, you're a nice man."

He drew in a slow breath. "When I'm not chewin' you out?"

"You're kind of nice even then." Her voice sounded husky, almost strained. "Sometimes . . . Most of the time . . . I don't know what to make of you. But I guess there's nothing really strange in that. I'm—I don't know very much about men."

"I figgered as much." He'd known it instinctively and known as well that he was glad she was innocent in the ways of men. As soon as he had time—as soon as they were out of this damned cave—he'd make it his business to teach her. His voice was extremely gentle when he spoke again. "You go on back to Peter." Perhaps by using the cricket's name it would make the insect seem more human to her. "Stay with Peter, baby. And stay out of this tunnel. Go back to the river you told me about. You'll have water there." He licked his dry lips and when he spoke again, he heard the ragged edge to his voice. "Be careful, baby. I don't want nothin' happenin' to you. Do you hear me? You be damn careful over there."

"I will, Rogue." Her voice had a catch to it. "But I don't want to go just yet."

"Miranda, I have to—"

"I know," she interrupted quickly. "I know you have to go, but I'll wait here, like always, until you're gone."

"If that's the way you want it," he said gruffly. "But you remember what I said. You be careful over there. An' whatever you do, don't let this setback get you down. We're gonna lick this cave yet."

"I know." Her voice was shaky. "But, Rogue? If something happens? I mean . . . if you can't break through to me in time . . . I just . . . I mean . . . I'm not afraid of death." The last words were uttered swiftly. "I'm really not. What bothers me most about dying, is doing it alone . . . here in this damnable dark."

"Miranda, stop it!" he rasped harshly. "Don't talk about dyin'! That's *not* gonna happen to you."

"I know," she said in a small voice. "But I just wanted you to know how I feel. I just wanted to know that . . . if something like that does happen, you won't leave me down here . . . you'll find a way to bring my body back to the surface?"

Rogue gritted his teeth and blinked his stinging eyes to clear away the moisture. "Yeah," he muttered. "I'll find a way. You got my promise on it."

"Thank you, McClaren," she whispered. "Now go on. Go back to Charlie."

Rogue left her alone, his heart knotted and aching for her, feeling as though he were abandoning her. She had no one to keep her company except for that damned cricket she'd found. God help her if anything should happen to the insect.

A stinging white shaft of pain streaked through Miranda's leg as she made her limping way back to the phosphor cavern. Was it only her imagination, or had the pain increased? Worry creased her brow as she remembered the way the wound had looked the last time she'd washed it. Was it becoming infected? She knew it was a distinct possibility. Perhaps she'd been foolish not to tell Rogue about it. But then, what could he have done? There was no way he could get medicine through the blocked passage to her.

Lord! she silently groaned. Didn't she have enough to be concerned about already, without having to worry about blood poisoning?

Just the thought of such an event sent fear shuddering over Miranda. As soon as she entered the chamber with the phosphor walls, she bent to examine the wound. Was it her imagination, or was her calf badly swollen? She couldn't be sure. The light was too dim, too shadowy.

Miranda knew she'd have to strike a match to examine it closer. Her fingers were already in her pocket when she remembered how few remained.

She dared not waste them. There was wood on the riverbank. If she could find enough, then she could light a fire. Perhaps she could even have some coals that would last for awhile.

With the decision made, she turned her attention to the cricket she'd left behind. "Peter," she called softly. "Where are you, Peter?"

Hearing a scuffling noise around the fallen rock, she hurried forward, convinced it was Peter making the sound. At first glance, she could see nothing, because it was darker around the rocks. When she heard the movement, she bent down, just in time to see a small wing disappear into the mouth of a salamander.

"God, no!" she cried, springing forward. "You nasty thing, you! You've eaten Peter!" Grabbing up a small stone she threw it at the salamander and it went scuttling for the crack in the wall.

Tears gushed from Miranda's eyes. She knew she was being silly, crying over a cricket, but Peter was all she had. In the short time since she'd found him, he had become her companion, her pet.

Dashing over to the crack in the wall, she threw several small stones into the crevice, hoping to kill the creature that had eaten the cricket. But she couldn't get enough force behind the throw and knew she was falling short of her mark.

She reached for another stone and felt something move onto her hand. Her gaze darted swiftly, and fixed on the small cricket with a missing hopper that had crawled onto her palm.

Relief washed over her. "Peter!" she exclaimed, lifting the insect until it was level with her nose. "I thought that nasty salamander had eaten you." As though Peter sensed her anxiety and meant to soothe it, he began to chirrup.

Stroking the cricket's velvety cloak, she transferred the insect to her breast pocket, then hurried as fast as her injured leg would carry her toward the river canyon. Each step she took sent a stabbing pain through her calf.

The cattle had stampeded when the shooting started. Perhaps the distraction helped Colby and his men, or it may only have been that Geraldo's band had little stomach for a battle. Whatever the reason, the outlaw band—all except Geraldo and two of his men, now dead—had fled the scene.

It had taken Colby and his men the rest of the day to round up the stolen cattle. When it was done, Colby headed back to the ranch house while the others drove the cattle to a safer place.

The sun had long since set when Colby rode into the ranch yard. Although he'd hoped to find Rogue and the others there, he was disappointed. Instead, he found Chance Carter waiting for him.

"Howdy, Chance," he said, dismounting stiffly from his horse. "What brings you out here?"

"About time you got back!" Chance exclaimed. "I've been waiting here since morning. If I'd known you were gonna be gone so long, I'd've gone somewheres else for help."

Chance's words made no sense to Colby, but he didn't even try to figure them out. His mind was on Rogue. "You seen Rogue, Chance?"

"Not for several days," the other man replied. "That's why I'm here. We need some more help."

"I'd like to help," Colby said gruffly. "But we're kinda hard up ourselves right now. Them damn rustlers is plaguin' us again. Just had a shootin' battle with 'em. Left three dead men out on the north pasture. An' as if that wasn't enough, we got two men lost in the cave down on Squaw mountain. Rogue took Charlie an' Rusty an' went to get 'em out." His heavy brows pulled together. "Can't for the life of me figger out why in hell it's takin' so long to find 'em."

"I know all about that," Chance said. "I've been in the cave helpin' 'em. The professor's daughter is gone now. She fell into some kind of deep hole."

"Gawd!" Colby said. "That little gal? Is she dead?"

"No. At least she wasn't the last I heard," Chance replied. "I guess she's still all right." He told the other man what had been occurring since they'd gone into the cavern, then finished by saying, "Charlie sent me after more help."

"Why in hell didn't you say who was needin' the help?" Colby growled, spitting a long stream of tobacco toward the ground. "They're Rogue's hands. If he's wantin' 'em down there, then that's where they'll go." He frowned heavily and added, "Just as soon as they get here."

"How long will that be?"

"Shouldn't be much longer. Maybe another hour or so. They're takin' the stock over to that box canyon so's it'll only take a couple of men to guard 'em."

"Maybe I should go out there."

"They'll be here afore you could get there," Colby replied. "You might just as well settle down and rest yourself while you wait."

Chance didn't have to be told twice. He was bone-weary. And, anyway, he told himself, he might miss the others if he rode out to meet them. Colby was right. He uttered a weary sigh and leaned back against a supporting post to wait.

Rogue felt frustrated as he left the well-cavern. Chance hadn't returned yet, but when he did, someone would ride to Austin to seek professional help. Rogue just prayed they would find it.

It took all his strength to pass the crevice leading to the blocked tunnel and continue on, but he did so. While at the well-cavern, he'd remembered the chamber where he'd almost drowned — the one that had claimed Rusty's life — and he was intent on crossing it.

God, let it lead to her, he silently prayed.

He passed over the cave coral without incident and hurried past the empty shell that had once been Rusty and continued on. He was already beyond the point where the rock wall had given way before he realized it. Then, turning to look back, he located the spot with difficulty — there was no

239

sign of the wall that had been there only a short time before, but a large slab of rock still remained, lying propped at an angle against the far wall—then he hurried across the floor that tilted upward on the far side.

A quick search and, as he'd hoped, he found a large tunnel—partially obscured by a huge outcrop—about four feet across and seven feet high. But instead of angling down as he'd hoped, it curved upward. Even so, he took it, unhesitatingly—after all, what else was there to do—and after a few hundred feet, the tunnel began to curve down.

Although he had the urge to throw caution to the wind and run down the passage—so sure was he that he would soon find Miranda—with the knowledge that he'd thought the same thing so many times before with disastrous results, he slowed his pace and became wary.

That was the only thing that saved him when he entered the wind tunnel.

When he heard the low moaning, Rogue's heart gave a leap of hope. Could Miranda's river be close by? His steps quickened and he rounded a curve in the tunnel, then found himself buffeted by winds so strong that he was swept off his feet.

His fingers tightened around the handle of his lantern just before the light flickered, then went out. The wind wrapped around him like a living thing, moaning and howling, trying to rip the clothes from his body as it slammed him against the far wall with enough force to knock him senseless.

Although Rogue fought hard to stay conscious, it was a losing battle. His head was reeling and he could almost swear there were bright points of light, dancing around his eyes.

Blinking rapidly to clear them away, he fought against a rising nausea. He couldn't give in to the sickness, couldn't lose touch with reality.

Even with the wind buffeting him, he felt smothered. The points of bright light disappeared, replaced by a red haze that slowly formed around him. Rogue knew it was an illusion, but it was smothering, all-consuming.

Desperately, he squeezed his hands into fists, stabbing his fingernails into his palms, relishing the resulting pain. He had to stay awake. He had to! If he lost his senses, this damned tunnel would probably kill him.

Twenty-one

Miranda's thoughts returned to Rogue as she made her way down the slope to the river. She remembered the way he'd called her "baby." His voice had been so tender, so caring as he'd tried to soothe her fears.

Oh, Rogue, she silently cried. *Will I ever see you again? And if I do, will you still call me "baby"?*

No one had called her that since her mother had died. She'd always been "Miranda" to her father and he'd always spoken to her as though she were an adult. It was only now—since Rogue had called her "baby"—that she realized how much she'd missed being spoken to with such tenderness and concern.

Not that her father hadn't been kind to her, but he'd expected so much from her. Too much, she realized now. Because of it, she'd had to grow up too fast.

Silently mourning her lost childhood, she half-limped, and half-slid, down the slope to the river bank, trying to ignore the pain of her swollen leg. It wasn't that hard to do, because suddenly the ache in her heart seemed to be much greater.

Rogue, having won the battle against the blackness that had threatened to overcome him, crept cautiously along the wall toward the wind tunnel. What could be causing such terrible winds? he wondered. The answer was beyond him, for he'd never encountered anything like it—outside of a tornado—before.

Hugging the wall behind him, using it for support, he began the long journey across the wind chamber in total darkness. Although he knew such a trip could be dangerous, he also knew he must take the risk. It would be useless to light the lantern. The wind would extinguish the flame instantly. But he couldn't let that stop him. The tunnel could very well lead to Miranda.

As he rounded the curve, a roaring sound, not unlike the sound of a waterfall on a rampage, bombarded his ears while winds of terrible velocity buffeted him from all sides, first blowing against him, then away from him. He felt as though he were fighting his way blind through a howling blizzard.

His mind tried to deal with the ambiguity of the situation. What could be causing the wind to behave in such a manner? Could it be gases from below? Or maybe barometric pressures inside the caverns that caused it? He certainly had no way of knowing, and even less time to dwell on it, so intent was he on keeping his feet beneath his body.

And the very precise, slow way he moved was the only thing that saved him when the floor suddenly dropped from beneath him. He swayed for a moment before stopping his momentum enough to step back. Then, as slowly as he had approached the chasm, he retreated, knowing that he'd come to a dead end.

After Miranda reached the bottom of the canyon, she gathered enough wood for a fire, then used one of her matches to light it. When the flames were leaping and dancing cheerily, she seated herself close by and stretched her legs out. Hitching up the leg of her riding skirt, she bent to examine the wound.

Her eyes widened in horror as she stared down at the torn flesh. The wound was oozing a thick fluid and her calf was swollen. She touched the area around the wound and sucked in a sharp breath. God! It was so painful and so horribly swollen, almost twice its original size, and the color was an ugly bluish red. She knew, without a doubt, that it was infected.

Lord, help her! What could she do? Although

she knew a little about medicine—there'd certainly been times when she'd had to cleanse wounds while exploring with her father—she'd never been faced with anything so grave as her injured leg.

Had it already gone too long? Was her blood already poisoned beyond help?

Miranda unlaced her boots and removed them. Then, with great difficulty, she pushed herself to her feet, then limped over to the river's edge. After sloshing the chilly water on the wound, she slumped down on the sand and began to cry.

Helplessly, unable to stop her tears, Miranda cried, her shoulders heaving with her sobs, until she was totally drained.

It wasn't until her sobs had become a hiccup that she became aware of the cricket's steady chirping. It was as though it had sensed her deep distress and was attempting to cheer her with its musical voice. It sang endlessly, its song washing over her like a cooling salve until finally, her eyes closed and she slept.

When Miranda woke, she didn't want to open her eyes because she already knew what she'd find; the eternal darkness that was always with her now. When she did look, for want of any other choice, she lifted her lashes to the shadowy world that had become her prison.

Are you going to lie there and wait to die? a silent voice questioned. *Isn't it about time you tried to get yourself out of this place?*

"No, I'm not!" Miranda muttered. "I won't give up. I *can't* give up."

Although Miranda's leg throbbed painfully, she tried to ignore it as she tore a strip from the bottom of her ragged skirt, and wound it around a thick green stick. She'd been lucky to find it. Since it was green, it wouldn't burn as quickly as the dry wood and would be more suitable for a torch.

When she'd completed her makeshift torch, she shuffled painfully toward the cliff. There was nothing for her down here. No way out. And she was almost certain there were tunnels leading off the phosphor chamber.

It seemed to take hours to reach the ledge because her legs were as unsure as hinged stilts. But finally, she reached the upper chamber. After a quick search, she found what she was looking for. On the far side of the cavern were two tunnels. After lighting the torch, she entered the right one and limped down it. Soon, it began to slope upward, and her heart began to pump erratically, her breath coming in tortured gasps, but still she continued on. All too soon the ceiling lowered, but rather than turn back, Miranda dropped to all fours. She had to go on, couldn't turn back yet. Her knees began to bleed, as the scabs were torn off by the rough rock floor. The walls closed in on her, the path growing narrower, the climb steeper.

Miranda licked dry lips over and over again, as her nostrils dilated, trying to breathe in the air that was becoming stale, almost scarce.

Then, abruptly, the passage came to an end, cut off by the ceiling that had dramatically lowered.

Swallowing hard, Miranda examined the cul-de-sac with terror-palsied hands. But there was no way out. She had no choice, she'd have to go back.

Even as she made that decision, her hands raked across a softer area. She held her torch closer, the better to examine the claylike substance. It was gray in color and had a grainy texture.

Something tugged at her memory. She'd seen something like it long ago. Was this the same thing? Was it possible she'd found some *moonmilk?*

Reaching out, she scraped a little away with her fingers and examined it again. It *looked* like moonmilk. She brought a small quantity to her mouth. It *tasted* like moonmilk. Oh, Lord! If it was, then perhaps she had found a way to save her leg!

She'd learned about the substance during her explorations in France. There, in a little town in the French Pyrenees, not far from the place where she'd been trapped underground for so long, she'd heard of the claylike substance found in many European caves. During the fifteenth and sixteenth centuries, many physicians had used moonmilk for its healing properties. It was used as a dressing for wounds, and it acted as a dehydrating agent and could stop bleeding. It would be centuries before the active substance it contained, a substance also found in streptomycin, would be identified.

Without hesitation—for what was there to lose—she scraped off some of the grainy clay and applied it to her leg. If it was moonmilk, then perhaps she would see an improvement in her leg. If not—she shuddered. She didn't want to think of the consequences.

"I'm ashamed to admit it, Peter," she said, her voice a shaky whisper. "But I'm scared. I'm finally down to that. I'm just plain scared. I know I'm going to die in here, and I don't want to. I don't even know how to. What does one do? Just lie down and wait for death to come? God, it would be so easy. I'm weak, I'm starved, I'm sick and I'm smelly and scabby and skinned and bruised and scared, and oh, God! On top of all that, I've just found Rogue! How could fate be so cruel? How could love be over before it had really ever begun?"

Miranda.

"He's calling me," she told the cricket. "I'll have to go and you'll have to come with me. That salamander is around here somewhere and he wouldn't be above making you his dinner."

She made her slow way back to the phosphor

chamber and went into the passage. She felt the emptiness inside and waited quietly until she heard the footfalls in the distance, saw the tiny pinpoint of light from his lantern.

"Miranda," the voice came quietly, seeming almost certain in the knowledge that she'd be there.

"I'm here," she said.

"I'm sorry it's taken me so long to get across to you." He sounded as exhausted as she felt.

"I know you're doing everything you can, Rogue. I have faith in your ability to get me out of here." Even as she said the words, Miranda knew them for a lie.

"Just keep on thinking that way. Okay?"

"I will."

"He cleared his throat. "Is Peter with you?"

"Yes. He's in my pocket."

"Lucky cricket."

She smiled. "You have a way of making me feel better."

"I'm glad, Miranda." There was a long silence before he spoke again. "It may be awhile before I come back here."

"Why?" She could hear the panic in her voice. "What are you going to do?"

"There's another tunnel that needs checking out. I've left it to the last."

She didn't like the sound of that. There was something different about his voice. "Will it be dangerous?"

"No."

"You're lying to me, McClaren. Don't do that."

"Perhaps it will be a little bit dangerous. But isn't everything down here?"

"Then don't attempt it."

"I must."

"No! I would rather die here than have you lose your life while trying to save me."

"Why?" His voice was hoarse. "If I was in your shoes, I would want everyone to move heaven and earth to get me out."

She laughed harshly. "You *are* in my shoes. Do you think they can get you out of there so easy? When you jumped in that well, you probably signed your own death warrant." She began to cry. "You're a fool, McClaren. A damn fool that's trying to be a hero. Well, I won't have it! Do you hear me? I just won't have it!"

"Hush, hush," he soothed. "How do you think it makes me feel to have you crying over me like this."

"I'm not crying over you," she denied. "I'm crying over me."

"Like hell you are. I know you better than that, professor."

"Stop calling me that!" she snapped. "I'm not a professor. I'm just a woman worried about a darn fool man who's bent on killing himself just to prove he's a hero!"

"Calm down, Miranda." His voice was soft.

"God, I wish these rocks weren't between us. If only I could touch you." His voice became husky. "I've been wondering what it would feel like to take you in my arms, to nuzzle my face in your silky copper hair."

Her breath caught in her throat, her fingers dug into her palms. "Why are you saying such things to me?"

"In other circumstances I probably wouldn't," he admitted. "But here, surrounded by the dark, it makes me feel better to say it. I'd like to hold you against me, to kiss your lips and feel your breasts pressed against my chest."

Heat swept over Miranda and his words caused an ache in the pit of her stomach, a slow, empty ache that needed to be filled. "McClaren," she whispered brokenly. "Don't do this to me. Can't you hear how much I'm hurting?"

"I hear, professor. And I hurt too. Every part of me hurts. Do you know I've never even touched your hand in friendship, and yet my body seems to know you well. Just as though it remembers the silky feel of your bare skin against mine, the way your neck would move back so my lips could taste the soft, sweet flesh under your ear. God! I can hardly believe I'm saying these words to you!"

Neither could she. Miranda could hardly credit her senses with what she was hearing, what she was feeling. It was as though he were making love to her with his voice.

"Will you forget all that when you do get in here to me?" she asked. "Are you going to be the cold heartless rancher I met only a short time ago?"

"Never," he said. "Too much has passed between us now. Way too much." He was silent for a long moment, then, "Professor?"

"Yes?"

"I have to leave now. Go back to your river and wait for me there."

"McClaren?"

"Yes, professor?"

"Be safe."

He laughed softly. "Of course."

Miranda listened to the sound of his receding footsteps, still hardly able to believe what had just happened. He had actually made love to her without touching her. The sound of his voice remained in her memory as she made her way back to the phosphor chamber.

Twenty-two

Although it was only midafternoon, the Raven Saloon was already crowded when the man known only as Smith by Geraldo and his bunch pushed aside the batwing doors and stepped inside. Immediately, his nostrils flared, assailed by the pungent smell of sour whiskey.

His searching gaze slid around the smoke-filled room, stopped to rest for a moment on Mary Belle, the dark-haired beauty who was Elmer Raven's latest acquisition. Smith's eyes narrowed thoughtfully, dwelt momentarily on the cleavage exposed by the flame red, low-cut gown she wore, then lifted to her face. He'd never seen the like of her before. Rumor had it that the girl was still a virgin . . . that Elmer Raven was saving her for his private stock.

Smith's lips twisted into a smile that never reached his cold, blue eyes. As soon as he had the time, he'd find out for himself whether or not she was a virgin and neither Elmer — nor any other man — would dare to interfere.

He was brought back to the present as the piano player—having finished his break—hit the first chords on the instrument, producing a sharp, tinny sound. Smith jerked his gaze toward the man, quickly dismissed him and searched the room for his partner in crime.

Smith found the man seated at a corner table with three other men, each of them seeming oblivious of everything except the cards they held in their hands.

The saloon girls had already begun to circulate, and as Smith started across the room, one of them—a girl he knew only as Hazel—stepped in front of him.

"Need some company?" she asked.

"Not yours," he answered rudely, shoving her aside.

Shrugging her shoulders, apparently unmoved by his refusal, she left him alone and stopped to offer her services to one of the other customers.

Smith continued on across the room until he reached the table occupied by the card players. Then, stopping behind the man he'd come to see, he gripped him by the shoulder to get his attention.

"What do you want?" the man said, frowning heavily at Smith.

"I gotta talk to you," Smith said.

"I'm busy," the man with the cards said, turning his attention back to the cards in his hand. "You'll have to wait."

"It's important," Smith growled.

"So's this," the other man said. "I got a hunderd riding on this hand." He waved toward the bar. "Go wet your whistle. We'll talk when I'm finished." His lips stretched into a smile as he looked at the other man. "After I've taken these gents' money."

Smith spun on his heels and stalked to the bar. Dammit! There was a hell of a lot more than a hundred dollars at stake. He shoved himself up to the bar between men who moved aside immediately to allow him space. Although his lips never moved, he smiled inwardly. That's the way it had always been, ever since the day his daddy first brought him into the saloon. He was a big man around these parts. A man feared by others, a man who had enough power to make others suffer if they messed with him. Soon his power would be even greater. With all the wealth he would soon have at his fingertips, he would run for congress. Hell! He might even run for president of the United States of America.

Yeah, why not? His eyes flashed hotly to the man playing cards and this time, he did smile. Even Trace Carradine—alias Jones—would jump when he called.

Rogue's eyes itched—he knew they must be bloodshot—and fatigue had become a heavy burden. Even so, he refused to stop to rest until he'd checked out one last tunnel.

Although the temperature in the cavern was cool, sweat beaded his forehead. He grunted with exertion, pushing the lantern in front of him while he wiggled his body farther into the passage that could not even be called a crawl way now because there was not enough distance from floor to ceiling to do more than lie flat on his stomach and inch his way forward like a snake.

"This has got to work," he said, taking comfort in the sound of his own voice. He was at his wits' end now. Every avenue, every crevice big enough to squeeze through had been checked out . . . except this one.

The passage had so many twists and turns that the light from his lantern penetrated only a few feet in front of him. Another bend lay directly ahead; a bend that was so sharp he was unable to see past it.

Proceeding with caution, realizing the floor could drop away without any warning, he held the lantern in front of him and probed the depths around the curve.

After satisfying himself that the floor was still there, he pushed his upper torso into the bend . . . and discovered another bend just a few feet away.

God! Was this all for nothing? Was it going to be just another dead end? He rubbed his hand across weary eyes that felt as though they were filled with sand. What the hell was he going through all this for, anyway? he wondered. He'd probably never break through to Miranda. She would be in that damned cave until the day she died! And without food, that day couldn't be far away.

Miranda had decided it was past time she found something to eat. Actually, she'd come to that decision after she'd seen the big catfish swimming in the pool below the waterfall. Its pale, almost colorless body suggested it had been in the dark cave for years, feeding on the algae that were somehow able to grow on the bottom of the pool that was separated from the main body of water by a sandy shoal fingering out into the river, allowing a thin veil of water to pass over, but apparently not the fish.

Or maybe the fish was satisfied where he was.

Miranda didn't know the answer, nor did she care. Since she'd laid eyes on the fish several hours earlier, her every thought was directed toward catching it.

An extensive search of the riverbank had rendered up a forked stick that would make the base of a net. Although she had a small amount of thick cord in her pocket, there wasn't enough to weave a net, so she left it where it was and ripped several strips from the bottom of her riding skirt. By the time she'd fashioned the improvised net, her riding skirt had been shortened to midthigh.

But she didn't mind. Not if the loss of her skirt would net her the fish.

She was at the water's edge when she remembered Peter. Scooping the cricket from her shoulder, she bent over a hollowed out log nearby and gently placed the cricket on it. "You better stay here, Peter," she said softly. "This fishing stuff can get out of hand sometimes. If you fell in the water you could wind up being that big catfish's dinner."

As though it understood her words, the cricket began a steady chirruping and crawled toward the inner recesses of the hollow.

"That's a good boy," she said. "But you be careful. There may be salamanders down here by the river, and you know they wouldn't think twice about going into that log after you."

Unwilling to get her clothing wet, Miranda stripped it off and tossed it carelessly on the sandy bank, then entered the pool. Water swirled around her calves, cooling the heated flesh around her wounded leg. She took another step, felt the water gliding past her knees, sloshing against her thighs. It was deeper than she'd thought.

She took another step, felt the water around her waist, then moving upward to caress the swell of her breasts. Miranda sucked in a deep breath as the cold water touched her erect nipples. If it got much deeper she'd never be able to net the fish, much less carry it to the bank.

Even as the thought occurred, the bottom

sloped upward; water slid down her breasts, past her waist, stopping on the fullness of her hips.

Her gaze fastened on the rock where the catfish was hiding, and she swished closer. Suddenly, her feet slipped on the algae growing on the bottom; she flailed out with both arms, finally regaining her balance.

Darn it! She had to catch that fish!

Suddenly, the big catfish darted from beneath the rocks and streaked in front of her.

Excitement surged through her veins as she lowered her net and scooped toward him. When she lifted it up, she found several minnows flopping in the bottom of it, but nothing larger.

Dumping the minnows back into the water, she searched for the catfish. He was nowhere to be seen. Realizing he had retreated beneath the rocks again, she pushed her net under them, gave it a wide sweep, then yanked it out of the water.

Her eyes widened as she saw the strips of fabric moving, jerking rapidly as something heavy flopped inside. "Peter!" she screamed. "I did it, Peter! I got him!"

The net jerked again, the weight of it almost knocking her off balance, and she scrambled for purchase against the slippery bottom. "Oh, no," she said, hurrying toward the bank. "You aren't going anywhere. You're about to become my dinner."

Slipping and sliding, she managed to reach the bank without losing her catch. She moved at least twenty feet up the river bank before deciding she was far enough from the water, so that, in the event the fish managed to get away, she could catch it before it flopped its way to the river again.

Bending over the net, she dumped the contents out on the red sand, then stared in amazement at the creature attempting to right itself.

A turtle! Dammit, instead of the catfish, she'd caught a turtle.

Miranda was overwhelmed with frustration. Now that the excitement of the catch had left her, she was shaken by weariness. Her legs trembled and she dropped to the sand. She didn't think she had the strength to try again. Not just yet. Not until she rested for awhile.

Something moved in her peripheral vision. She turned and saw a perch flopping madly, attempting to make its way back to the river. Although it wasn't very big—not much more than a mouthful—she'd have to be content with it for her meal.

Wrapping her arms around her body, attempting to warm her chilled flesh, she sat there looking at the perch. If she'd managed to catch the large catfish, she wouldn't have had to go in the cold water again for awhile. Miranda knew enough about her body to know that a constant loss of heat could soon bring on all sorts of illnesses.

Leaving the fish where it was, she slid into her garments, replenished the fire with wood, then set about cleaning her catch. When she'd finished, she raked a few coals aside and laid the fish across them.

The steady chirruping of the cricket told her Peter had crawled out of the log. "I didn't catch the big one, Peter. Just a lousy turtle." A flicker of movement caught her eyes and she turned to see the turtle making its steady progress toward the cricket on the log.

Alarm streaked through her and she scooped the small insect up with her finger. Rounding on the turtle, she said, "Get away from here. Go back to your home in the water before I make *you* my dinner."

As the words left her mouth, her eyes narrowed on the turtle. Why not eat the turtle? she wondered. She'd never eaten one before, but she'd heard the meat was delicious. She continued to study the creature. Somehow, she hated to eat it, but if she didn't, if she let him go, the turtle was likely to eat Peter while she slept.

Miranda knew she was being ridiculous, but she couldn't bear the thought of losing the cricket; Peter's singing helped keep her sane. And she was almost certain she would need all the help she could get before this ordeal was over.

If it ever was.

Don't think like that, an inner voice warned. *That way lies madness.*

She studied the armor plating on the creature that was still moving toward the log, its beady eyes seemed to be focused on the cricket perched atop the breast pocket of her shirt.

How do you go about killing a turtle? she silently wondered.

The bend had proved to be an S curve that was so difficult, so tight, Rogue was barely able to maneuver his way through it. When he was on the other side, the cavern walls began to widen. Although it was only by a few inches, there was more room to maneuver.

Moments later the passage took a downward curve, going farther into the depths of the earth, and it was just entirely possible the tunnel might break through into the ceiling of the cavern where Miranda was imprisoned.

Rolling onto his back, he stared up at the ceiling a scant four inches away from his face and allowed himself time to rest. But only for a moment, then he began to inch his way forward again.

When he heard the muted roar, excitement surged through him. Although he'd been fooled before, this time it had to be Miranda's waterfall he was hearing.

A sense of urgency possessed him and he moved forward faster. He was nearly there. Nearly there. *Miranda,* he cried inwardly, *You won't be alone much longer.*

Miranda's head jerked and she started to her feet, then slowly settled back down again. Rogue's voice had been different this time. Not nearly so close. As though the distance between them was filled with a heavy, impenetrable substance . . . like tons and tons of rock.

Shuddering, trying to shake the dread covering her, Miranda took Peter out of her pocket, stroking his velvety coat, his stiff, leathery forewings, seeking comfort from the act.

Somehow she knew that Rogue wasn't in the passage. Some inner sense told her so. And even though he thought he was getting closer to her, she knew he wasn't. Instead, Rogue was getting farther away.

Her gaze fell on the turtle again. The armor plating would make a nice cooking pot . . . if she could separate the top piece from the bottom. Her eyes misted as she held Peter up to her face. "I don't really want to kill him," she confided. "But it might become necessary."

The cricket began his melodious song again.

When the passage became a chimney, Rogue strapped the pack on his back and began to climb downward. He was sure now—positive that he would soon reach the cavern where Miranda was trapped.

Rogue realized he was probably coming through

the ceiling of the cavern, so he was making certain he had plenty of warning before the drop. According to Miranda, it was a long way down to the floor, but he would worry about that later. Right now he was only interested in reaching the cavern.

If only the light from the lantern would reach farther, but it seemed to be reflected back to him. He really didn't have time to figure out why. He must keep his mind on his descent, keep his back secured on one side and his feet and hands pressed firmly against the other.

He was coming up on a bend and he prayed that he'd be able to negotiate it. He went on, cautiously, one hand clutching the lantern while the other hand pressed hard against the wall, helping his feet as he worked his way down and around the curve.

Suddenly, his feet slid, he pressed harder with his back and free hand, trying to retain his position on the rock while looking down to examine the rock below him.

His eyes widened, just before he slipped.

He lost his grip on the lantern, heard it clatter against rock just before the blackness surrounded him. And then he fell.

Twenty-three

Killing the turtle was easier said than done. Miranda had decided the easiest way to accomplish the task would be to crush the creature's head with a rock, but the turtle refused to cooperate and kept pulling its head back into the shell.

She was about ready to give it up when she thought of turning the creature onto its back. Grabbing the turtle shell at the back end, she flipped it over and almost instantly the turtle stuck its head and feet out and waved them frantically, trying to right itself.

Picking up the fist-sized rock beside her, Miranda muttered, "I don't really like doing this, but it's your life or mine," and brought the rock down with all her strength.

She kept her eyes away from the creature's crushed head while she cleaned it with her small folding knife and cut the meat into strips, carefully trimming away the fat and laying it aside. It would come in handy when she made a torch.

While the aroma of cooking meat teased her nostrils, and made her stomach growl with hunger, Miranda searched the riverbank for a stick to use for the base of her torch. Her efforts were soon rewarded. A few feet from her campfire she found a stout limb about two inches thick. She broke off the end — leaving a length of about eighteen inches — and held it aloft. If she coated strips of fabric with the turtle fat and wound them around the stick, the result should be a slow-burning torch that would last long enough to enable her to search the passages for an exit.

Peter, perched on her shoulder, began a steady chirruping. "I know," she muttered, as though the cricket had uttered a reproof. "Rogue told me not to explore alone, but he doesn't realize how bad it is here. He thinks I'll be all right until he comes. But I won't, Peter. I think my leg is real bad. I guess I washed the moonmilk off when I went fishing. I'll have to find some more of it, and maybe, while I'm looking for it, I just might find the way out of here." She looked toward the upper chamber. "I have to," she went on. "He's been trying to get in here for days. By the time he reaches me — if he ever does — I may have gangrene in this leg."

Black desolation settled over her as she heard herself say the words. Until now, she wouldn't even allow herself to think them, much less say them aloud. But she'd only been fooling herself. Her leg was terribly swollen. Painful to walk on.

She didn't dare wait any longer. No, she'd run out of time. If she didn't act now to save herself, then it just might be too late.

When Rogue regained consciousness, he became aware of the smell of kerosene fumes. They were almost overpowering in their intensity.

Coughing, trying to clear his lungs of the fumes, he searched for the lantern. It was within easy reach, and surprisingly, still intact. Soon, he was surveying his surroundings by the flickering light.

He was in a rounded rock hole, about twelve feet in circumference and a little more than five feet in height.

He coughed again as his lungs filled with the fumes. He had to get out of here before he suffocated, but he'd need both hands to do so.

Hooking his right foot beneath the lantern handle, he stuck his head through the hole and straightened to his full length. With the lantern below him, he was working in shadows, but his searching fingers caught in a crack and gripped hard.

Bracing his back against the rock wall, he used his hands and free foot to climb through the hole, grunting with the effort it took. Once above the round bottom, he transferred the lantern to his right hand and started to climb up the circular hole, using the few crevices and bulges there to work his way upward again. He realized that, at the pace he was going, it would take hours for him to get back to the chimney rock, but he would not let himself think about that, nor about anything else. Instead, he concentrated his efforts on finding the right holds for his hands and feet so he could thrust his weary body forward.

As a safeguard, Miranda scratched an arrow at the mouth of the tunnel before she entered. Then, satisfied she'd done everything she could to let Rogue know where she'd gone, she limped down the passage, the light from her torch flickering erratically against the passage walls, diffusing itself into nothingness among the dark recesses.

Although the tunnel sloped upwards—the direction she needed to go—Miranda wondered if she was making a serious mistake exploring the tunnel on her own.

"But what else could I do?" she muttered.

Could I do. Could I do, the cavern echoed back.

"Rogue will never break through to me. Never."

Never, never, never, echoed the tavern, seeming to mock her fears.

Although Miranda worried about leaving the dubious safety of the phosphor and crystal cave, she knew she must while she had the strength to do so. But as time passed and the stabbing pain in her leg became more intense, she fought the urge to return, to go in the other tunnel that contained the moonmilk.

There was only a trace of it there, she reminded herself. Not enough to do much good. She needed more of it, and there was just the slight chance she would find some in this tunnel. If not the moonmilk, then perhaps the way out.

She was still worrying the matter over in her mind when, quite suddenly, she heard a faint sound in the distance. Miranda stopped, cocking her head to listen intently. Was that the sound of dripping water?

Holding her breath, she waited, ears straining for the sound. There it was again . . . somewhere in the tunnel ahead of her, barely heard, yet unmistakable.

She limped forward again, faster, fifty feet, then paused to listen. Again, she heard the drip of water. Although the sound was distinct, it was still far away.

Beneath her feet was a smooth rock floor that continued to lead upward in a gentle curve. She held the makeshift torch in front of her, examining the walls as she went. When the floor began to slope downward, her spirits went with it.

As though sensing her depression, the cricket began a steady chirruping.

"It's no use, Peter," she said. "We're going down again. We'll have to turn back."

Even as she turned, the edge of the light shimmered with a sliding liquid gleam and she realized there was water on the floor ahead. Was it seepage from the rocks? Or perhaps another subterranean river?

Curious, she went to investigate.

Her footsteps were quicker, the light flicking over the rock in eager search.

The tunnel narrowed until it became little more than twelve inches wide. As the walls squeezed inward, she saw a narrow gap to her left not more than ten inches wide. And curiously, it didn't, like the other cave, give onto darkness. Instead, the darkness slackened beyond it.

All thoughts of returning vanished. She had to see what lay ahead. She squeezed her narrow frame through the crack, feeling the rock scrape against her already raw skin as she did. But still she forced her body forward, her eyes probing the shadows ahead.

The darkness had given way to gray shadows now. Ahead of her the passage curved sharply to the left; beyond the curve she could see the light, and the drip of water was clear and loud.

When she rounded the corner she stopped short.

Directly ahead was light. Not artificial light, but the light of day. The passage opened to a gallery of moving green. Miranda's heart beat fast with hope. Had she found another exit to the outside world?

It must be. Why else would there be grass, and clusters of blue and pink flowers and the leaves

270

from a slender tree situated at the mouth of the tunnel.

She almost ran the rest of the way, ducking under the arch and coming suddenly into a little glade.

Miranda stared in amazement. There was the source of water . . . a spring. It supplied enough water to create a miniature waterfall that fell into a pool not more than ten feet in circumference.

Her gaze lifted and found rocky shale above her. She realized at once she hadn't found a way out. A quick tilt of her head and her eyes found the opening, at least forty feet above her. She was in a small enclosure, perhaps fifty feet across—a light-well.

Perhaps centuries ago this had been a circular cave, not unlike the ones she'd already been through. But here, the roof had fallen in and let in the sun and the seeds of grass and wild flowers. The spring had fed them, so that now, in the heart of the mountains, was this little well of light filled with vivid color.

Cra-a-a-ck!

Miranda jerked as the sound thundered above her, seeming almost to shake the walls of her prison.

Cra-a-a-ck! It came again.

And then the rain fell. Sheets of water that drenched her hair and shoulders and body as she stood with upturned face, unwilling to lose sight of the world outside.

She shifted her shoulders with the sudden chill caused by her wet clothing and the damp earth around her. She moved beneath a nearby ledge and stood with her arms hunched against her sides, and waited, listening to the sound of the thunder, the lightning and the falling rain.

The rain continued to fall. How long would it last, she wondered? While she waited, she studied the walls of the enclosure. Was it possible to climb them? Even as the thought occurred, she quickly dismissed it. The rocky shale would crumble around her if she tried to scale the walls.

Miranda shivered and sneezed. Realizing she was borrowing trouble staying where she was — she had to dry her clothing — she darted across the light-well and entered the tunnel again.

She was searching for some dry wood to build a fire when she felt a sudden urge to return to the blocked passageway. "Rogue must be on his way there, Peter," she muttered.

Eager to see him, to tell him what she'd discovered, she attempted to light her torch. But it would not light. It was too wet.

Even so, she must go. She felt compelled to do so.

Hoping she could make it through the tunnel in the dark, she kept her hands on the sides of the passage and made her way through the fissure. Soon, the gray shadows gave way to blackness and her eyes ached with darkness. Miranda had to exercise all her self-control to stop herself from returning to the light.

The echo of her coward pulses seemed to fill the tunnel as she felt her way through, afraid that somehow, she would miss a turn and become lost. Once the fear was so overpowering that she stopped and struck a match. The match flared and the little circle of light given off danced away through the faintly echoing spaces of darknesses.

The way seemed longer than before, the rocks more plentiful, and she was out of breath when she finally reached the phosphor cavern. She allowed herself no time to rest before hurrying across the cavern and entering the tunnel. Then Miranda made her way down the tunnel to the rockslide. Once there, she cocked her head and listened for footsteps.

For a long moment there was only silence, then she heard him! His footsteps were slow, and far away, but there was definitely the sound of someone coming toward her.

His voice, when it came, was strangely hoarse.

"Miranda!"

"I'm here," she said quietly. "Are you all right?"

"Yes," he replied heavily.

"Something's wrong!" she said sharply. "What is it?"

"Nothing's wrong," he answered. "I'm just tired."

"When was the last time you rested?"

"Can't rest," he said. "Not enough time."

"You aren't going to help me if you make yourself ill," she said. "You have to rest. You should go back to the big chamber with red sand and get some sleep. But first," she infused excitement into her voice, "first, let me tell you what I found. You'll never believe it."

"I'm at the point where I'll believe almost anything."

"I found a chamber where the roof had caved in," she said.

"Where?"

"Down one of the tunnels that leads off the—"

"Miranda." His voice was angry, harsh. "I told you not to go off on your own."

"It wasn't far," she said. "And I was afraid you weren't coming back."

"Dammit! Don't you think you're in enough trouble already? Do you have to go looking for more?"

Hurt streaked through her. How could he speak to her that way? Surely he knew how bad things were for her. She had to get out, must have medicine for her leg.

He doesn't know that, a silent voice reminded. *You didn't tell him.*

Her voice was husky, strained, when she spoke again. "Don't you want to hear about the light-well?"

For a moment there was a long silence. Then, "You said the roof caved in? You could see outside?"

"Yes," she replied. "But I don't think it's a way out. The walls are made of sandstone. I think they'd crumble if I tried to climb them."

"You're probably right. Stay the hell away from it."

"I will," she replied. "I wish you could see it. It was a beautiful little glade. There's a spring there and flowers and trees. And it was raining. I actually felt the rain on my face."

"It was raining?"

Something in his voice gave her pause.

"Yes."

"Miranda. Stay away from it. The walls might collapse and you could be caught under the rubble."

"But—"

"Dammit! Stay away from it. You have no business going off in the dark that way anyway. You could have lost your way and never found your way back here."

"I have a torch," she said stiffly.

"How did you manage that?"

"I wrapped strips of fabric soaked in turtle fat around a thick stick. It smoked a lot, but otherwise, it was all right."

He gave a heavy sigh. "You're somethin' else, professor. Not many people would've thought of doin' that. But don't go off like that again." He didn't sound quite so angry now. "God, I don't ever recall being so damned tired."

"You need rest, Rogue. You're pushing yourself

too hard. You've got to stop it. Don't you realize you can't help me if you make yourself ill?"

"You're right," he said. "But I don't want to leave right now."

"Then sleep there. Sleep as long as you want to and know that I'll be over here, only a few feet away from you." Her voice sounded strangely intimate even to her own ears and she wondered if he heard it as well. She began talking soothingly, telling him about the different places she'd gone with her father, the caverns she'd explored and the things she'd seen, trying to make them sound funny and interesting. When his questions finally ceased, Miranda realized he'd fallen asleep.

She envied him his ability to sleep so easily. It had been so long since she'd slept . . . so long. Yet, she dared not sleep now. Her leg was throbbing painfully, making her aware that she needed to do something about it.

Miranda pulled her leg around until she could see the injured calf. Although the flesh was puffy around the wound, and it was still swollen and discolored, the wound had closed and it was no longer oozing pus. Surely that was a good sign.

Expelling a long sigh, relieved and weary, she rolled the torch on the rocky floor to smother the flame, then leaned back against the wall and forced herself to relax. Her eyelids flickered, then drifted slowly down. When her chin dropped, her eyelids jerked up, then fell slowly again. Moments later, she was fast asleep.

Rogue woke to silence and was immediately alert. For one short moment he thought he was alone in the passage, but a slight movement beyond the rockslide, followed by a muffled groan, told him he was wrong. Miranda was still there, and judging by her heavy breathing, she was fast asleep.

Unwilling to wake her, he lay in the darkness listening to the comforting sound of her breathing, longing to be close enough to hold her in his arms. He realized now that he'd been almost at the breaking point when he'd entered the blocked tunnel. His mind was so tired that he'd barely been able to think, but the sleep he'd acquired — along with Miranda's presence — had calmed his jangled nerves, renewed his strength and his ability to think clearly. Surely, now that he was rested, he could find a way to free Miranda.

Granted, he hadn't been so tired in the beginning, but neither had he known the extent of the tunnels that riddled the cavern. Now he did know and, since he'd tried every damned one of them, he could turn his efforts elsewhere.

If he couldn't get to her from inside the cave, then he'd have to get out of the cave and try from there. She'd spoken of a light-well. Although she'd said the walls were sandstone, it could still be the answer — the way to reach her. If he could find the place she spoke of, maybe they could set crossbars up and lower a rope down from that, keeping away from the sides.

Yeah. It just might work.

First though, he had to get out. The rock chimney appeared in his mind's eye. What lay beyond the barrier? If the chimney continued up, then there might be an exit on top of Squaw Mountain. Although the rock blocking it was hard, might even be some kind of marble, surely the small pick in his pack could chip it away.

He nodded with satisfaction. Yeah. He was almost certain he could do it. And after he got out—providing he did—then he could hotfoot it back to the ranch and get some help. He'd certainly need some. There was no way he could build the crossbars and lower himself into the light-well alone.

His thoughts turned to the underground river. In the dense woods at the base of Squaw Mountain, there was a narrow river fed by several springs. At one particular spot, the river plunged over a waterfall into a deep pool. As far as he'd been able to determine, there was no other exit for the water; only the pool. Rogue, who was naturally curious about this land he'd inherited, had been so busy he'd had no time to explore it yet, but, according to Colby, the water was sucked into a hole at the bottom of the pool.

It had to be Miranda's underground river. There could be no other explanation. But that knowledge wouldn't help him get her out. A man would be a fool to try to get to her that way.

Suddenly he heard her stirring. "Miranda," he said softly.

"Yes?" she inquired, sounding as though she covered a yawn.

"Miranda—I heard you waking up."

"Are you feeling better now?"

"Much better. I was all tuckered out. Now I'm ready to tackle this damn cave again."

"Rogue." Her voice was soft. "You must take better care of yourself. You know you're my only hope of getting out of here."

"Yeah," he said gruffly. "I know. I just didn't know what I was up against down here. Now I've got some idea, an' I've developed a real healthy respect for this place." He looked at his flickering light. Dammit! He'd left it burning while he slept and now it was low on fuel again. "Miranda, did you leave your torch lit?"

"No. I put it out before I went to sleep. Besides, I don't need it in here. I know every step of the way back to the phosphor chamber. I'll save my light for later."

He wanted to say so much to her, to tell her how much she had come to mean to him, but the words wouldn't come. That wasn't surprising though. He'd never been one for pretty words. Even so, he wished he could say them, but instead of telling her how he felt, he spoke of his intentions. "Miranda, I've exhausted every tunnel I can find. Now I'm going to try something else."

"Will it be dangerous?"

"No. I'm going to climb all the way up the rock chimney. I'm almost sure it exits on the top of Squaw Mountain. When I get out of here, I'll search out that light-well you found. I'll come to you that way."

"No!" she said sharply. "I told you those walls are made of sandstone! They'd crumble beneath your weight."

"I've figgered out a way," he said gruffly. "I'll use crosspieces and tie a rope in the middle. That way I don't have to use the walls."

"It might work," she said slowly. "Yes!" Her voice gained confidence. "I think it would work. But why don't you just stay over there and go tell Charlie about it. He can send for help and—"

"He's alone, Miranda," Rogue said grimly. "The help he sent for never arrived. Somethin' must've happened to Chance."

"Oh, God, no! First Rusty, now Chance. How many people will lose their lives trying to save mine."

"Stop that!" he said sharply. "We don't know what happened to him. Maybe he just couldn't find any help."

"If that were the case, then he would've come back," she said.

"Yeah, I guess he would've." He expelled a heavy sigh. "Don't blame yourself, baby. Chance volunteered. He wanted to help. He was like that." Rogue realized he spoke of Chance in the past tense and hastily corrected himself. "He *is* like that."

"I guess you're set on going ahead with your plan," she said in a tearful voice. "But promise me something, Rogue. Promise me that you'll be real careful."

"You got my promise," he replied. "And, Miranda, keep away from that light-well. Do you hear me?"

"Why can't I wait there for you?"

"There might be some falling rock when I come down an' I don't want you to get hurt." They were both taking it for granted that his plan would work. "Wait down by the river. Do you hear me?"

"Yes. I hear you. And I'll wait there. I promise."

Leaving her was the hardest thing he'd ever done, but somehow he managed to go.

Twenty-four

Miranda's thoughts were in turmoil as she limped painfully through the tunnel toward the phosphor chamber. Chance and Rusty were dead. And, no matter what Rogue said, the blame for their deaths rested squarely on her own head. How could she cope with the guilt? Added to the guilt she felt over Janie's death, its weight seemed almost unbearable.

Suddenly, a white-hot stab of pain streaked through her leg, beginning somewhere near her ankle and running all the way up her thigh. It was a pain so agonizing that she dared not ignore it. Instead, she slumped down on the rocky floor of the tunnel and, with trembling fingers, extracted a match from her ever-dwindling supply and lit the torch.

Then, holding the flaming torch aloft, she twisted her swollen leg so she could better examine it, then quickly sucked in a sharp breath.

There was no sign of the moonmilk she'd spread over the wound—the stuff had probably washed off in the river—and it had all the signs of gangrene. The area around the wound was a distinct purple, angry-looking and swollen, while the cut itself was fish-belly white, oozing a foul-smelling pus.

"Oh, God, no! Please!" she whispered. "Don't let it be gangrene!" Even as she uttered the prayer, she knew it was too late. Her eyes fastened on the telltale red line running up and down her leg.

Shuddering with fear, she wedged her torch between two rocks and wrapped her arms around her upper torso. *Gangrene!* Just the thought of it was enough to make her tremble. She knew enough about gangrene to know the infected area must be cut away—had met a mountain climber in France who'd suffered the loss of a leg to gangrene. The man had considered himself lucky to be alive.

Get hold of yourself, a silent voice warned. Do something! "What?" she muttered. "What can I do?"

Miranda tried to think of some way to stop the infection, to keep it from spreading. "Cut it," she said aloud. "I have to find some more moonmilk. The wound will have to be opened and the poison squeezed out, then maybe I won't—" She couldn't finish the sentence, couldn't think about losing her leg to gangrene. No! She had to get up, had to find more of the moonmilk, had to take herself down to the river where she'd have water to cleanse the area.

Even as Miranda worked out her plan of action, she felt hesitant about returning to the river. Perhaps she'd do better by going to the light-well. There was a spring there and— No. Rogue had told her to wait for him at the river. She'd get the moonmilk—if there was enough left to scrape away—and then she'd go to the river and do what she must do.

"God, please give me the strength for it," she said aloud. "Please, just give me the strength to do what has to be done."

The cricket, as though sensing her deep distress, climbed out of her breast pocket and up her blouse. When it was perched on her shoulder the insect began his cheerful song.

With one thought in her mind—to get more of the healing clay—Miranda pushed herself to her feet and, with an unsteady gait, circled around the stone formations that blocked her way to the tunnel.

Since Rogue knew he'd be unable to hold the lantern and work, he lit the small piece of candle—all that was left in his supply pack—and used melted wax to secure it atop a protruding rock. Then, bracing his back against one wall while his feet were pressed against the opposite one, he chipped away at the stone blocking the chimney.

Although the hole was small, he could see

enough beyond the barrier to know that the chimney continued to rise. He felt encouraged by that fact and worked feverishly, hacking away at the rock, taking no notice of his aching joints, his torn and bruised flesh. What did they matter when he was certain he'd found the way out?

God! Let me be right! This has to be a way out of here!

Suddenly, with a shower of rocks, a larger portion of the barrier gave way. He reached beyond it, found a handhold and levered himself through. Then, extinguishing the flame on the candle, he stored it in a pocket, hooked the lighted lantern over his left arm and began the climb.

His breath came in short gasps, sweat beaded his forehead, but still he went on, and even as he did, his mind puzzled over the muffled roaring that was getting louder all the time. It didn't make sense. If he was coming out — as he'd thought — on top of Squaw Mountain, then what was making the sound? Unable to find an answer, he continued upward until finally, his searching hand found nothing but emptiness above him.

Startled, he jerked his head back, his gaze trying to penetrate the shadowy darkness above him. Was it another chamber? The sound was louder now, but barely audible over the thundering of his heart.

Suddenly, his nostrils twitched. Were his senses deceiving him, or was that water he smelled? The fresh scent of water, combined with the thundering roar could only mean one thing. He was near a waterfall.

Miranda's waterfall? His heart leapt with hope. Could it be the waterfall, or was he faced with another wind chamber?

Bunching his muscles, he heaved himself through the hole. His eyes widened as he held the lantern aloft. He was sitting on a ledge in another large cave.

No! It wasn't a cave. His eyes narrowed on the lighter area about fifteen feet away. They caught on a shimmering liquid gleam and he recognized it for what it was.

A waterfall!

He was in a hollowed-out space behind a waterfall.

Rogue looked down into the hole from which he'd just emerged, saw the yawning blackness, then lifted his gaze toward the wall of water facing him. Although he'd never been here before—not here on this ledge behind the waterfall—he knew the place.

It was as though a piece of missing puzzle had been found, making the whole suddenly recognizable.

Yes, he exulted. He did know the place. It was Colby's waterfall, located near the northern boundary of the Lazy R. The river, fed by more than twenty springs, plunged over a stairstep of marble rocks, falling into a deep pool where it seemed to end. But Rogue knew that was an impossibility. No river containing so much water could just come to an end. It had to feed a subterranean river.

Miranda's river.

Springing to his feet, he crossed the large chamber behind the waterfall, searching for a way out. Although the waterfall completely covered the face of the cliff, he soon discovered the narrow ledge—about six inches wide—that had been carved out of the rock by tons of water falling when the river was at the flood stage.

Hitching up the pack that dangled from his left shoulder, Rogue hugged the cliff and moved across the ledge into the waterfall. Although he'd prepared himself for the cold water, the force of it caught him unawares, almost knocking him from the ledge before he was able to right himself.

With water streaming down his face, he left the waterfall and slid out into the fresh air.

Blinking rapidly to clear the water from his eyes, he shoved the wet tendrils of hair away from his face and tilted his head back to look up at the sky. Although it was turbulent—angry gray clouds roiled swiftly overhead, holding the promise of a storm—it had never looked so good before.

Rogue breathed deeply of the fresh air that already smelled of rain. He felt like shouting with happiness—he was back on solid ground again. God, he'd actually done it. He'd left that godforsaken underworld behind him. He'd never have to breathe that stale air again, never have to fight his way through that everlasting darkness—that suffocating, stifling darkness that held dangers he'd never even imagined existed.

How could people actually like going in a place like that? How could Miranda and—

Miranda! God, she was still down there, and here he was congratulating himself on being free, forgetting all about what she was going through. Dammit, what kind of man was he anyway? He had to get her out of there!

His gaze narrowed on the hole on the bottom of the pool. It was small, circular, perhaps two feet in circumference, but it was partially blocked by two large flat stones.

There was movement around the stone, a circular movement not unlike a small whirlpool. This *had* to be the entrance to Miranda's river. But to try to reach her that way would be foolhardy. It could very well result in his death.

Rogue, becoming aware of water dripping into his eyes again, wiped his damp sleeve across his face while he hurriedly circled the pool. It would take him a couple of hours to reach the ranch house, but there would be help available there.

Just a few more hours, Miranda. Hold on just a few more hours and I'll have you out of there.

Rogue took off at a loping trot. His heart pumped wildly as he ran, trying to pace himself, knowing that he dared not risk collapsing. He was halfway to the ranch house when he saw the riders top the hill ahead.

He strained his eyes to see through the mist and felt as though a great weight had been lifted from his shoulders when he recognized the foremost rider as Colby. Moments later, the riders surrounded him.

"Rogue!" Colby exclaimed. "Boy, am I glad to see you! After what Chance here had to say, I was afraid you might be dead."

Rogue frowned. Chance Carter was alive. He'd reached the ranch house and Colby. Why hadn't they gone to the caves? It was a question that he uttered aloud as one of the riders urged his horse nearer and Rogue narrowed his gaze on him. "Where've you been, Chance? Why didn't you get some help like Charlie told you to."

"Couldn't, Rogue. Had to wait for somebody to get back to the ranch," Chance explained. "Where's Miranda?" His gaze traveled to the cedar brake beyond Rogue as though he expected to see Miranda emerge from the thicket.

"She's still trapped in the cave," Rogue said shortly.

"Then what're you doin' out here?" Chance asked.

"Standin' here answerin' questions!" Rogue snapped. "I was on my way to get the help you never brought."

"Well, hell! I—"

Colby cut through Chance's explanations. "We were ridin' there now, boss. I sent Lefty to town to round up some help. We got more trouble here

289

than we can handle. We found the stock, found the rustlers too. Killed part of 'em and run the others off. Thought it was all over, but it looks like the gang is bigger'n we thought, else there's two bunches hittin' on us, 'cause—"

"I don't have time for that now," Rogue snapped. "You'll have to take care of it! Right now I need to find the place Miranda told me about. She called it a light-well."

"Light-well?" Colby frowned down at him. "I never heard about no—"

"It's a hole in the ground—prob'ly thirty or forty feet down—an' I figger it's on top of Squaw Mountain. Miranda said there's a spring at the bottom an' lots of growin' things." His gaze moved over each of the riders. "Any of you ever seen a place like that?" Each of them shook his head.

"Then we'll just have to look for it. Colby, forget about the rustlers for the time being. I want every man jack riding for the Lazy R to look for that damn hole in the ground."

Colby nodded his head. "Consider it done, boss." His gaze went to one of the riders, a slim young man not more than twenty years old. "Slim, give the boss your hoss and double up with Danbridge. Since neither one of you weighs very much, his mount won't have no trouble carryin' the pair of you."

Nodding, Slim dismounted and handed the reins to Rogue. It was only after he was astride that he realized it was raining, but even then he gave it no more than a passing thought.

The rain fell steadily as they made their way up the mountain, but Rogue and the others ignored it as they went about searching for the light-well. Several hours later Rogue was near despair. Although they'd searched the mountain thoroughly, the only holes they found were made by gophers and other small woodland creatures.

Rogue joined Colby beneath a large cotton-wood tree. "We might as well quit lookin'," Colby said. "There ain't nothin' like that up here." His shrewd gaze met Rogue's. "Do you think she could've imagined it?"

"I don't know," Rogue said. "She's been under a lot of strain . . . maybe she did. But she seemed so certain about it."

"What do you want us to do now?" Colby asked. "Should we keep on lookin'?"

"No. We'd be wastin' time." His lips tightened. "I've got to do somethin' about gettin' her outta there, Colby. But I don't know what to do. There's gotta be another way in there. I—"

He broke off as a jagged streak of lightning split the heavens above. Thunder boomed across the sky, followed by another streak of lightning.

"Damn!" Colby growled. "You'd think we didn't have enough troubles already without this rain beatin' down on us. Looks like it's gonna get a whole lot worse too."

Rogue took a swipe at the water trickling down his face, but it was quickly replaced by more. Apparently the storm that had been brewing in the north had finally reached them.

The horses shifted restlessly around him, obviously unsettled by the loud noise. Another streak of lightning split the sky and a big bay reared up high, pawing at the air with his hooves as his rider fought to control him. The other horses were made even more restless by the bay's fear.

"We better get under cover," Colby said. "Looks like we're gonna have a cloudburst!"

A cloudburst. The words triggered something in Rogue's memory. He wiped the water from his face again, visualizing the waterfall in his mind . . . and the pool, gorged with water, swollen almost beyond its banks, certainly much higher than it usually was.

Suddenly, he realized the implications. *Dammit! He'd sent Miranda to the river!*

Cra-a-ack!

The single clap of thunder was so loud that it seemed to shake the ground beneath his feet. The rain increased, falling in blinding sheets around him.

Thunder boomed again, followed by a brilliant flash of lightning, seeming to mock the knowledge that chilled Rogue's blood—the knowledge that Miranda was under the ground. He'd made her promise to wait at the river, and the rain was falling so heavily that the volume of the water would quickly increase. And so would Miranda's danger.

It was almost a certainty the river would flood the cavern.

God! She would drown!

He couldn't wait! There was no time to waste. He had to get back to her, to warn her of the danger.

Rogue reined his mount around. "Get some help in there to Charlie," he cried. "I'm goin' back down there!"

Colby grabbed the reins before the horse could move. "Wait a minute, son. If you got a better way of gettin' in there to the girl, then maybe you better tell us about it."

"I don't have a better way," he said. "Just somethin' I'm gonna try. I think the hole in the bottom of that pool is big enough for a man to go through and I'm sure it leads to the cave where Miranda is trapped."

"Are you crazy?" Colby growled. "You ain't gonna try to get to her that way? It ain't possible. You might just as well take your gun and blow your brains out."

"There's no other way. If she's not warned, then she could drown." He yanked the reins out of Colby's hands and spurred the horse toward the waterfall, ignoring the shout behind him. He had no time to argue the matter.

It seemed to take forever to reach the waterfall. He dismounted and looked at the hole in the bottom of the pool. Was it big enough for him to enter? And could he hold his breath long enough to reach Miranda?

God! He hoped he could. If he couldn't, his life was soon to be over.

Setting the lantern aside, he jerked off his boots, stripped off the heavy pack and opened it up. Pulling out some tins of sardines and the last package of matches, he stuffed them in his pockets, wishing he could take more. But he didn't dare overload himself. The weight and bulk would be a disadvantage—could even cause him to hang up halfway down the river tunnel.

He gave an inward shudder at the thought, wondering if he was doing the right thing. Then, taking himself firmly in hand, he poised on the bank, took a deep breath and dove straight into the whirlpool. He felt the water's pull immediately and moved with it.

When he felt the bottom, he reached for one of the rocks blocking the hole, managed to pull it aside, then reached for the other. His plan was to clear both of them away, then surface for another deep breath. But it didn't work that way. As soon as he shoved aside the second rock, the force of the water sucked him into the hole.

God! He hadn't time to get another breath and his lungs were already half empty. He'd never make it. His lungs were burning and he was going to die . . . going to die . . . going to die . . .

Twenty-five

A chill shook Miranda as she stumbled through the tunnel where she'd found the moonmilk and she gave an uncontrollable shudder. The moisture-laden air made her hair curl damply around her face and her breath came in short gasps while her heart beat in double time. The indescribably stale smell of the tunnel made her feel faintly nause-ated and it was hard to keep going, but she knew she must. She dared not stop because she might not have the strength to get up again.

"God, Peter," she gasped. "I didn't think it was so far. Have I missed it?"

The cricket gave no sign that he heard her, but then, what had she expected? He couldn't answer her, could only sing his chirruping song, and right now she wasn't in any mood to hear it. She must concentrate on putting one foot in front of the other, on keeping her eyes on the tunnel ahead. How much farther could it be, anyway?

God, she was hot . . . so damnably hot!

Suddenly she realized the light in the tunnel was

brighter, as though the torch flame was being reflected back toward her over and over again. That couldn't be possible though, so it must be an illusion. Her pulses pounded loudly in her ears as she went on, rounded a curve, then stopped. She was finally there! Finally at the end of the tunnel where she'd found the moonmilk.

Realizing she was swaying on her feet, she uttered a little groan and dropped to the floor for a short rest against the cool rock walls. Something about that thought seemed out of place, but she couldn't quite make it out.

Lordy, she was hot! The thought had only just occurred when she wiped her free hand across her face, expecting to find sweat there, but although her face felt hot to the touch, no moisture had accumulated there. Instead her flesh felt incredibly dry.

She roused herself, barely able to summon the strength to move, and crawled to the opposite wall where there was a scant trace of the healing clay. Then, slowly extracting her knife, she scraped at the wall, dropped the scrapings into her right pocket, then scraped again to remove what little had remained there. When she'd finished the task, she rolled the grainy claylike substance into a little ball then replaced it in her pocket, hoping there was enough to help her leg.

She was struggling to regain her feet when another chill shook her frail body. She waited until the shaking had passed, then tried again to instill strength into legs that seemed to be made of rubber.

She had to keep going, couldn't stop now. Not until she'd done something about her leg. God, it had looked awful! She would certainly lose it, and possibly her life as well if she didn't cut away the poisoned area, but she had to get back to the river before she started.

Don't think about it! an inner voice screamed. Think about something else. Think about Rogue.

Rogue. Yes, she'd think about him. He was coming to save her. Please, God, let him hurry. I need him so desperately.

Miranda limped slowly down the tunnel, her legs moving automatically as she headed for the phosphor chamber and the underground river located below. She wouldn't allow herself to think about how far it was. She forced her thoughts in another direction instead . . . on Rogue, and the way he'd looked the last time she'd seen him, so many days ago.

His face had been wooden, expressionless, and yet she'd thought of a thundercloud when she'd looked into his dark eyes. He'd seemed ruthless to her, his rage almost beyond control, his dislike for her evident in every line of his body. But it had all been a sham . . . a facade that he'd presented to her. He wasn't like that at all. Instead, he was kind, so gentle with her, so caring about her fears. Even when he was gruff, she'd sensed the concern barely hidden by his words.

A man like that was worth his weight in gold. Had he meant it when he'd said he cared for her? She wanted to think so, needed to think so. In the beginning she'd thought he cared more for his ranch than he did for her father's life. She realized now that she'd been wrong. He'd thought she was like someone named Dallas . . . someone who'd hurt him badly. His voice had been different when he'd spoken of Dallas. Someday, Miranda decided, someday, Rogue would tell her what had happened.

His voice had been so different when he'd spoken of his mother. Miranda remembered the gentleness she'd heard then, the sound of his voice when he'd described her. Vanilla and spice and fresh-baked cakes, he'd said. What a wonderful description that was.

Rogue's upbringing had apparently been very different from her own. Her father had never married again. Was it because he had never gotten over her mother's death?

Did he blame himself for not being there when she needed him? Miranda had often wondered about it, but the professor, when questioned about her mother, would answer abruptly and quickly turn the conversation in another direction. She'd learned early that if she was to have his company, she must not talk about the past.

His housekeeper, Sarah, had often complained loudly about his neglect of his daughter. More than once, they'd exchanged bitter words. After one such confrontation, Miranda had feared her father would dismiss Sarah. But instead he had taken his daughter on his next trip.

Although Sarah hadn't approved of that either, she'd kept silent. Miranda had a feeling that Sarah cared deeply for the professor, perhaps even wanted to be the mistress of his house and mother to his little girl. But her father would never marry again. Despite his wanderings, he had loved her mother and her death had wounded him deeply. Miranda didn't think he would ever get over it.

Life was so unfair. It could bring people together in the oddest ways, just long enough for them to become involved . . . even loved . . . by another. Then, when it was least expected, something happened to separate them, leaving at least one with a broken heart.

Feeling a burning sensation in her fingers, Miranda realized the flame had eaten away the wood to just a few inches from her fingers. How much farther was it to the phosphor chamber? Although she tried to hurry her pace, each step she took sent pain streaking up her leg.

Rogue slid through the tunnel like a long drink of whiskey sliding down a thirsty man's throat. He could feel sharp rocks tearing at him, ripping his clothing, was aware of the tunnel widening slightly before closing in around him again.

How much farther was it, he wondered. Even as

he tried to hold onto the thin thread of consciousness, he felt the encroaching blackness threatening to smother him, knew if he allowed it to happen, he was lost.

His shoulder struck something hard with enough force that his breath whooshed out of his lungs. A red haze formed around his vision and he fought against it, beating at the rocks around him with his fists, barely feeling the resulting pain.

Suddenly, without warning, the protruding rock broke away and he slid through the gap. His lungs burned so badly they were at the point of bursting as the force of the water tossed him back and forth as though he were nothing more than a limp rag. His body struck against a rock and pain lanced all the way down his shoulders and back. It was dark, so damnably dark.

Rogue didn't know whether his vision was going or whether there was no light . . . but he did know he was drowning . . . drowning . . . drowning . . .

Rogue!

The cry was silent, coming from the heart. It caught Miranda halfway across the phosphor chamber. Her head jerked toward the river canyon.

Something was wrong! Rogue was in trouble. She knew it as well as she knew she still lived.

Her gaze slid toward the yawning mouth of the blocked tunnel, then slid away again. He wasn't there. She knew he wasn't. She looked toward the canyon again, feeling compelled to go to the river.

The river!

God, he was coming through the underground river!

Miranda knew it was so! Knew as well that he wasn't going to make it! Rogue was drowning. She knew it, could actually feel the water in her own lungs, could feel herself choking as though she were there with him. God, he *was* drowning!

Forgetting the pain of her swollen leg, she ran toward the cliff and scrambled over the side, mindless with terror, sending a shower of fallen rock before her as she slid, fell and crawled toward the river.

She landed at the bottom in a crumpled heap, drew in short gasps of air, then, calling on what little strength she had left, Miranda regained her feet and began to search the river.

Moments later, she found him.

The waterfall had flung him into the pool below and his limp body bobbed lazily in the current.

Miranda screamed. The sound started low, almost a growl, and raised itself higher and higher, full of pain, loss and anguish. "Rogue! God, no! Don't be dead! You can't be dead!"

Help him! an inner voice said. *Get the water out of his lungs! Force it out! You can save him if you try!*

"Yes," she muttered. "I can do it. Damn you, Rogue. You're not going to get away from me so easy. I won't let you."

Dragging him out of the water, she turned him on his back, turned his head toward her and began to pump his chest, intent on forcing the water from him. She was encouraged by the sight of the water gushing from his mouth each time she pressed against his chest. When the water stopped coming, she stopped pumping, but still he lay motionless.

Putting her face close to his lips, she felt for a breath of air. There was nothing. She tried for a pulse. Still nothing. Feeling hysteria rising inside of her again, she willed it away. "Damn you, Rogue!" she grunted. "You're not going to die! Do you hear me? I won't let you die!"

Pinching his nostrils together, she opened his mouth, and began to blow her breath into him. She blew rhythmically, breathing in a deep breath, blowing it into his mouth, sucked in another long breath, and blew into his mouth again. Over and over, she kept it up, pausing every few moments to pound on his chest, hoping to make his heart start beating again.

But it was no use. He continued to lie . . . motionless. God! He was gone!

Tears filled her eyes and trickled down her face, faster and faster and faster. A scream of agony began from somewhere deep within. It was a shriek that halted before it erupted when she heard a harsh rasping sound, as though air was being taken into a rusty pipe.

Her eyes jerked back to the man on the ground and she saw his eyelids flicker. He coughed and water gushed from his mouth. Rolling over, he began to cough out the water still in his lungs. And when he was done, he rolled over and looked up at the girl who knelt over him.

"Well, I'll be damned!" he swore. "It worked! It really worked!"

"You fool! You damned fool!" She struck him hard against his chest, not caring as he winced with pain. "What did you think you were doing?" She knew tears were streaming down her face, but she couldn't stop them from falling. "I thought you were dead! I thought you were dead!" Both fists were flailing him now as she continued to shriek the words hysterically. "I thought you were dead! I thought you were dead! Damn you! Damn you! Damn you!"

Twenty-six

Rogue wrapped his arms around Miranda and pulled her close against him. Although her blows hurt like hell, he knew it was hysteria driving her, knew as well the only way to combat it was to hold her against him until she calmed down. And, if truth be told, he didn't mind having her in his arms, not even a little bit. He was glad of the excuse to hold her so tight, but he wished she wouldn't cry so hard.

He stroked her tangled hair and whispered soothingly to her; all the while an ache was growing in his midriff as convulsive sobs continued to shake her frail body. "Don't cry, baby," he muttered. "Everything's all right now. Don't take on so." His stomach knotted; he was near losing control of himself. "Stop it, now. You've been a good girl, managin' to keep yourself alive in here. You got a lotta courage, baby. Just hold on to it a little longer. Don't fall apart on me now. Not when I need you most."

He tried for a lighter tone, knowing he had to

do something because her crying was an ache in his gut, each wrenching sob threatening his fragile control. "Just look at me, professor. I got blood all over me." Although he couldn't see the blood, he could feel its warmth trickling down the side of his face, realized the sharp rocks had cut his head. But the wound was of little concern to him at the moment. The pain in his head mattered not the least compared to the one in his chest.

He lifted her chin, trying to make her look at him, but her eyes were unseeing, her eyelids squeezed tightly shut. "Don't you care that I'm bleeding like a stuck hog?" he asked.

Her eyelashes flickered, then slowly lifted and she stared up at him through tear-drenched eyes.

Feeling as though he were on the right track, he continued. "The rocks in that tunnel nearly beat my brains out. We'll prob'ly have to rely on yours now. Come on, baby," he coaxed. "Are you gonna let me bleed to death?" She gave a hiccuping sob and her gaze narrowed on his forehead. Immediately, she sucked in a sharp breath, raised her hand, and he felt a feathery light touch—a mere brushing—against his skin.

She looked at her fingers, at the dark stain on them and went stiff, pulling herself out of his arms, leaving him feeling curiously bereft. Drawing a long, shuddering breath, she spewed out her feelings. "That was a d-damn fool thing you d-did. The rocks didn't b-beat your brains out! You didn't have any to b-begin with!"

She bent to tear a strip from the bottom of her riding skirt and his gaze fastened on her long, bare legs. Lordy, she had beautiful legs! His pulse quickened and his heart beat in double time, and although he knew he was staring, he couldn't make himself look away.

"Bend down so I can reach you," she ordered, pulling his gaze back to hers. "Now keep still while I see how bad it is."

He remained obediently still until she began to wipe around the wounded area, then he uttered a protest. "Take it easy, that's sore!"

"I don't wonder!" she snapped, seeming oblivious to his pain. "But don't expect any sympathy from me!"

"Sympathy be damned," he said, curling an arm around her waist and pulling her against him. "Sympathy is not what I had in mind."

"Let me go, you fool!" She struggled out of his arms. "How can you make jokes at a time like this. Even a fool wouldn't have tried a stunt like that!" Her overbright green eyes had darkened, reminding him of a West Texas tornado, and they held an equal amount of fury. "You were dead when I pulled you out of that r-river! You had stopped b-breathing, damn you!" Her mouth compressed into a thin line, her hands curled into fists and she looked as though she were going to start beating on him again. "I had to pump the water out of your chest. I had to beat on your heart and when that didn't work, I breathed air into your lungs."

Her voice was rising again and he grabbed her hands and uncurled her fingers. "I get the picture," he said gruffly. "You don't have to say any more."

"Nevertheless, I *am* going to say more. If I hadn't been here, then you wouldn't be alive now! And I nearly wasn't here!" She glared at him furiously. "I was in the tunnel, dammit! If I hadn't felt something was wrong and come back down here, then . . ."

His hands tightened over hers and his expression became hard. "You were where?" he asked.

Her face paled and a flush began to stain her cheeks. "I — I was in the tunnel — well, just out of the tunnel. I had to go there. I had to have — "

"You told me . . . promised me, that you'd go straight to the river and wait for me. You talk about me not havin' any sense! Good Lord, woman. Don't you know why we're in this mess?" He stuck his face to within inches of her own. "Hasn't all that schoolin' you took taught you anything? You must have noodles for brains! How could you even think about goin' off on your own like that when — "

"D-don't yell at m-me!" she stuttered. "I should've k-known you'd say something like th-that! I should have known you'd b-bring up my s-schooling." To his horror, her eyes had filled with tears again.

"Okay," he said gently, using his fingertip to

catch a tear that hung on the end of her dark lashes. "We'll forget about it. Okay?"

His eyes devoured her face, touched on her disheveled hair, the scratches on her skin, barely visible in the diffused light. "You've been through hell, haven't you, baby?"

She sniffed, lowered her lashes, and turned her head away as though she was ashamed of her tears. When she spoke, her voice was weary and strained. "It hasn't been all fun and games." He clutched her shoulder, intending to offer her comfort, but she shrugged it away and turned back to him. "You talk about me having no brains. I've heard it said it takes a fool to know one." She turned back to him. "You were outside, weren't you?" Although she made it a question, it seemed more like an accusation. "Why did you come through that river tunnel? You told me you were going to find the light-well."

Her words jolted his memory, brought back his sense of urgency. "Because it's raining like hell out there. I was afraid the river would flood the cavern." His gaze probed the watery depths. "Can you tell if it's any higher than it was?"

She followed his gaze. "No. It could be, but I really can't tell. It doesn't matter though. The canyon is too deep for it to make a difference. I don't think any river—no matter how big—could generate enough water to flood it."

For the first time, he let his eyes wander around the canyon. A good part of it was in shadows, the rest exuding a strange, diffused light, very similar to what he'd expect from thousands of fireflies. His eyes widened. "My, God! You weren't making any of it up!"

"Did you think I was?"

"Not intentionally," he said. "But I thought maybe you'd imagined it." He looked up, trying to see the ceiling, but such a feat was impossible. He shook his head. "You can't even see the ceiling. How could such a place exist without anyone knowing about it? Damn! It's like a world within a world. If it was lighter in here, and the ceiling was painted blue, you could almost believe you were under a sky."

Her lips twitched slightly. "If you painted the ceiling blue it would cover the phosphor rocks and make this place dark."

He grinned. "I guess you're right. We'll have to be satisfied with that color green." Rogue's eyes devoured her face, then returned to meet her gaze. Not for the first time, he was aware of her over-bright eyes, a fact that he'd put down to her tears. But the tears were gone now and her eyes, coupled with her flushed face, alarmed him. "Miranda? Are you okay?" He placed his palm against her forehead, found her skin hot to the touch and his heart began to pound with dread. Something was wrong . . . terribly wrong with her.

Colby had hesitated too long after Rogue rode

off. Although he'd ridden hard to catch him, he'd arrived at the pool just as the other man dove into the water.

"Rogue, don't!" he shouted, even knowing it was too late to be heard.

Springing from the saddle, he hurried to the pool, saw Rogue fumbling with the rocks around the hole. He knew that the instant the water took hold and sucked Rogue down, he would be hurting for air.

Dammit, the boy had actually done it!

Colby's shoulders slumped and a lump rose in his throat. He squatted back on his haunches and stared into the water, his gaze fixed on the place where Rogue had disappeared, unaware of the rain pelting his slicker. He remained there for long minutes that seemed like eons, waiting to see if Rogue came up again, but his waiting was in vain.

Still, he couldn't leave yet. When his legs began to tingle, he knew he had to move. His arthritic legs wouldn't easily accept such a position. His movements were automatic as he rose to his feet and stepped back beneath an overhang to get out of the rain.

Finally, becoming aware the rain had ceased, he heaved a sigh and mounted his horse and rode back toward Squaw Mountain. He wouldn't let himself believe Rogue was dead. Not yet. Right now he had to find that hole on Squaw Mountain. He'd get that girl out somehow or another, and pray to God that Rogue was with her.

He was halfway to Squaw Mountain when he saw two riders approaching. Recognizing them as Lazy R men, he pulled up his mount and waited for them to arrive.

"We got more trouble, Colby," the older of the two said. "The cattle's been stampeded again."

"Dammit! What in hell is goin' on?" Colby growled. He scowled at the two men. "If the cattle is stampedin' what're you two doin' here?"

"We got the stock under control again, but figgered we'd better come for you. We caught one of the men who helped stampede the stock."

"Then maybe we can find out what's goin' on now." He looked at the younger of the two. "Everbody else is up on Squaw Mountain. You ride there an' tell them to keep lookin'."

"What're they lookin' for?" the young man inquired.

"A hole," Colby said. "A deep one. You seen anythin' like that up there?"

"No. I sure ain't."

"Then look for one. I want the lot of you to keep lookin' until I say stop." Without another word, he reined his horse around and urged the bay forward. He had no doubts that he was doing the right thing. There were plenty of others looking for a hole that prob'ly didn't even exist. If it did, they would find it. If Rogue were lucky enough to make it through that river tunnel, they would find a way to rescue him, but he'd have nothing to come back to if Colby

311

didn't stop the rustlers.

It seemed to take forever before he reached the place where the cattle were being held. Although the stock were still restless, it wasn't anything out of the ordinary. And the herd didn't seem to be missing any cattle so perhaps they hadn't lost any during the stampede. He reined his mount toward a tree where he saw a small knot of men gathered. He recognized them as Lazy R riders. At his approach, they stepped aside, allowing him to see the man bound to the tree.

Colby studied the man—a stranger to these parts—carefully. He was about forty, with dark thick hair and eyebrows, a scrawny, rough-looking man with a blunt nose. "He done any talkin'?" Colby asked as he slid from the saddle.

"Not so far," said the nearest man. "But we ain't pushed him yet. Was waitin' for you to come." He looked past Colby. "I take it Rogue ain't back yet."

"You take it right," Colby grunted, not bothering to explain further. He strode to the bound man. "Now the way I see it, mister, you got two choices. You either talk to us, or you get drug by my horse."

The man's lips curled into a sneer. "You ain't gonna scare me with your threats."

"Ain't aimin' to scare you none," Colby said. "Just tellin' it like it is. One of you men untie him."

The outlaw's lips stretched into a thin smile.

"You just made a right decision, mister."

"Reckoned so myself." Colby waited until the man was unbound from the tree, but with hands still tied, then directed the nearest man to bring his mount.

"Whatcha up to?" the outlaw asked, his eyes darting frantically around the small circle of men, sliding over each in turn before returning to Colby.

"Take the rope offa my saddle and tie it around his wrists," Colby directed, ignoring the man's question.

"Hey!" the outlaw exclaimed. "You ain't really gonna drag me, are you?"

Colby ignored him, taking the other end of the rope and securing it to the big bay's saddle horn. He looped the reins over the saddle horn, keeping his back to the others, his ears tuned to the sounds of the outlaw squalling out his fear as he was dragged behind the bay.

"You can't do this," the rustler cried. "It ain't decent. You can't—" he gasped with pain as the rope was tightened about his wrists. "Wait a minute!" he yelled. "Don't do this! It ain't legal! It ain't— Wait! I'll talk! I'll tell you whatever you want to know!"

Colby turned back to him. "I ain't so sure you got anythin' I want to hear," he said. "We caught you in the act. If we get rid of you, then we get rid of the problem."

"No! You won't! Me an' the boys, we're just

hired hands. The same as Geraldo and his bunch was. We ain't interested in the stock. We just got paid for makin' trouble for you. For keepin' your boss busy so's he won't notice what else is goin' on."

"What do you mean by that? What else is goin' on?"

"I don't know. I swear to God I don't. We was hired by some fellers callin' themselves Smith and Jones."

"A likely story."

"It's the truth. So help me God. Those two fellers gave us a hunderd dollars apiece to keep you fellers busy. An' they said if we run off any stock, then we could have 'em."

Colby studied him beneath beetled brows. It sounded crazy. Why would anyone hire someone just to devil Rogue? Who would hate him that much? As far as Colby knew, no one. Rogue was well liked in the county.

"You ain't gonna drag me now, are you?" the outlaw whined. "You're gonna turn me loose, ain'tcha?"

Colby snorted. "Who said anythin' about turnin' you loose?" he asked. "A man would be a damn fool to do that."

"What're you goin' to do? I told you all I know."

"For now we'll lock you in a shed. Just until Rogue gets back. He'll be the one to decide what's to become of you."

Colby left the man and turned to look at the cattle. He turned back to the Lazy R riders. "Guess most of you better stay out here," he said. "They ain't no tellin' what'll come down next. Seems like somebody's bent on causin' a lotta grief for the boss. It'll be up to us to see it don't happen. Looks like it might be a heavy job too." He turned away again, his mind focused on the problem of finding the men who called themselves Smith and Jones. At least it was something that would take his mind off Rogue's fate.

Twenty-seven

Fear sent icy fingers through Rogue's chest, twisting into his guts, curling around his heart and squeezing it into a tight knot of pain. "You're burning up with fever, Miranda. How long have you been like this?"

"I don't know. I guess a few hours, or it might have been longer, maybe days."

"Do you know what's causing it?" His eyes narrowed on her head, slid down her face and neck, then back up again to meet her gaze. "Do you have an injury?"

"Yes . . . my leg. It's cut, and I . . . think it's bad. That's why I was in the tunnel, because of my leg."

"Let me see." He bent to examine her closer. "Which leg is it?" His palms ran over her left leg, found nothing more than scratches and reached for the other one.

"It's the right one," she said. "My calf."

But she needn't have answered. He'd already

316

spotted the trouble. His breath caught as he examined the swollen area around the wound, saw the telltale line streaking up the length of the leg. God, it was bad. Was he too late to save her leg? If it must be removed, could he bring himself to do it? And how could it be done? He had no instruments, nothing to use except his knife, which would be useless in such a case.

His gaze fastened on the wound itself. Thick rivulets of pus oozed from a dark slash about two inches long. At least it was draining a little of the poison away, but not nearly enough. The flesh around it was raised and looked puffy and swollen. There was a small amount of dried blood beneath the wound as well as some kind of white, grainy-looking stuff.

He ran his finger over it. Was it some kind of sand? It felt more like clay.

"It needs to be lanced," she said in a small voice. "And I have a little moonmilk in my pocket."

His eyes flicked up to hers. "Moonmilk?" Was she raving?

"Yes. I scraped it off one of the tunnel walls. There wasn't much of it there, but maybe it'll be enough to draw the poison out." She looked at him. "I'm so tired, Rogue, so damn tired. I don't think I can stay awake."

She had wilted considerably. He took her hand in his. "You must, honey. There are things I need to know. We've got to take care of that cut. It's full of poison. It'll have to be opened and it's going to hurt like hell."

"I know," she sighed, leaning back against the sand and closing her eyes. "But I think you'll have to do it by yourself." The last words were barely uttered before she gave a heavy sigh, then went limp.

"Miranda?" he muttered, patting her face gently. "Wake up, Miranda."

Miranda couldn't obey him; she didn't even hear him, because she'd lost consciousness. With a muttered curse, he tore off a piece from the bottom of his shirt and, after wetting it in the river, bathed her face, hoping she'd come to her senses. But it was no use. She didn't even stir.

He looked at the gash in her leg again. Perhaps it was for the best. He'd clean and lance the wound while she was out. Maybe that way, she could be saved some pain.

Taking off his wet shirt, he dipped it in the water and washed her leg. Then he left her to search for some wood. The pieces were small, but wood was plentiful. It didn't take long to gather enough for a fire.

Then, with his heart beating fast, he set about tending to her wound. He heated the blade of his knife to sterilize it, then using the tip, he opened the wound and watched the thick pus flow out. He was on the point of binding it when he remembered what she'd said about the moon-milk.

Searching through her pockets, he found a small ball of grainy white substance. It had to be the stuff she spoke of, but why had she gone for it? Since she'd had it on her leg, then maybe it contained healing properties.

Did he dare take a chance on it?

No, not yet. He'd wait awhile. See if lancing it had been enough.

Rogue felt bone-weary. He knew he could do no more for her at the time. After moving to higher ground, he built another fire and lay down beside her, pulling her against him. Then, having done all he could, he closed his eyes and went to sleep.

Rogue didn't know how long he slept, only knew that her shivering woke him. He jerked awake, his eyes on her, but she still slept. Her body was hot against him . . . was her fever higher than before? He looked at her leg. The calf was still swollen, angry-looking and the red line still stretched from the wound up to her thigh. Nothing had changed, unless it had worsened. He shuddered. He was helpless against blood poisoning. If only he had some medicine.

Suddenly she groaned and opened her eyes. "Rogue? Are you really here? It wasn't a dream?"

"No, it wasn't a dream," he said gently.

"I'm so cold," she said. "So cold." She looked at him with fever-glazed eyes. "Why is it so cold?"

"You have a fever," he said. "But don't worry."

Her eyes widened and for a moment they were clear. "My leg. I forgot to tell you. You have to

319

lance it, and you have to put some moonmilk on it."

"The moonmilk, Miranda. Is it a medicine?"

"Yes. Put it on my leg. It'll take the fire out. The moonmilk is cold, just like the moon. Put some on my leg, Rogue." She was rambling.

"Is that the only reason you want it on the wound, Miranda?" She'd closed her eyes again, but he shook her slightly until she opened them again. "You have to tell me, baby. What does the moonmilk do?"

"Cools it," she crooned. "Makes the fire go away. Put some on."

"It might be dangerous, honey. The stuff might make the infection worse."

"No." For a moment she seemed lucid. "Doctors in . . . France . . . used it. Has a drawing power . . . heals some way. Put it on for me. Can't do it myself." Her eyes closed again.

"Miranda, don't go back to sleep yet. Are you sure about the moonmilk?" He knew he was grasping at straws, but there was nothing else. And if there was even a chance the stuff—the moonmilk—would really help, he had at least to try. "Honey, where did you get the moonmilk?"

There was no answer. She had lost consciousness again.

Rogue took one last look at the girl and entered the first tunnel. During the past few hours she had gotten worse. He had only one hope left. He would have to find where she'd gotten the stuff she'd called moonmilk and to do so, he would have to leave her.

If Miranda had followed her father's methods, then she'd have taken the right tunnel. After lighting the small piece of candle in his pocket, he entered the tunnel and followed its length until it came to an abrupt end.

His heart jerked crazily. He was on the wrong track. Although he'd examined the walls carefully, he'd found no trace of the grainy claylike substance. He turned, on the point of retracing his steps when the light swept over a lighter stain on one wall. And the area looked as though it had been gouged with something sharp.

Bending closer, he lowered the candle, sweeping it over the spot. He could see residues of a milky sludge that had apparently leaked down one wall, seeping across the rocky walk and down onto the floor.

Scraping one finger across the substance, he felt the grainy texture, found it was the same as the stuff he'd found in Miranda's pocket. But there was so little of it, how could he possibly find enough to make the poultice he would need?

Miranda's lashes fluttered against her pale cheeks as consciousness returned. She opened her eyes and stared up into the diffused greenish glow that did little to chase away the shadows in the upper chamber of the phosphor cavern. Her brows pulled into a puzzled frown. What was she doing up here? She couldn't remember going to sleep, couldn't remember climbing the slope. The last she could remember, Rogue had—

Rogue! She struggled to push herself to her elbows, the better to search the chamber, but found the act took more strength than she could muster. "Rogue?" she called, her eyes darting back and forth, probing the shadows around her.

Only silence was her answer. Complete, absolute, silence. Her eyes misted with tears. Rogue wasn't here. It had all been a dream. *But he seemed so real, felt so real,* her heart cried. "A hallucination," she muttered in a strangely hoarse voice. "Nothing more than a hallucination."

He hadn't been anywhere near her. The blocked passage kept them apart. Her memory of being held in his arms was only her subconscious mind making her believe her dreams had come true. Nothing more.

Miranda shuddered with cold and realized it was a chill induced by high fever. Her injured leg must be worse; she could feel the blood throbbing through it, stabbing into her calf with each beat of her heart.

Blood poisoning. Just the thought made her blood run cold. She felt almost certain it was already too late to save her leg, probably even too late to save her life.

322

Rogue!

Her eyes turned toward the yawning mouth of the blocked passage. If she could reach it—if she could crawl down the tunnel, then perhaps she could hear his voice just one more time.

Gathering her strength around her like a cloak, she turned herself over and positioned her hands below her upper torso. Then, bunching her muscles, she lifted herself from the waist up and began the slow crawl toward the tunnel.

After determining that the moonmilk had leaked into the tunnel from somewhere above, Rogue dug his knife out of his pocket and chipped away at the rock near the ceiling. Although it had looked as if it were a harder type of rock, it turned out to be nothing more than limestone, and it gave easily beneath his blade. It took little more than an hour before he'd made a hole big enough to put his head and shoulders through.

Holding the ever-dwindling candle aloft, his lips twitched into a smile. He'd found a tunnel that went straight up. And, although the walls were composed of limestone—too crumbly to climb— his efforts had been rewarded. One whole side of the tunnel was covered with the milky sludge that Miranda had called moonmilk. And the stuff would be plentiful. If it did contain some mysterious healing agent, then she'd surely get well.

Suddenly, Rogue felt a sense of urgency. He dug several handfuls of the grainy substance out of the wall and shaped it into soft balls which he dropped into his pocket. Uttering a silent prayer that it would be enough to make a difference, he withdrew from the upper chamber and hurried back to the phosphor chamber.

His heart gave a leap of fear when he saw that Miranda was no longer where he'd left her. Moments later he found her, face down near the mouth of a dark tunnel.

Colby sat astride his mount at the base of Squaw Mountain, wondering if he'd made the right decision in calling off the search. He pulled a plug of tobacco out of his shirt pocket, bit off a hefty chaw, shifted it to his right jaw, then went back to studying the top of the mountain.

It had been a day and a half since Rogue had disappeared into the river tunnel. All of the daylight hours since that time Colby had had men searching for that damned hole, but they'd come up with nothing except those dug by varmints, nothing big enough, nor deep enough to be the hole the girl had spoke of. Therefore, it couldn't exist. Her mind had invented the whole thing.

He cocked his head to listen, heard the wind sighing through the cedars, heard the slight creaking of the branches, the sound of a mockingbird in the distance, but there was no human sound. No one raised a voice to call out for help.

Heaving a dispirited sigh, Colby spat a long stream of tobacco at the ground, shifted in the saddle, and after one last look up the steep side of the mountain, he urged the big bay forward.

He had no idea that had he been able to climb that steep rock, he'd have found what he'd been searching for. Perhaps ten feet above his head, located on a sharp incline, was a pile of rocks layered by heavy stones, held in place by a narrow ledge. Completely hidden from above by several cedars growing at the edge of a cliff were two boulder-sized rocks, resting a mere seven feet apart. And between those rocks, where they joined with the rocky cliff, was the opening they had searched for; an opening that would remain hidden from sight for years to come.

If he'd waited just a few minutes longer; if he hadn't been in such a hurry to meet with the experts who'd come to help in the search, he might've heard the voice that called out to him.

"Colby? Can you hear me? Can anyone hear me? I'm down here! I'm in the light-well!"

Twenty-eight

Needles of sunlight pierced Miranda's closed eyelids. Although barely awake, she was aware of the different situation, of the incredible brightness around her. Opening one eye, she squinted against the light, searching her memory for the reason it felt so wrong.

Suddenly, her other eye popped open as memory flooded over her. There hadn't been this much light in the cave! Had her ordeal finally ended? Was she outside in the sunshine now?

A face came between her and the sunlight; she recognized it immediately and her heart leapt with gladness. It was Rogue. He'd finally found her.

Running her tongue over dry lips, she verbalized her questions. "Is it over? Are we outside now?"

"I'm afraid not, baby," he said roughly, leaning closer to her. "We're just in the light-cave that you told me about." He wrapped his arm around her and pulled her to a sitting position, holding her there by his strength. "It shouldn't be long before we're out of here though. My men are up there looking for this place now and they won't stop until they find it." His palm cupped her chin and tipped her head toward him. "Are you thirsty? You've been running a fever for a long time."

Now that he'd brought it up she realized that she *was* thirsty—incredibly so. Her tongue felt swollen twice its size. "Yes," she replied hoarsely. "I need a drink of water." She tried to sit up and groaned. "I think every muscle in my body aches."

"I'm not the least bit surprised," he said. "You're covered with cuts and bruises. And that leg of yours was enough to lay anybody low. It's a wonder you were able to keep going."

Her leg. Was it still swollen? She looked anxiously at him. "Is my leg still bad? Am I going to lose it?" She flexed the muscles in her calf, glad that she could still feel it. That meant her leg was still attached.

"It's better," Rogue told her. "I don't know if it's because I opened it and drained out the poison, or if it's because of that stuff—the moonmilk—that you wanted on it."

"More than likely a combination of both," she said. "The moonmilk does contain a healing agent, but there was only a small amount of—"

"I found some more," he interrupted. "You were so insistent about it and I didn't know what else to do. The stuff may've been what pulled you through. For awhile I was afraid you were too far gone for anything to help—was afraid the leg would have to go." His voice was rough, ragged and uneven as though he'd been under a good deal of strain. "Thank God it didn't come to that."

The thought made her shudder. She didn't want to think about it. "You . . . you were going to get me some water?"

"Yeah, but it'll be better if I move you to the spring." He lifted and carried her as though she were a child, then with his cupped hands, he dipped water from the spring-fed pool and brought the cooling liquid to her mouth. She swallowed greedily, gulping handful after handful until her thirst was quenched.

Then, propping her up against the nearest wall, Rogue handed her a piece of baked fish.

"You've been fishing?"

"Yeah. Not in the ordinary way, though. I used my shirt for a net and scooped the fish out of the river. Baked it on a flat, heated rock. Now eat it up."

She did, and it tasted like ambrosia to her. When she'd finished eating, she lay back on the sandy floor, tired beyond belief.

They slept that night in each other's arms — to keep away the cold — Rogue had told her. It hadn't been necessary for him to justify sleeping beside her; it was an arrangement that suited her perfectly.

Held close against the warmth of his body, she slept long and hard, waking after sunrise to find him silently studying her. His voice was husky when he spoke, his words totally unexpected. "What have you done to me, Miranda Hartford?"

"I — what do you mean?" She stared up at him

wonderingly, taking in the craggy roughness of his unshaven face, aware of the strength contained in him.

"I never thought I'd feel this way about any woman . . . never thought it could happen to me."

"Wh-what way?" Her breath felt trapped, unable to jerk through the tightness of her throat, her eyes unable to move from his.

Instead of answering, he said, "A man could drown in your eyes, baby." He reached out and picked up a tousled curl, lifted it to his face and moved it slowly across his lips. "Your hair is like spun silk, so soft and shiny." He let the curl slide through his fingers, then traced her jawline with a callused finger. "I'm not much for fancy words, never have been, but a man needs pretty words when he looks at you. Nothin' else could even begin to describe you."

Miranda felt almost mesmerized by him, unable to move even if she'd wanted to . . . and she didn't. God help her, she loved this man. She didn't know how it had happened, didn't know when it had happened, only knew that it had.

She loved him!

"What do you think about when you look at me that way?" he asked gruffly, bending his head to kiss the tip of her nose. He moved slightly, his lips brushing against her earlobe, then she felt the wetness of his tongue tasting her skin. She shuddered as delightful tremors danced through her body.

Instinctively, her arms circled his neck and she moved her head until her lips were positioned beneath his. All he had to do was lower his head just the tiniest bit, and yet he hesitated. For a long moment they stayed that way, then he drew back slightly.

Unwilling to let him go, her arms tightened.

"You feel so good," he groaned. "It's been a long time since I held a woman in my arms. Too long."

Miranda didn't care about the other women he'd held, didn't want to hear about them. All she cared about was the here and now. Why didn't the fool kiss her? She had no experience with men but she'd been almost certain that he was going to. Hadn't she given him enough encouragement? What else could she do short of initiating the contact herself?

Darn it all! Why were women supposed to wait until the man had made the first move? But then, hadn't he already done so? Was he waiting for her to make the next one? No, she couldn't. He would think her too bold—like that other woman, the one he'd called Dallas.

She could do nothing except wait and she was feeling slightly foolish now. Perhaps she'd read him wrong. Maybe he didn't want to kiss her. He'd been silent so long, his eyes never leaving hers. What had he said about holding a woman? It had been a long time? "Why has it been so long since you've held a woman?" she asked.

The edges of his lips curled slightly and she could have sworn there was a twinkle in his eyes. "I haven't had the time—or the urge, in a long while."

"You're holding me now," she said. Actually, he had drawn back slightly so that she was holding him more than he was holding her, but he didn't contradict her.

"So I am." There was definitely a twinkle in his eyes . . . she was certain of it now.

"So you feel the urge — ?"

"Yeah, honey. I do." His arms gathered her close, his mouth dipped down and fastened on hers.

Miranda sighed deeply and closed her eyes. His kiss was heavenly, gentle and tender . . . all that she'd expected it would be. But what she hadn't expected was his mouth lifting from hers so fast. She'd wanted the kiss to last longer.

Feeling disappointed, she opened her eyes and stared up at him. Is that all there is to it, she wondered. Although the kiss had been wonderful, the effects hadn't been lasting. She wanted more . . . much more.

As though she'd spoken aloud, he said, "Are you sure?"

She nodded quickly, saw his head lower again and closed her eyes.

This time his kiss was different, hard, demanding. Her breath came in quick gasps as his hands smoothed over her flesh, touching here and there, covering the fullness of her breast, then moving down to follow the curve of her hips. She lay in the crook of his arms, almost melting beneath his touch.

God, it felt so good. She'd never dreamed this moment could happen, never dreamed she could feel this way. Was it always thus when a man kissed a woman? She didn't really think so. If it was, then

331

why had she never heard about it? Why wasn't it shouted from the rooftops? No. It must not be this way with everyone. This feeling must be reserved for only a special few.

Suddenly, he broke the kiss and lifted her hand to his mouth. He kissed the tips of her fingers and slowly worked his way to the palm, licking the sensitive hollow with the tip of his tongue. She uttered a tiny gasp of arousal, felt a tightening in her lower belly.

Immediately, he rolled her onto her back. Cupping the weight of one breast in his hand, he teased its peak into hardness with his thumb. His knee forced its way between her legs to spread them apart.

The soft bristles of his unshaven chin teased her skin while his warm male lips courted hers, exploring every curve and hollow with ease and sureness. The pulsepoint in her neck was pounding against his finger, betraying the rapid beat of her heart as her lips clung to his.

Her hands explored the flexible, strong bands rippling along his upper arms. She was aware of her breasts swelling to fill the large hands that cupped them in their palms while a thumb drew lazy circles around the rosy peak of her breast, hardening it into an erotic button.

The heat emanating from his hard flesh spread quickly through hers. This hot, languorous passion was something she'd never experienced before. It produced an everchanging array of sensations.

Each time her skin tingled under his caress she

wanted to stop the moment and hold it forever, but the heady male smell of him would crowd the sensation out, or she would taste the lazy fire of his kiss, forgetting everything else until another sensation overwhelmed her.

Shaping her hips to the thrust of his, she tried to ease the throbbing ache that was slowly consuming her. His hands fumbled at her clothes and she felt cool air against her skin as he stripped them away and tossed them aside.

Then, removing his own garments, he returned to her, fitting her body against his nakedness. Fastening his lips over hers again, while at the same time parting her legs, he probed at the center of her thighs.

Miranda felt a momentary pain as he entered her womanhood, thrusting quickly into the moistness within. The heat of his body seared into her and she felt a quickening rush of blood through her veins.

A tightening low in her stomach twisted her into a coiled knot of need and she whimpered low in her throat, moving against him, silently urging him to satisfy some nameless need within her, to release her from the unbearable tension that held her in its grip.

Unable to wait longer, she surged against him, heard his quickly drawn breath and found a satisfaction in it. She moved again, felt the hardening of the shaft within her and then he was moving, drawing her into a whirlpool of raging desire that reached down into her innermost depths and threatened to drown her in rapture. Faster and faster he moved, plunging deeper and deeper, until the world seemed to explode in a dazzling display of lights that illuminated every corner of her being.

When it was over, they lay together. Tiny beads of perspiration dampened her skin as she gazed at him, her eyes soft and wondrous.

"I never dreamed it could be like that," she said.

His strong lean features wore a bemused look. "Neither did I," he said gruffly. He bent his head and placed a kiss on the tip of her nose. "Did I hurt you?"

She laughed huskily. "No. Did I hurt you?"

He gave a short burst of laughter. "That's the first time a woman's ever asked me that question."

She blushed wildly. "I just meant . . . you have cuts and bruises on your body and we — we — " She broke off and struck him lightly on the shoulder. "You know what I mean."

"Yeah, and no, you didn't hurt me." He smoothed a hand across her cheek and pushed away the tendrils of hair clinging to her damp skin. "I wish I didn't have to leave you."

"Leave me?" Alarm streaked through her. "What do you mean?"

He gave her a crooked smile of regret and rolled away from her. "I have to go find us some food," he said. "Or would you rather starve?"

"I've tried that, thank you. And I didn't like it very much." She felt curiously bereft, deprived of the warmth of his body. "Are you going back to the river?" A foolish question, she realized. Where else would he get food?

"Yeah. We're lucky there's fish in it."

"Let me go with you," she said.

"No. You better stay off that leg for awhile."

"I wish you didn't have to leave me alone." Her voice was forlorn.

"I do too. But we can't live on love."

"Love?" Her breath caught in her throat as her gaze held his.

"Did you think it was something else?" he asked softly. "What other name would you put on what we just shared?"

"I—I didn't know how you felt—what you were thinking—" Her voice broke and she couldn't go on.

Snatching her against him, he smoothed back her hair and held her gaze. "Now you do. I love you, Miranda Hartford. Make no mistake about that. This feelin' I have for you couldn't be anything else."

"And I love you," she whispered, her eyes misty with happiness. "I never thought I would love a man, Rogue McClaren, but I do love you."

"Just hold that thought until I get back," he said. "Then I can do something about it."

"You won't leave me alone very long?" she asked anxiously.

"No. You won't ever be alone again. I promise you that, baby. I'll always be here for you."

Another quick smile and he was gone.

Colby rode the bay toward the ranch house. He

felt almost certain the rustler had told him the truth. But who the hell were Smith and Jones. The names were obviously phony . . . common names like those tacked onto a couple of gents who didn't want their real names thrown about.

Why in hell would they want to cause trouble for Rogue? The rustler had said it was to keep Rogue and his men so busy they wouldn't notice what was going on, but what could be happening that Rogue wasn't supposed to know about? For the life of him, Colby couldn't figure it out.

Dammit, why hadn't he moved faster? Why hadn't he stopped Rogue from goin' into that hole? He'd been too slow, hesitated just that little bit too long before goin' after him. It was a damned crazy idea, so crazy that maybe it had worked. Colby hoped to hell it had. Otherwise, Rogue was probably dead.

Unable to consider such an event, Colby turned his attention to Squaw Mountain. Had he made a mistake in calling off the search? Was there a hole up there somewhere?

He sat alone at a table in the shadowy corner of the room, a well-dressed man, wearing a pin-striped suit that spoke of affluence. But it was a false impression that he gave. At the moment he had very little money to speak of, but he expected that to change soon. If things went as he planned, and they seemed to be doing so, soon he would be a man of great wealth.

With a sardonic smile, he reached for the glass on the table in front of him, hefted it, swirled the contents, then tipped his head back and swallowed the fiery liquid, feeling its heat all the way down to his stomach. Although it was only cheap whiskey, he pretended it was the finest burgundy, knew that soon he would have a well-stocked cellar of his own. All he had to do was wait . . . let a little time pass, enough to do the work he required. That was all. He didn't have to lift his hand again. Time would take care of everything for him.

Heaving a sigh of contentment, he poured himself another drink and leaned back in his chair and allowed his eyes to slide around the room, to finally rest on the dark-haired girl in the flame red dress who'd offered to keep him company earlier.

Perhaps later he would take her up on her offer. Right now, he would allow himself the luxury of contemplating the wealth that would soon be his for the taking.

A shriek of laughter from across the room drew his attention and he saw a slightly tipsy barmaid barely escaping from a customer's fumbling hands.

For some reason, the sight stiffened his lower body and he looked at the dark-haired girl again. A man had stopped beside her and the two were talking together. Perhaps, the man in the pin-striped suit decided, it was time to call her over. Before another bought her for the night. His lips curled into another smile. After all, he told himself, there'll be plenty of time later to contemplate his golden future.

Twenty-nine

"You won't ever have to be alone again . . . alone again . . . alone again."

As the words echoed over and over in her mind, Miranda took comfort from them. Already, too much of her life had been spent alone. Granted, Sarah — their housekeeper — had been there for her, but the woman was filled with bitterness toward the professor and, perhaps even without her knowledge, that same bitterness had colored her relationship with Silas Hartford's child.

Unwilling to dwell on the past, Miranda focused her thoughts on Rogue and what had passed between them. "Rogue McClaren," she whispered, rolling the name across her tongue. "What a beautiful name." She giggled. "What a beautiful man. Rogue McClaren. *Mrs*. Rogue McClaren." She smiled, liking the way that sounded. "Miranda Hartford McClaren." Yes. It definitely sounded right.

With her lips curling into a smile, she reached for her clothing, twisting her leg as she did so and

338

wincing as pain lanced through her calf. With a worried frown, she bent to examine it, found it was still covered with the grainy claylike sludge Rogue had applied.

Although it was still swollen and sore, she could see at a glance that it had greatly improved; there was no longer the telltale streak running up her leg and the color—where before it had been a purplish red—had faded now to a bright pink.

Again, she reaching for her clothing, pulled her undergarments toward her. Her nose wrinkled distastefully as she studied the soiled material. Her clothing would certainly benefit from a good wash.

She became aware of the gentle, tinkling sound the waterfall made as it fell over the limestone into the pool below. Her gaze caught and held on the verdant ring of fern growing at the water's edge. How could such a thing be? she wondered. Didn't fern need sunlight to grow?

Crossing the light-well, she knelt beside the pool and looked straight up, examining the hole high above her, and realized that the afternoon sun could very well reach the fern . . . indeed, it must do so, otherwise the fern would not be able to grow.

Miranda looked into the pool and frowned at her reflection. Her hair was dirty, hanging in tangles. In fact, she looked frightful. How could Rogue stand to look at her?

Did she dare bathe in the pool? She didn't want

to spoil their drinking water. Her gaze lifted, searched for—and found—the source of the water. It trickled out of the limestone, covering an area about three feet wide and falling into a hollowed-out rock, not unlike a deep bowl, before spilling over to make the waterfall.

A puzzled frown creased her forehead. Water falling at such a rate would surely need an outlet. She searched the bottom of the lower pool, judging its depths to be two or three feet. Perhaps water escaped through the bottom of the pool and traveled to some other place in the cavern.

Unable to find the answer, and too eager for a bath to let it bother her overmuch, she stepped into the water, allowing the cooling liquid to wash against her heated calf. Lord, it felt good, and it was much deeper than she'd imagined. The absolute clarity of the water made the depth deceptive.

Miranda waded deeper, felt the water swirl around her hips . . . felt the stones on the bottom poking at her bare feet, and still she went on. She was about four feet from the edge—in the center of the pool—when the water reached her midriff.

She shivered when the water lapped against her breast, paused momentarily, then went on. Another foot and she was at its deepest point. The water covered her shoulders, lapping at her chin.

Taking a deep breath, she went under, soaking her hair thoroughly, rubbing her hair vigorously between her palms, wishing she had some shampoo. When she'd done the best she could with it, she waded out again, combing her fingers through the tangles, then turning her attention to her soiled garments.

When she'd finished, Miranda donned her wet clothes, knowing they would dry faster on her body, then stretched herself out where a narrow beam of sunlight played across the rocky floor. Heaving a sigh, she allowed herself to relax; her eyelids fluttered down, then closed. Another moment and she was fast asleep.

Miranda didn't know how long she slept, only knew that she was still alone. She sat up and looked at the yawning mouth of the tunnel. How long had Rogue been gone? Had something happened to him?

Her heart jerked as panic washed over her. *Stop it,* a silent voice said. *Your clothes are still damp. He hasn't been gone very long.*

She tried to forget her worry, told herself to think of something else . . . think about the way he'd looked when he admitted his love for her. He'd seemed almost as bemused by what had happened between them as Miranda was.

The whole thing was still hard for her to believe.

She remembered the feel of his arms around her, the feel of his naked skin—so warm and silky—against her own. It had seemed so natural, so right, the culmination of their love . . . a lovely, beautiful, passionate coming together.

Her body had a sudden urge to feel him against

her again and she uttered a sigh of longing. How long must they wait before they could make love again? She felt a sudden heat in her cheeks, realized she was blushing. Was she wanton, wanting him again so soon?

She sighed again and turned over to stare up at the sky above her. As she watched, the greenery that edged one side of the patch of blue moved back and forth, swaying beneath a gentle wind.

Miranda strained her eyes, narrowing them on the hole so far above her. Rogue had said his men were searching for it. Would they find it? She listened hard for the sound of voices, heard nothing save the tinkling of the waterfall . . . and that in itself seemed strange.

She frowned, wondering why she found it so.

Suddenly she knew, and with the knowledge, she felt alarm. She hadn't heard the cricket chirruping for a long time. Where was he?

Anxiously, she searched the light-well, crawling on hands and knees, searching the shadowy areas, but there was no sign of the cricket. She felt a stab of guilt as she realized Peter must have been left behind.

Remembering the salamander, knowing he'd make a quick meal of the injured cricket, she scurried toward the tunnel. Although Rogue had taken the torch, Miranda felt sure she could find her way through the passage without a light. And since she hadn't the foggiest notion how long it would take Rogue to catch a fish, she knew she dared not wait until he returned. The cricket's life could be hanging by a thread. And, although she might already be too late to save it, she knew she'd at least have to try.

Rogue, having caught the big catfish that Miranda had been after, was on his way back to the light-well. He crossed the large cavern, his eyes skimming across the phosphor walls as he marveled at the way the phosphor combined with the crystals to make the soft diffused glow.

Suddenly, his eyes caught on a darker patch on the wall and he bent closer to examine it. Instead of the greenish color he'd come to expect, there was a streak of gold running through it.

Pyrite. His lips twitched as he recognized the ore. It had fooled so many people with its glitter that it had been labeled "fool's gold." Rogue, having seen both the real thing and the fake, knew the difference.

"Too bad it's not real," he muttered. "I might've been a rich man."

He'd never thought much about wealth before, never really wanted it. But when he thought about Miranda, and their future together, he knew he wanted enough money to give her everything she desired. Would she be happy living on a ranch? God, he hoped so, because now that he'd found her, he intended to keep her.

Something moved in his peripheral vision and

his gaze narrowed on it; a cricket crawling out from beneath a rock. When he saw the insect was missing one hopper, he realized it had to be Miranda's cricket and reached for it.

Unhesitatingly, the little creature climbed up on his finger, clinging tightly with the remaining five of its tiny legs. He was on the point of entering the tunnel when he heard the sound of footsteps.

Miranda kept one palm pressed firmly against the passage wall as her anxious gaze probed the darkness ahead. Surely it couldn't be much farther to the phosphor chamber.

The darkness became lighter, almost a shadowy gray. Miranda heard the sound of footsteps a moment before she saw the torch and the bulky shadow beyond it.

"Rogue?" she called. "Is that you?"

"Who else? What're you doin' in here? I told you to wait for me." He sounded angry with her.

"I'd forgotten all about Peter," she exclaimed. "When I couldn't find him, I was worried."

"No need," he said, coming nearer. "I found the cricket in the phosphor chamber. He's in my pocket." He stopped beside her, studying her in the flickering torchlight. "When are you going to learn to stay put?"

"Are you angry with me?"

"Not that. Just worried about you. You shouldn't be running around without a light."

"I've been through here before. I knew I could make it."

"Nevertheless, you've gotta learn to stay put." He looked at her leg. "Does it hurt?" he asked.

"No. But it's still swollen enough to slow me down."

"Another reason you shouldn't've left the light-well. Besides, one of us needs to stay there in case somebody stumbles across the hole at the top."

"I'd forgotten they were looking for it," she said. "It won't take us long to get back there."

When they reached the light-well he tossed the fish onto the floor and turned to her. "Sure you're all right?"

"I'm sure," she said, her gaze narrowing on the fish. "That looks like the catfish I've been after."

"Too late," he said. "It's my catch."

The catfish would probably weigh at least seven pounds and would give them a goodly supply of fish oil. She uttered her thoughts and he agreed with her. "We'll eat our fill and dry the rest for later." He eyed her ragged skirt. "We'll use my shirt for torches. That skirt is as short as it's going to get."

"Don't you like to see my legs?" she teased.

"Yeah," he said. "And so would my men."

She blushed furiously. She hadn't thought about that.

He gathered up several dried branches and set about making a fire. Then, leaving her warming near the flames, he searched the cavern for a moment, returning to her with a long flat stone about double the width of his hand. Placing four stones of a like thickness around the flames, he placed the flat stone on them to heat.

Despite the thinness of the cooking rock, it took a long time to heat. When it finally felt hot to the touch, he laid slabs of fish on it and soon the aroma of cooking fish teased their nostrils.

"There's some watercress growing at the edge of the pool," she said. "Would you like some with the fish?"

"Anything green would taste good," he replied. "Show me where."

Together, they gathered a double handful of the watercress and carried it back to the fire. He tested the fish, pronounced it done and hurried to wash a couple of flat rocks to use for plates.

"I feel bad letting you do all the work," she said.

He smiled at her. "You need to stay off that leg as much as possible. When we've finished eating, I'll get some more of that stuff that you call moonmilk. We'll keep some here in this cave so there'll be plenty at hand when you need it."

She relaxed against a log—it had obviously fallen from the hole above them, probably blown in by a severe storm—and watched him scoop a portion of fish on a clean rock and hand it across to her.

Feeling famished, she ate greedily, finishing off a large portion of fish and half of the watercress.

Then, wiping the fish oil off her mouth, she sighed with contentment. "Maybe it wouldn't be so bad to stay here for the rest of our lives," she said.

"Don't even think that," he said. "We're gonna get outta here. Make no mistake about that. If Colby don't find this cave in another couple of days, though, then I reckon we better start lookin' for another way out."

"I'll do whatever you want," she said. "It doesn't matter to me as long as we're together."

He pulled her into his arms and held her close against him. She felt his breath, warm against her ear, and she snuggled closer. "I never thought I could feel this way, Rogue. Not ever. It's the most wonderful feeling in the world . . . loving and being loved."

"Yes," he agreed softly. "It's good."

"Only good?"

"More than good."

"How much more?"

He laughed softly and bit the lobe of her ear. "How can you measure a feeling?" he asked. "Should I say bigger than this cave? Bigger than my ranch?"

"Still not big enough," she said. "I'm so full of love for you that it's beyond measure."

"I am too." His reply was followed by a long, passionate kiss.

Miranda wrapped her arms around his neck and pulled him closer, pressing her body harder against him. A flame flickered to life deep within her body and slowly began to burn, leaping and swaying, dancing like a performing ballerina. Her breath quickened, her fingernails dug into Rogue's shoulders and he responded immediately. With a muttered groan, he tore away her clothing and pushed her back against the ground. A moment later his lips were all over her, cutting off her breath, teasing, tantalizing, until Miranda thought she would go crazy from wanting. Then, when she thought she could stand no more, he entered her, and again, she was lifted to heights she'd never even dreamed possible.

Thirty

The late afternoon sun trailed golden fingers across the wall as Miranda—her naked body still flushed with recent passion—lay in the circle of her lover's arms.

High above them a light wind played through the trees, sending the fresh scent of cedars into the light-well to tease their nostrils with its fragrance.

Miranda's gaze locked with the rancher's. She felt warm and protected, surrounded by his love. Only one thing dimmed her happiness. The uncertainty of her father's fate.

"What's wrong, baby?" Rogue asked, pushing an errant curl from her eyes. "What's botherin' you?"

"I was thinking about Poppa," she said. "I wish I knew what happened to him. One way or the other." She meant whether he was dead or alive but couldn't bring herself to say the words.

Apparently Rogue knew what she was saying

though. "Quit worryin' about him. Your pa can take care of hisself. Right now he's prob'ly settin' up there with Charlie cussin' a blue streak 'cause I let you get into this mess."

"Do you really think so?" She wanted desperately to believe it. "I can't understand why he went off like that. He should've stayed near the landslide."

"He'll tell you all about it when we get outta here," he said huskily. "But you gotta believe he's okay, baby. The people I sent for—those cave experts from Austin—they would've found him by now."

"I hope so. I have to believe he's safe."

"He is," Rogue said firmly. "And soon we're gonna be too."

"I feel safe now," she said. "With you beside me I can take whatever this cave has in store for us."

"This cave can't think, honey. We can. Just keep that in mind. We'll be out of here soon."

"I know." Although she wasn't so sure about that, she said the words he wanted to hear. "Rogue?"

"Hmmmm?"

"Will you tell me about Dallas? Why do you hate her so much?"

His arms tightened momentarily, then slowly relaxed again. "Yeah. I guess you oughtta know what happened." He expelled a long sigh, then began to speak. "Dallas was the wife of my brother, Michael. She was rich, spoiled and—" he gave her a long look, "—had some kind of college degree."

She quirked an eyebrow. "Is that why you disliked me? Because of my education? You thought that made me like her?"

"She looked somethin' like you too. Had the same color hair and that look that you have."

"What look?"

"The way you look at a man, babe. The way you're lookin' at me now. Most girls, they kinda flutter their eyelashes and look away, like they're afraid to meet your eyes. An' the older ladies look at a man like they think he's needin' a good feed . . . you know, like a mother does, but you an' Dallas . . ." His voice trailed away as though he wondered if he should continue.

"Yes?" she asked, tilting her chin to hold his gaze. "How do I look at you?"

His lips quirked. "Like you're doin' now. Like you're the same as me. Like you're gonna knock my block off if I say somethin' you don't like."

"And that's it?" Her eyes widened with surprise. "You disliked me because I looked at you as an equal?"

"It's that suffragette stuff," he explained. Suddenly, his eyes narrowed. "You *don't* believe in it, do you?"

"Certainly I do."

His chest lifted in a sigh. "I'm afraid we're gonna have some trouble over that."

"Why should there be trouble? What's wrong with the women's movement?"

351

"I want a wife, Miranda. Not a do-gooder. Not someone whose life revolves around some damn cause. Not someone like Dallas."

She felt curiously hurt. "And you believe I'm like that? That my life revolves around the women's movement? Aren't you prejudging me?"

"Yeah." He looked long into her eyes. "I guess I am, babe."

"And you've decided you don't want me?" She tried to pull away but his arms tightened around her.

"No. I want you. Make no mistake about that. I'm just givin' you fair warnin' that I'm not my brother. I won't let you tie me up in knots and run circles around me. If you're expectin' anything like that, then you better put it out of your mind right now."

"Consider it done," she whispered. She felt so happy to know that he wanted her, even though he suspected her of being the type of woman he'd so carefully avoided, that she decided to forgive his way of saying it. At least for the time being. "And to put your mind at rest, I'll tell you that, although I agree women should have equal rights, I've never been much of a joiner. I'll be more than happy to make a home for you and our children."

"Children?" he questioned, his eyes soft and gentle.

"You do want children?" she added.

"Yeah. Dozens."

"Maybe five or six to start with."

352

"Then another five or six to go on with."

"You're going to keep me busy."

"That's the plan."

"I'd like to meet your family, Rogue. I always wanted to be part of a family."

"I'll share mine with you until we have our own."

"Dallas as well?"

It was said as a joke, but instantly, his expression became dark. "You won't be seein' Dallas. She's not part of the family."

"She left your brother?"

"She killed him!"

Miranda gave a sudden gasp of horror. "Killed him? I'm sorry. I had no idea. What happened, Rogue?"

"I don't like to remember, babe." His eyes were dark and brooding. "Michael was a gentle soul. He didn't like to see anything suffer. He was only six years old when he decided to become a doctor."

"He was a doctor?"

"No." His voice was bitter. "He didn't get that far. Because of Dallas."

"What happened?" she asked again.

"He went away to college. Met Dallas. Married her and came home again, all in the space of one year." His tone was clipped, harsh, his hands tightened into fists.

"He changed his mind?"

"She changed it for him. She was older than

him, had already been there three years when they met. She graduated one day and they married the next. Then he brought her home. I don't know what she had in mind, but ranch life didn't appeal to her. She wanted to go home—back to New Orleans. They did for awhile, but Michael had no training. The only work he could find was in a factory. It didn't pay enough for Dallas to live the way she wanted and her family—they'd wanted her to marry money—had washed their hands of her, so they came home. From that day forward she made Michael's life a misery." His voice became bitter. "Michael thought she'd be okay when they had children, kept wonderin' why they didn't. One day, during an argument, she told him why. They'd made babies all right, but she knew about herbs, had mixed up somethin' that made her lose 'em."

"Oh no!"

"When Michael found out, he was like a wild man. He went to the nearest saloon and, before the night was over, he was dead."

"How?" She squeezed the word through the lump in her throat.

"He got into a fight with a drifter. I think he wanted to die. Maybe Dallas didn't actually hold the gun, but it was her finger that pulled the trigger."

She could actually feel the pain tearing at him. "I'm sorry," she whispered. "So sorry."

He buried his face in the curve of her neck. She

354

stroked his hair, her heart aching for him. "Did you really think I was like that?" she whispered. "Did you really think I could deliberately end a life we had created?"

He pulled back and cupped her face in his palms. "Charlie said I let Dallas color my thinkin' and I guess I did. No. You couldn't do nothin' like that. You care too much about life, honey. The way you saved that damn cricket proves that."

Peter. Where was he? She hadn't heard him for some time. "Have you seen Peter?" she questioned.

"Yeah, babe. I put him over there." He pointed at the nearest wall. "Last time I saw him he was still climbin' toward the sunshine."

Her brow wrinkled with worry. "Do you think he'll be safe out there?"

"Yeah. He'll be fine. He's prob'ly already found a lady friend. Just like I did."

"I hope he has. He deserves to find a mate. Peter helped me hold on to my sanity. He provided me with company when I needed it badly."

"I know. And I'm grateful to him."

A flicker of movement far above them caught her eye and she froze, her gaze riveted on the hole. Was it the cricket she'd seen?

"What is it?" he asked, following her gaze. "Did you see something up there?"

"I thought I did." She watched for a moment longer, but saw nothing, other than the limbs edging the hole. "Maybe it was Peter."

"No." He sat up straighter. "You couldn't've seen the cricket that far away."

"Then perhaps it was the wind blowing the leaves across the hole." She moved out of his arms. "I'm sure I saw something. Maybe we better get dressed."

"Why?" he asked lazily, pulling her back against him and cupping her right breast in his palm. "I like you this way."

"That's obvious," she said struggling in his embrace. "But just suppose we're about to be found."

"All right," he said gruffly, releasing her. "You made your point. I'll let you put your clothes on."

"Thank you," she said dryly. "I appreciate your consideration."

"Don't be smart!" he said, smacking her on the backside. "I just might change my mind." His eyes narrowed on the hole again and he frowned. "Maybe you did see somethin' after all." He stood up. "Hey! Is anybody up there?"

"Rogue!" she protested. Grabbing up her clothing, she raced for the mouth of the tunnel, hiding herself there while Rogue continued to yell.

"Colby! Is that you? We're down here!"

There was no answer. No sound, except for the wind sighing through the branches and the merry tinkling of the water as it splashed into the pool.

Miranda listened intently as she donned her garments, continued listening for a reply that never came.

"Guess there's nobody up there," Rogue said gruffly. "I thought, for a minute, I heard somebody talkin'." He eyed the limestone walls, then ran his palms over the nearest one. "There's no way we could climb this," he said. "The walls would crumble if we tried." He looked toward the sky again. "It's gettin' late. We better start thinkin' about leavin' here."

"Leaving?" She looked at him with puzzled eyes. "Where would we go, Rogue?"

"I don't know, honey. There's a couple of tunnels we haven't checked out yet. We oughta at least try 'em."

"But if we leave here—what if they come while we're gone?"

"They'll come down and look for us. Colby knows what to do." He squeezed her shoulder. "Don't worry about it none. We're gonna get outta here."

"I know. And I'm not worried. I just thought it would be better to stay here." Her eyes pleaded with his. "There's fish in the river. We'll have plenty to eat. And there's lots of wood here for a fire. Maybe we'd better just wait until Colby finds us."

"No." He shook his dark head. "We have to keep lookin' for a way out, Miranda. We can't leave it all up to the others."

His insistence made Miranda realize he thought they wouldn't be found. "All right," she said. "We'll go on if you think we should."

357

His smile sent her fear into hiding. Whatever happened, they were together. "Since we're going to leave, maybe you better get some more fish . . . just in case we're gone for awhile."

"Might be a good idea," he agreed.

"I'll have to make another torch. There's plenty of wood for the base, but I think my skirt's about used up. I could tear some strips off the bottom of my shirt—"

"Use mine," he said. "And maybe you could weave some kind of carrying basket out of the fern."

"Why didn't I think of that?" she said, her eyes skimming over the fern growing in such abundance around the pool before returning to him.

"Two brains are always better than one," he said with a grin. "Have you ever done any weaving before?"

"No," she replied. "Have you?"

"Yeah. You gather some fern while I build a fire. The smoke might help the searchers find us."

"I never thought of that."

"Like I already said, two brains are better than one." He wrapped his fingers around a thick limb, dragged it to the fire and began breaking it into shorter pieces.

Miranda gathered an armload of fern, then joined Rogue beside the fire. He had a stack of wood nearby, ready to replenish the flames when the wood burned down.

After showing her how to weave the reeds together in the shape of a narrow basket, he gave her a hard kiss, told her to stay put and then he entered the tunnel. With a casual wave of his hand he left her alone.

Thirty-one

The air was moist, hot and heavy; it plastered Miranda's hair against her head as she stumbled through the tunnel, hurrying to keep up with Rogue. They'd been walking for hours, and although she felt exhausted, she was unwilling to complain.

The floor slanted downward at such an angle that negotiating it had become awkward. Although Miranda had become doubtful about going farther, she kept silent, allowing Rogue to make that decision.

He'd have to make it soon though. The torch was almost gone. Soon there would be nothing to light their way except the small piece of candle he carried in his pocket. It wouldn't last through the journey back to the phosphor cave.

Miranda wondered if Rogue had forgotten, wondered if he was even aware how close they were to total darkness. He'd said two brains were better than one. Was she making a mistake in not speaking out?

"Rogue," she began. "Maybe we should — "

"Hush!" he commanded. "Listen for a minute."

Holding her breath, she did exactly that. Her heart picked up speed when she heard the subtle roaring that meant there was water somewhere up ahead.

Wrapping his fingers around her wrist, he hurried forward, dragging her with him. "If I'm not mistaken, that's another underground river. It just might be a way out." He held the torch aloft, stepped forward, then gasped, "Oh, God!"

Miranda felt the tug on her wrist, realized he was losing his balance and knew instantly what had occurred. It was like reliving the nightmare. It happened so fast there was no time to react. The torch lit his way as he fell.

Without a thought for the consequences — knowing that anything was better than being left alone again — she flung herself into the abyss.

Instantly, she felt a disembodied lightness as the shadows closed around her, wrapping her in a smothering embrace. Miranda was totally unprepared for the jarring blow on her buttocks, just before she was enveloped by the sweet darkness . . .

The late afternoon sun shone down on Colby as he guided his bay around the grove of cedars, his eyes alert for signs of trouble. When he reached the screen of willow trees edging the banks of the Colorado river, he paused momentarily to study the ground around him. Except for a few tracks left by wild game, there was nothing.

His nostrils flared, taking in the odor of sweating horseflesh mingled with his own less-than-fresh scent. He'd been riding since dawn and it was hotter than hades. Had been since the rain two days ago. Even now the air hung around him like a wet blanket, heavy and damp and suffocating.

He untied the black kerchief that circled his neck, and he wiped his face with it. Then he retied it, fastening it so the knot hung at the back of his neck. He could stand the heat — he'd lived with it for more than sixty years now. He could stand the dirt — it went hand in hand with the life he lived. What he was having trouble tolerating was being unable to find the men responsible for rustling Lazy R stock.

Pulling a pair of field glasses from his saddlebags, he scanned the area for any sign of movement, but there was nothing. He was at the point of putting the glasses away when a motion to the left made him pause and swing the glasses toward it. He saw a rider in the distance, moving eastward, toward Squaw Mountain.

Immediately, Colby changed directions.

Replacing the field glasses in his saddlebag, he forded the river and followed the rider at a distance, unwilling to be seen until he knew the man's identity.

Since the rider made no effort to hide his tracks, there was a good chance that he knew he was being followed. Colby's narrowed gaze swept the area, searching out the places for possible ambush. He didn't intend to be taken unawares.

His hands clutched the reins as the bay picked a cautious path up the hill, over the ferns and lichened granite. When he reached a point which gave him a clear view of the terrain, he waited, silently peering through the field glasses into the distance.

His patience was finally rewarded. A rider, maybe half a mile ahead of him, emerged from the trees, moving at a fast walk. He looked neither to the right or to the left, just rode straight ahead. From his stance in the saddle, the loose way he held his body, it was clear he was unaware that he'd been spotted.

Keeping under cover until the rider disappeared into the cedar thicket at the base of the hill, Colby waited. Then, nudging the bay in the flanks, he began his descent. Once on the valley floor, he picked up speed, still marking the passing sign and checking in all directions. It shouldn't be much farther now. He'd have to be careful.

For some reason, he wished he wasn't alone.

Rogue felt the wetness close around him, then something struck him hard against the back. God! Could it be Miranda? Had he pulled her down with him? He reached out, his fingers brushing human flesh. It *was* her! His fingers circled her wrist, pulling her to him as they continued to sink, the water pressure becoming more intense with each passing moment.

When he felt a solid surface beneath his feet, he kicked hard against it, immediately surging upward, pulling Miranda with him. When he broke the surface, he held her against him with one arm and used the other and his feet to stay afloat.

The force of the water fought with him, trying to tear the frail body from his grip. He heard a mighty roar ahead, then his head struck solid rock. He went under, fought for a moment for his senses, then came up gasping, still clutching his precious burden in his arms.

Suddenly, as though the river had vomited them out, Rogue felt sand beneath his body. He shifted his hold on Miranda. She seemed limp, almost weightless. "Miranda? Are you okay?" His heart gave a jerk of fear when she didn't answer.

He shook her hard. "Miranda! Say somethin'! Speak to me, baby!"

She gave a coughing groan, then coughed again. He felt water spewing from her mouth with each hacking cough. "That's the way, honey," he said. "Get it outta your lungs." He held her loosely, allowing her room to breathe while she continued to cough, expelling water from her lungs, until finally, her tremors passed and she lay still.

"Miranda?" His voice was soft; he was determined not to frighten her. "Are you okay now, honey?"

"Yes." Her voice was curiously husky. "I — I think so." She began to cry. "I thought I'd l-lost you again."

"Shhh. Hush up now," he said softly. "You didn't lose me. We're still together. Wherever the hell we are. At least we're still together."

She sniffed, then asked, "Where are we?"

"I don't know."

His fingers fumbled for the matches in his right pocket, withdrew the waterproof packet and unwrapped it. Pulling out a match, he struck it against the side of the box. It didn't light with the first strike . . . nor the second one. "Dammit!" he swore softly. "They can't be wet." He struck the match against the box again and it flared suddenly, then began to burn. The flame was erratic, bending this way and that, as though encountering puffs of wind.

Quickly, he cupped his other hand around the flame. "There's a draft in here somewheres," he muttered. "Reach into my left shirt pocket and get the candle out."

Hurriedly, she dug into the pocket and pulled out the candle. "Here," she said.

"Hold the wick to the match," he muttered.

After the candle was lit, Rogue shielded the flame with his hand and turned his attention to his surroundings. He was standing in waist-deep water a few feet from the riverbank. Located to his right was a tunnel from which water poured into the cavern. His eyes slid to the other side of the chamber, perhaps fifteen feet distant, found another tunnel there — where the river made its exit.

His eyes measured the distance from the ceiling to the water. Five or six feet. He waded toward it, carefully shielding the flame as it bent sideways in the draft.

"Do you think we can get through there?" Miranda asked, following closely behind him.

"I don't know," he said. "We're fixin' to find out."

They reached the mouth of the tunnel and Rogue tried to gauge the depth of the water with his eyes. The water was too murky. "Hold the candle for a minute," he said, passing it across to her.

"What are you going to do?"

"I'm going to check the depth." He waded downstream a few feet, felt the water slide up his chest until it reached his shoulders. Then, suddenly, the bottom dropped away and he went under.

He kicked his feet and broke the surface again.

"Rogue!" Miranda's panic-stricken voice echoed through the cavern. "Are you all right?"

"Yeah." He swam toward her until he felt solid rock beneath his feet. "Looks like we'll have to swim if we go that way." He looked back at the tunnel again. "How good are you at swimming, babe?"

"Good enough to keep from drowning . . . at least . . . I guess it would depend on how far I have to swim."

"Me too." He took the candle from her and waded ashore. "Let's see if there's another way out of here."

366

Miranda followed him to the bank. "This chamber is only about twenty feet in circumference," she said softly. "Notice how porous the walls are? Probably more so than in the tunnels. That accounts for the chamber. The limestone wore away faster at this point. She looked at him and although her expression was calm, her voice wobbled slightly. "We seem to be having a bad run of luck. It may take us a while to get out of this one."

"You may be right, babe. But don't ever think we're stuck here. We *will* get out." He smiled down at her, feeling amazed that she could still be so brave about the whole thing. She was such a frail little thing and yet, she was unaccountably strong. Another woman would have berated him for his carelessness. But not her. Not his Miranda.

Although Miranda tried to put on a brave front, she really wasn't feeling courageous. Rogue thought it had been courage that made her take the leap into the chasm with him, but that wasn't it at all. No. It had been fear that drove her . . . fear for his life and the fear of being left alone again.

"What do you think, Rogue? What should we do now?" She felt good that she'd managed to keep the fear out of her voice. Her gaze searched the small cavern again, for perhaps the fourth time. But nothing new came to light.

"I don't know yet," he said, cupping her chin in his palm. "But we'll think of something, professor.

You're a smart young lady. Between us we should come up with something. And it's not really that bad. At least we don't have to backtrack. We're already together and every move can be forward."

"Thank God we are together!" She followed Rogue across the chamber, saw him bending toward the shadows. "What did you find?" she asked.

"Wood."

"Great!" she said. "We can have a fire and dry out our clothes."

"I wasn't planning on burning the wood," he said. "It looks like there's several pieces lodged in this crevice." He began to pull at the wood, but it was stuck hard in the crack in the wall.

"Hold this." He pushed the candle at her, then used both hands to tug. Suddenly the wood came loose and he went sailing across the cavern.

Miranda, feeling suddenly terrified that he would be carried into the water, dropped the candle and made a dive for him. Suddenly the flame went out, leaving her in total darkness. "Rogue, where are you?" she asked.

"I'm still here," he said. "What happened to the candle?"

"I dropped it." Her voice was shaky as she swept her hand across the floor, felt the candle momentarily before it rolled away. "There it is." She moved again, scooped up the candle an gave a startled yelp as hot wax burned her flesh.

"Take it easy," Rogue said. "There's nobody in here except me and you."

"I forgot. I have the candle now if you have a match." She heard him fumbling for his matches, a moment later they had the candle burning again. She laughed uneasily. "Sorry about that. I guess I'm nervous."

He nodded, but seemed to be paying little attention. Instead, he studied the wood he had pulled loose then returned to the crevice and dug out another piece.

"Rogue?"

"Ummm?"

"If we aren't going to burn the wood, then why do you want it?"

"I have a plan. If we can find enough wood, we can make a raft to take us out of here."

"Do you really think that's possible?"

"I'm not sure." He turned to look at her. "We don't know how far that river goes, honey. We might not be able to swim all the way. If we have a raft we wouldn't have to swim." He smiled wryly. "It's at least worth a try."

He was right. Dripping some hot wax on the floor, she secured the ever-dwindling candle and hurried to help him. Her eyes caught on the top of the tunnel . . . and widened. There was a ledge up there that ran as far as she could see. Not really a ledge, she silently corrected herself, but more of a narrow bridge made of rock with an empty space of perhaps three feet above it. And caught in the cavity were three good-sized limbs.

"Rogue," she said, "Look at the top of the exit

369

tunnel on your left. There's a cavity above the ceiling."

"I know. But it won't help us, honey. It's too thin to support our weight."

"That's not what I'm talking about," she said eagerly. "Don't you see the limbs caught up there? Wouldn't they help with the raft?"

He turned toward the tunnel. "You're right," he said. "They would." His brows pulled together in a frown. "I'm not so sure we can get 'em out though. They're too far over the river."

"Yes, we can. We'll use the fishing line." She pulled the roll of line from her pocket and handed it across to him. "See if you can make some kind of hook for the end."

He studied it for a long moment, then said, "You got a hairpin?"

She shook her head. "No. Sorry. It won't be that easy."

He grinned at her. "Guess I'll have to rope it then."

Miranda thought he must be joking. But it seemed he meant it. Making a big loop, he weighted the circle with pebbles, spaced an equal distance apart, then tossed it toward the nearest limb. To her complete amazement, he managed to get the line around the limb. In an amazingly short time all three limbs lay at their feet.

While Miranda helped him tie the limbs together something tugged at her memory; something about the wood being lodged in the ceiling. When the an-

370

swer came to her, she wished she'd remained unaware.

The limb could only have gotten there in one way. The chamber must have been completely flooded.

Miranda looked down at the cavern floor. Was it her imagination or was the water already rising? Feeling the need to hurry, she said, "I'll lash what we already have together while you gather some more." Although she tried to keep the fear from her voice, she didn't quite succeed.

After a quick glance at her, he looked at the river and his eyes narrowed, moving back and forth as though measuring the distance. "Maybe you better get the limbs and let me do that," he said. "Looks like we're gonna need them real quick and I can do it faster."

Realizing he was right, she rose and began to search for more of the dried wood, hoping they could get enough together to carry them safely out of the cavern which would very soon become a deathtrap.

Thirty-two

Colby pulled the big bay up in the cedar thicket and wrapped the reins around a sapling. Then, senses alert, his eyes searching the area around him, he made his way through the tangled mass of cedars growing near the base of Squaw Mountain.

He was halfway through the grove of trees when he heard a horse whinny. The sound was followed by hoofbeats, headed away from him. Muttering a curse for leaving his own mount behind, Colby was on the point of backtracking when he heard the sound of voices.

His brows pulled into a heavy frown. Apparently the rider he'd followed had met someone. Had the meeting been planned? If so, who was it? And why? There was something definitely wrong here.

Colby's gaze lifted beyond the cedars to Squaw Mountain, rising two hundred feet above him. Why in hell had they chosen this place to meet? The whole thing had a peculiar stink to it . . . much like finding a polecat in the woodpile.

He crept closer, carefully avoiding the dry roots

and fallen branches that might give away his presence. The voices were more distinct now and they had a familiar ring. Colby circled a plum thicket, making sure to keep enough shrubs between himself and whoever had stayed behind.

Barely twelve feet separated him from the clearing when he stopped behind a thick cedar, parted the branches and peered through.

Immediately, Colby's eyes widened. Hell! He knew them all right. At least, he knew two of them. Jory Cavanaugh from the Flying W, and Trace Carradine — who owned the neighboring Bar C ranch — squatted on their haunches, in earnest conversation with a third man.

His age was hard to determine — maybe late twenties — and he was dark and unshaven. His build was lean and rangy, and his dark stringy hair — looking as though it could use a good wash — hung past his collar. Colby, judging by the man's rough appearance, figured him for a drifter.

"I ain't so sure about that, Mr. Jones," the drifter was saying. "You say it'll be easy, but that ain't the way I heard it."

Colby's gaze skittered back and forth, quickly covering the area in the clearing as he looked for another man . . . someone the drifter had called Jones. But, other than the three men and their horses — tethered nearby — the clearing was empty.

"Who said different?" Trace Carradine inquired, arching a sandy colored brow. "Who have you been talking to about this?"

"One of the boys run into what was left of Geraldo's bunch. He claimed Geraldo was dead, said that old man—McClaren's foreman—and some of them Lazy R riders found 'em just shy of Turkey Creek. Killed Geraldo and a couple of others. That true?"

"What if it is?" Carradine asked, pinning the man with his gaze. "Are you going to let an old man scare you?"

"I ain't stupid," the man said. "And neither was Geraldo. Now he's dead."

Carradine's lips curled into a sneer. "Geraldo only thought he was smart. He could've made it if he'd used his head. I talked to one of his men. He told me what happened. Geraldo underestimated McClaren's foreman. He should never have stopped when he did."

"Whatever the reason, he's still just as dead," the man pointed out.

"Nothing worth having is without risk," Carradine said. "Now make up your mind. Are you in or out?"

The other man looked uncomfortable. His eyes shifted away from Carradine's. "Like I said—"

"You better think carefully about your answer, mister," Carradine warned softly. "Mr. Smith and myself . . . well, we don't like loose ends." He straightened slowly, his hand hovering a mere two inches above his holster. "And if you're not with us, then I'm afraid you'll be considered a loose end."

"I didn't say I wasn't with you," the man said

hastily, rising to his feet. "I was just after advice about how to go about the whole thing."

"I guess you're just going to have to figure that out by yourself," Carradine replied. "I don't care how you go about it, but I want McClaren's bunch kept busy." His eyes were stone cold as he held the man's gaze. "Now, as far as I'm concerned, this conversation is finished."

"Yessir," the other man replied, backing slowly toward his horse. "Me an' the boys are gonna take care of everthin'." He threw a quick glance at Jory Cavanaugh and spoke again. "It was nice seein' you again, Mr. Smith. Real nice."

Cavanaugh didn't reply. Instead, he remained silent as he'd done throughout the entire conversation.

Colby remained where he was, puzzling over the conversation he'd just heard. It was obvious now who Smith and Jones were. But what in hell were they up to? Dammit! Colby silently cursed himself for not having had the foresight to bring someone with him. If he hadn't been alone, he could've found out right now what in hell was going on.

His eyes were hard as they studied Jory Cavanaugh. He'd known Jory since Rogue had inherited the Lazy R and, although he'd known Jory was ambitious, he'd never suspected him of dishonesty. Although Colby was usually a good judge of character, it seemed — in this instance — he'd been wrong.

Now Trace Carradine was another matter. Colby

had never trusted him. He'd come to the Lazy R a few months after he'd bought the Bar C Ranch and introduced himself to Rogue. Colby, he'd ignored. The foreman had suspected he was considered too far beneath Carradine's station in life to be noticed.

Colby's lips twitched. Maybe Carradine was already learning that he should have taken more notice of the foreman.

Cavanaugh strode to the base of the cliff and peered at a plum thicket growing there. What in hell was he looking for anyway? Colby wondered. Surely he didn't think he'd find plums at this time of year!

"Make damn sure it's covered," Trace growled.

"Nobody gonna find it," Jory replied, turning to face the other man. "Hell, it's been here for ages an' nobody's been the wiser."

"That old saddletramp found it, didn't he?" Trace said coldly.

"Yeah. But he was looking hard down here. The way I heard it, he was down here looking for a pocket watch he'd dropped off the cliff. Said the watch was special—had belonged to his pa—so he wasn't about to stop looking until he found it."

"I heard the story too."

"I know. I was just making a point. A man would have to be looking long and hard to find it. And he wouldn't do that unless he lost something or already knew it was here."

"Maybe so," Carradine replied. "But I think I'll put a man to watching this place."

"Suit yourself." Cavanaugh strode to his horse, a big black gelding. "You going straight home?"

"No. I've got business in Llano." Trace joined Cavanaugh beside the horses. "Let me know if anything develops around here."

They mounted and rode away.

Colby puzzled over Carradine's words. What exactly did he mean? What did he expect to develop around here? He waited until the sound of hoofbeats died, then shoved his way through the cedars intent on inspecting the plum thicket.

Carradine and Cavanaugh were trying to hide something. But why use the Lazy R to do so?

A few minutes later he found the split in the face of the cliff.

Deep within the cavern Miranda watched the water level rise. Slowly, but surely, the water engulfed the rocky floor and crept up the walls.

Miranda watched it all happen with a desperation that threatened to choke her.

"Oh, God, Rogue, hurry!" she cried, feeling the water lap against her thighs. The current was strong and she fought against the pull of the water. "It's getting deeper and deeper. It won't be long before the water will completely flood the chamber."

"Just a few more minutes, babe," he said grimly. "I'm working as fast as I can."

He wove the line over and under the logs, lashing them as tightly as he could, with nothing more than the thin line to work with. All the time he worked, Miranda wondered if he was wasting his time. It was a makeshift raft at best, made up of fishing cord and flimsy logs. It might very well come apart the minute they climbed on it.

The cold water lapped higher, sending a cold chill against her breasts and swirling upward. Oh, Lord have mercy! It had risen at least another four inches! "Rogue! It's taking too long." The water covered her breast, crept toward her shoulders. "Maybe we should forget the raft!" Her voice was almost squeaking with fright. "Rogue!" Her fingers frantically circled his upper arm, tugged at him. "We've got to get out of here! We're going to have to swim for it!"

"No, babe. It's too late for that. The current's too swift!"

"But we have to do something!" she cried. "Don't you realize what's happening? This chamber will fill completely up. We won't be able to breathe!"

"I'm nearly finished. Just one more knot. Put your free arm around my neck and hold on tight," he said harshly. "No matter what happens, Miranda. Don't let go!"

Without hesitation, she transferred the candle to her left hand and slid her right arm around his neck. She had no intention of letting him go. Whatever happened . . . whether they lived or died, they would at least be together.

She uttered a silent prayer. *Please, God! Let it*

work. Let the raft hold us up. Don't let it end here. Not when I've only just found him.

The water had reached her chin by the time Rogue tied the last knot. "Don't let go," he grated. "I'm going to try it!" He pushed at the raft, and Miranda felt it give beneath their combined weight. "It won't take both of us," he said. "I want you to climb on it."

"No!" she snapped, tightening her grip around him. "I won't leave you here."

"I don't figger on stayin'!" he snapped. "I'm goin' to go with you all the way. But the raft won't hold both of us. I'll hang on to the side."

Miranda could no longer touch bottom and the water was lapping at Rogue's chin. She looked at the river tunnel. There was still a foot of clearance there, but if they waited much longer it would be gone. Their only chance was to go downstream and hope they would find another large chamber like the underground canyon. But still she hesitated. "I'm afraid we'll get separated," she cried.

"We won't." He was treading water now, trying hard to hold the raft steady while the current tried equally hard to swirl it away from them. "Grab the raft, Miranda. Then get on it."

Realizing he wouldn't budge until she obeyed, Miranda gripped the raft with one hand and tried to pull herself aboard. The wood sunk several inches beneath the water . . . the candle hissed and sizzled and the flame was snuffed out, leaving them in total darkness. "It won't hold me," she cried, shoving the candle deep in her pocket. "It's useless!"

"No!" he snapped. "Don't panic! We'll both hang on the sides."

She felt him fumble with the raft, then one arm tightened around her waist. "I've got a good grip on both you and the raft," he said. "Now, honey, listen to me. I know you're scared, but we're gonna come through this okay. Hold to the raft. Hold on tight. And, whatever happens, don't turn it loose. You hear me?"

Miranda nodded her head, then, realizing he couldn't see her response, said, "Yes. I hear you. And I'm holding as tight as I can."

"Good." The raft swayed, moved farther into the river and Miranda knew he must be shoving it there. "Still okay?" he asked.

"Yes," she replied. "S-still okay." She wanted to say more . . . wanted to tell him she loved him, but before she had a chance to do so, the current grabbed them, flinging them forward at a tremendous pace. The raft grated against something— Miranda guessed they'd struck the rock wall around the mouth of the tunnel—paused momentarily, then slid slowly to Miranda's left.

Panic engulfed her. The river tunnel was narrow . . . they might miss it completely. The current might keep them swirling around the chamber until it was completely flooded.

God, they would drown in here!

Suddenly, the raft canted sideways, then moved a few more feet to the left. Limbs grated against rock, then moved again . . . slowly at first, then faster. Faster and faster the raft swirled, seeming to be caught in a whirlpool.

"Rogue!" Miranda cried, her head spinning dizzily.

"Hang on!" he shouted. "Here we go!"

And they did. With a speed that seemed unreal, they entered the tunnel and sailed away into the blackness.

Thirty-three

The sun hovered just above the western horizon, hanging there like a huge fiery ball in a painting of red and lavender, reminding Colby the day was fast coming to a close. Already shadows were lengthening, spreading through the rocks, creeping around the cedars and shrubs, and, although Colby knew he didn't have much time, he was unwilling to leave until he discovered what Trace and Jory were so intent on keeping hidden.

The crack he'd found was a small one. Maybe four feet high and three feet wide, easily hidden by the plum thicket.

Dropping to his knees, Colby peered inside.

It was a deep crack, angling straight into the mountain for perhaps twenty feet or so. Much to his surprise he could see all the way to the end. He didn't stop to wonder why, only felt relief there'd be enough light to make a search of the place.

He was on the point of crawling inside when the wind gusted, blowing loose dirt and sand into Colby's eyes. "Dammit," he muttered, his eyes stinging with pain.

Blinking rapidly, he tried to rid himself of the offending grit. His eyes teared, his vision became blurred.

Suddenly, he heard a soft sigh and stopped dead in his tracks, the hair rising at the base of his neck.

He wasn't alone. There was someone else in here.

Dammit! He couldn't see anyone.

With one hand hovering beside his holster, he wiped his eyes and peered into the shadows. There was nothing . . . nobody in here except himself. He was just getting jumpy, scared of his own shadow.

Disgusted with himself, he moved on, his knees digging into the thick mat of leaves lining the floor. Where in hell had they come from? He pushed them aside, searching for whatever was hidden there, determined to find it. He was almost at the back of the opening when he stopped, cursing himself for a fool. It was too damned light in here!

He looked up . . . and sucked in a sharp breath. The ceiling had completely disappeared. Instead of a hole, he was in a crevice. High above his head was a crack — more a split in the rock — that went straight to the top of the mountain.

Elation set his heart to pounding. Had he found the place Miranda spoke of? The place Rogue called the light-well?

The water was cold, almost icy, numbing Miranda's fingers as she clung desperately to the raft while the river—a howling maelstrom of fury—tried to tear her loose.

There were times when she thought it might succeed. Minutes passed . . . seeming like hours. God, how long *had* it been? How could they survive this? Where would it all end? *Would* it ever end?

Maybe it would be best if she ended it herself. All she had to do was let go and—

Even as the thought surfaced, she shoved it aside. She couldn't do anything so foolish. Why had she even entertained such a notion? She'd been in worse situations before. All she had to do was hang on and they'd get out of this one.

Suddenly, she heard the crunch of wood scraping against rock and felt Rogue's arm tightening around here.

"The raft is caught on something," he said.

Miranda realized he was right. The raft had stopped its forward flight. Instead, it bobbed and swayed in the water, seeming to be held in place by some kind of obstruction. It dipped slightly, pushing beneath the water, then bobbing up again as it moved sideways.

"I can touch bottom," Rogue said, his hand lifting slightly.

"Don't leave me!" she cried, her voice sounding hollow. "Leave me, leave me . . ." the panic-stricken voice came out of the darkness, sending shivers of fear trailing down Miranda's spine. *Goose!* she silently chided herself. *It's only an echo.*

"Rogue?" Her voice was calmer. "Did you hear the echo? I think we're not in the tunnel anymore."

"My thoughts exactly," he said from beside her. "I think you can stand now, honey. I'm going to light a match so we can see where we've got to."

He was right. When she straightened her legs, they brushed against rock. She stood there, shivering while he fumbled for the matches. "They're nearly gone, aren't they?" she asked.

"What's nearly gone?"

"The matches."

"We've got a few left, honey. Don't worry about it."

But Miranda did worry about it. What were they going to do when they no longer had a light?

Suddenly, the match flared, sizzled and flared again. She held her breath, willing the match to stay alight, watching the flame flicker erratically, bending this way and that as it fought to survive in the drafty river tunnel.

Her gaze hurriedly swept the shadows around them, mindful of the need to familiarize herself with their surroundings before the match burned out. As she'd hoped, they were in the bend of another large cavern.

The match sputtered, fizzled, it wouldn't last much longer.

"Come on, babe," Rogue said roughly. "Let's get outta the river while we can see where to go."

He looped his fingers around a pole, dragging the raft behind him as he waded to the river bank, leaving Miranda to hurry after him. Her gaze moved quickly around the chamber, taking in the high ceiling—a fact which caused her great relief— dripping with formations, before her eyes went sweeping lower again. She was conscious that Rogue was dropping the raft, just before the light went out, leaving them in total darkness again.

"Rogue?" Something puzzled her.

"It's okay, honey. Don't worry about anything. I'm right here beside you."

"Rogue, would you light another match?"

He took her hand in his. "Honey. I don't think I should."

"Why?"

"We're nearly out," he admitted. "There's only a couple left in the box."

Her jaw clenched tightly. She'd known they were running low. They had to be. But she'd seen something, was almost sure she had—something that seemed out of place.

Suddenly, she remembered the candle and dug it out of her pocket. "I have the candle, Rogue. Would you light it for me?"

"Babe, we have to save the matches." He pulled her against him, wrapped both arms around her. "Does that make you feel any better?"

"Yes," she admitted. "But I still want you to light the candle. I saw something across the cavern. I think we ought to check it out."

"What did you see?"

"I'm not sure, Rogue. It looked like some kind of

material. I'm not sure. I saw it just before the light went out."

"Your mind was prob'ly playin' tricks on you, honey. It was makin' you see what you wanted to see."

"Why would I want to see material?" she asked crossly.

"Settle down," he said, patting her back as though he were soothing a child. "Where did you see it?"

"In here."

"Yeah. But which direction?"

She thought about it for a minute. "I think it was to our left. Maybe ten or twelve feet. There were several formations there and I thought I saw something under one of them."

"Okay. We'll check it out. But we won't light the candle just yet. Tuck it back in that pocket — no! Give it to me. You might lose it."

Although her mouth pressed into a thin line, she handed the candle to him. She'd managed to keep it safe until now without losing it.

Holding tightly to his hand, she moved with him through the darkness, stepping carefully across the floor, ever mindful of the dangers that could be hidden from them.

Suddenly he jerked to a stop. "Dammit!" he muttered.

"What is it?" she asked.

Instead of answering, he released her.

"Rogue?" Miranda could hear the panic in her

voice. "What is it? What's wrong? Why did you let go of me?" She was afraid to move, remembering the way the floor could give way to a chasm so swiftly.

"Stay where you are, babe," he said gruffly. "I'm going to light the candle."

He was going to light the candle when he'd insisted it must be saved? Why? Her heart fluttered wildly while she waited in the darkness. What had he found . . . or thought he'd found, that warranted such a measure?

She held herself rigid as he struck the match then held it to the small piece of candle. Rogue's large frame blocked her view as light flickered around them, chasing away the nearest shadows.

Miranda's gaze swept quickly around the chamber, dwelling on the calcite formations hanging from the ceiling like icicles, dropping to the popcorn-shaped crystals puffed out on the walls, then moving over the stone shelves shaped like birdbaths that marked the surface of a pool that had long since receded.

Jerked out of her study by a movement, she watched Rogue kneel beside something on the floor. Her breath caught in her throat, threatening to choke her as she saw what he was bending over.

Although it seemed nothing more than a bundle of rags, Miranda knew it was more. She couldn't tell whether it was male or female—it could be either—only knew that it had once been human. The way it lay—so still, crumpled like an old bag of rags—made her aware that the figure—whoever it had been—was beyond help now.

Horror seeped through her. Lord! Don't let it be Poppa! Not like this! Not here! Even as she uttered the silent prayer, she realized the figure was smaller than her father. But who could it be? Had someone else accompanied Poppa and Roger in the cavern?

She didn't want to look at the empty husk, but found herself unable to tear her eyes away. "Is—is it Poppa?" she asked fearfully.

"No. It couldn't be," he replied. "Whoever it was has been dead for years."

Relief flowed through her, mingled with a terrible sadness that whoever it had been had come to such an end. "Can you tell how he—or she—died?"

"Looks like it was a man. And his right leg is broken. Prob'ly couldn't go any farther. More'n likely starved to death," Rogue said grimly. "We'll never know for sure."

"I wonder how he got here?"

Rogue delved his hand into the dead man's right pocket, pulled out a pocket knife and a few coins, then tried the other one and found a few more coins. Miranda turned away while he searched the corpse, finding it distasteful, and yet, knowing it must be done.

"Thank God!" Rogue's voice spun her around again.

"What is it?"

"He had some matches left," Rogue replied. "Don't know how he managed that. There's no sign of a lantern or candles." He looked at the box of matches in his hand. "Now why would anyone have a whole box of matches left if he didn't have any other means of light?"

Thirty-four

Miranda, realizing Rogue had forgotten about the necessity of conserving the candle, hurried toward a twisted limb that had long ago been cast out of the river. She broke it into several smaller pieces and stacked them together.

As though Rogue knew what she was about, he strode over and knelt to light the wood. The wood caught quickly; he snuffed out the candle and shoved it into his shirt pocket, then squatted beside the fire, adding wood to it as she found it.

There seemed to be a plentiful supply, most of it dry and hard as though it were almost at the point of becoming calcified. Miranda kept her eyes turned away from the dead man as she continued to search for wood, keeping well to the opposite side of the chamber from the corpse.

It was purely by accident that she saw the dark shadow of a tunnel several feet beyond the dead man.

"Rogue?"

"Yeah." He looked up at her. "What is it, babe?"

"Look over there!" She pointed to the spot. "Maybe that's how he got here!"

"Well, I'll be damned!" he said, rising to his feet. "You just might be right."

Stepping gingerly around the corpse, she hurried to the place. As she'd suspected, it was a tunnel. "There's some scrapes on the floor," she said. "Like someone's been through here." She turned to look at him. "It may be the way out!"

"It just might be at that." He knelt to peer into the hole that was chest-high to him. "It's certainly bigger than a lot we've been through." He looked up at her. "We're going to need some light, babe." He looked at the dead man. "Maybe if we use the shirt . . ."

"Rogue? It doesn't seem decent."

"I know. But we've got no choice. Bring me some more of that wood. I saw some roots. That should work even better."

She did as he asked and soon he was twisting the roots together then covering them with strips torn from the shirt.

"Wish we had some more fish oil," he said grimly. "I'm not sure how long this thing is going to burn."

"Maybe it won't have to burn long," she said. "Maybe it's only a short way to the surface."

"If that was so then why didn't he—" Rogue gestured with his thumb—"crawl out of here. No,

392

babe. I think we're still quite a way from the surface."

After lighting his makeshift torch, he shoved it into the tunnel. The flame bent sideways. "Look, babe. The flame is bending that way. There has to be a draft flowing through here." He crawled into the tunnel. "Stay close behind me," he said.

Holding the torch before him, Rogue crawled into the hole and moved quickly down the passage. Before they had gone fifty feet the ceiling began to lift until they were able to walk upright through the passage.

They would have missed the air tunnel if Rogue hadn't been watching the flame so intently. Suddenly it bowed in the other direction. He stopped and went back a few feet, searching the rocky walls until he saw a narrow crevice, not more than six inches wide. It was the air tunnel. And there was no way they could use it to escape.

Despair flooded over Miranda at the moment of realization. They were still trapped. There was no way out for them.

"Don't worry," Rogue said. "The draft was coming from there, but that don't mean much. This might still be a way out."

"You don't mean that. You're just saying it."

"I do mean it," he said firmly. "That man came in here somehow. And it was more'n likely he did it through this tunnel."

Realizing he was right, Miranda followed him down the passage, hurrying to keep up with him.

They rounded a corner and Rogue came to an abrupt stop.

"What is it?" she asked hurriedly, her heart racing with dread.

"Stay back!" he commanded shortly.

"What did you find?" she asked, peering around his shoulder, totally unprepared for what she saw.

He sat against the cavern wall, his head tilted forward as though he were only resting. "Poppa!" she whispered, feeling as though she were going to pass out.

"Don't look, babe," Rogue said harshly.

But she ignored him, moving on rubbery legs across the floor, then sinking to her knees beside him, folding her arms around herself as she swallowed back the obstruction in her throat. "No, Poppa," she moaned. "No, no, no."

"There's nothing you can do for him," Rogue said, lifting her to her feet. "Come away while I take care of him."

Blindly, she obeyed. She felt wounded to the core. Her father was all she had left in this world. Now he was gone too. "Roger," she said suddenly, remembering her cousin.

"There's no one else here," he said. "Maybe your cousin is still alive. After I— What the hell!" he exclaimed suddenly. "Miranda! He's still alive!"

"Alive! Poppa's alive!" The tears she had held at bay suddenly burst free, almost blinding her as she sprang forward and fell to her knees beside her father.

Rogue examined him and turned to her. "Looks like he's got a broken ankle. Some kind of head wound too."

"But he's not dead?"

"No. His pulse is faint, but it's still there."

Her emotions overcame her and she began to sob in earnest. Poppa was alive. They still had a chance to save him.

"Stop it, Miranda," Rogue said gruffly. "Don't fall apart on me now. Not when I need you most." He tore off a strip of his shirt, wiped at the dried blood on the back of her father's head, then used it to bind the wound. He was tucking the ends into the bandage when the professor groaned.

"Poppa!" Miranda called out. "Poppa, can you hear me? It's Miranda, Poppa!"

"Mira . . . ?" Silas Hartford mumbled, his eyelids fluttering as though he were attempting to open his eyes. "Is that . . ."

"Yes, Poppa," she said quickly. "It's Miranda."

"Let me lay him down, babe," Rogue said, gently easing her aside. "He'll rest better that way." He carefully lowered her father until he was in a reclining position.

Miranda picked up her father's hand. It was cold and felt paper-thin.

His eyelids fluttered again then lifted and he stared up at Miranda. "You're here," he rasped.

"Yes," Miranda said shakily. "I'm here now. I'll take care of you."

"Knew you would." His lips curled slightly as though he were trying to smile. "Always did. Thought you'd never . . . come." It seemed to take a great effort for him to talk. "Sarah said . . . you were . . . sick." His eyes moved over her disheveled hair. "Have you been . . . crying, my dear? Shouldn't . . . told you I'd be . . . back. Needn't . . . worry." He lifted his hand, touched her hair momentarily, then let it fall again. "It's been . . . so long, Mary . . . so long . . . so long." His eyelids fluttered, then closed again. He expelled a long sigh, then his head fell to one side.

"Mary," Miranda whispered shakily. "He didn't know I was here. He thought I was mother." She choked back a sob of pain. "He didn't know who I was, Rogue! He's delirious."

"Calm down, honey," he said gruffly, pulling her into his arms. "He's alive. Don't think about anything else. We'll get help for him."

"How, Rogue? We can't even help ourselves!" She looked up the tunnel. "Why is my father alone? Where is my cousin, Roger?"

Roger Hartford, seated across from Trace Carradine in the Silver Dollar Saloon, was unaware of the events taking place in the cave. If he had been aware of them, he wouldn't have been so complacent, so sure of himself and content with what he

396

speculated would be a rosy future for himself. Just the thought of it sent a smile across his face.

"What're you so happy about?" Carradine asked.

"What's not to be happy about?" Roger asked, reaching for the bottle of whiskey on the table. After pouring himself a fresh glass of the amber liquid, he swallowed it quickly.

Soon it would be over. Soon he would have what he wanted. He poured himself another drink, wiped a few drops from the pin-striped suit he wore, then met the eyes of the other man.

"Plenty," Carradine said. "I know better than to count my chickens before all the eggs are hatched."

"What does that mean?"

"The professor might not be dead," Carradine said. "You admitted he was still alive when you left him."

Roger Hartford lifted the glass to his lips, then took a hefty swallow before he answered. "No. He wasn't dead when I left, but he sure wasn't going anywhere."

"I don't like it," said the other man. "You should've made sure he was dead. What if he gets out of there?"

"I told you he's not going anywhere," Roger said. "He had a broken ankle. There's no way he could walk out. That's why he didn't object to me leaving him there. He thought I was going for help." He laughed shortly. "He knows by now that he was wrong."

"You don't think much of him, do you?" inquired Carradine.

"Not much," Roger said. "But he didn't know that. I made sure of that. What about your end of the deal? You were supposed to get rid of McClaren's stock."

"I'm still working on it. Geraldo's bunch left the country. Had to find somebody else." He eyed Roger speculatively. "You got that map on you?"

Roger grinned. "No. I don't carry it with me. Thought it would be better to put it in a safe place."

"Why don't you give it to me?" Carradine said. "I could put it in my safe. No one could get at it there."

"That's okay," Roger said. "Thanks anyway, but I'd feel better hanging on to it."

"Suit yourself," Carradine said shortly. "How long do you think it will be before the old man dies?"

"He may be dead already." He pinned the other man with a look. "What're you going to do if McClaren finds the way out of there?"

"I don't think we have to worry about him anymore," Carradine said with a grin. "One of my boys heard he tried to get back in the cave through a river tunnel. They figured he drowned."

"Still, you can't be sure of it."

"No. But we've got both entrances covered. If

he shows his face above ground, the boys know what to do."

"Let's hope they do a better job than that Mex, Geraldo, did."

"Don't keep shoving that down my throat," Carradine growled. "Just make sure nobody knows what's under the ground. And, Roger . . . I think it would be a good idea for you to go back down there. Just to make sure the professor is really dead. After all, we don't want any witnesses. Do we?"

"All right," Roger said, pouring himself another whiskey. "I'll go and make sure this time. But there's no way the old man can still be alive."

Roger felt a sinking feeling in his stomach. He didn't want to go down again, couldn't bear the thought of facing Uncle Silas again—if he were still alive.

But Roger knew Trace Carradine was right. He would have to go back.

Because, if Silas Hartford *had* survived, the whole thing could blow up in their faces.

Thirty-five

Rogue found the professor's lantern near his pack, both left within easy reach. A quick check of the supplies sent Rogue's eyebrows soaring. The pack appeared to be well stocked, containing several tins of food, small utensils, matches, candles and fuel.

He sat back on his haunches and puzzled over his find. Why in hell hadn't the professor used the supplies? Why had he been sitting in the dark when there was fuel for the lantern?

Although the lantern lay on its side, it was within easy reach. So was the food supply.

He shook the lantern and heard the slosh of liquid. There was still plenty of fuel inside. It must have gone out when it was overturned.

Striking a match, he set it to the wick, snuffed out the small piece of candle — barely more than half an inch now — and crammed it into his pocket again.

His gaze slid to Miranda, still kneeling beside her father. "Miranda?" She remained unmoving, seeming totally unaware of his presence. "Miranda?" he said again.

Slowly, she lifted her head to look at him.

"Your pa's gonna be okay, babe. But we have to get some food in his belly."

"We don't have any," she replied. "I lost the basket when we fell into the river."

"I know, honey," he said gruffly. "But that's okay. We don't need it now. There's plenty of food in the pack."

"Food in the pack?" Her gaze dropped to the canvas bag, then returned to him. "Why didn't he use it?"

"I think he couldn't," he said gently. "He must've been too weak . . . may've been unconscious since that blow to the head." He pushed the lantern toward her. "We're gonna need wood for a fire, honey. Since there's none here, I'll have to go back to the river."

"Not by yourself!" she cried.

Lifting her to her feet, he held her close against him. "You'll have to stay here," he said gently. "We can't leave your pa alone." He felt her tremble and tilted her chin toward him, forcing her to meet his eyes. "There's no other way, babe. But you got nothin' to worry about. There's food in the pack and plenty of candles."

"Something might happen to you," she said, her voice shaking. "Something always happens when we're separated."

"Now stop that!" He shook her gently. "Nothing's gonna happen to me. The river's not very far from here. I'll be back before you know it."

"Promise?" she whispered.

"Cross my heart and hope to die."

Her lips quivered, then lifted into a smile. "Then go on."

Rogue pulled her against him for a quick hard kiss and Miranda returned it with fervor. She slung her arms around his neck and pressed her body hard against his.

He was breathing hard when he set her aside and loped down the passage that led to the river.

Miranda went through her father's supplies while Rogue was gone, laying most of them on the floor while she decided what to use. Her father's pack was better equipped than hers had been, but there was nothing unusual in that. After all, he'd known when he left Austin that he would be exploring the cave.

She'd been searching for her father and fully expected him to be at McClaren's ranch.

Laying aside a can of beef stew, she shook her father's shoulder. "Poppa. You must wake up. You have to eat." There was no response. Her father remained still, unmoving.

When she heard the sound of footsteps drawing nearer, she set aside the things she'd need to make coffee.

Tossing the wood into a pile, Rogue knelt to lay the fire. When he had a modest blaze going, she made coffee—using the small pot her father always carried in his pack—and heated a can of stew.

Again, she tried to wake her father, but still there was no response. Had they come too late to save him?

She worried the question over in her mind while she poured coffee in a cup, and carried the steaming liquid to Rogue. "There's only one cup," she said. "We'll have to share it."

"You first," he said, picking up the can of stew. "Do you want the stew heated?"

"Not unless you do."

While he opened the can, she lifted the lid off the cracker box. Soon they were leaning against the wall, sharing the stew and crackers and coffee.

Although the coffee warmed her and the stew filled her empty stomach, Miranda barely tasted it. Her father's condition was foremost in her mind. "Did we find him too late, Rogue?"

"Don't even think that way, babe. The head wound's not too bad. He may have a concussion, but he's mostly sufferin' from lack of food and water."

"There was a lot of blood on his head."

"Dried blood," he reminded gently. "The cut's not too deep. Won't even need stitches."

Miranda's gaze remained fixed on her father.

"He had plenty of food and water, Rogue. More than enough to last until we got here."

"I know, babe. But that blow on the head was more'n enough to knock him senseless. He must've woke up long enough to knock the lantern over. There's no tellin' what happened then. Maybe he passed out again, or maybe he just couldn't find it in the dark."

"He must have passed out," she said, anguish surging through her. "Poppa wouldn't just sit there in the dark and starve himself."

"I'm sure he wouldn't," he said gently. "But there's no sense in speculatin' on what happened here. Your pa's the only one that knows, an' he damn sure can't tell us."

"We have to get him to a doctor."

"I know, honey. And I've been thinkin' about it. He's too heavy for us to carry."

"I'm not going to leave him here," she snapped.

"I don't expect you to," he said, turning to meet her eyes. "The professor's gonna wake up before long. When he does, you need to get some food into his belly."

"You're going to leave me, aren't you?" She'd known all along he would. There was really no other choice.

"Yeah, babe. I have to." He wrapped his arms around her. "You'll be okay, honey. You know you will. You've got guts you haven't even used yet."

"No. I'm a coward." She burrowed her face in his shoulder. "I've always been a coward, and right now I'm scared stiff, afraid if you leave me you won't be back."

His hands tightened convulsively, digging into her waist, left bare by her torn shirt. But she didn't mind the pain. Instead, she welcomed the feel of his fingers against her flesh.

"I'll be back," he said gruffly. "Didn't I go through the river tunnel to find you? You'll never get away from me, babe. I'd follow you to the ends of the earth if I had to." He tilted her chin, held her eyes in a mesmerizing gaze. "Now give me a smile before I leave."

"I don't feel much like smiling," she said woodenly, pulling out of his arms and looking across at her father. "I'm sorry to be such a coward."

His words caused a tiny smile to pull at her lips but her expression was serious. "I am your girl, Rogue. Don't you ever forget it either." Her eyes filled with moisture. "Are you going right now?"

"Yeah." His head dipped down and his lips brushed her forehead. Then, pushing her lightly from him, he rose to his feet and looked up the tunnel. "I'll leave you the lantern," he said, his mind already on his journey.

"No. You take it. I have the fire . . . and the candles. We'll be all right." *Don't go,* she silently begged. *Please don't leave without me.*

405

He took the lantern in hand and bent to kiss her, but she met him halfway. She wasn't going to let him leave her so easily. Wrapping her arms around his neck, she fastened her lips to his.

When Rogue finally released her, his breath was coming in unsteady jerks, a fact that Miranda found immensely satisfying. She drew a shuddering breath, but before she could speak, he was gone.

Colby went over every inch of the crevice, even digging through the leaves that matted the floor, determined to discover what Trace Carradine and Jory Cavanaugh were hiding there. But his efforts went unrewarded.

Even so, his search had not been fruitless. True, he had found no hidden treasure, but neither had he found any sign of the place the Hartford girl had described.

However he *had* found another hole. Located just above his head, the hole—barely two feet high—went straight into the mountain. How far, Colby had yet to determine, but first he'd need some kind of light.

Cursing himself for not carrying a lantern, Colby left the crevice and hurried to his mount. He'd set a couple of men to watching the place until he had time to check it out. Right now there were more pressing matters.

The sun was sinking below the horizon when Roger returned to Squaw Mountain. Although he felt uneasy about going back into the cave, he knew Carradine was right. He had to make sure his uncle was dead.

Leaving his mount tethered to a tree, he removed the lantern he'd tied to the saddle and entered the crevice, making his way across the spongy mat of leaves.

Roger moved swiftly, knowing there was nothing to fear. He'd been there enough times to know the place well, to discover the cracks and narrow ledges that allowed him to climb up the wall to the dark hole.

He paused at the entrance — just long enough to light the wick — then crawled inside, pushing the lantern before him. Roger tried not to think about his uncle. He'd do whatever he must when the time came. Instead, he turned his thoughts to Miranda. He hadn't wanted to cause her pain, felt regret at doing so, and yet, there'd been no other choice. Although Uncle Silas hadn't seen the vein of gold, he would have, had they continued with the exploration.

No. He'd had no choice. Uncle Silas couldn't be allowed to live. But at least Roger had been spared having to kill Miranda.

God! Would the tunnel never end?

The light danced along the walls as Rogue stumbled up the seemingly endless passage. He took heart from the fact that the floor continually slanted upward, but it twisted and turned continuously until he wondered how much progress he was really making.

Suddenly, the tunnel opened into a large room. He held the lantern before him, his sweeping gaze searching the chamber. Stalactites clung to the ceiling high above him while calcite formations grew out of the walls. His gaze dropped lower.

"What in hell?" he muttered, staring across the empty expanse that should have been the floor, but instead, was only a place of shadows.

It was then that Rogue realized the vastness of the chamber. Regardless of the fact that there was rock beneath his feet, it wasn't a floor, but a wide ledge.

He made his way carefully to the edge and knelt to peer into the abyss. Despite the lantern light, he couldn't see the bottom.

His gaze swept the chamber. There was no way down that he could see. Could he go forward? Perhaps. Although the ledge narrowed considerably, it continued around the wall as far as he could see.

Realizing he had no choice, Rogue continued across the ledge, hugging the wall behind him as it became narrower and narrower until there was only a mere ten or twelve inches of rock between himself and the abyss.

His heart thudded within his chest, his eyes flickered here and there, as he studied the area ahead of him. The lantern was looped through his arm to free both hands and it continually swung back and forth, the light dispelling the shadows only momentarily, before swinging away.

That was the reason he almost passed the opening. He would have if he hadn't been pressed so tight against the wall.

Suddenly without warning, the rock behind him dropped away and Rogue lost his balance. He stepped back, trying to keep himself upright and felt his foot sinking.

"What the hell?" he muttered, flailing out with both arms.

But his attempt to keep himself upright was in vain. He fell backwards, his heart jerking and jumping like a drunken butterfly.

Expecting to plunge down into a pit of darkness, Rogue found himself, instead, striking something hard. The blow had enough force to send his breath whooshing out of his body.

Then, before he could pick himself up, he heard footsteps echoing through a tunnel, coming from somewhere behind him.

Thirty-six

A feeling of dread swept over Miranda and she wrapped her arms around her upper torso and stared into the fire. How long had Rogue been gone? she wondered. It seemed like days already, but she realized it couldn't have been more than a couple of hours.

Her gaze flicked to her father. He remained unmoving, showing no sign of life. She must try to wake him, must get some nourishment into him.

Picking up the can of milk, she moved to his side. "Poppa," she said, shaking his shoulder roughly. "Poppa! You've got to wake up!"

Suddenly he groaned and her heart gave a crazy jerk.

"Poppa!" she said again, slapping his cheek lightly. "Wake up, Poppa. You must eat something."

Without warning, his eyes popped open and he stared up at her. "Miranda?" he questioned hoarsely. "Is . . . that . . . you?"

"Yes, Poppa," she said, her voice shaking with emotion. "It's me." Tears filled her eyes and spilled over. "Will you drink some milk?"

"Milk?" he muttered peevishly. "Don't like milk . . . know that." His fingers gripped her arm. "Where you . . . been? I . . . waited and waited . . ."

"I had a hard time finding you," she said, lifting his head onto her lap. "You need something to eat, Poppa. But you're awfully weak. You need to drink the milk."

"Told you . . . don't like . . . milk." His voice, although feeble, held a note of impatience. "Get . . . bottle in—" His eyes moved sideways seeming to search for something, then skittered back to her. "My pack," he muttered. "Where . . . is . . . pack?"

"It's here," she said quickly. "It's right beside you."

"Brandy," he said. "Need . . . brandy."

She delved quickly into the pack, realizing—from the hoarseness in his voice—that brandy was exactly what he needed.

Finding he was unable to drink from the bottle, she fed it to him with a spoon, watching him carefully each time he swallowed, fearing that he would choke.

The brandy seemed to help . . . at least he was more lucid and less irritable with her.

"Would you drink some milk now?" she asked.

411

He nodded his head and his lips twisted slightly. "If you think . . . will help." He turned his head, searching the passage, then meeting her eyes again. "Where . . . Roger? Don't see . . . Roger."

"No. He's not here." She bent over him and held the can of milk to his mouth. "Here, drink this."

He swallowed several times, then turned his head away. "Enough," he muttered. "Where's Roger?"

"I thought you could tell me," she replied, sitting back on her haunches. "You were alone when we found you."

He looked puzzled. "Roger stayed . . . behind?"

"Behind where, Poppa? Where did Roger go?"

"For help . . ." He pinned her with his gaze. "Didn't you know?"

"No, Poppa. You were here alone. I haven't seen Roger."

Although obviously puzzled, Silas Hartford was too weak, too exhausted, to worry about his nephew's whereabouts.

"Tired," he muttered, his eyelids closing. "Need sleep."

"Go to sleep then," she said softly. "I'll stay right here beside you." And she did. Long after he'd fallen asleep, long after the fire died down, Miranda continued to sit beside him, and all the time she wondered where her cousin was.

"Hartford?" Rogue called. "Is that you?" Feeling like a fool for asking the question, for who else could it be, Rogue got to his feet, picked up the lantern, and strode up the passage.

Although there had been no answering call, Rogue knew he hadn't just imagined the sound. He had heard something . . . someone. Holding his breath, he listened to the silence. Nothing. Maybe he'd been wrong after all.

Dammit! He'd been in the cave too long. Now he was hearing things. And wasting time.

Muttering a curse beneath his breath, he strode quickly up the passage, turned a corner and stopped dead in his tracks.

Roger Hartford stood a few feet away from him, staring at Rogue with astonishment — or was it just plain fear? — written on his face. If Rogue hadn't been so worried about Miranda he might have noticed the man's almost immaculate appearance. Rogue's eyes were red-rimmed from lack of sleep, while Roger's eyes were clear. And, although his face had a four o'clock shadow, Rogue's lower face was covered with short bristly chin whiskers.

"McClaren?" Hartford questioned. "Is that you?"

"Yeah," Rogue said. "It's me. I wondered where you got off to."

"Did . . . did you find Uncle Silas?"

"Yeah. We did."

"He's not—he's—how is he?"

"Just barely alive."

Roger peered past Rogue's shoulder, his gaze probing the darkness beyond. "Where's Miranda?"

"She stayed with the professor while I came on. Did you find the way out?"

"Yes," Roger said, his lips twitching, pulling into a nervous smile. "Back that way." He bent his elbow, jerking his thumb past his shoulder. "It's not very far. We can go back and get Miranda and Uncle Silas now." His body was held tensely as though he waited for Rogue to make the first move.

"We may need some help moving the professor," Rogue said. "He won't be able to walk." Even as he said the words he realized that Roger would already know that. "Why didn't you go for help?" he asked, his dark brows pulling into a frown.

"Help seemed so far away," the other man replied. "And I was so worried about Uncle. I got lost in one of the tunnels." He jerked his thumb behind him again. "There's several of them back that way. Anyway, I was gone so long, that I was afraid for him."

"Maybe you should go on," Rogue said. "You could go to the ranch house for help while I go back and wait with Miranda."

"No," Roger replied. "I don't think that's a good idea. You said my uncle's in a bad way.

414

Wouldn't it be better if we try to get him out of here?"

"Yeah. I guess you're right." Rogue, eager to get back to Miranda, hadn't really taken much convincing, but there was something about Roger's explanation that bothered him.

But he was probably just imagining things.

He spun on his heels, bent on retracing his steps down the passage, his thoughts turning to Miranda. He hadn't liked leaving her alone, knew she was afraid something would happen to keep him from returning.

"We'll have to go slower now," he said, realizing they'd reached the large chamber. "I don't trust this ledge very much. I'll be damned glad to leave here. It's been—"

He broke off, his breath whooshing out of him as a heavy blow struck his midsection hard enough to send him sprawling forward. The lantern spun out of his hand as the floor fell away and he plummeted down into darkness.

Miranda was so tired her nerves throbbed, but she dared not lose herself in sleep for fear her father would wake and need her. Her eyes burned dryly and she felt drained, hollow and lifeless. When she heard the sound of approaching footsteps, her heart jerked, then leapt with joy. She could see a light in the distance. It must be Rogue, coming back for them.

"Rogue!" she cried, hurrying toward the distant light. "Thank God you're back! Did you find the way out?"

"It's me, Miranda," a deep voice said, and, although it was familiar, he was certainly not the man she had expected. "I've come to take you out of here."

"Roger?" She looked past his shoulder, her gaze searching for Rogue, but the corridor beyond was dark, empty. "Are you alone?" she asked.

"Yeah." He stepped into the small chamber, then stopped abruptly, his eyes taking in her appearance, dwelling for a moment on her bare, scratched arms and legs. "What in hell happened to you?"

Her lips tightened grimly. "You wouldn't believe everything that happened to me. It looks like you and Poppa had it rough too." Her brow wrinkled as she took in his barely wrinkled, pin-striped suit. "At least Poppa gives that appearance." Her gaze flashed back to him. "Why does he look so bad, Roger? Where have you been?"

"I left him to search for a way out," he said quickly.

"How long ago?"

"I don't know, Mandy. I think maybe it's been a couple of days. I knew Uncle Silas was bad . . . knew he needed help, but I got lost." Tears flooded his eyes when he looked at his uncle. "Say he's all right," he begged, dropping to his knees beside his uncle. "Don't tell me he's dead, Mandy. Please don't say that."

Her heart went out to her cousin. She hadn't realized he cared so much. "He's not dead, Roger," she said gently. "And I think he's going to make it. He's weak . . . terribly frail, but he woke up for a few minutes. Long enough to take some brandy and milk."

"Thank God," he said fervently, wiping a shaking hand over his eyes before leaving his uncle.

She asked the question that was uppermost in her mind. "Did you see Rogue McClaren? He left us to search for a way out."

He seemed to hesitate, his eyes flicking away evasively, before returning to meet hers. "Yeah, Miranda. I saw McClaren."

Something about the way he looked at her caused her breath to stop, to become trapped in her throat. "Where is he?" she whispered, apprehension knotting her stomach.

"He won't be coming," he said grimly.

"Wh-what do you mean?" Fear, stark and vivid, glittered in her eyes and she began to shake as she waited for him to speak.

"He fell, Miranda."

"Fell where?" Her eyes never left his face as she waited for him to answer her question.

"He fell into a pit, Mandy. A deep one. There was no way he could have survived the fall."

Thirty-seven

Colby felt frustrated. Dammit! He couldn't be in ten places at once. He needed more riders. Already shorthanded, he'd set two men to watching that hole in the mountain and another one riding for the sheriff. That left only four men to guard the herd. Not nearly enough if they had to fight off rustlers.

And, as if he didn't have enough trouble on his place already, his horse had thrown a shoe.

Grimly, he returned to the ranch, turned the bay loose in the corral and saddled a gelding. He was on the point of leaving when he heard the thunder of hoofbeats.

Since Rogue allowed none of his horses to be mistreated, Colby knew something was wrong.

That was enough to put him in the saddle.

The rider came closer, his battered black hat pulled low on his head. He reined up in a cloud of dust, his mount rearing back, pawing at the air with his front hooves.

Colby's hard eyes narrowed on Zeke Raglan, waiting for him to speak.

He was a tall man with narrow shoulders and a weather-beaten face. Although he was fifty years old, he looked at least ten years younger.

"You were right, Colby," he said. "Somebody's rode in . . . Looked a stranger to these parts. He went straight to that hole in the cliff like he knew it was there."

"Is he still there?"

"Was when I left. I didn't wait around to see if he came out. You said if—"

"I know what I said," Colby growled. "Well, don't just set there. let's ride." He kneed the gelding, and the horse gave a jerk then leapt forward.

Colby hadn't expected results so soon or he'd have kept watch himself. He wondered who had gone in the mountain. Zeke said it was a stranger. Could it have been the same man Jory and Trace were talking with? What the hell was so important about that hole? Whatever it was, Colby figured it was past time he found out.

Miranda felt as though she'd been kicked in the stomach. God! It couldn't be true! Rogue couldn't be dead! He just couldn't! She would have known it, would have felt him die. There was a bond between them, a tie that couldn't be broken without her knowing it.

How then could he be dead?

"It's not true," she whispered, verbalizing her

denial. "He's not dead! He couldn't be, Roger! I'd have known it . . . would have felt him die . . . would have . . ."

He looked at her curiously. "He's dead, Miranda. You can take my word for it. I saw him go over the edge."

She shook her head. "He survived the fall. He didn't die."

"Nobody could have survived that fall." He turned his attention to his uncle again. "Forget the rancher, Mandy. We've got to think about Uncle Silas now." His gaze swept over the professor's drawn features, then swept back to meet her eyes again. "I tried to take care of him. I really did. I would have carried him out of here on my back, but he was too heavy for me. You know that, don't you?"

"I know," she said dully, still trying to deal with what he'd told her about Rogue. But how could she deal with such a thing? No matter what Roger said, Miranda knew it couldn't be so.

She clenched her fists tightly, leaving nail prints on her palms, welcoming the resulting pain. Her body shuddered; a cold wave swept over her as reality took over.

Rogue must be dead. Otherwise, why would Roger tell her such a thing? It had to be true, and yet, she found herself unable to believe it.

Miranda felt chilled, her legs rubbery, her knees refusing to lock in place. She swayed for a moment, feeling as though she were going to faint. "No," she whispered, her mind still trying to deny the death of her love. "It can't be true!" Her voice rose, became an agonized wail. "No, no, no!" She wrapped her arms around her upper torso, rocking herself back and forth.

She was vaguely aware of her cousin's astonished gaze just before he bent over and slapped her hard.

Gasping with shock, she pressed her hand against her cheek and looked up at him through moisture-filled eyes.

"What on earth is wrong with you?" he cried in a high-pitched voice. "Why should you care if McClaren is dead?" Wrapping his fingers around her upper arm, he yanked her to her feet. "Did you have something going with him, Miranda?"

Miranda, finding herself unable to stand without support, leaned against the wall. "He was—" She broke off and swallowed hard. How could she explain the way they'd felt about each other . . . the plans they'd made together. Now they'd never be married, never have children, never have any kind of future together.

But, God! How could she bear to face a future without Rogue?

Something sparked in Roger's eyes. His lips tightened, the way they did when he was angry, but when he spoke, his voice was kind. "You don't have to say any more, Miranda. I guess, considering the circumstances, it was only natural the two of you would become close. But he's gone now and he won't be back. You've got to think about Uncle Silas now. We have to get him to a doctor."

Sudden shame washed over Miranda and she wiped away her tears. How easily she had forgotten her father's needs. How selfish she was not to have remembered. Roger was right. They had to get Poppa to a doctor, and they must do it quickly.

But how could they carry him?

"We made a raft," she said hesitantly. "Rogue and I. Maybe we could use it for a litter. You look strong, Roger." He did look fit, amazingly so. "Between us maybe we can carry Poppa out of here."

"It's worth a try anyway," he said quickly. "Where is the raft?"

"Down that way." She pointed down the tunnel. "It's beside a river."

"I know the place," Roger said. "There was a corpse down there." He showed no emotion, no pity for the unfortunate soul. "We were there when the rock fell from the ceiling and struck Uncle Silas on the head." His lips curled, then pressed tight against his teeth. "I did the best I could for him, Mandy. You know that, don't you? I couldn't carry him by myself. I was too weak. That's why I went for help. But I got lost in the tunnel."

"You've already explained, Roger," she said

dully. "I know you did everything you could. If you'll just get the raft . . ."

"Yeah. I'm going." His eyes darkened. "I just wanted you to understand why I left him."

"I do understand." Her voice was lifeless, a monotone.

He studied her for a long moment as though undecided about something, then turned abruptly and strode away.

Left alone, Miranda gathered up the scattered supplies and put them into the pack — more from habit than anything else, for they surely wouldn't be needed now.

Her mind, as well as her body, felt numb. She just couldn't accept Rogue's death as a fact. It didn't feel right to her, therefore, it couldn't be so.

But if he wasn't dead, then where was he?

When Rogue fell into the abyss, he had flailed out with both arms, desperately searching for something — anything, to break his fall.

He heard a snap, just before his seeking hands brushed something solid. His fingers curled, wrapping around the object and he came to an abrupt halt.

Rogue swayed in the darkness, hanging on for dear life, knowing there was nothing between him and death except his ability to cling to the object.

What was it anyway?

It felt like a rock. A hard, narrow rock. Maybe a ledge. Or perhaps just a protrusion. How long would it hold his weight?

Desperately, realizing his lifeline might break at any given moment, he shifted his grip, edging slowly to the right until his fingers encountered empty space.

God! If only it wasn't so dark! If only he could see just a little bit.

Slowly, he moved to the left, searching for something more substantial to support him. When he felt dampness beneath his hand, he jerked it away. Wet rocks would be too slick, too unstable.

Rogue hung there, unable to go up or down, clinging like a fly to the cliff, wondering just how long he could hold on. He tasted bile in his throat and swallowed hard, willing himself not to be sick.

God! How long could he hang on?

How in hell had he wound up like this? He'd felt a blow against his back just before he fell, knew that Roger must have pushed him, but why? Was he mad? And if he was, then Miranda was in danger.

Desperation filled Rogue as he shifted his hands again. Dammit! He had to do something before Hartford could harm Miranda. But he was so damned tired, and his fingers so numb that he could hardly feel the rock beneath them now. How long could he continue this way? How long until he fell?

"Damn you, Hartford!" he muttered. "If I get outta this, you're gonna pay!"

He shifted his right foot and felt something sharp scraping against his left knee. What in hell was it? Some kind of rocky protrusion? Or maybe a ledge?

Just the thought gave him hope, renewed his strength. He moved his left leg, bending it out and lifting his foot. If it *was* a ledge of some kind, then he just might have a chance.

When Colby, followed closely by Zeke, reached the clearing at the base of Squaw Mountain, Rowdy Granger left his hiding place among the rocks and joined them.

"He's still in there," Rowdy told them.

"How long's it been now?" Colby asked.

"A couple of hours," Rowdy replied. "Can't figger out what he's doin' in there so long."

"I think it's time we found out what's so interesting about this place," Colby said, sliding from the saddle. "You stay out here and watch, Rowdy. Zeke, you come with me."

Colby drew his gun and Zeke did likewise.

Dropping to his knees, Colby crawled into the hole, his eyes quickly scanning the interior, searching for an intruder, but there was no one there; the crevice was empty, completely undisturbed.

"They ain't nobody here," Zeke said, his voice puzzled.

"No," Colby replied, his gaze lifting to the yawning mouth of the tunnel. "He's gone in the mountain, an' we're goin' after him. Zeke, you go back and fetch my lariat. Maybe you better bring yours too." He looked back at the other man. "And, Zeke. Take that lantern off'n my saddle and bring it along. I 'spect we're gonna need it."

While Zeke crawled back out of the cave, Colby climbed up to the hole above and edged his body inside a few feet. There was nothing unusual about the hole, except that he could see no end to it. Colby wasn't able to determine how far it went into the mountain, but guessed it must be a far piece since the man who'd gone in hadn't come out again.

What in hell could be here that would interest so many people? he wondered.

It was damned well past time he found out.

Thirty-eight

Rogue's heart thudded in his chest as he pressed his back against the wall of sheer rock behind him. He was exhausted, completely and totally drained. It had taken every ounce of his strength to secure himself on the ledge. His lips twisted wryly. A narrow ledge was not necessarily secure.

Every muscle in his body ached and he felt much the way he had last fall when he'd been bucked off a wild mustang, but that was the least of his troubles.

No. For the first time in his life, Rogue was afraid to move. He *dared* not move, because his position was too precarious. One slip could send him plunging to his death below.

"Damn you Hartford!" he swore loudly. "Damn you to hell!"

Realizing he was accomplishing nothing, Rogue dug his fingers into his pocket and extracted a match. He'd need a light to assess the situation.

He struck the match against the rock. It

flared momentarily, then began to burn steadily. Holding the match above him, he peered up the face of the cliff. There was a rocky protrusion a few feet above him, obviously the one that had saved him. But, God, it was flimsy. It's a wonder he'd been able to catch it, an even bigger wonder it had held his weight. Other than that, there was nothing. No crevices or cracks to help him climb.

The match sputtered, then went out and he dug for another one. When it was aflame, he held it out, peering down into the abyss.

The chasm was deep. Too deep for the meager light to reach the bottom. He'd have to find something to drop into the blackness.

He fumbled for a coin, found one, dropped it into the darkness and waited for the sound that would tell him it had reached the bottom.

Although he listened intently, he heard nothing. Not even a soft sound. He shuddered to think how far it must have gone.

It looked like that way was closed to him too.

Anger surged through him, rage that had to be let out. "Damn you, Hartford!" he cried again. "Damn you to hell!"

"Rogue? Is that you, boy?"

The voice jerked Rogue's head up. "Colby?" he asked eagerly. "Is that you?"

"Damn right it's me," Colby answered.

A light appeared above Rogue, then he saw Colby's head edging over the cliff. "What're you doin' down there?" Colby growled roughly.

"Get me the hell outta here!" Rogue shouted.

"Just hold your horses," Colby snapped. "Got a rope comin' down now."

Roger Hartford had no intention of using the raft for a litter and wondered why he was even going to the trouble of fetching it. But even as he wondered he realized why he was acting in such a fashion.

He was stalling for time, unwilling to get on with Miranda's murder.

Murder.

It was an ugly word, but there was no other name for what he planned to do.

How could he even be considering such a thing? He didn't want to hurt Miranda, but what else could he do?

His mind worried over the problem as he made his way down the passage to the river chamber. His gaze slid over the human remains and he controlled a shudder.

It had seemed fitting to strike Uncle Silas while he was bending over the corpse. Roger's lips twisted in memory. "I should've struck the damn fool harder," he muttered. "Now it's to do all over again."

Roger still didn't know why he had carried his uncle up the passage to the smaller chamber. Maybe it was because Silas was conscious and—

even at that point in time—Roger didn't want to admit to what he'd done. Not with his uncle looking straight at him, giving him that all-knowing look that Roger had always found intimidating.

But Silas wasn't so smart. Roger was certain Silas had believed the explanation cooked up by his nephew—that a rock had fallen from the ceiling and struck him. There was really no reason for him not to believe it. Certainly he had no idea of his nephew's animosity.

No. Roger had always been able to keep his feelings hidden. Perhaps because he knew he must. If the old fool had even suspected how Roger really felt, he wouldn't have continued to support him.

Circling the body, Roger had found the litter and dragged it back up the passage, hurrying now, wanting the deed finished. Although the raft wasn't really heavy, he was sweating when he reached the small chamber where Miranda waited.

She bent over her father, looking so worn, so fragile, so absolutely beautiful in her tattered garments. How could he even consider destroying that beauty?

Miranda had always been special to Roger, even when they had been children together. That's why it was so hard to think about killing her now.

His eyes flashed wildly. It was really all Uncle

Silas's fault! If he had died as Roger had intended, it would not have become necessary to kill Miranda. As the only surviving male member of the family, he would control everything she owned.

If Silas Hartford were dead.

But, dammit! There was no way of killing him without Miranda's knowing what he'd done.

His lips tightened into a thin line of displeasure. He should've known the old skinflint was too mean to die. Although Silas was a wealthy man, he'd thought Roger would settle for the measly monthly income Silas had settled on him. But Roger had no intention of making do on such a pittance. Not when Silas had more money than he could ever use . . . and the Hartford family home as well, when by rights half of it should have gone to Roger. Never mind that Roger's grandfather had settled an equal amount on both his sons. The old man had known Roger's father for a wastrel, and should have done something to insure Roger's future.

Roger looked down at Silas Hartford, not even bothering to hide his hatred. He'd felt good when he'd struck his uncle. Had wanted to strike him over and over again, but the old man had turned and faced him.

Dammit! Roger thought petulantly. Why had the old fool turned around and looked at him?

Roger's gaze went to Silas's ankle and a wide grin spread across his face. The old fool had fallen unconscious before his nephew left him, leaving Roger to do as he wished. Although Roger could have taken that moment to kill him, he hadn't done so, knowing that if the old man was found, several blows might become suspect. Instead, he had taken a perverse pleasure in breaking his uncle's ankle, rendering him helpless, unable to leave the cave alone.

Roger felt almost overcome with mirth at his ingenuity. He had been so clever and his rewards would be great. He would have the family fortune plus half the gold found in this cave.

He was silently congratulating himself when Miranda looked up at him. "I think he's bet—" She broke off, a puzzled frown marring her forehead. "What's wrong, Roger? Why are you staring at Poppa that way?"

She knew! Dammit, he should have known he couldn't keep secrets from her. His hands clenched into fists and he stared at her throat, so white, so delicate. He hadn't wanted to do it that way, hadn't wanted her to see what he was about. But now, he had no choice.

"I don't want this to happen," he said, feeling hot and cold at the same time. His gaze was earnest as he met her wide green eyes. "You know I've always cared for you, Mandy. Ever since you were a little girl."

"I know, Roger. You were always good to me."

"I was, wasn't I?" he said eagerly. "So you see

how hard this is for me." He reached out, his fingers clutching her upper arms tightly. "Uncle Silas was never there for you. It was me you went to, the one you counted on. I was your champion. Your knight in shining armor."

She looked puzzled. "I know, Roger."

"I never wanted you to be hurt. I tried to keep you out of it, even after I found out about the gold." He realized he was talking too fast, but he couldn't seem to help himself. He had to make her see, had to make her understand. "None of it would have happened if Uncle Silas hadn't given me such a pittance to live on." His voice became a whine. "He could've done more. He had plenty of money. He wouldn't have missed a few thousand dollars a month."

Her lashes swept down across her cheekbones, then snapped up again, her wide green eyes suddenly fearful. "You're hurting me, Roger." She tried to shake him loose, but he tightened his fingers, digging painfully into her already-bruised flesh.

He could see she was scared, and he deeply regretted being the cause of it. The kindest thing would be to finish her as quickly as possible.

Looping the rope around his waist, Rogue pulled it tight, then positioned his hands one above the other and tugged hard, giving the signal to pull him up. His muscles bunched, became taut, as he prepared to leave his perch; the rope tightened and quivered and the tension increased.

He felt the vibration as the rope was drawn across the overhanging rock above. His feet swung free of the ledge, and he began to spin round in the air.

Come on, he silently urged. *Do it! Get me out of here.*

He moved upward, spinning around like a top. His head spun dizzily as he moved, swaying and spinning over the abyss, fearing any moment the rope would break and he would fall.

The rope quivered, then stopped, leaving him dangling like a spider at the end of its line. The rope jerked, went up an inch, then dropped two inches. He could hear the sound of voices above, but he couldn't understand the words.

What ·in hell had happened? Was he too heavy for them?

Suddenly, the rope jerked again, paused, then gave another jerk, and slowly, but surely, he began to rise again.

He kept his head tipped back, saw the overhang coming nearer, until at last he could see the men above, could see the way they strained to pull him up.

It seemed an eternity before his hands reached the top, before he slid them out, gripped the ledge and clung, staring eagerly into their tense faces.

Even as he watched, he saw their muscles tense, their hands clench as they gave the final haul that pulled him over the edge.

He landed on hands and knees at the feet of his rescuers, then dropped to his stomach to catch his breath, but only for a moment. He dared not delay, not with Hartford on the loose.

Rogue had no idea why Roger had pushed him over the ledge, only knew that he had done so, and a man like that could be dangerous to everyone around him.

And he was probably with Miranda at this very moment.

Miranda stared up into Roger's overbright eyes, realizing she was dealing with a man who was mentally unbalanced. "Let me go, Roger," she said, managing to keep her voice steady despite her fear. "You're hurting me."

"I don't want to, Miranda," he said peevishly. "But I don't have any choice. Surely you can see that. I'm tired of being a nobody. I want the money *and* the gold."

She gripped his hands, trying to pry them loose from her shoulders. "You can have it all, Roger," she said, her voice wavering slightly. "I don't want any part of it. Just let me go."

"Oh, no, Mandy. You know too much. You'd tell everyone about me if I let you live. No. You'll have to die."

"Please, Roger," she coaxed. "Let me go. I

435

won't tell a soul. How could I when I don't know anything about it."

"Don't lie to me!" he spat. "You know. I saw the way you were looking at me. You know I killed Uncle."

What little color Miranda had drained completely away. "You did that to Poppa?" she asked, her voice expressing her horror.

"Don't pretend you didn't already know," he said in an aggrieved voice. "That won't work." His eyes narrowed on her pale face. "But even if it's true, it no longer matters. Because now you know. And you couldn't keep your mouth shut. Not about your father or about McClaren."

God! He had pushed Rogue into that abyss!

"You'd tell somebody," he babbled on. "Then I wouldn't have the gold. I must have that gold. Nobody can keep it from me. Not after everything I've done to get it."

His hands gripped her neck, his fingers digging into the tender flesh of her throat and Miranda screamed out her terror, striking out with her fists at the deranged man who was bent on squeezing the life out of her.

His eyes widened. "Don't scream," he muttered, jerking his head aside to dodge her blows. "And don't yell like that. It won't be bad, Mandy. I'll make it as easy as I can for you. All you have to do is hold still and I'll just squeeze a little harder and it will soon be over."

Miranda couldn't make a sound, his grip was

too strong, but she wouldn't give up so easily. She grabbed a handful of hair and yanked hard, and although he grimaced with pain, his grip only tightened.

Her head began to spin, and spots floated in front of her eyes, but she wouldn't give up, knowing that if she did, she would surely die. Although her strength was fading fast, she lifted her knee and struck him a blow that connected with the softness between his legs.

With a heavy groan, Roger released her, his hands covering his man parts, as he bent over himself.

Miranda, unable to stand alone, fell in a crumpled heap to the floor. She lay there, sucking in huge breaths of life-giving air, barely aware of her cousin a few feet away.

Not until he turned his attention to her again.

"Bitch!" he snarled, leaping toward her with outstretched hands. "You're going to regret that!"

Quickly, Miranda rolled away, gaining precious time as Roger collided with the floor. But she had only gained a little time, not nearly enough to get away from him. Even so, she could do no less than try.

When he made another leap, she rolled again, but this time, he had anticipated her. He threw himself across her body and reached for her neck.

"Get away from her!" a voice snarled.

And then, almost miraculously, Roger was lifted away from her.

"You!" Roger spat, his color receding to an unnatural paleness. "You can't be here. You're dead."

"No," Rogue's dark eyes were cold and chilling and there was a hard ruthlessness in his face as though he would enjoy tearing Roger limb from limb. "You botched the job, Hartford. But I'm givin' you the chance to try again."

Miranda saw the insane glitter in her cousin's eyes just before he leapt for Rogue's throat. "No!" she shouted hoarsely.

Rogue fended the attack with an elbow to her cousin's chin. Roger grunted then, doubling his hands into fists, he sent a right winging toward Rogue's face.

With a quick side step, Rogue dodged the blow, smashing a left to his opponent's nose. It connected, causing blood to spurt out as though a fountain had been opened.

Enraged, Roger swung a kick at Rogue with his left foot; it caught Rogue on the knee and his legs folded beneath him and he sprawled forward. Roger was quick to take advantage, aiming another kick at his opponent.

"Rogue!" Miranda cried, crawling toward him.

"Leave him be," Colby said, wrapping his fingers around her wrist. "The boy will do just fine and that cousin of yours has got it comin' to him."

Miranda swallowed hard. How could she stay where she was and watch her cousin kick Rogue senseless? Even as she asked the question, Rogue rolled away from the other man and came up swiftly. He wasted no time, lunging at Roger and smashing another blow to his nose. He followed it quickly with another blow then a quick right to the chin that floored Roger on the spot.

Miranda was vaguely aware of other figures moving to stand over Roger, but her attention was on Rogue. He favored one leg as he knelt on the rocky floor and pulled her into his arms, burying his head into the curve of her neck. She could feel him trembling against her.

"Are you all right?" she asked, her voice wobbling slightly.

"I'm okay, babe," he said gruffly, pulling back to look at her. "How about you? Did he hurt you?"

"No," she replied, sliding her arms around his neck. "He told me you were dead."

"I nearly was," he replied. "If Colby and Zeke hadn't come along I don't know what would've happened." He looked over at Roger. "What was it all about anyway?"

"I'm not really sure. He talked about money, said Poppa didn't give him enough and he rambled on about a gold vein he'd found in here."

"A gold vein?" Rogue looked at her cousin. "Is that what this is all about?"

Roger remained silent, his eyes glassy with

rage as he wiped his sleeve across his bloody nose.

"There's no gold in here," Rogue said, his lips curling contemptuously. "Don't you know the difference between gold and pyrite?"

"Pyrite?" Roger glared at Rogue. "What's that?"

"It's fool's gold." Miranda answered the question. "Just plain fool's gold, Roger."

"It couldn't be," Roger said. "There's more than fool's gold in here. I didn't go through all this for nothing. I have a map showing where the gold is."

"Let me see," Rogue said.

Roger hesitated for a moment, then, apparently deciding he would gain nothing by withholding the map, he reached in his pocket and handed it over.

Rogue studied it quietly for a moment then handed it back. "It's the same vein I found and it's completely worthless."

"No!" Roger cried. "You're lying."

Rogue shrugged. "Believe what you will. But it's fool's gold all right." He studied the other man. "How did you plan to mine this gold, with it under my property?"

"I think I can answer that," Colby growled. "He had some kind of deal going with Trace Carradine and Jory Cavanaugh."

"Trace and Jory?" Rogue lifted his eyebrows. "When we get out of here you'll have to tell me all about it." He turned his attention back to Miranda. "Right now, I've got other things on my mind." He took her hand in a tight, protective grip. "Come on, babe. Let's get outta here."

Miranda was more than willing to comply.

Thirty-nine

An errant sunbeam slipped between the window curtains and played across Miranda's eyelids, stirring her from sleep. She could hear the vibrant sounds of robins singing from somewhere nearby and realized it must come from the old oak tree growing just outside the bedroom window.

Rogue's bedroom window.

The bedroom that she now shared with Rogue.

Feeling as contented as a cat after a warm bowl of milk, she let her eyes wander around the room.

It held a mixture of old and new furniture. The bed upon which she lay was a four-poster, mahogany with a white fringe coverlet that hung over the sideboards. Rogue's housekeeper, Martha, had put a large bowl of flowers on the table at the foot of the bed. A large mahogany bureau stood against a far wall while nearby, placed near the window, rested a caned rocker.

Granted, the room was stark, but Miranda didn't mind. When Rogue could spare the time, they would go after her things. Poppa had agreed to let her have her mother's spinet. It would look good in the parlor.

Her lips curled into a smile and she turned her attention to the man in bed with her: the man who was creating such a delicious warmth against her back. Sleep softened his granitelike features.

Miranda still found it hard to believe they were married. The waiting had been hard, but Rogue had insisted. They would wait until her father could give her away.

And so they had. Even though it had been a whole month, they had waited . . . and they had abstained from lovemaking. Her lips twitched. That had been Rogue's decision, not hers. And she had reason to know he'd regretted that decision. The waiting had been hard on both of them.

She smiled again, remembering the way he'd made love to her last night—their wedding night—with the energy of a man who'd been starved for weeks and had finally had a feast set before him.

He had been insatiable.

But then, so had she.

Why didn't he wake up?

How could he continue to sleep when the robins sang so wondrously, when the sun shone so brightly? She turned in his arms and placed a kiss on his bare shoulder. Although he stirred slightly, he slept on. Feeling totally dissatisfied with his response, or lack of it, she trailed her lips along his shoulder until she reached the base of his neck.

Rogue stirred again, uttered a sigh, then lay still, his breathing undisturbed.

Darn it! How could he keep on sleeping like that? It was the morning after their wedding day. It would be their first full day as husband and wife. Was he already so bored with her that he would sleep the morning away?

Well she wouldn't have it!

Grasping the sheet covering the lower half of his body, she slid it toward his thighs until she exposed that which she sought.

It lay soft and still, surrounded by shining black curls, so different from the wild, throbbing man-thing that had pierced her over and over again last night.

How could she make it so again? Was it an impossible task?

She moved her hand toward it, then jerked it back, wondering at her boldness.

Her eyelashes lifted and she studied his face. He gave no sign of waking.

Becoming impatient, Miranda opened her mouth and trailed wet kisses across his chest, stopping momentarily at each flat male nipple to circle it with her tongue.

Although he jerked slightly, he gave no other sign of response to her ministrations, continuing to breathe evenly, his chest rising and falling slowly.

She leaned back on one elbow and stared up at him. His eyelids were firmly closed, his expression relaxed.

Her lips shaped into a pout. She wasn't ready to leave the warm bed. She wanted him to wake up. Wanted him to kiss her, to make love to her, but he remained fast asleep, as undisturbed by her efforts as an unfeeling rock.

Miranda remained positioned on one elbow while her eyes strayed over him. He was totally masculine, his muscles clearly defined even in sleep. The only thing soft about him was the limp, pale, male thing that still rested comfortably in its bed of curls.

Still unwilling to leave him, she bent over and placed a kiss on his lips. "Rogue?" she questioned softly. "Rogue, are you awake?"

He remained unmoving, his breathing never changing.

Her lips tightened. He couldn't do this to her. They had only just been married! Dammit! She would *not* let him sleep the morning away.

She would just have to try harder.

Worming her way lower in the bed, she flicked her tongue across his right nipple and was rewarded with a startled jerk and a quick indrawn breath.

All right! She was getting somewhere now.

She flicked her tongue again, drawing a wet circle around the nipple, feeling his muscles tense beneath her ministrations.

Drawing back momentarily, she cast a quick look upward, but his eyes were still closed.

She'd have to take more drastic measures.

Sliding lower, she dipped her tongue into his navel. His reaction was immediate. His stomach tightened, his lower body stiffening.

She looked up for an instant, saw his eyes wide and staring and a smile curled her lips. She wasn't done with him yet. She'd teach him that he couldn't sleep through her kisses.

Opening her mouth, she attacked his navel again, her tongue digging into it eagerly.

Her heart was beating so fast that she barely heard his choked, "Miranda."

Thoroughly enjoying herself now, Miranda trailed wet kisses across his flat, silky stomach, savoring the salty taste of his flesh, moving lower and lower, as her hand preceded her mouth toward his maleness, no longer soft and pliant, but an erect, throbbing shaft.

Although she'd meant to tease him, something was happening deep inside her own body. A fire was slowly being stoked, sending heat through her lower belly as she continued to minister to his silky flesh.

But suddenly, it was over.

With a strangled gasp, Rogue gripped her upper arms and yanked her toward him. His lips fastened on hers as he shoved her back on the bed, spreading her legs and driving his shaft toward her.

She gasped with pleasure as he entered her, filling her body with his maleness. Then, they moved together in that age-old rhythm of love, climbing higher and higher until they reached their peak.

When it was over she lay beside him, feeling replete and completely satisfied.

She looked up at him. "No regrets, Rogue?"

"Regrets about what, babe?"

"About our marriage."

"Never," he whispered. "Never, my love. When the preacher said the words over us, he made you mine. And nobody can ever take you away from me."

"I'm yours?" she asked wryly. "Like your horse and your ranch? Am I just a possession, Rogue?"

"You know better than that," he growled, his arms tightening around her. "You're not a possession, babe. You're my wife. But you *are* mine. Make no mistake about that. You belong to me now."

"Belong to you." She tasted the words on her tongue for a moment, then arched a brow at him. "Do you belong to me?"

"Yeah, babe. I guess I do."

"Then that's all right," she said, beaming up

at him. "I'll be your possession as long as you'll be mine."

He laughed huskily. "Agreed," he said, his eyes holding a glint in them. "I'm glad that's settled, because I have something else besides talkin' in mind."

"What?" she inquired, wondering if matters of the ranch had already claimed his attention.

"Well . . ." He drew away slightly and looked down the length of his body. "If I remember right," he said, "you left off about along there." His finger pointed to a position just below his navel. "I'm thinkin' maybe I stopped you too soon."

"Rogue!" she cried, feeling her cheeks begin to burn. "You don't really mean—"

Her words went unsaid as his lips closed over hers and by the time he finished kissing her, he'd covered her entire body and she'd forgotten everything, caught up as she was in a series of explosions that left her shuddering with ecstasy.

When it was over, she stared up at him through misty, wondering eyes. There was much about life she hadn't learned in college, but Rogue seemed more than capable of teaching her the rest.